Sex... Love... Lies & Deceit

RISHA ROZAY

Copyright © 2019 by Risha Rozay.

ISBN: 978-1-970135-21-3 paperback

Published in the United States by Pen2Pad Ink Publishing.

Requests to publish work from this book or to contact the author should be sent to:
ribandz23@gmail.com

Risha Rozay retains the rights to all images.

CONTENTS

INTRODUCTION

Sex, Love, Lies and Deceit is a fictional story that takes you on an adventure into the life of a young transsexual woman by the name of Candy. WARNING: Be prepared to be entertained, as this novel is going to give an inside look at a lifestyle you probably know little to nothing about. Join us on this incredible ride where dreams become nightmares, friends become enemies, secrets becomes truths and fantasies becomes realities. This book is a ravishing page turner filled with chilling tales of sex, love, lies and deceit. It will keep you on the edge of your seat and leave you wanting more!

6

CHAPTER 1

How It All Began

"What the fuck?" Candy said to herself as she was thrown into the back of a police paddywagon. She sat there for about an hour alone, contemplating on how she let herself get wrapped up in some bullshit like this. She furiously banged against the wall of the paddywagon with her head; and that's only because her hands were cuffed behind her back.

"Why the fuck am I still sitting here?" she screamed. "Can you just get me to booking so I can bond the fuck out?"

The two cops sitting up front ignored her while conversing back and forth with the other officers involved in the whole operation. Just then she heard one of the officers come over the walkie-talkie radio, "Hey fellas we got two more."

One of the officers up front looked back through the cage and said, "Be patient little lady, we got some company coming for you."

"Fuck some company! I want to bond out...these cuffs hurt!" she screamed as she twisted her wrist back and forth in a desperate attempt to find comfort.

Moments later the back door of the paddywagon flew open and two more girls were put in. One of them was crying. She looked to be about 18. She was a white girl with beautiful crimson red hair that hung slightly past her shoulders.

"Everything will be alright." Candy said to the hysterical brunette.

"I take it that this is your first rodeo," the other girl said sitting directly across from Candy, looking at her like she just knew she didn't belong here.

"Yeah, this is my first time," Candy replied. "Why do you ask?"

"Because you look like a needle in a haystack. What's a goody two-shoes like you doing selling pussy anyway?"

"That's none of your damn business." Candy replied. She dropped head down as if she was ashamed.

"No need to be ashamed Pocahontas. My mama always told me as long as you got a pussy you a never be broke," the girl replied.

Yea, that part but I don't even have a pussy, Candy thought to herself.

"This is a minor setback for a major comeback. They gone get us down to booking, process us, take our fingerprints and our mugshots. If you got somebody that'll bring you a hundred and fifty dollars down there to bond you out, they'll let you go. My sugar daddy gone meet me down there. You look like the innocent type, so I doubt you want to contact your parents and tell them you been busted for prostitution. I'll have him pay your bail too and you could just reimburse me when we get out." the girl said to Candy with a slick smirk on her face.

"Why would you do that for me?" Candy replied. "You barely even know me and besides they took all my money when I was arrested."

"Oh, you can work it off...you pretty as fuck, so I know you run it up."

"I ain't working for nobody!" Candy said raising her voice.

"Slow down Lil Mama...bring that shit down a notch. I'm just joking, but hey I'm Alexis and if you need help, I got you. You ain't even got to pay me back. Pepper Ann on her own." she said looking over at the white girl who at this point had been bawling so hard, her face was almost the same color as her hair.

Alexis was beautiful. She wore her hair 22 inches or better, long sleek black Brazilian sew in bust down the middle; she was bright-skinned with pretty brown eyes and resembled Lisa Raye from *The Players Club.*

The white girl who'd been crying the whole time suddenly managed to stop.

"Can you help me too?" she asked in a whining voice.

"Yeah I can help you, but you gone to have to work it off Snow Bunny," Alexis replied.

Just then, the door flew open and four more girls were thrown in.

"Good job boys!" one of the officers said.

"See what happens when you go fishing? Off to booking..." he said as he slammed the door. The seven women were apprehended in a prostitution sting at a Super 8 hotel on Harry Hines in Dallas, Texas. This area was well-known for sex trafficking. The officers set up shop in one of the hotel rooms and responded to Backpage and Craigslist ads from women in the area. This led to the arrest of the seven girls they held in custody in the back of the paddywagon. When they got to Dallas County jail, they were removed from the back of the paddywagon one by one. A female officer took five of the women, one of which included Pepper Ann.

Candy and Alexis were the only two left.

"Why they leave us here?" Candy said confused.

Just then one of the male officers that transported them said, "Okay gentlemen, follow me."

"Fuck you mean gentleman?" Alexis replied.

"Save the shit talk!" the officer quickly replied, "You got a dick don't you?"

Candy looked over in total shock and said, "Alexis you're trans? I never would have guessed!"

"Girl, just call me Lexi and for what it's worth, I never would have clocked your tea either."

After about 3 hours of booking and processing, they still sat in a holding cell waiting for Lexi's sugar daddy to come and post their bail. It didn't seem like that was gonna happen though. Lexi called him numerous times and each of her calls went unanswered.

"Ok gentlemen, lock down. It's time for shift change," said the same rude ass officer who processed them. He unlocked the door to their cell.

"If the circumstances were different and we were anywhere other than jail, I would punch his fat Peter Griffin lookin ass right in his mouth," Lexi said under her breath.

"You can continue your collect calls after shift change," the officer said locking the door to their cell.

Candy burst into tears, "What the fuck are we gone do now?" She said though muffled tears.

"Bitch, shut the fuck up with all that cry baby ass shit. Imma think of something," Lexi replied as she began to pace back and forth in the tiny cell. About an hour into the new shift change, a young black officer came around to do count. He strongly resembled the actor Shemar Moore, except he was slightly darker. Nevertheless, this man was fine. He paused for a moment when he noticed a familiar face.

"Diamond," he said with a smile on his face looking at Lexi.

"Hey Officer Hancock," Lexi replied cheerfully. That wasn't his name; it was just something she liked to call him. He became a regular of hers a couple years ago. Lexi liked him as a client. He fell in the category of what she liked to call 'easy money'. He only liked his dick sucked real sloppy and extremely wet. He also wanted you to stroke it and jack it off while doing so.

"You two know each other?" Candy said sounding surprised.

"I need your help...can you get me outta here?" Lexi said as she stood up from the bottom bunk.

"Get me out of here too!" Candy yelled.

"Us!" Lexi said. Get us out of here," she said looking back at her new found friend.

"Give me a minute, let me finish my count and I'll see what I can do," the officer said as he stepped out of the cell. Moments later he returned. This time he pulled the door all the way up behind him and stepped in. "I can make this all go away, but what you gone do for me?" the officer said unzipping his pants and releasing his big black 11-inch dick.

"I got you Daddy," Lexi said as she dropped to her knees, grabbing hold of his massive cock.

"You too Pretty Red," he said licking his lips at Candy and gesturing for her to come over.

"Unt un, oh hell naw! Ya'll got me fucked up!" Candy said shaking her head.

"Look here Pocahontas! Bitch you better get yo ass down here and do what you need to do. You wanna go home don't you? So quit fucking actin like you too good to suck dick!"

Candy quickly came to her senses and both girls went to work tag-teaming his dick, choking and gagging all over Officer Hancock's throbbing penis. Lexi was shocked Candy actually had a decent head on her shoulders. She went crazy on that dick and actually ended up doing most of the work. She seemed to be really enjoying herself.

The officer moaned with intensity as he approached his climax. He pulled both the girls heads together and released his heavy load on their faces. Lexi then leaned over and kissed Candy while the semen dripped from their lips.

"Keep her around I like her," the officer said zipping up his pants. "You ladies are free to go." He made all of their charges disappear and processed them through bond out, as if their bail was posted.

Once they were on the outside, Candy fell to her knees and kissed the pavement. She was extremely happy to be free. She had never been incarcerated before and this entire ordeal made her promise herself to never to end up in a predicament like that again.

Candy stood up looked over at Lexi and said, "We can never speak of this ever again."

"I already forgot about it," Lexi said with an innocent smirk on her face.

This is going to be the beginning of a great

friendship Candy thought to herself...or would it?

CHAPTER 2

I'll Take You to The Candy Shop

I'll take you to the candy shop. Want a taste of what I got...I'll have you spending all you got keep going till you hit the spot woah woah. The sounds of 50 Cent blared through Candy's portable blue-tooth speaker. This was her theme song and she played it to help motivate herself when it was time to get money. She told herself she was through with this lifestyle, but she had to do what she had to do.

"Woah woah yes bitch, that's my shit," Candy sang as she danced in the mirror admiring her reflection. She walked back over to the bed and sat down. "Bitch I can't believe my phone hasn't rang all day. I haven't received one call from a date."

"Have you posted any recent ads?" Lexi replied. Four years had passed since they first met and became best friends.

Alexis was twenty-four, five foot seven, and one hundred and sixty-five pounds with a nice perky rack her sugar daddy paid for a couple years ago. She also had ass injections that she paid for herself. She had to turn a lot of tricks to do it too. But it didn't matter to her; she was always a firm believer that if you work hard you play hard. She was very passable as a woman. Her friends and clients often refer to her as Diamond from *The Players Club*, so she rolled with it.

Diamond actually made her a lot of money over the years. Back when the *Player's Club* movie came out, Diamond was damn near every man's fantasy. In a way, Lexi was helping these niggas fantasies become reality.

"Yes bitch, I just posted two ads on BackPage and I also posted on Craigslist."

"Bitch, why would you do that? I've told you numerous times, that's the quickest way to get yourself wrapped up. Bitch, ain't no damn money on Craigslist, ain't shit on there but Dallas P. D. You trying to get booked again. Sometimes I think when I talk to you; it goes in one ear and out the other."

"I know best friend," Candy replied. "But I'm so desperate right now; I really need to come up with this money to get Cane out of jail. His bond is five thousand dollars. The bail bondsman said if I bring him ten percent which is five hundred dollars, by twelve tomorrow he would get him out. I gotta get this money though bitch. I need my man and I know if I hesitate, then it's a possibility they might find out he's on parole back in Illinois."

Cane was Candy's boyfriend of eight years. They started dating their senior year of high school. Cane fell in love after watching Kendrick Rodriguez blossom into this beautiful woman named Candy. He knew that one day he would make her his wife. Cane had known Candy since the sixth grade, but they never really spoke to each other. Their freshman year in high school is when Candy really started catching his eye. By that time little five foot two Kendrick with the glasses, who was always getting picked on by the other kids for being soft, begun to blossom. He got rid of those awful glasses and got contacts. He also took down his shoulder length braids and got a relaxer. He was now going by the name Candice. Jamal "Cane" had never really been attracted to boys before. He was the star of the football team and could have any girl he wanted, but it was something about that short Puerto Rican and black girl that he sat next to everyday in third period.

One day he built up enough courage to speak, "Hey my name is Jamal, but everybody calls me Cane." She smiled. "I know who you are," she replied, "My name is Candice, but you can call me Candy."

"Candy Cane, I like that," he replied. "See we go good together," he said in a laughing, but serious kind of way. They were inseparable ever since.

Candy was twenty-five, Puerto Rican and black about five foot four, one hundred and fifty pounds...she hadn't grown much since school. She was very small and petite with B cup breast and she had a nice little fat ass, all natural of course. Candy hadn't had any work done, but she'd been on hormones for about three years. She loved how the process was coming along. She also was very happy with the growth of her titties and felt as if she was finally becoming a woman. She wanted to remain as natural as possible. That's how Cane liked her and she promised him she would always stay that way. So she hardly ever wore weave and she wore very little make-up. She didn't really need it and was passable without it. She used to relax her hair, because she liked it straight; but Cane loved her hair in its natural curly form. So she stopped relaxing it and would just flat iron it from time to time.

"Well, girl you know if things were under different circumstances, I would give you the five hundred dollars, but I'm not finna give you money to get this bitch ass nigga out of jail, just so he can go right back to beating yo ass like Tina Turner."

"Candy, you know how I feel about him. You deserve so much better," Lexi said as she got up from where she was sitting to come over and sit next to Candy on the bed

"I know best friend. He promised me he's gonna do better. He just gets so angry about the fact that I have to sell my body for us to survive."

"If he would get off his ass and find a job you wouldn't have too," Lexi replied.

"I understand that, but he's a felon girl...it ain't that simple."

Money over everything, that's my attitude... the sounds of Trina blared from Candy's purse.

"Hold on girl let me get that... Thank you for calling the Candy Shop where the panties drop... this is Candy at your service."

"Hi Candy, my name is Stan. I found your ad on BackPage how much for the hour?"

"My donation for the hour will be three hundred roses, are you affiliated with any law enforcement?"

"No, I am not," the date replied.

"Ok love, well text me a picture. I'll reply with the address and you can be on your way."

"Ok darling, I'm sending the picture now. See you soon."

"Ok, thank you for choosing the Candy Shop...see you soon!"

"Great, sounds good to me," the date replied."

"Girl I gotta date...about fuckin time!"

"Ok, girl get that money, I'm finna get out of

here. I'm supposed to be meeting Oscar at Razoo's for a late lunch. He's been so busy at the firm, he barely has any time for me."

"You should be happy," Candy said. "Shit that less work you gotta do and your coin gone come regardless."

"Period," Lexi said as she stood up and collected her purse and keys from the table. "Ok girl call me later," Lexi said on her way out the door.

"Will do," Candy replied while locking up the door behind her. Candy turned her music back on and began to prepare herself for the date she had on the way.

"I'll take you to the Candy Shop..." she sang under her breath as she stepped into the shower.

CHAPTER 3

The Struggle of Being a Side Chick

You see, I look too good for this necklace and I look too good to be havin kids. You know I look way too good to be innocent, I'm conceited I got a reason... the sounds of Remy Ma blared through the speakers as Lexi did eighty down 635. She was already late for her late lunch with Oscar and she knew he would be furious. Oscar was Lexi's sugar daddy. He began as just a regular date.

See Oscar was the kind of date every girl wanted and wished they could luck up on, but the chances were slim to none. Oscar was tall, dark and handsome. And even though he was in his early fifties, he looked every bit of thirty-five. He had a wife and four children; two of which were away at college. He loved his wife dearly, but he also loved the attention of a beautiful transsexual as well. He referred to it as an acquired taste.

He'd secretly seen Lexi for about three years

and began to gradually grow serious feelings for her. He made sure that she lived comfortably, just as comfortable as his wife. She drove a 2014 Dodge Charger and had a condo up in Highland Hills out in Frisco. She had an allowance of twenty thousand dollars a month and all she had to do was be his and only his. Which meant she wasn't allowed to sell sex anymore, which was fine with her. Oscar Delanni was one of the highest paid attorneys in Texas and the highest paid black attorney in Dallas.

Lexi couldn't help but feel some type of way after spending the majority of her day with Candy and all along knowing that she betrayed her. Lexi had been sleeping with Cane for about a month behind Candy's back. Deep down she felt horrible about it, but there was something about Cane that she just couldn't resist. She always had a thing for chocolate brothers, but Cane, he was that special kind of dark chocolate. He was her acquired taste. He stood about six foot two, two hundred and 10 pounds, muscular build with tattoos, and he always wore a clean shaved bald haircut. Usually she wasn't attracted to bald men, but in this case, she made an exception. Lexi and Cane originally hated each other, because he couldn't stand her cocky attitude and she couldn't stand the way he controlled her best friend.

But their hatred for each other was quickly forgotten. Their first sexual encounter wasn't really supposed to happen. It just kinda did. Candy had a date and usually she sends Cane to wait outside while she's working. Just so happened, this day it was raining something serious. Lexi happened to pop up at the same time that Candy's date was arriving and she noticed Cane standing outside in the rain. Now she didn't like the nigga, but she wouldn't wanna see the man just standing there getting soaked. So, she told him to get in. At first he was reluctant to take her up on this offer. He was being a bit of a hard ass.

"I'm good," he replied.

Lexi said, "Boy it's raining, get the fuck in the car." After about a minute, he figured what harm could it do and got in.

"I still don't like you bitch," he said as he shut the door.

"Oh, bitch trust and believe I still hate you too. I should have left yo bitch ass out there to catch cold or something. Hopefully the rain would wash some of that dirt off yo black ass, bum."

She turned on the heat so he could warm up. She reached in the back and grabbed her red and black Aeropostle hoody from the back seat and handed it to him.

"Come up out that shirt; it's soaked."

"I'm good." Cane replied while shivering.

"Look, I know we may not like each other and can barely see eye to eye, but I'm tryna help yo black ass." she snapped back. He took the sweater and slowly removed his shirt.

Accidently the word "Damn," parted ways from her lips.

He looked over at her and said, "Oh you like what you see hun?"

She sarcastically replied, "You aight."

"Just alright," Cane snapped back. "Bitch, I look good."

"I mean you cute or whatever, but look that's none of my business," Lexi said as she began to thumb through the radio stations.

"You been wanted to fuck me Bitch...I be seeing how you look at me. All that not liking me shit was just a facade so Candy wouldn't pick up on it."

She quickly fired back, "Bitch ass nigga, ain't no muthafuckin body waaaa...." Before she could finish her sentence, Cane leaned over and kissed her. She let it happen for a moment then she pulled away and slapped him. Cane laughed.

She tried to make light of the situation and changed the subject. "So why you outside anyway...can't you stand in the lobby?"

"Hell naw, dude at the desk a bitch. He said I look like a thug and it's bad for business." Lexi wasn't really paying attention to the conversation; she was too busy thinking about that kiss.

She looked over at Cane, "Nigga you know you was out of line right? Your girl is my best friend."

"Ok...and?" Cane spat back. "What the fuck is that supposed to mean? What she don't know won't hurt her."

The car fell silent for a moment. It seemed as if time stood still for about thirty seconds. Before you knew it, Cane went in for another kiss. This time she didn't stop him. He pulled her over into the passenger seat on top of him. She wanted to stop him, but her body wouldn't let her. It just felt so good. He continued to kiss her as he raised her tight, fitted maxi dress over her head. He never put on the sweater, so he still sat there shirtless, chest glistening from the moisture that covered his body. He couldn't help himself. He was passionately kissing her, massaging her ass and gripping her cheeks. He then lifted her bra and took one of her succulent 36c cup titties into his mouth. She couldn't help but moan. He turned her around facing the dashboard and lifted her a little higher. Cane pulled her G-string to the side and began eating her ass like groceries. Lexi moaned in total pleasure.

The sound of Dej Loaf played through the speakers, *Aye that's my shawty I like what you be doing with yo body and can't nobody get this pussy wet yo and can't nobody fuck me like you can no, no no no...* She was so wet, the bottom of his face was shining. He then eased her down on his thick, fat cut, ten and a half inch dick.

In that moment, she felt like her soul immediately left her body. He began to make love to her like no man had ever done before. His rock hard dick was sliding in and out of that tight wet hole, sending chills up her spine with every thrust...

It was already a quarter after two when she sped up into Razoo's parking lot. She was supposed to meet Oscar for lunch at 1:30, so she knew he was finna be pissed. Just as she was getting out of her car, Oscar came walking out.

"Baby let me explain." Lexi said jumping out of the car.

"Ain't shit to explain...You already knew I was pressed for time Lexi," Oscar said angrily walking towards his car. "How many times must I tell you time is money? Bitch, get in the truck!" he demanded as they approached his vehicle. She got into the passenger side of his 2015 Range Rover + Limited Edition. He quickly undid his pants releasing his average uncircumcised penis and said, "Here suck this dick." She pulled her hair back in a ponytail and did as she was told And after about fifteen minutes of pleasure, he came in her mouth. He handed her a napkin and said,

"Here, clean yourself up." Lexi wiped her hands and mouth, then fixed her hair. Oscar popped the locks. "Now get the fuck out of my truck..." he said. "I gotta get back to work." She exited the vehicle and he sped off into traffic almost hitting a black Ford Focus. Lexi knew he was still upset. She just stood there for a moment feeling used and disrespected.

I wonder do he handle his wife like this...probably not, she thought to herself as she walked back to her car.

CHAPTER 4

What Kind of Birds Don't Fly

You have a collect call from (Cane) an inmate at the Dallas County jail to accept the charges press one-beep... This call is subject to monitoring and recording, you are now connected.

"Hello," a male voice spoke into the phone.

"Hey bae," Candy said.

"Bitch, what the fuck took you so long to answer the phone? This is my third time calling."

"I know bae, I'm sorry I was with a date. I just came up with the five hundred dollars for the bail bondsman and a lil extra to cover the room for another month and to turn up when you get out."

"Bitch, don't you know it's eleven o'clock and its Saturday! Them mufucka's close at twelve today!"

"I already know bae. Lexi on her way to come

take me down there right now...the bitch shoulda been here by now," Candy said in an angry tone.

"Ok bae, I'm sorry I got so angry with you bae. I just get so upset at the fact just knowing that I have to share you. And you expect me to just be Ok with it. You're mine, you belong to me," Cane said through the phone in a dominant tone.

"I understand that Cane, but this monthly hotel fee, our phone bills, food, shopping expenses, habits and other necessities we need is not gonna pay for itself. You already know I'm yours. I always have been and always will be Mrs. Candy Cane," she said trying to sound sexy.

"No matter what," Cane replied.

"No matter what," Candy responded.

You have sixty seconds remaining.

"Ok bae, Imma let you go. Make sure yo ass make it down there before twelve."

"Ok Daddy, I love you."

"I love you too ma...see you soon."

Thank you for using DPCS, goodbye. The call was disconnected.

Cane sat on the edge of his bunk with elbows on his knees and his face in his hands. He felt like shit after talking to Candy. He put her through so much and she was still by his side. He knew he didn't deserve her. His mind went back to the last time he made love to her. He reminisced about how he fucked her in the shower right after he came in from his little secret sex session with Lexi. He felt so guilty about it. He knew what he was doing was wrong, but it was just something about that bitch that turned him on. He couldn't stand her ass...he actually hated her guts, but damn did that bitch have some good pussy. He couldn't stop thinking about it.

Sex was always good with Candy and it's been good for the past eight years. But sex with Diamond, which was what he liked to call her, was spectacular. He told himself if he called her Diamond, he wasn't fuckin Lexi. He wasn't cheating on his girl with her best friend. Somehow that made sense in his twisted fucked up brain. He'd been in jail since last night after another one of his drunken episodes. They were becoming more and more frequent. He had gotten drunk in a bar in the lobby of the hotel while he was waiting on Candy to service a date. After he had about six too many, he went upstairs and picked a fight with Candy after seeing her date leave. This guy wasn't like those average white guys that usually come. This was a tall light skin swole mother fucker. Cane couldn't help but to picture him fuckin his woman and quickly grew furious. After about an hour of a heated argument, he became very aggressive, belligerent and things even got a bit physical. He told himself that he would never allow himself to get like that again; especially after that incident landed him in prison for two years.

The loud speaker came on in his cell, *Jamal Cane pack your shit, your bond has been posted.*

"Damn that bitch move quick, it hasn't even been an hour yet. I swear I love my bitch." After dressing back into his street clothes, Cane walked out the doors of the Dallas County jail. He couldn't believe that he was really back breathing fresh air and damn it felt good.

"Aye, you got another cigarette bro?" Cane asked another guy who was released right before him.

"Yea, I got you my nigga," he replied as he handed Cane a Newport.

"Thanks bro, I'm Cane by the way."

"I'm Yella," he quickly responded. Cane could tell by this fella's attire that he was a workin man.

"Aye bro, where you work at?"

"Aww shit, I work at Lube Pros over in Plano."

"What ya'll do there?" Cane asked. He really didn't care what they did. He would do almost anything for stable employment at this point.
"Changing oil, tires and shit you know." Yella replied.

"Are they hiring?" Cane asked.

"Do you know how to administer oil changes and change and rotate tires?"

"Yea I do. I was in youth build's mechanical trade program. I was gonna be a mechanic before I caught my felony."

"Aww you a felon? Shit'd me too! But I'm a manager in that bitch now. From parole to payroll my nigga," Yella said as he took a long pull from his square. "Look take my business card, put in an application and give me a call in a couple days. I can get you in."

"Damn bro, straight up?" Cane said in total shock. "That's what's up my nigga. I'll put it in tonight. Good looking out."

"No problem," Yella replied. Just then a black Chevy Suburban sitting on 26s pulled up in front of the jail.

Future banged through the speaker, *Let's fuck up some commas.*

"Alright my nigga, this my bitch here. I'm out. Make sure you hit my line bro."

"Will do my nigga," Cane replied.

"Aye, one more thing before you roll, do yo girl got a phone I could use? My shit is as dead as Michael Jackson and I need to call my bitch and let her know I'm out."

"Yea I got you," Yella hopped in the passenger seat. "Bae, let me see yo phone. This Mercedes bro, Sadie this Cane," Yella said as he introduced the two. Mercedes had carmel skin tone, hazel eyes that he could tell were contacts, a Marilynn Monroe lip piercing and quite a few tattoos. She wore her hair in a red short cut bob with a feathered bang.

She was a bit on the plus side, but she was cute to be a big girl... he thought to himself. Cane didn't know her tea until she spoke.

"Hey wassup love?" She said in a raspy, but very masculine tone.

Damn this bitch sound like Barry White, Cane thought to himself. "What's good ma?" he replied. Yella handed Cane the phone.

She picked up on the second ring, "Thank you for calling Candy Shop where the panties drop. This is Candy at your service."

"Bae I'm out! Call Lexi to come pick me up."

"Ok my love stay right there," Candy said, "I'm finna call her now."

"Ok, but tell her to come now. I'm standing out front," Cane said and hung up.

"Thanks bro, Imma be in touch," he said while handing Yella back the phone.

"Alright my nigga, be smooth, hit my line," Yella said as they drove away.

"Will do," Cane replied as Sadie sped off with the music blasting.

Approximately thirty minutes later, Lexi pulled up with Xscape playin on the CD, *You're my little secret and that's how we should keep it...* as he got in, she turned the music down.

"What kinda birds don't fly? Lexi asked.

"What kinda hoes don't lie?" Cane replied. "Bitch if you woulda came and get me last night like the fuck you said you was going to do I wouldn't be in this predicament!"

She placed her hand on his inner thigh, "Baby, I can explain."

He simply replied, "Excuses are useless, drop me off." She really didn't have an excuse. Her conscience was just fuckin with her so she decided not to go get him even though she couldn't stop thinking about that dick. Cane really wanted to fuck her, but instead he would make her wait and leave her ass feigning for a while. This was all a part of his plan. He already had her dickmatized. It was almost time.

CHAPTER 5

Treat Him Like A King

"Baby daddy just made bail today. He a thug nigga he'a shoot today," she was walking around her hotel room singin this funny song that she had came across on YouTube by the Hudson brothers.

Them brother are hilarious, she thought to herself.

She picked up her phone and dialed a number, "What's good wit it Mami?" A Latin male voice spoke into the phone.

"Hey, Diablo...look Papi I need you to bring me a fiddy. I'm at the room."

"Ok chica, I'll be there in twenty minutes."

"Ok love, see you soon," she said as they hung up. Thirty minutes later her phone went off

"I'm outside," his ass never really came on time.

His twenty minutes usually meant an hour, so she was surprised he got there as quick as he did.

"Ok, I'll be right there," Candy said putting on her shoes to run outside and meet him. She walked up to the late eighty's model Chevy Caprice Classic and hopped in the passenger seat.

They completed their transaction and she got out, "Thanks Papi."

"No problem Mami," he said as he drove off.

Just then she looked over and noticed Lexi's car parked on the other end of the parking lot. Her and Cane were just sitting there and from what she could see they seemed to be arguing. She started walking towards the car, but Cane immediately noticed her and hopped out. Lexi snatched off into traffic.

"What was that all about?" Candy asked.

"You know, same old shit," Cane replied with a nervous look on his face.

"No, I don't know. How about you fill me in...I'll wait," Candy said crossing her arms across her chest.

"Well it's like this, shorty feel some type of way about me putting my hands on you. I assured her that it was the last time. I love you Bae..." Cane said with a voice of compassion. "... and I promise to never hurt you again."

"I love you too Daddy and Imma check that bitch. I told her to stay the fuck out of my business," Candy said standing on her tippy toes to give her man a kiss. "I'm so happy you're out. I almost lost my mind without Bae." Cane released a sigh of relief. She bought it, he couldn't believe she bought it. He was getting nervous for a minute there.

They tightly fell into each other's embrace, "It's only been a day," he said looking into her eyes. Candy noticed he had an aroma of Chanel perfume on him, the same kind Lexi wore. She knew the fragrance so well. Candy bought her a bottle of it for her birthday a few months ago. It was the only kind of perfume she wore.

She thought to herself, "Damn was this bitch all over him or did this nigga put on some of her perfume?" She quickly cancelled that thought out of her head; maybe she sprayed it while he was in the car. She felt stupid for the first thought that came across her mind. They hate each other. "You're over reacting," Candy she told herself.

It was about a quarter after one when they walked into their hotel room. Candy had a nice, hot bubble bath waiting for Cane when he arrived. Rose petals greeted him at the door. He followed them into the bathroom where the petals were beautifully scattered in the tub.

He quickly undressed and got in. He slid down into the hot tub of water to relax and unwind for moment. About twenty minutes into his bath, Candy knocked at the door.

"Can I come in?" she asked.

"Come on in Bae," Cane replied. Candy changed into something sexy. She walked in wearing a fire red teddy with the ass part missing. She put on a pair of red bottom heels and a rose in between her teeth. She also carried a tray of chocolate covered strawberries and a glass of champagne.

He thought to himself, "Damn life is good, I don't deserve this."

"Are you enjoying yourself Daddy?" Candy asked as she handed him the glass of wine. She laid the rose on his chest.

"Yes baby, of course I am." Cane replied.

After he finished taking his bath, he walked out of the bathroom completely naked, his dick hanging. Candy lay in bed with rose peddles scattered over her body. A rush of excitement quickly came over her as she watched him walk over to her licking his lips. The sounds of Sons of Funk played on her iPad through her portable Bluetooth speaker.

Shole feels damn good to me when I'm pushing

in side of you, can't explain the way it feels all I wanna do is be with you... As Cane stood at the foot of the bed, fully erect, admiring his woman, a sudden feeling of guilt came over him. He cheated on her, beat on her and still she showered him with affection and treated him like a king. In that moment, he realized he couldn't lose her. He knew he had to cut it off with Lexi. Fuck what he planned. Candy meant more to him than anything in the world; he couldn't jeopardize losing her.

"Bae I don't deserve you."

"Yes, you do. I just want you to realize what it is that you have and stop taking it for granted. You better realize what side yo bread is buttered on."

That night he would make passionate love to her and explore every inch of her body with his mouth. Then in the morning he would take the ten thousand dollars Diamond gave to him before Candy almost caught them. It's the reason they were sitting in the car so long in the first place. Lexi was reluctant to give him the money, but its kind hard of to tell Cane 'No' after he put good wood down on you. Cane had big plans for the money. Even though it wasn't a lot, he was going to use it wisely. He planned to buy Candy a really nice engagement ring and propose to her. He made his mind up; Candy was the woman he would share his life with.

After about three hours of passionate love making, Candy poured up a couple glasses of

Hennessey that chilled in a bucket of ice. Then, she brought out a plate and retrieved the package she copped from Diablo from her purse.

She looked at her king and said, "Now let the real party begin."

She'd only done coke on a few occasions, but she knew it was something that Cane really enjoyed. So tonight, she would get higher than a giraffe pussy, climb on top of her man and ride him until his dick went soft.

Cane looked at her and said, "Is it my muthafuckin birthday? Damn a nigga need to beat yo ass more often." She shot him one of those looks, that if looks could kill, he would have died immediately. "Chill out Bae, I'm just kidding," Cane said while giggling.

"Kidding my ass," Candy replied sarcastily.

"You know I love you ma. That was the last time on my mother's grave." She knew he was telling the truth then, because Cane didn't play when it came to his mother. After all, he beat his stepfather so severely; it left him a coma. Cane left the man for dead and a neighbor found him in the alley behind their building, barely clinging to life. Cane attacked him for introducing his mother to heroin. The addiction eventually led to her death. He didn't like to talk about it though, so Candy hardly ever brought it up. But, she knew that cocaine was his only way of easing the pain. Liquor only made him angry. But, when he did a combination of the two, he was calm and mellow. His eyes lit up like a kid on Christmas day when she broke down the bag on the plate. She smiled, making him happy was all she wanted to do.

"So now I see why the name Cane stuck with you. It didn't have shit to do with your last name." He broke out into laughter as he reached for the plate.

"That's bullshit...even though I do love cocaine," he said leaning down to snort his line.

CHAPTER 6

Jealousy At Its Finest

Lexi sat at a stop light a couple blocks away from Candy's hotel, when a sudden rush of emotion overcame her. She burst into to tears, completely overwhelmed with emotion. Everything was becoming so real to her. She wanted it all to be a bad dream or a horrible nightmare that she could just wake up from. She deceived her best friend, the only friend she ever really had.

Lexi was trapped in this fucked up side-chick ass relationship with a man who spoiled her, but treated and talked to her like shit. Then to top it all off she was falling in love with her best friend's boyfriend, a man that she knew she could never really have as her own. She sat there for a moment soaking in her sorrow. She quickly snapped out of it when the car behind her honked letting her know that the light turned green.

Just then her gas light came on. She quickly

pulled into a Quik Trip and hopped out to go pay for gas. She looked cayute and she knew it. She wore a grey and white cropped top jumpsuit from PINK and white high-top Air Force Ones.

"Thirty on pump six please and a pack of swishers."

I need to smoke after this shit, Lexi thought to herself. On her way out the door, she bumped into some light skinned ass nigga with oil stains all over what appeared to be his work uniform.

"Excuse you, Miss Lady."

"Oh, my bad," she replied.

"You good beautiful, I'm just fuckin wit cha. Say where yo man at?" He asked her.

"Who said I had a man?" She quickly responded.

"Pretty lady like yourself, I just would have expected you to be taken."

"Maybe I like the single life," she replied as she started walking back to her car.

"Hey I didn't get your name!" He yelled across the parking lot.

"That's because I didn't give it to you," Lexi

responded, slightly looking back over her shoulder. She pumped the gas and got back in the car. Just then her text notification went off. It was from Oscar. *Meet me at Olive Garden on Spring Valley tomorrow for lunch. Be there at noon and don't be late.*

I can't stand this motherfucker, she thought to herself.

"I won't." She replied and dropped the phone back in her purse. She looked at the clock on the radio, it was still early in the day. What was she gonna do?

She felt as though she had no life. She decided on getting her nails touched up and an eyebrow and bikini wax. Then she would call up her thirsty as cousin Jazz to see if she wanted to hit up Black Orchid tonight. Jazz was always thirsty when it came to going out with Lexi, because she knew they would be right in V.I.P with all the ballers and sometimes celebrities. She also hated going out with Jazz, because every time she went out with Jazz, she'd disappeared with a different nigga and left her there drinking by herself. Who else could she call? Candy was her only friend. She was sure she wasn't gonna hear from that bitch until tomorrow and she didn't have any other friends.

Just as she pulled up at the nail shop her phone rang. *Imma boss ass bitch bitch bitch bitch bitch bitch imma boss ass bitch...*

"Hello? What it is hoe wassup...bitch this Jazz."

"Oh, wassup bitch, I was just finna call. Do you wanna go out tonight?"

"Duhh bitch, you shoulda known I do, that's actually why I was calling you. My home girl told me Webbie and Boosie gone be in Black Orchid tonight. I'm tryna go home with one of em."

"Bitch Aunty Sherry must have known yo ass was gone be a hoe that's why she named you Jazzibelle."

"Naw she ain't know. Shit'd you know all eleven of her kids got named after someone in the bible. When I would come home crying because kids would make fun of me, my oldest sister Eve would alway say, "Honey, it's just a name, just make sure that you don't live up to it. I did just the opposite."

"Bitch, yo ass crazy. But Ok, Imma let you go. I gotta get in here so I can get these eyebrows fleeked. I'll be through there to get you about ten."

"Ok bitch. I'll be ready." Lexi hung up and got out of the car.

"Alexander Terrell Jackson," a familiar voice spoke just as she hit the locks on her car.

"James Lee Cole," she sarcastically replied.

"Bitch its Jamiya."

"I would say bitch its Alexis, but you already knew that," she said with a disgusted look on her face. Miya was another T-girl she met while she doing time.

She was only in a few months before Miya had gotten shipped off to prison. She was in for credit card fraud and was one of the coldest rutters to walk the streets of Dallas. Rutter was a word well known in the gay community for people who cracked cards. She cracked cards since she was 17 and the bitch was 28 now. That bitch paid for her complete transition at some elderly white woman's expense. Miya was about six feet tall dark skin with a big ole booty. People referred to her as Serena Williams, but Lexi always called her Venus, because the bitch was ugly and not passable at all.

"What's been up girl, it's been so long. Life's been treating you well I see," Miya said as she glanced over at Lexi's car.

"Yes it has...how long has it been, four, five years?" Lexi said pulling her purse up on her arm. It's been four since they sent a bitch upstate and sat me down for a minute. But I'm back down bitch. I been out for three months now."

"That's what's up bitch, stay the fuck out trouble. Look what you doin tonight? Me and my cousin finna pop out. Black Orchid finna be crackin.

I heard Webbie and Boosie supposed to be in the club tonight. You can roll if you want to."

"I would love to, but bitch I'm broke as fuck! I've been tryna find a new hustle. Crackin cards was all I knew. I guess a bitch finna have to post an ad or something, because something gonna have to give. A bitch can't be broke, but I been tryna lay low a least till I get off parole."

"Don't trip bitch I got you. Matter fact, let me go get these nails and eyebrows together, then we can hit up North Park. Imma cop you sumtin fly to step out in. You want yo nails done?"

"Hell yea, bitch! OMG thank you so much Lexi, you a real ass bitch."

"No problem Boo. I haven't forgot about that care package you plugged me with when I first came on the deck." Miya smiled as they walked into the nail shop.

CHAPTER 7

A Man That Don't Work Don't Eat

Cane woke up early the next morning and walked to the Waffle House down the street to get Candy some breakfast. She was still sleep when he got back. He woke her up tickling her feet and sucking her toes.

"Stop bae, you so nasty."

"Wake up sleepin beauty. I brought you some breakfast in bed," Cane said in an animated voice.

"Aww thanks baby. You shouldn't have," Candy replied.

"This is only the beginning. I plan to take you out for dinner as well."

"Where McDonalds?" she said sarcast-ically.

"No, I was thinking something a bit more upscale. I was thinking Jasper's."

"Cane that restaurant is expensive. We don't have that kind of money and I ain't finna dine and dash with yo ass."

"Don't worry, I got you Bae...just trust me. While she was eating breakfast, Cane called up Yella. He needed a ride and it was time to start putting his plan in motion.

"Hello."

"Aye bro...this Cane from yesterday. We chopped it up in front of the jail house."

"Yea, I remember. What it is my nigga?"

"Aye bro, I was just letting you know I put in that application."

"Ok, I'll pull yo application when I get back to work tomorrow. I'm off today."

"Ok cool. Aye bro, do you think you can do me a really big favor?"

"That depends on what it is my nigga." Yella replied.

"If you ain't doing shit, I need you to give me a ride to Town East Mall, so I can pick up something for my girl."

"Aww, no problem. I got you nigga. Let me take

a shower and shit and I'll be right there. Where am I picking you up from?"

"I'm at the Motel 6 right off 635 it sits to the right of the LBJ, heading east. I'll text you the address."

"Ok blood. I'll be there in about an hour."

They said their goodbye's and hung up. Cane stepped back into the room. He stepped in the hallway while he spoke; he didn't want Candy to get suspicious of his conversation.

"Bae I'm finna go take care of some business with my boy. I'll be back later."

"What boy do you have that I haven't met and is just now hearing about? And what business do you have to take care of in Dallas that don't involve Candy?" She aggressively asked.

"Don't trip ma, some things a nigga gotta do alone" Cane replied.

"Ok, I trust you so I ain't gonna trip. But don't go doing nothing stupid Jamal," she was serious now. She only called him Jamal when she was serious.

"I promise I ain't on no bullshit."

"Ok, but you still ain't told me about this new friend you done met."

"His name Yella. I bumped into him yesterday when we were being released."

"And when will I meet this yella character?"

"You will meet him in due time."

Cane went to take a shower. By the time he finished getting dressed his phone started ringing

I aint a killa but don't push me revenge is like the sweetest thing next to eating pussy... Cane was a big Tupac fan.

"Hello." It was Yella. "I'm outside blood."

"Ok, I'll be right out." He hung up and went over to the side of the bed where Candy lay. She'd fallen back to sleep. He kissed her on the forehead. He decided against waking her, she looked so peaceful sleeping.

"I'll be back soon my love," he whispered.

He walked out the lobby of the hotel where Yella sat out front and hopped in the truck. Yella smoked a blunt and listened to Drake's *Hot Line Bling*.

"What up bro?" Cane said to him.

"What it is my nigga?" Yella replied while passing the blunt to Cane.

They drove off into traffic. "Aye bro, can I ask you a personal question?" Cane asked Yella as they approached a red light.

"Yea, what's up?" Yella replied.

"Don't take offence to this, but is your girl a tranny bro?"

"Yea she is, but why did you ask that...what you a homophobic or some shit?"

"Naw hell naw, my girl is too. That's what I was gonna tell you."

"Aw ok, shit'd me and Sadie been together five years. We met in the joint, she was my cellie at first."

"That's wassup nigga. Shit me and Candy been together eight. We went to high school together."

"Damn ya'll married by common law," Yella replied.

"Yea, but I wanna do it the right way now. That's why you taking me to the mall. I'm going to get her an engagement ring. I'm finna ask her to be my wife."

"Damn that's what's up my nigga. Congratulations!"

"Don't congratulate me yet, she hasn't even

said yes."

"That's yo girl. Ya'll been together eight years, she's gonna say yes. She don't want no other nigga but you...that's obvious."

"You right bro. How about you and yo girl join us tonight for dinner. Candy is dying to meet you. We're having dinner at this upscale restaurant called Jasper's."

"Yea I'm down. Sadie would like that too. She swear a nigga don't ever do shit nice for her."

Just as they were exiting off the highway, Cane noticed a huge sign off to the right side of him. *Now leasing stop in today to find out about our move in specials.*

"Aye bro, stop right here...let me check out these town homes. I gotta get the fuck out of that motel."

Yella pulled into the entrance of the Peach Tree Apartments. They got out and walked into the leasing office.

"Hello gentlemen," the black lady behind the desk said to them.

"Hello ma'am. Well, I was riding by and noticed your sign. It said something about move in specials?" Cane asked while shaking the woman's hand.

"Yes you have come to the right place. Well let me show you one of our vacancies and I'll tell you all about the specials as you look." The apartment was an immaculate two bedrooms, two bathrooms, enclosed patio, high ceilings, and all new appliances. He was sold.

"I'll take it," he said.

"Great, well our move in special is eight fifty for the first month's rent, application fees and deposit will be waived.

"How long does it take for the application to go through?"

"Well about forty-eight hours," she replied.

"How about this I drop the eight fifty for the rent then put about five hundred in your pocket and you let me move in today?"

"Well I can lose my job for this, but I'll just change the date on your application and fabricate your background check. I can use that five hundred," the woman replied.

"Great!" He paid her and she gave him the keys to his home. Now they were off to the mall to get this ring. After he bought the five-thousand-dollar ring, he went and spent three thousand on furniture,

"Damn this money is going fast," he thought to himself, "but it's all worth it." He couldn't wait to see the look on Candy's face.

CHAPTER 8

If You Like It Then You Should've Put A Ring on It

Candy straightened her hair and put on a little make up. She wore a royal blue and iridescent stoned gown with a small train and the back out. She also wore some small iridescent stone earrings and silver stiletto pumps. She stood out front because Cane told her to be standing out front at six o'clock. He also told her to dress formal. She had that gown for years since she had bought it for prom. Cane was still in the closet then. He wasn't ready to share his truth with the world. So she saved the dress and she was excited to finally have a reason to wear it. Just then a limo pulled up and the driver got out, came around and opened the door.

"Ms. Cane, I'm Jewarrd. I'll be your driver for the evening."

What the hell? Driver, limo, upscale resta urant... damn is my nigga selling drugs and I don't know it? Candy thought out loud.

It was about 6:30pm when they arrived at Jasper's; the driver came around and opened the door for her. She stepped out onto a red carpet, she felt like a celebrity. When she walked into the restaurant, she couldn't believe her eyes. Everything was so beautiful. She walked up to the hostess stand.

Before she could even speak, he said, "Ms. Cane, right this way," as she followed him. She thought to herself, *How the fuck does all these people know my name?*

When she arrived at the table, she saw Cane dressed in what appeared to be an expensive suit. She noticed two people she hadn't ever seen before; Lexi and her rich lawyer friend was also seated. Lexi was wearing a strapless all white Ferragamo gown and her plus one was wearing white as well. The girl with the red hair, whom she didn't know, was wearing a red form fitting dress that hugged her at the knees. And the light skin fellow who was with her wore a red and black Versace pantsuit. Cane wore a grey pants suit from Armani Exchange, accented with a royal blue under shirt.

He must have known I would wear this dress; Candy thought to herself and smiled.

"What's all this?" Candy asked. "Lexi, what are you doing here? She said as she approached to take her seat.

"Cane invited me," she replied smiling.

"You look beautiful."

"So do you," Candy replied. Cane stood up and pulled out the chair for his lady. Candy looked at the two guests and spoke.

"Hello I'm Candy, how rude of my honey not to introduce me."

"Hi, I'm Mercedes," the female spoke.

"And I'm Nayshawn, but you can call me Yella," the man replied.

"Oh, you're the infamous Yella. I've heard so much about you," she said to him adjusting her seat comfortably.

"All good things I hope," he quickly replied.

"Oh yes of course," she responded. Just then the waiter came over to take their orders. They sat there chatting for almost an hour before their food was brought out. The food was amazing. After everyone ate and ordered desert, Oscar told the waiter to bring them one of their most expensive bottles of wine and the check.

"Dinner is also on me everyone. My treat," he said out loud. Just then another waiter came out with three gift boxes and placed them in front of Candy.

"Wait there must be some mistake, it's not my

birthday," Candy replied.

"Are you Mrs. Cane?" he said.

"Yes," she said with a confused look on her face.

"Then these are yours. Its no mistake, enjoy the remainder of your evening," he said as he walked away.

She looked at Cane and said, "What is this?"

He said, "Open them and see, but you must open them from biggest too small." She looked over and saw Lexi recording, but she thought nothing of it. She just figured maybe she was posting on Snapchat or something. She opened the first big box and it was filled with magazines and coupons from David's bridal.

"What the hell am I gonna do with this stuff Jamal?" She opened the second medium sized box. This box had four sections in it and one section there was the neckless Cane gave her last Christmas. In the next section was a pair of keys. In the third section was a diamond studded bracelet that she knew belonged to Lex's grandmother. She never left the house without it and Candy noticed that she didn't have it on.

"What the fuck kinda gifts are these?" She thought to herself. "I'm gone at least wait until I open this last box before I check his ass for playin wit me." The very last section held a beautiful pair of royal blue diamond earrings. "I'm finna put these on right now," she said as she glanced over at Cane.

She opened the small box last. There was a folded-up piece of paper inside it that said:

Something old
Something new,
Something borrowed
Something blue,
A love like this I never knew
Please allow me to share the rest
Of my life with you.

When she looked up after reading this, Cane was down on one knee at her feet,

"Candice Hymena Rodriguez, will you do me the honor of being my wife?"

She burst into tears, "Yes, yes I will!" she replied as he placed the ring on her finger. He got up and gave her one of the most passionate kisses he had ever given her in his life.

"I want the world to know that I love you."

She smiled and said, "Well tell the world my love...shout it for the whole world to hear!"

Cane leaned down and whispered in her ear, "I

love you baby, you are my world."

She stood up and shouted, "I'm gettin married!" The entire restaurant clapped in applause. She looked at Lexi and said, "Bitch did you know about this and didn't tell me?"

Lexi replied with tears in her eyes, "I just found out today, but my gift to you is I want you to wear my grandmother's bracelet on your special day and I want to pay for your dress. I'm so happy for you sis."

"Thanks love," Candy replied. She looked over at her fiancé, "Ok love, there's one thing that is still a mystery to me, what was the keys for?

"Something new," Cane replied. Those are the keys to your new two-bedroom town home at the Peach Tree Apartments."

"Bae I'm ecstatic! How did you do all of this?"

Before he could speak, Lexi spoke, "I gave him a loan."

Yella chimed in, "...and I gave him a job."

Lexi's rich lawyer friend spoke up, "Well since everyone is in such a giving spirit, I want to pay for the wedding." He was getting drunk and when he got drunk, he got generous. He cut Candy a check for twenty-five thousand thousand. Candy broke down into tears; she couldn't believe this was all happening. She was really getting married. She was finally gonna become the real Mrs. Cane.

"Somebody pinch me, I must be dreaming."

CHAPTER 9

If The Shoe Don't Fit Don't Force It

Sadie and Yella were riding the President George Bush Turnpike on their way home when Sadie out the blue blurted out, "Bitch why the fuck you can't do something like that for me?"

Man, bitch you better watch yo muthafuckin mouth before yo lips beat you to the hospital. You must've had to many glasses of wine," Yella said infuriated.

"I'm just sayin bae; we've been together five years now and were not getting any younger."

"Look Sadie, I'm not finna have this conversation with you right now."

"It's a conversation that needs to be had Nayshawn. I'm tired of playing house nigga this ain't Disney. Where is the future in all of this?" Sadie said gazing out the window.

"Well if you're tired then take yo ass to sleep bitch. I'll propose to you when I'm ready. If you're the woman that I decide to share my life with."

"If I'm the woman you decide to share your life with and just what the fuck is that supposed to mean Yella?" She spat back sitting up in her seat.

"Are you sayin that you don't know if you wanna be with me?" She screamed at him as tears started falling uncontrollably down her face. He didn't respond. "Stop the car."

"Yo ass over reacting Mercedes!" Yella screamed.

"Stop the fuckin car!" She shouted. Yella came to a complete stop causing both of their bodies to jerk forward. Sadie hopped out and began walking up the side of the highway. He slowly drove alongside her.

"Girl get yo tale in the car, yo ass trippin. Mercedes you know I love you, now would you bring yo ass on?" He got aggressive after a while. "Look you're the only woman I want and I promise we will make that commitment when the time is right."

After about a half hour of persuading her, she got back in. She really didn't give a fuck about what he was saying, those six-inch red bottoms were doing a number on her feet; and it was a long walk back to Louisville where they lived. So, she gave up and got in. They didn't speak the entire rest of the way home.

Yella really did love her and she knew that, but what she didn't know was that the reason he didn't want to marry her. It was because he had been sleepin around on her and he wasn't ready to commit. He was fuckin a different bitch every other day and he wasn't ready to give that up and just commit to being with one woman. He was only twenty-six, he was young dumb and full of cum, marriage could wait. Yella didn't have no type. He didn't give a fuck how you looked as long as you had a hole that he could penetrate, he was goin in. He was fuckin trannys, real bitches, even had slept with a couple niggas, but that wasn't really his preference. You had to be an extremely feminine bottom for him to make an exception, but Yella had his eyes on a new prize. He wanted Lexi and he wasn't gonna rest until he got her. Ever since he bumped into her the other night at the gas station, he couldn't seem to get her out of his mind. He made a note in his mental to get her number from Cane.

The next day while he was at work, Sadie packed all her things and moved out. She went to stay with her sister Porchia. Sadie had two sisters, Porchia and Alexus. Their mother had cursed her when she named her Stanley after her crackhead father. So after she decided on transitioning she changed her name to Mercedes so that she would fit right in with her sisters, which she looked just like.

It was after five when Yella got home from work he was exhausted. The day had been so busy at work, he barely had enough time to pull Cane's application and set up his interview. He told him to just come in and do his paper work and he was hired on the spot. By the end of the day he was drained. He just wanted to lie in the bed with Sadie and relax and probably watch some Netflix. As he walked through the door he was prayin she had cooked. He worked five days a week and three out of the five of those days he came home to a home cooked meal. This day was different. The house was cold.

"He walked in, "Honey I'm home." No response. He walked into the bed room, half of the dresser drawers were pulled out. Their walk-in closet was in shambles and there were hangers on the floor scattered everywhere.

"This bitch done left me, she really left me." He was furious and heartbroken all at the same time. He ran outside, jumped in his truck and drove everywhere he thought she might be. He went to her mama house, he went to her best friend's house and he went to her sister Alexus' house.

She has to be at Porchia's, he thought to himself. When he pulled up, Porchia's kids were playing outside in the yard. When they saw his truck, they ran in the house and locked the door.

He was for certain that Sadie messy best friend, mama, and sister had warned her that he was on the way. He walked up to the porch and knocked at the door.

Porchia's ghetto, purple weave wearing ass came to the door. Without opening it, she yelled, "Keepa knockin but cha can't come in."

"Porchia let me talk to Mercedes."

"She don't wanna talk to you," Porchia screamed from behind the door.

"Tell her I love her and I'm sorry. I want her to come home now ya hear."

"I ain't tell her shit nigga. Fuck you nigga," she replied while looking out the peephole.

Yella began kickin at the door. "Open this mufuckin door! Mercedes...Mercedes... Sadie, please don't do this to me." Sadie sat on the bed in her sister's room with her hands over her ears, but still hearing everything. She started crying she couldn't hold back the tears.

"Yella get the fuck outta here, you scaring my kids! I'm finna call my baby daddy to come whoop yo ass."

"Bitch, call yo baby daddy hoe! You know how I rock!" After about ten more minute of kicking at the door and yelling Mercedes name, he finally gave up, got in his truck and left. He was gone get her back. He couldn't lose her like this, not like this. He called Cane up.

"Aye bro what you doing?"

"Shit my nigga chilling wit bae."

"I'm finna slide on ya, is that ok?"

"Yea that's cool, come on," Cane replied as they hung up.

He sparked up a blunt and took a big pull of it. He desperately needed to clear his mind. And he knew the perfect remedy.

"Fuck that bitch if she wanna go; let her go," he told himelf, but he knew he was lying. He was in love with that girl, but he was gone use this time to get close to Lexi. Until Sadie comes to her senses and brings her ass home that is.

CHAPTER 10

Is My Mind Playing Tricks on Me?

After everything that transpired yesterday, Lexi wasn't really feeling like her self. After her lunch date with Oscar, he dropped a bomb on her that his wife was starting to become suspicious. She reviewed their bank statements and was suddenly becoming suspicious to the twenty thousand dollar transactions that was made monthly for the past three years. She really did some digging. He tried to cover it up by telling her it was a payout for investments and stocks, but he knew she didn't buy it. Then he went on to tell her that because of all this, she would be seeing less of him. He would also have to cut her living expenses down to five thousand dollars a month. He would continue to pay her rent, utilities, and other bills; and that she would only see him on Sunday's, during the hours that the wife and kids were at church.

Lexi was distraught. He spoiled her, showered her with money, gifts and affection and now he was threatening to take it all away.

"How the hell am I supposed to survive off of five thousand dollars a month," she thought to herself. She was really enraged when he offered to pay for Candy's wedding. How the fuck was he gonna pay for this bitch wedding when he was cutting her allowance like a kid with bad grades. It wasn't fair. Why did this bitch get everything, the perfect man, the perfect relationship, now she's gonna have this perfect wedding and go on to live this perfect life? "Happily ever after, where the fuck is my happy ending?" She cried laying in the middle of her California king sized bed. "Where is mine!" She screamed.

She wanted to be happy for her best friend, she really did, but her heart was overtaken by envy. She wanted it to be her. She felt as though she deserved it. When Oscar cut that bitch a check for twenty-five thousand dollars and said this should cover it, she burst into tears. Everyone thought they were tears of joy and that she was happy for her friend. But no, they were tears of sorrow.

"Bitch that's my money for next month," she thought herself. "I should have never invited his ass. I coulda brought any broke ass nigga," Lexi was pissed.

Just then her phone went off, *Imma boss ass bitch bitch bitch bitch bitch bitch imma boss ass bitch;* she let it go to voicemail twice. On the third time she picked up because the caller seemed so insistent.

"Hello!" Lexi screamed into the phone in an angry tone.

"Damn sexy, you too beautiful to be sounding so angry...did I disturb yo beauty rest or something?"

"Who the hell is this..." She replied "...and how did you get this number?"

"This Yella sweet heart, you bumped into me at the gas station and you saw me at Candy and Cane's engagement dinner yesterday. My nigga Cane gave me your number."

"Well lose it," she said into the phone then she hung up. He called back three times she didn't pick up.

She picked up and called Candy.

Please listen to this call back tone while the subscriber you are trying to call is being located.

Go best friend, that's my best friend, that's my best friend, yea you betta fuck it up best friend, won't chu won't chu throw it in a circle ya,

"Hello," Candy answered.

"Bitch ask yo black ass bald head ass fiancé why did he give his dusty ass light skin home boy my number."

"He gave Yella your number? I'm finna curse his ass out, but girl he aint here right now. He gone with that nigga matter fact. What Yella want with yo number...don't he gotta girl."

"My point exactly," Lexi replied.

"Bitch when you gone bring yo ass over here so we can start planning this wedding. I want to have it in a couple months."

"Bitch why so soon?"

"Because I wanna go on and get it over with already. Maybe I was thinking that we could do it on my birthday, July 28th."

"Ok bitch, well I gotta run some errands, I'll be through there about five."

"Ok bitch, see you soon."

"Alright, in a minute," Lexi replied and they hung up.

When she pulled up at the Candy's room it was 5:30pm. She was a little late and her stomach was in knots. She didn't wanna come at all. She started thinkin about everything and she realized that she was a really bad friend. She brought Miya along with her. She invited Miya to come stay with her for a little while after she found out she was staying in a shelter. She knew that she was tired of being cooped up in that house, so she invited her to come along. She was dying to see Candy anyway even though they weren't big fans of each other when they were locked up.

Yella and Cane pulled up as they were getting out the car.

"Hey beautiful wit yo mean ass," Yella shouted. Lexi kept walkin. "Why you hang up on me boo?" She flipped him the bird and walked into the lobby.

"When they got on the elevator, Miya asked, "Girl he was fine...who is that?"

"This lame ass nigga named Yella. He been on my heels heavy. I ain't goin."

"Yella...wait a minute...Yella, I know that name from somewhere. Yella light-skinned big dick Yella? Girl I heard some shit about him," Miya said anxious to spill the tea. "Girl don't fuck with him, his name out here bad."

"Didn't plan on it," Lexi said as they walked up to Candy's room. Lexi knocked at the door, Candy opened it.

She looked over at Miya, "Why you bring her here Lexi?"

"Bitch shut up, that shit old! And besides, she has some great ideas for the wedding and you can use the extra help moving this shit into yo new place."

"Yea, I got some good ideas for the wedding," Miya chimed in.

"Ok, but let me hide my credit cards before y'all come in." Miya rolled her eyes.

"Bitch calm down, I'm just fuckin with you," Candy said as they walked in. "I'm moving out of this piece of shit finally."

"What the fuck you gotta move...clothes?" Jamiya said. "Y'all got it bitch, I can't break no nail, I just got them done."

"I know, I paid for them remember?" Lexi replied sarcastically.

"See you ain't have to do all that Miss Thang, don't front," Miya spat back.

"I was thinking ten thousand should be enough to cover the wedding. I'll spend five on a small little weekend honeymoon at Disney World, then go on a cruise."

"Bitch you ain't nothing but a big ass kid," Lexi said jokingly. "Just go to the cruise."

"Bitch and you know this man," Candy said in her best Smokey impression. "I always wanted to go to Disneyland. I was gonna use five thousand to furnish my house and the other five to get me a cheap car."

"I thought Cane already bought furniture," Lexi asked as she rolled her eyes.

"He did only for the bedrooms. Plus he bought some TVs and video games, you know shit niggas like. I got to put that women's touch and I want my shit done right," Candy said smiling, looking as if she was day dreaming.

"Well that sounds like a plan," Lexi said sarcastically.

But Candy had caught it, *this bitch jealous,* she thought to herself.

CHAPTER 11

You Can't Have Your Cake and Eat It Too

It was Saturday morning, Cane looked at his phone and noticed he had three missed calls from Yella. Candy was gone shopping with Lexi getting things for the house. Today was the day that they move in. He and Candy packed all their belongings the night before, so everything was good to go. He spoke to Yella last night and he told him to be ready in the morning.

How the fuck did you oversleep nigga? You gotta lay off that Christina, he told himself. Him and Candy had been partying and making love nonstop since the engagement.

"Let me call this nigga back," he said out loud. He dialed the number and it rang three times before Yella picked up.

"Bout time my nigga," Yella spoke into the

phone when he answered.

"I overslept bro. Bae ass did that to me last night. I swear it's like she can't keep her hands off me since I proposed. If I would have known it would be this sweet I woulda done it years ago."

"Yeah bro, I wish I woulda made that commitment. Sadie ass still ain't talkin to me. I've been going by her sister's house everyday sometimes two and three times a day. I just miss her bro...I don't know what to do."

"I'm sure she miss you too bro, just give her a little time...she's gonna come around bro," Cane replied.

"I damn sure hope so, but enough about that shit are you ready...are you up?"

"Yea bro, I'm up. The shit all packed and ready to go," Cane responded.

"I'll be there in twenty minutes."

"Ok cool," Cane said just before hanging up. Thirty minutes later Yella was calling saying that he was out front. After packing all of their belongings into Yella's truck, they sat there for a few more minutes. Yella rolled a blunt so they could blow on the ride back to the new place. When they pulled into the parking lot, Yella noticed that Lexi's car was already there.

"Ya girl move quick, don't she boy?" Yella said pointing at the Rent-a-Center truck pulling into the parking lot behind them.

"Yea, that's why I love my bitch. She don't play no games," Cane replied.

"Let's gon' head and unload this shit, so I could go in here and holla at Lexi evil ass. Imma hit that, watch."

That last comment didn't quite set right with Cane. Even though he told himelf he was done, he didn't wanna think about Yella fuckin Lexi. He still felt like she belonged to him.

They unloaded the truck and took everything in the house. Candy was busy showing the movers where everything went. He was walking in the kitchen where Lexi and Yella were when he heard a comment that pissed him off.

Lexi said, "If I did you wouldn't know what to do with it." The two exchanged laughter and the conversation fell silent when they noticed him standing there.

He shot Lexi an evil look. "Aye bro, I need you to help me mount this flat screen on the wall."

"Ok, here I come bro," Yella replied. He couldn't believe it, this bitch was really talkin to this nigga all sexual and shit. How could she do this to him? Yella ran out to the truck to grab a cigar.

"Now is your chance," he said to himself. He walked in the kitchen and snatched Lexi up by her arm.

"Bitch you bet not fuck that nigga, I'm not playin with you Lexi...you better not fuck him."

"Cane, let me the fuck go," she said as she snatched her arm away from him. "I didn't plan on fuckin anybody, but if I did, in what way does it concern you?" She said while running her finger across his engagement ring Candy brought him the day after he proposed. She was tryna piss him off, but it really just turned him on. Just looking at her made his dick rock hard. Just then Candy walked in.

"What's going on in here?" Candy asked.

"We were just..." Lexi spoke, but Cane cut her off.

"We were just going over ideas for kitchen decorations.

"Since when do you have a passion for decorating?" Candy replied.

"Since today," he said as he walked back into the living room. Candy wasn't stupid. She knew they wasn't talkin bout no damn decorations, but she didn't say nothing. Her and Lexi walked out on the patio and Lexi lit up a square.

"Bitch when you start smokin?"

"Bitch when I started stressin."

"You need some dick! Sex is a major stress reliever."

"You're right. I do," Lexi said as she stuck her head in the door and yelled, "Yella, you wanna fuck?"

Yella started undoing his belt. "Hell yea," he said.

"Not right now nigga. I'll text you my address, be there by nine and bring a condom...a couple of em," she yelled. Cane was beyond pissed at this point. This bitch really had the audacity to disrespect him like this. He felt like his blood was boiling. He had to release some of this anger.

"Candy, let me holla at you in the room," he yelled outside.

"Ok bae, coming." When she came in the room, he attacked her kissing her and ripping away at her clothes. "Honey stop, we have guests."

"Fuck them," he replied.

"What has gotten into you Jamal? You're

behaving like an animal!"

"Imma show you," he kept saying over and over. He turned her around aggressively and bent her over the new bed they would share.

"Show me what?" Candy asked in a trembling tone, "Cane stop!" After lubing her up with his saliva he entered her with force. Candy began franticly screaming, "Stop stop, bae stop Jamal you're hurting me." Tears began to fall from her face.

Lexi came to the door, "Girl are you ok?" Cane busted his nut and left Candy there crying.

"She cool, "Get the fuck out! Both of y'all get the fuck out my house," he yelled.

"I don't know what the fuck your problem is nigga, but imma go'on and go. Call me tomorrow bro."

Lexi said, "You bet not hurt her."

"Bitch get yo hoe ass the fuck outta my shit," he said as he pushed her out the door. Cane didn't know what had come over him, he just felt so demonic. When that feeling faded, he knew he had fucked up; especially when two hours had passed and Candy still hadn't come out the room. She layed in bed and cried herself to sleep. She just she just didn't know what come over him. She just figured he must have been drinking or gettin high this morning. The whole ordeal made her want to call the whole thing off. But, she loved him. So what if he raped her.

CHAPTER 12

Hold Up Wait A Minute

Lexi was really feelin fucked up after she left Candy's house. She was worried about her friend. She had called her about ten times, left four voicemails and about twenty text messages.

"I hope that nigga ain't jump on her," she thought to herself. She was purposely trying to piss him off by inviting Yella into her house to have sex. She just didn't expect for him to take it out on Candy. She wasn't planning on fuckin him for real. All this shit was beginning to become a bit too much for her to handle.

As she pulled into her parking garage, she parked along side of what appeared Oscar's truck.

"What is he doing here? It's not Sunday and I ain't gotta see him yet." She looked at the clock and it was almost 4pm. Lexi keyed into the front door of her condo and expected to find Oscar waitin on her with some Chinese take out or something. But no chop suey, no fried rice, what she found was her home girl on her couch, missionary style, getting her suey chopped. There was a stench of bowel movement in the air.

"You two in my muthafuckin house?"

Oscar jumped up and she attacked Jamiya. She quickly leaped on top of her and began aggressively punching her, screaming at the top of her lungs.

"Bitch how dare you? I was nice enough to let you come live in my home and this how you repay me? You fuckin my man, bitch you fuckin with my money, get your shit and get the fuck out."

Oscar had never seen this side of Lexi and he was shook. He felt like he was lookin at the devil himself.

"And you..." Lexi turned to him.

"Look at your pathetic ass, standing there covered in shit. What you have to say for yourself?" He didn't speak.

"Now just like you strolled up in my shit and layed down the pipe. I got some shit I wanna lay down. I wanna lay down a couple demands. First, you're gonna raise my monthly income back up to twenty thousand dollars. Second, you will never threatin me with cutting my cash flow again, not only will your wife hear from me personally, but every news anchor in Dallas will as well. Last but not least, go in the bathroom, get a towel and clean yourself up and get the fuck out of my house. I'll see you tomorrow at the regular time."

He went into the bathroom, took a shower and left. He felt so ashamed. How could he let that ugly girl talk him into doing this? He needed a drink. Jamiya was scared to walk out of the guest room after packing her things. Her head was pounding, a tooth was missing and to top it off, her hair was destroyed in the fight. Lexi paid three hundred dollars for those bundles and installation and she straight ripped them hoes right from her scalp.

"I'm gonna get her back, if it's the last thing I do," she said to herself as she walked out the door. She was so distraught, because she considered Lexi a really close friend. They confided in each other and they held one another's secrets. "Yea, I shouldn't have fucked her trick, but shit'd she fuckin her best friend man...how could she get down on me when she doin the same shit. I was just tryna make a couple dollars."

It was 8:30 p.m. when Lexi stepped out of the shower. Her phone was ringing off the hook.
She picked up quick.

"Damn who died," she said jokingly.

"What happened to the address you was

supposed to be textin me?" Yella said into the phone.

"You couldn't possibly think I was for real," she replied.

"I was hoping you wasn't just pulling a nigga leg. I really wanna make love to you. I want to explore every inch of yo body with my mouth. I wanna have my tongue so far in you that I can taste your emotions."

"Damn boy, I've heard of eat the booty like groceries, but damn taste my emotions...Ok, you win. 3983 Stonehill Drive Apartment 3 Building 6. The gate code is 2319."

Yella showed up an hour later, wearing nothing but a robe and some Jordans. Lexi had on some red and black Bulls boy shorts and a black bra.

When she opened the door, she greeted him with only one word, "Ready?"

In his best Trey Songs voice, he replied "Yeeaahh!" She showed him to the room where the mood was already set. Candles were lit and *Oreo* by R. Kelly played on surround sound. She poured him up a glass of Moet. After he finished it, he motioned for her to come closer. She came over and stood in front of him as he sat at the foot of her bed. He slowly eased her out of her panties. She unsnapped her bra and let it fall to the floor. He picked her up and laid her down on her back. Then he dropped the robe and kick off his J's.

"I'm gonna cherish every moment of this," he said as she was staring at his monstrosity of a cock.

"Boy, I don't know where he thinks he's putting that thing...all that can't fit in me!"

"Don't worry baby, I'll take my time. You'll be fine." Her heart felt like it was about to start beating out of her chest. He lifted her legs and started eating her ass like it was Thanksgiving Day. I mean he must've been down there about an hour. Then he stopped abruptly, started sucking her toes, then he went back down eating her ass. Then he did the unthinkable. He slid her cock in his mouth.

Now Yella wasn't really a fan of queenie weenie, but there was something about this girl that made him wanna try new shit. He reached over on the night stand and grabbed the KY Touch. He put some on the tips of his fingers and applied them to her, then he squirted some in his hand and began stroking himself, as he slipped her back into his mouth.

After another twenty minutes of pleasure, he came up to lift her legs and slid in. He could tell from her facial expressions that it was painful to her. He slowed down and kept easing in slowly. Once he was completely in, he began slow stroking. Not before long, she got used to it and started doing tricks on it; riding it, throwing it back and all. When he got ready to cum she told him,

"Pull out," but he pinned her down and said,

"Sharing is caring. I've shared a part of me with you and now you belong to me."

Just then there was a knock at the door. She threw on her robe and went to get it. It was a black woman who appeared to be in her late 40's.

"Can I help you?" she asked. The woman reached her hand out.

"Alexis Jackson, I'm Deborah Delanii, Oscar's wife. So nice to finally make your acquaintance." Lexi's mouth dropped.

CHAPTER 13

Expect the Unexpected

Sadie sat in the waitin room at the Dallas Medical Center. Ever since she left Yella and moved in with her sister, she hadn't been so well. She wasn't able to keep anything down. Every time she tried to eat, she would throw up. The glands in her throat were so swollen; it was becoming almost impossible to swallow. Then to top it all off, she had a really bad case of the runs. She was running to the bath room every five minutes. She didn't know what was going on with her, but she figured that she had the flu or some sort of virus. What ever it was wasn't letting her rest until she addressed it.

Just then the nurse called her name, "Stanley Russell?" She didn't say anything. She wouldn't answer to that name. She didn't accept disrespect of any kind and to her address her as anything other than Mercedes Russell was disrespectful. After the nurse went back to the back office, Sadie stepped to the desk to complain. She told the woman at the desk that she was transgender and that she would only be addressed as Mercedes Russell.

"That's what my ID says, that's the only name I'm responding to...I had my name changed legally."

The woman replied, "Well your file says..."

"I don't give a fuck what the files says," she said cutting the lady off. The lady apologized and buzzed Sadie to the back. When she got situated in the room, they directed her to the nurse who called her by her birth name. She went into the room.

"I'm so sorry ma'am, no one told me you were transgender."

"It's ok love. Now you know, so can y'all just tell me what the hell is wrong with me," she said gettin up on the bed.

"Ok, not a problem," the nurse replied, "Can you start by telling me what brings you in this evening?" Sadie gave her a list of her symptoms.

"Ok ma'am, let's start with some blood and urine samples." After taking her blood and having her pee in a cup, the nurse checked Sadie's vitals. She informed her that her blood pressure was high and that her temperature was high as well. They would have to start an IV.

After getting everything set up, the nurse looked at Sadie and said, "I'm gonna get these down to the lab for testing and the doctor will be in shortly." Sadie relaxed and chilled in the hospital bed playing Candy Crush on her phone. About an hour of that, the nurse and the doctor came in wearing masks.

"Good evening Miss Russell, I'm doctor Renaldi. I will be caring for you this evening. I have good news and bad news, which do you care to hear first?" He asked her.

"Let's hear the good," she replied.

"Well your lab tests are back and you don't have the flu."

"Ok...and what's the bad?" She said quickly.

"Our test studies show that you are in fact HIV positive and that your immune system is very weak. Something as small as a common cold could make the difference between life and death." Sadie burst into tears screaming.

"How is that possible?" she screamed. You have to test me again; there must have been a mistake!" The doctor then informed her that her viral load was extremely high which meant she contracted the disease quite some time ago.

"We will do everything we can do to try and stabilize you, but the disease has become aggressive, Miss Russell. It might be too late to get it under control. There's a good chance it could turn into full blown AIDS.

Only time will tell; but we can assure you that we can make your stay as comfortable as possible. You're gonna be here for a while. We want to start treating you as quickly as possible. I'm cannot be too certain of what the future might hold at this point. All we can do is expect the worse and hope and pray for the best."

"Expect the worst! Fuck you mean, expect the worst? I'm cool...I got the stomach flu. Y'all must have got my lab results mixed up with someone else. I demand a retest."

"We can retest Miss Russell, but I will advise you not to get your hopes up." Then he turned and exited the room. A million and one things ran through her head. She didn't know how to feel and she couldn't stop crying.

She wasn't accepting this, "They're lying. You need to go to another hospital," she told herself. She then snatched out all the IVs and whatever else they hooked up to her and left. She wasn't finna stay there and wait on another test. That doctor seemed pretty sure.

Fuck a retest; I know how to fix this, she thought to herself. She went home to her sister's house and wrote three letters, one to her mama and one to each of the twins, Porchia and Alexus. She then went into her sister's closet to retrieve the .25 small handgun.

Her sister's baby daddy kept it around for their protection in case he wasn't around. He taught Porchia and Mercedes how to use it, so if the moment came, they would know exactly what to do.

She walked outside and jumped into the rental car. She stopped at the liquor store down the street and got herself a fifth of Hennessey. Then she called Yella's phone about thirty times. He didn't pick up.

Fuck it, imma just pop up, she thought to herself. She noticed the truck was gone when she pulled up at Yella's place. He ended up spending the night with Lexi. She went to his weed stash he kept in the night stand by the bed. She grabbed a dime and a pack of swishers, then went in the living room to roll up. She smoked both blunts and wrote Yella a letter explaining to him how she really felt and why she did the things that she did. When she finished, she kissed the letter and left red lip prints under her signature. She opened the fifth and downed it like a gallon of water. Then laid in the bed, said a prayer of salvation, put the gun in her mouth and pulled the trigger.

She wanted Yella to be the one to find her; after all it was his fault. He was the one that took her life.

CHAPTER 14

It's Too Late To Apologize

That Monday morning, Cane called Yella to apologize. He hadn't spoken to him since everything happened Friday. Since it was his first day at work, he needed to make things right, especially since he needed a ride. The first two times Cane called, he didn't answer. He picked up on the third call.

"What's up nigga?" Yella asked when he answered.

"Shit bro, I just got up. I just wanted to call you and apologize for the other day. I really showed my ass and I feel terrible about it. Candy hasn't even talked to me, since that day. I don't know what to do bro. I just feel like I'm losing her."

"You good bro, I know you didn't mean no harm. But look, I know it's yo first day on the job and I don't want you to be late. Imma swing by there and come get you. Then we can go by my house so I can grab my uniform. After that, we gon' head to work.”

“Ok cool,” Cane replied.

“I’ll be there in a half hour,” Yella said as they said their goodbyes and hung up.

Thirty minutes later, Cane was sitting outside smokin a cigarette when Yella came flying up into the apartments.

“Damn bro, what’s the rush?” Cane said getting into the truck.

“I’m tryna hurry up and get home. Sadie’s sister Porchia called me asking if I’d seen Mercedes. She said Sadie left them all letters saying that she was gon’ be good. She said don’t worry about her and that she was sorry, but she had to do what she had to do.

Porchia just figured she meant she was coming home...that she was coming back to me. So I’m tryna get home. Baby there waiting on me. Porchia seemed really worried about her, because she wasn’t answering her phone and she hadn’t seen her since Friday night. When Porchia got in from the club Sadie was gone. So, I told her to meet me at the house. I stayed the night out and I’m on my way home now.”

“See bro, I told you she was gone come around,” Cane said. “...and stayed the night out where at my nigga?" he asked lighting up the blunt Yella had in the ashtray.

"I spent the weekend with Miss Hard-to-Get herself."

"No muthafuckin way," Cane replied.

"Yes, muthafuckin way and baby the truth you hear me nigga?"

Cane made a note in his mental to smack that bitch next time he saw her. Not before long they pulled up at Yella's apartment. Porchia and her baby daddy Reggie was already there waiting.

"She's here Yella, she gotta be. Her rental car is here," Porchia said as she exhaled a breath of fresh air. She's gonna curse the bitch out for scaring her like that. She knew the bitch was probably asleep with a hangover and her phone turned on silent. When they walked through the door, they were hit with a funny smell.

"You got a dead rat in here or something bro?" Cane said as he walked over to open up a window. Porchia looked at the table and walked over to it. Yella she wrote you a letter too. She picked it up. She couldn't help it she was nosy. She read it and her stomach fell to her feet. Yella didn't see all that. He walked to the back towards the bedroom. The next thing he saw was an image that will stick with him for the rest of his life.

He screamed, "No Sadie, no!" and everyone came running back there to see what the fuss was about.

As soon as Porchia walked into the room, she broke down and began screaming, "Call the police! Call an ambulance! Call somebody!"

She turned to Yella who fell to his knees at the side of the bed and cried like a little bitch. She kicked him in the back of his head and began punching him, "Bitch I don't know why you crying...it's your entire fault," her baby daddy grabbed her.

"My fault...how is this my fault bitch? You know what? Just get the fuck out of my house," he started screaming as he pushed her out the door.

Reggie stepped up then and said, "Aye bro, keep it verbal, no need to get physical."

Yella replied, "Bitch ass nigga fuck you!" Reggie swung on him and they got to bangin right there in the hallway. Cane immediately broke them up, "Look y'all, it's not the time or the place for this shit. That damn girl is lying in that bed dead. Instead of calling the police or the morgue or somebody y'all niggas wanna fight."

Reggie spit blood from his mouth onto the floor, looked at Yella and said, "This is far from over my nigga."

"Get the fuck out!" Yella replied. Reggie and Porchia sat in the car to make phone calls to friends and family, while Reggie made some calls to his homies. After she called her mom and sister, Porchia started reading the letter Sadie left Yella again. She hadn't got all the way through it when she stopped at HIV positive. She wanted answers. She needed to know why her sister did this. The letter was three pages long and page by page she slowly discovered the truth. Yella and Cane called the police. Not before long they heard sirens blaring in the distance.

Porchia handed Reggie the letter and said, "Read this bae, you and yo boys gone have to get this nigga. I want him dealt wit. That bitch gotta die!"

"Bro how about you pack a bag and come stay at my place for a while," he said as he pulled Yella up, who had fell back on his knees at the side of the bed; where Mercedes' lifeless body laid, almost completely covered in blood. About 10 minutes later, the police crime scene investigators and the Dallas County Morgue showed up. They immediately began taping off the the area surrounding the apartment.

One of the responding officers first on the scene stepped to Yella and Cane and said, "Can you to fellas come down to the station to answer a few questions for me?"

"Sure, just let me call into work and we can head

on down there." Yella called in for him and Cane and they went in for questioning. Sadie's mamma pulled up in the car with her other sister, just as the coroner was bringing her body out.

She jumped out of the car, ducked under the tape and ran towards the bodybag screaming, "My baby, my baby, Lord Jesus not my baby!" For the first time that day, a tear fell from Cane's eye. It hit him. This shit was real, Sadie is really gone. Yella cried like a baby. This was the first time he had cried in years.

"My bitch gone, she really gone," he said as Cane pulled him in for a hug.

"Be strong bro, we gone get through this."

CHAPTER 15

All Good Things Must Come To An End

It was about eleven in the morning when she woke up. Yella left for work a couple hours ago. She was still worn out from their weekend of passionate lovemaking. She dreaded getting out of bed, but she agreed to meet Oscar's wife for lunch today. After she had showed up at Lexi's doorstep the other night, Lexi turned her away and told her that it wasn't a good time. So she agreed to meet her for lunch on Monday. She attempted to call Oscar, but he wasn't accepting any of her calls.

She got up to get dressed and headed over to this little Italian bistro on Oak Lawn. When she arrived, there Deborah sat quietly sipping a white wine, waiting for her. She wore a beautiful red sundress accented with red Chanel sunglasses. Lexi wore a black blazer with a form fitted white blouse underneath and her black Giuseppe boots. She didn't wanna overdo it, but she also didn't want to look cheap. Seein Miss Thing in a sundress made her regret wearing those expensive ass shoes. They were cute, but very uncomfortable.

"How are you doing?" she asked Lexi as she took her seat.

"I'm blessed and you?" Lexi replied, without giving her a chance to respond. "Let's cut the crap, how did you find out?" Lexi asked with the *I was waitin on you at the door* look on her face.

"About six months ago, I grew suspicious of these twenty thousand dollar transactions my husband made into this private account. I already had my suspicions about him cheating, so I hired a private investigator to do some digging for me. But that's not what led me to your door. I found out about you two months ago, but the reason I made the visit to your home was because that night, the very night I visited you...my husband was talking in his sleep. He kept apologizing to you, saying that he was sorry and that he would be ruined if you went to the media."

"So, that's where I stepped in. I came over that night to tell you that whatever transpired between you and my husband has come to an abrupt end. You will not be seeing him again. You will not be receiving any more of our money and you will not be going to the media to air any of his dirty laundry. I've allowed you to fuck my husband, but let's be clear bitch, I will not allow you to fuck with my bag."

Oscar is on set with 20/20 right now shooting a segment on men of power who live double lives and he's letting everything out for the world to see. So I'm sorry hun, but this well has run dry," she said as she finished her drink. She got up and walked away from the table. "Oh here's a parting gift, she placed a check for ten thousand dollars on the table. Stay blessed," she said walking away.

Lexi sat there in silence for a moment just to allow everything to soak in. Was this really happening? Had her lavish life suddenly come to an end? Would she really have to go back to escorting? She started crying as she sat there picturing herself performing oral sex on those old smelly white men, "I can't go back to that," she thought, "Hell naw."

"Can I get a cranberry and vodka?" she yelled out. No one seemed to hear her or maybe they just weren't paying attention. Can I get a fuckin cranberry and vodka?" she yelled again this time at the top of her lungs.

A waiter came over, "I apologize ma'am, I'll be right with you," he said as he went to fetch her cocktail.

She called Candy so that she could fill her in on everything that transpired. Candy didn't answer, but she replied with a text, *Can't talk right now I'm at the police station. They're questioning Yella and Jamal...it seems as though Mercedes killed herself.*

"What the fuck..." she said out loud. "What county?"

"Dallas County," Candy replied.

"I'm on my way."

Lexi finished her drink and left a ten-dollar bill on the table. Then she jumped in her car and rushed down to the police station. When she pulled up, dozens of news people were standing out front. She figured they wanted to get a statement from Yella and Cane about the recent death of this young woman.

When Lexi walked into the jailhouse, all eyes were on her. Candy and Cane were sitting in the waiting area. When Lexi approached, Cane shot her an evil look.

"Damn, why you muggin me. I ain't kill the girl," Lexi said nonchalantly. Cane didn't reply.

"Cane just finished giving his statement," Candy said. "We're just waiting on Yella to finish up."

"So, what happened?" Lexi asked.

"Girl, I don't know. All I know is they were on their way to work. They stopped at Yella's house so he could change into his uniform and they found her dead."

"That's crazy girl, she just seemed so happy at your engagement last week. What would make her wanna do something like this?"

"Maybe she found out you was fuckin her man," Cane said under his breath.

"What was that?" Lexi said picking up on the shade Cane threw.

"I don't know, this shit is all a mystery to me," Candy replied. Just then Yella and the homicide officer Kenneth Zurcowski walked in. Lexi recognized him from episodes from the First 48. She walked up to Yella and gave him a hug. He embraced her and started crying. The four of them exited the building with Lexi and Yella holding hands.

Suddenly they were swarmed by media, "Nayshawn Rice would you like to give a statement?" one reporter asked.

"Get that damn camera out of my face!"

"Is it true that your lover committed suicide because you were sleeping around with another woman?" asked a thirsty news reporter. "Are you the mistress?" she said pointing the mic at Lexi.

Sadie's thirsty ass best friend contacted the news station. She wanted to expose Yella for the dog he was. They all had to ride with Lexi, because Yella and Cane rode down in a squad car. Candy took the train to meet them there. When they left, they stopped at Applebees for a bite to eat, but neither one of the fellas had much of an appetite. After they left, they drove back to Yella's house so he could gather some of his things and get his truck from the parking lot. But, when he arrived he was in for a rude awakening. His truck was destroyed. Every window was busted, every tire flat and the words, *you're dead* sprayed painted all over the truck. Lexi didn't know what the hell was going on, but things were becoming more and more awkward by the minute. Yella punched her dashboard.

"Hey, hey, hey don't fuck up my shit cuz somebody vandalized yours." Just then Cane reached from behind her and smacked the shit out of her.

CHAPTER 16

Too Much Pressure Can Bust A Pipe

"Now Cane, why the fuck would you hit that damn girl?" Candy asked hitting him in the chest.

"Bitch ass nigga, you got me fucked up! Get the fuck out my car!" Lexi screamed holding her face.

"Why would you hit her?" Candy continued to ask him as he sat silent with a blank stare on his face.

"Fuck that!" Lexi screamed. "I don't need no muthafuckin explanation. All I need is for this bitch to get the fuck out my car!"

Then Yella spoke, "How is he supposed to get home Lexi? You're overreacting."

"That's not my fuckin problem, he better beat his fuckin feet. I'm not overreacting shit and yo bitch ass can get out with him. You can't even defend me clown! Both y'all some clown ass niggas."

"Ok Lexi, just chill for a minute. You might not need an explanation, but I do," Candy said. "Now why the fuck did you hit her? And that's my last time asking you."

"I slapped the bitch because I felt like it. I'm sick of her smartass mouth and bro just lost his girl. Now's not the time for that shit! Fuck her and her cocky ass attitude. I'm sick of the way this bitch constantly tries to make everything about her. This man just lost his girl, his car is destroyed and she talkin all this shit like that fuckin dashboard was made of gold."

"Bitch, I don't give a fuck if it's gold or not, its mine," Lexi screamed. "Now can you please exit my fuckin vehicle? I'm really getting tired of asking you."

"Ok bitch, if you tired then take yo rat ass to sleep. I'm not getting out of a gotdamn thang! Now what the fuck you gone do about it."

"Ok can everybody calm down just a second?" Candy yelled.

"Oh bitch, you gone get the fuck out of my car one way or the other." She retrieved her purple tazer from her purse, got out and opened the back door.

"So are you gonna make this harder than it has to be?" Candy jumped out and ran around the back of the car.

"Lexi wait! Bae just get out...we'll call a cab."

"Naw fuck that, let that bitch tase me! She better have Jesus on speed dial cuz he's gonna be the only one who can save her."

"Bro just get out the car," Yella chimed in.

"Bae come on, I'm begging you," Candy asked. Cane then stepped out of the car. He pointed his finger in Lexi's face, touching it against her nose and said,

"Bitch you been touched by an angel." Candy went back around to get her purse out of the car.

"Bitch ass nigga, you don't scare me. I'm not Candy."

"What the fuck is that supposed to mean Lexi?" Candy asked.

"You're gonna watch that bitch word," Cane replied.

"It means just what it sounds like. He might be able to control you with that aggressive ass Ike Turner shit, but that shit don't move me."

"Just then Cane grabbed her by the throat, "Bitch what I just tell you."

"Lexi reached up and tased him in the neck."

Cane fell to the ground.

"Lexi, what the fuck!" Candy screamed. Lexi jumped in the car, but before she could pull off, Cane punched his fist through the window and grabbed her hair. Lexi immediately locked onto his arm and pulled off. She drug him almost to the entrance of the complex before he lost grip. Lexi felt her hair ripping from her scalp while he was pulling it; she knew she was gonna have some major bald spots. When Cane got up from the ground his legs and knees were scrapped up and bleeding badly.

"Imma kill that bitch," he said as Lexi drove out of the gate.

"Candy called a cab and they sat in silence on Yella's steps. When they made it home, Candy got the first aid kit and some peroxide and cleaned his wounds.

"Yella, there's clean sheets and towels in the guest room. Make yourself at home," she said as she began tending to her man. "You're gonna have to learn to control your anger. You can't just go around lashing out and attacking people when you're upset or you don't agree with something," Candy said to him. "I think you need anger management Cane. This shit is getting out of control."

"I know bae. I just get so upset at times and the only way I know how to respond is to get physical," he said with his head hanging down. After she finished cleaning him up, he laid down and took a nap.

Later that afternoon around 3, Candy took a cab to a nearby car lot and bought a 2001 Nissan Altima. It was used and wasn't in the best condition, but she only paid four thousand dollars for it and it was hers. She wanted to make sure an incident like the one that occurred earlier never happened again. She stopped at Kroger's on the way home to pick up some items to prepare dinner for Cane and Yella. When she got home, she was surprised because Cane walked to Walmart across the street and already had dinner prepared for her. He fried some pork chops, made some biscuits, broccoli, mashed potatoes and gravy.

Candy smiled, "I could get used to this," she said as she began putting the groceries up. After she finished, she stood there admiring her man.

"Well don't stand there," Cane said jokingly as he handed her the plate he prepared for her. "Let's eat." He called Yella in from the patio, "Bro dinner is done."

"Thanks bro, but I ain't got an appetite. I think imma just go back to sleep." He'd been real down since he found Sadie dead this morning. After they ate, they went into the bedroom and curled up to watch a movie on Netflix. They ended their night with passionate lovemaking. After they both climaxed, Cane drifted off to sleep. Candy got out of bed to clean the dishes and do some minor house work she hadn't got around to doing that day. Afterwards, she took a hot candlelit bath and relaxed in the peace and privacy of her own home.

Damn, it felt good to have yo own shit, she thought to herself. When she finished bathing, she dried off and walked into the bedroom. Cane was talking in his sleep. She stood there and listened. At first she found it cute at how he kept sayin, "Come here girl." She grabbed her phone wanting to get it video, but then he said something that completely caught her off guard. "Lexi stop playin and come here girl. I told you I'm sorry. You know how I feel about you ma."

Just then Candy turned off the camera and slapped his ass right out his sleep. He jumped up like Queen Latifa in *"Bringing Down the House"*, *Who want it wit lean.* "What the fuck you slap me for?" She pressed play on the phone and when the video stopped, she slapped his ass again.

CHAPTER 17

Jealousy and Envy Just Don't Mix

Lexi was leaving the hair salon when her phone rang. *"Imma boss ass bitch bitch bitch bitch bitch bitch imma boss ass bitch..."*

"Hello," Lexi said.

"Hi my name is Rebecka Chandler, I'm calling on behalf of David's Bridal. May I speak with Ms. Alexis Jackson please?"

"This is she," Lexi replied.

"Well, I was just calling you to inform you that the strapless ivory Armani wedding dressed you ordered is ready to be picked up. I also wanted to see if you wanted to keep your appointment for your fitting of the bridesmaid dress."

"I'm gonna have to get back with you on that, but I'm on my way to pick up the wedding dress."

"Ok our offices hours are…"

Lexi cut her off, "I don't need to know your hours. Didn't I just say that I was on my way and hung up?" Lexi was really pissed off. She forgot that she paid five thousand dollars for a dress she couldn't return. And on top of that, her and Candy weren't even on speaking terms. They hadn't spoken in two months. She figured Candy felt some type of way because she tased her man,

"Oh the hell well," she said out loud. "Lexi don't kiss no ass. I guess I can give the bitch the dress any way, I can't get my money back."

Lexi picked up the phone and dialed Candy's number. *The subscriber you are trying to reach cannot be located. Please check the number and try again.*

"Damn I know this bitch ain't changed her number. I guess I can just stop by there after I pick up the dress…seeing that it's only down the street from her house."

When Lexi pulled up at Candy's apartment, she sat in the car for a half hour contemplating on if she really wanted to knock on this door or not. She finally talked herself into it. When she knocked at the door, she heard Candy's voice coming from inside the house, "Coming," she yelled.

"What a pleasant surprise. What are you doing

here Lexi," she said when she opened the door. Lexi was holding a huge box.

"I was bringing your dress we ordered. It came in today."

"Oh, that was nice of you, but I'm not sure that I can accept that."

"What do you mean you're not sure you can accept it? This is the dress you picked out and it's not refundable. So, whether you like it or not you're stuck with it; you're taking this dress." Lexi dropped the box and turned to walk away.

"Lexi wait. I'm sorry, I'm acting like such a bitch. Thank you for the dress. I shouldn't take out my anger on you."

"It's cool," Lexi replied. "I'm the one that should apologize. I never should have let things get out of hand like that...I just wish I could rewind the hands of time."

"Come in and have a seat. I have something to ask you and I want you to be completely honest with me," Candy said with a serious look on her face.

"Yea sure what's up?" Lexi replied as she walked in. She took a seat on the living room couch.

"I don't know how to ask this, but it's something that has been troubling me for quite some time now.

I really need to know."

"What is it Candy?" Lexi asked?

"Have you and Cane ever been sexually involved with one another?" Candy asked.

"What? Where did that come from? Why would you think something like that?" Lexi asked looking surprised.

I hope this bitch ass nigga ain't said nothing, she thought.

"Well, that night after the altercation between you two, I overheard him talkin in his sleep...hang on I got it recorded." Candy got up and went into the room to get her phone. Lexi felt like she was gonna vomit. There was so many times she wanted to tell Candy what happened between her and Cane, but she knew there was a possibility she could lose the only friend she ever had. Candy walked back into the living room and handed Lexi the phone. After watching the video, Lexi felt like crying. She couldn't believe what she saw. He really did have feelings for her. She wasn't in it by herself. He had feelings for her too.

"So did anything happen, Lexi?" Lexi sat silent for a moment contemplating if she really wanted to tell the truth. She knew that the next words out of her mouth could either make or break her. *Just tell the truth Lexi. Now is your chance,* she kept telling herself. *She's not gonna hate you she just wants to know.*

Just as Lexi was opening her mouth to speak, Cane walked into the house. They looked at each other and was locked in each other's gaze.

"Nothing happened," Lexi said.

"Lexi what a pleasant surprise," Cane said sarcastically.

"You sound like yo bitch. It's good to see you too Cane."

"Cane, don't be such a dick," Candy said rolling her eyes. "Is that all you have to say to her."

"You're right, I'm sorry Lex. How are you? How has everything been?"

"I've been good, I can't complain. How about yourself," she replied.

"You know same shit, different day. Hey Lexi, I really do want to apologize for everything that transpired between us. I'm taking anger management classes now and making amends. It is one of our steps, so can you forgive me?" Cane asked her offering his hand. She shook it.

"Of course, I forgive you Cane. And, I apologize as well. We both showed our asses. I'm just glad we're all past that. Now we can get this show on the rode with this wedding. It's in two weeks and not to mention it's your 26th birthday Candy."

"I know, I know, I'm so excited! First things first, we have to book a venue for the reception. My parents, brother and sisters are flying out next weekend. Canes's grandmother and his two brothers are driving down three days befcre." Candy said clapping in excitement.

"Wow you're gonna have a full house. I have more than enough space at my house. Some of your family is welcomed to stay with me," Lexi said stated.

"That would be great Lex. I'll put my parents in our room. I can put Cane's grandma in the guest room, his brothers in the living room, my sisters in your guest room, my brother on your couch, and me and Cane will be on an air bed in the study."

"Sounds like a plan," Lexi said.

"I ain't sleepin on no damn air bed in my own house," Cane said aggressively.

"Bae, it's just for a couple days chill out."

"I guess," he said as he walked towards the bedroom.

"I'm so excited to see my family. I've booked an appointment for you, Marisella and Marisol to be fitted for your dresses next Tuesday."

Why do you and your brother Kevin have black names, but your sisters don't?"

"Because my mom named the boys and my dad name the girls, Maatisella and Maatisol. It's the way they're pronounced, but they're named after my Papa's sisters in Puerto Rico. None of us has met them. But, we all took my Papa's last name. My mom had to be true to her black side when she named us."

"Interesting," Lexi replied. "Can't wait to meet them."

CHAPTER 18

The Cards Never Lie

It was three in the morning and Cane sat on the patio of their apartment smoking a cigarette. A week had gone by since he came home from work and seen Lexi and Candy in the living room talking. It had been more than a month since the last time he saw her. Two months to be exact. He felt really bad about the ordeal that transpired between the two of them. It's just Lexi made him fill some type of way. He knew she was only fucking that nigga to get back at him. Over the course of these last couple of months that they've been apart, Lexi only came across his mind a couple times. He thought he was completely over her...or so he thought.

"I guess I was mistaken," he thought out loud. Because ever since he saw her last week, it's been so hard to get her off his mind. Just the other day at work, while he and Yella were on their lunch break, he was deep in a daydream reminiscing about the last time he made love to Lexi. He immediately snapped out of it when Lexi called Yella's phone.

He wanted to reach over the table and knock Yella's fronts down his throat, but he kept his cool. He was really learning how to control his anger.

I guess those anger management classes are working, he thought to himself. He slowly counted to ten while Yella conversed with Lexi.

Then he counted back down to one once he heard Yella say, "I love you too baby." How could she love this nigga already? She barely even knew this nigga." Cane tried his best to get his mind off off her, but somehow images of her just kept creeping right back into his mental.

"Aye my nigga, you wanna check out the new strip club in the South that just opened. If it's decent in that bitch, I think I might have yo bachelor party there," Yella said to him snapping Cane out of his trance.

"Naw, I'm good my nigga. I gotta go home after work. Candy done prepared a big dinner for the fam. Her people made it here from out of town yesterday and my big mama and my lil brothers will be here later today. You and Lexi are welcome to come if y'all want to." He only said that because he really only wanted to see Lexi.

"Ok nigga, we will be through there. What time does it start?"

"Just come around 7:30," Cane replied.

"Don't think you getting off the hook too nigga. We gotta hit up that strip club sometime this week. This is the last few days of your life as a free man, so I gotta give you a night to remember. I'm talkin pill poppin, panties droppin, bottles poppin, its all on me."

"Alright my nigga, we can go Friday. That's my last night as a free man as you say it, like I'm finna go to prison or some shit."

"Naw not like that nigga. I'm saying it like, nigga you finna marry this girl."

"That's like signing your soul over to the devil my nigga. I ain't never doing that shit."

"Well, that's your opinion nigga, but my baby deserves the best. I'm willing to sign my soul over to her."

"Nigga, don't you know that's gon' be the only thing you gon' be fuckin for the rest of your life?" Yella said.

"I know nigga. I'm ok with that shit. That's been the only thing I been fuckin for about seven and a half years."

"I thought y'all been together for eight."

"We have," Cane replied.

"Damn, my nigga. You gotta a side joint!" Yella said in disbelief.

"Naw nigga, its some shit that happened a little while ago. It's really not even nothing to talk about. Candy is all I want. I'll be fine with her for the rest of my life...baby the truth." Now all he had to do was convince himself of that.

"Come on nigga, let's get back to work. Our break been ova," Yella said as he jumped up from his seat.

When Cane made it home from work that evening, he was surprised to walk into the house and see Candy, her mom and two sisters along with his Big Mama preparing a huge meal. It looked like Thanksgiving in summertime. They really had outdone themselves.

"Jamal, boy you better get over here and give Big Mama some sugar." It's been a couple years since he'd seen his Big Mama. She raised him and his two brothers Jeremiah and Jermaine. After their mother's addiction spiraled out of control, she lost them to the system. Big Mama stepped up and took on all the responsibilities her daughter could not. She gave those boys a good life on a fixed income.

"Boy when you gone let ya hair grow on in? You walkin round lookin like the guy off the Pine Sol commercial," Big Mama said.

"Now that's the smell of a clean lookin ass boy," his youngest brother Jermaine chimed in.

"Jermaine Tyshon Cane, boy if you don't watch yo damn mouth, yo lips and yo teeth gone beat you to the hospital!" Big Mama yelled from the kitchen. "If you don't swallow em first." That's one thing about Big Mama, she didn't play and them boys knew if she said something one time she wasn't gonna have to say it twice.

Cane grabbed a six pack of beer from the fridge and walked into the living room where the guys were watching the game. He passed a beer to Candy's dad Hector and her brother Kevin. Then he turned and handed one to his little brother Jeremiah and left Jermaine sitting there with his hands out.

"You're only nineteen lil nigga...not on my watch."

"Big Mama know I be drinking, don't she Jerry?" Jeremiah didn't say anything.

"Y'all come show y'all big brother some love tho. It's been like two years and y'all just growing up on a nigga." They both stood up and embraced Cane with a group hug.

About an hour passed when Candy's mother Gena came into the living room and announced dinner was ready.

"Come gather round for prayer." Just then there was a knock at the door.

"Who is it?" Cane yelled.

"Me nigga!" Yella responded from the other side of the door. He and Lexi were dressed alike, both of them wearing red shirts, blue jeans and matching red and white Jordans. It kinda pissed him off, but he brushed it off. He gave Yella a fist dab and he hugged Lexi as she entered the door. Damn did she smell good.

"Y'all are right on time," he said. Lexi looked so damn good, he made up in his mind that he had to have that one last time before he made this lifetime commitment to Candy. He was gonna fuck Lexi one last time and then he would finally be able to put her out of his system. After dinner he was gonna pull her to the side and make his move.

CHAPTER 19

UnpreDICKable

It was Wednesday morning. Candy and Cane stood on the patio in a passionate lip lock embrace. Today was gonna be the last time she saw her man. The next time she saw him; he would be her husband-to-be on Saturday. Even though the wedding wasn't till Saturday, Lexi was whisking Candy and her sister away on a trip, she called the Final Retreat. She paid for round trip tickets for four to Miami. Lexi, Candy and her twin sisters were gonna fly out to Florida and have the time of their lives. Then fly back Friday morning, so Candy could become Mrs. Candy Cane once and for all.

She knew the day was approaching, but she couldn't believe it was almost here. These were her last couple nights as a free woman. She vowed to herself that she was gonna do something that she'd never done before.

"What's up bitches? Are you hoes ready to turn the fuck up? The Final Retreat is in full effect bitches," Lexi said as she walked through the door. The next thing she knew she was picking herself up off the floor.

"Show some respect," Big Mama said while sweeping up the kitchen floor with the same broom she just took across the back of Lexi's head.

"I apologize ma'am," Lexi said as she got up rubbing the back of her head. Jeremiah and Jermaine burst into laughter. Lexi rolled her eyes. She was glad that weren't staying at her house like originally planned. Them boys were irritating. Well, it really was only that young one. Candy's sister stayed with her and she really seemed to enjoy them.

Candy and Cane stepped back in the house,

"What's with all the commotion in here?" Candy said as she walked in.

Jermaine said in the mist of still laughin, "Big Mama creased yo home girl with the broom."

"Let me guess...you were cursing coming in."

"Yea bitch, why didn't you warn me?" Lexi said in a whispered tone.

"My bad girl, wasn't thinking," she said as she dashed off to the back. "Let me finish getting my bags and I'll be right out." Just then Cane came from the back carrying three luggage bags.

"Aye lil bro, y'all take these bags out to the car for these ladies."

"Am I getting paid?" Jermaine replied.

"Boy get off yo ass and fetch that luggage!" Big Mama yelled from the kitchen. "You were raised to be gentlemen, not sit on yo gentle ass. You do it just because those are ladies, not because you're getting paid," Big Mama said bending over to pick up the trash she swept.

Marisela and Marisol came from the back wearing matching white strapless sundresses. Cane's brothers jumped up to get those bags once they got sight of the girls. Lexi gave Sella the keys,

"Y'all can finish taking y'alls things out; I'm finna step out here and smoke a square." Lexi stepped out on the balcony. Cane was right behind her pressing his throbbing penis against her ass.

"Oh hey, good morning to you too, Lexi said pushing him away. "I'm doing great thanks for asking," she said sarcastically. He laughed stepping in towards her. "I'm not finna play with you Cane."

You don't have to. You did enough of that last night. I just wanted to thank you for blessing me with the best one last time." Lexi thought back on last night, which should have never happened to begin with. It's just that after Cane hemmed her up against the wall outside the other night; he told her that he had to have her one last time. His proposition was hard to resist.

"I'm ready to go hoe," Candy said stepping out on the patio where the two were just finishing up on their cigarettes. She handed Cane an envelope that contained three tickets. It's Isley brother tickets for our parents. I figured you might have your hands full while I'm away."

"Oh, thanks babe, you're a life saver. I didn't have the slightest idea on where to begin to entertain old people," Cane said sarcastically as he leaned in for one last kiss from his bride-to-be. Lexi felt sick to her stomach as she thought about last night.

"She really was a horrible friend," she thought to herself. But damn that dick was worth it. They fucked on the hood of her car in a park in the middle of the night.

"It was a beautiful day in Miami when they got off their flight. They retrieved their luggage, then caught a cab to the Ritz Carlton, where they stay for the next two nights.

This entire trip was paid for at Oscar's expense. Lexi recently found that she still had access to the credit card he gave her.

That wife of his wasn't so smart after all, Lexi thought to herself when she discovered that she still had access to the funds. She'd been swiping ever since. Once they made it to the hotel, the four of them got checked in. Lexi attempted to pay for four rooms, but Sella and Sol insisted on sharing a room. The identical twins were beautiful and almost a splitting image of Candy.

They were often mistaken for triplets. The only difference between the three was that the twins were a bit thicker than Candy was. After they got checked in, they went to a spa Lexi found for them. All four of them got bikini waxes and full body massages. After that they went to dinner at a four-star restaurant on Brickell Avenue. Then, they gambled the night away at the casino. Sella and Candy were the only ones to win.

The next morning, they ate breakfast in bed and got together for their hair and nails appointment. They had their hair done at studio D by Pablo, a well-known celebrity stylist. Afterwards, they spent the majority of the day shopping. They hit the beach so they could show off their new bikini waxes. And after lying on the beach and watching the sun set, they went back to their rooms to get dressed for dinner. They enjoyed a nice little French bistro they came across leaving the salon.

On their way back to the hotel, they stopped at a little shop with a sign in the window that said *Ten-dollar tarot card or palm readings*. Lexi decided on a palm reading. The little old woman spoke with a deep Haitian accent.

"Everything that you have done in darkness will soon be brought to the light," the little old woman said to Lexi. She snatched her hand away from the woman. The twins received their readings from the cards. She read the twins together, since they were connected by birth. The lady laid three cards down in front of each of them, then turned them over. Sella's card read: *Sadness, grief* on one and then *true love* on the other. The third card said *sad life,* which she would go through sadness of some sort, then fall in love and have a baby.

"You will soon endure something that will hurt your heart, but you will soon find love and bear a child." Sol's cards read: *Sadness, grief* and then *riches and happiness.* "You too will soon endure something that will hurt your heart as well, but you will soon find wealth and be happy yet again."

Candy decided on having her palm read. As the lady began tracing the lines in Candy's palm, the candles began to flicker as if someone was attempting to blow them out. Then the lady suddenly stopped and gave Candy a chilling look. She felt as though this woman was staring right into her soul.

"Get your affairs in order, the time is approaching." the woman said as she blew the candles out. She then placed a card in front of Candy and disappeared into the back.

"Wait, what is that supposed to mean get my

affairs in order?" Candy turned over the card. It was the card of death. She felt as though all the blood immediately drained from her body. Lexi grabbed her hand.

"Girl, you know this shit don't mean anything. Girl, this ain't real. That bitch just tryna scare you."

"Well it worked," she said as she jumped up and walk out the door. "Fuck this shit, lets hit the strip club," Lexi told the twins as they followed Candy out the door. "I need a fuckin drink," Candy said as they stepped out on the street.

CHAPTER 20

The Morning After

The next morning the girls were supposed to meet in the lobby by 9:00am. They could take a cab to the airport and board their plan by 10:30am, make it to Texas by twelve to get dressed and be ready to walk down the aisle by 2:00pm. Everyone was present, except for the bride-to-be.

"Where this bitch at? She gone make us miss our flight," Lexi said as she dialed Candy's number. *You have reach Candy Cane, I'm either busy or sleep, but I'll be sure to call you back, so do your thing at the beep.*

"This bitch still not answerin, y'all go on and start loading y'alls things into the cab. I'm finna run up to her room." Lexi walked over to the receptionist desk. "Hi, I'm sorry to bother you. I booked three rooms the other night and I lost the key to one of them. Can you make me a new one?"

"No problem ma'am. May I see some

identification?" the man at the desk replied.

"Sure," Lexi said as she handed him her ID.

"Ok, ma'am, which room did you need a key for?"

"Suite 329," she said as she tried calling Candy's phone again; still no answer.

"Here you go ma'am," the receptionist said handing her the key. "Would that be all?"

"Yes, thanks a lot," she said as she dashed for the elevator. When she stepped off the elevator, she bumped into the stripper from last night. Kash the Dicktator was his name.

"Hey big tipper," he said to her as he got on and she got off the elevator.

"What's up Kash?" she said as she stepped past him. When she got to the room, she keyed in and was distraught when she found Candy drunk, sleep ass naked, lying in a puddle of fresh vomit.

"Bitch get up...what the fuck, it's your wedding day! Did you forget?" Lexi said as she aggressively shook Candy out of her slumber. "Bitch get up!"

"I'm up," Candy replied. She got up and sat at the end of the bed.

"Come on bitch, you need to pull yourself together and get cleaned up. You got throw up all in your hair and this is five-hundred-dollar hair. I see you had fun last night after we left the strip club."

"Where the fuck did all these condom wrappers come from bitch? I done counted like four magnum wrappers that I've seen since I've come in here. They're everywhere in the bed and on the floor. Y'all was going rounds, huh? Who were you fuckin?" Lexi asked.

"Did you fuck that stripper?" Candy jumped up and ran to the bathroom to vomit again.

"I don't know," she said in between breaths as she let loose everything she drunk the night before. She finished puking, then stood up and turned on the shower. "I don't know best friend, I promise I don't remember anything from last night."

"Well get in the shower and I'll pack your shit then. I'll bring you up to speed on our way to the airport."

'That's not telling me who I fucked though Lexi. What stripper?" Candy asked very confused at this point.

"I have no idea," she said with a smirk on her face. "Get dressed," she said. "Stop trippin bitch, you wrapped it up."

"That's not the point Lexi. I'm about to get married and I just cheated on Cane...that's the fuckin point."

"Ok, fair exchange, ain't no robbery," Lexi sarcastically replied.

"What the fuck is that supposed to mean Lexi? Candy yelled from the bathroom.

"Nothing girl, just get dress before you make us miss our flight."

Lexi said she didn't mean anything by that statement, but she really did. Fact was that it kinda just slipped out before she could catch it. I guess that's why people say think before you speak.

Lexi gathered Candy's things and packed them into her suitcase. She started daydreaming after she got the bag all packed. Her mind drifted back the other night and the time she shared with Cane. He lied to Candy and told her that he and Yella were going to shoot pool and watch the game at a sports bar. Instead, he went with Yella to one of their friend's house, this guy named Black. Shortly after they got there, Lexi picked him up around the corner. They went to the park and Cane fucked her like he had something to prove. For that to be our last time together, he sure did make every second worth it.

I can still feel his fat, long, black dick pulsating

inside my tight hole, she thought to herself. *Cane came about three times and each one he released in me like he was tryna put a baby in me*, she thought.

"That was a night to remember," Lexi spoke out loud.

"Too bad I don't remember it," Candy said from the bathroom doorway startling Lexi.

"Bitch, what you jumping for?"

"Girl cuz you scared me, I didn't know you was right there. I got your bag packed. You all ready."

"Yea, let's roll girl...hold on let me grab my phone and charger, then we out." Just as Candy grabbed her phone, the message alert went off. "Who the hell is this textin me?" The message read: *Thanks for everything. Last night was amazing! If you're ever in Miami again, hit me up. I hope you liked the video I sent you. Stay beautiful. Yours truly Kash.*

"What the fuck...who is Kash and what video?"

"Kash!" Lexi yelled, "Bitch, so my suspicions were right. I bumped into him getting off the elevator. I figured he was leaving your room judging from the way he was all over you last night. I can't believe you don't remember. Your sister Sella got it all on tape."

"Apparently she's not the only one," Candy said as she pressed play on the video he sent her. Lexi came and sat next to her on the bed and together they watch her spontaneous night of entertainment. The video was only about ten minutes long, but it went down in just those few minutes. Lexi watched as her bestie bounced up and down on this man like a pogo stick. Then he flipped her over and laid her on her stomach then began eating her ass. Then to top it all off, he turned around and let her get back there.

"Bitch you topped him?" Lexi screamed.

"I can't believe this Lexi."

"I can't believe it either," Lexi replied.

"You can't believe I cheated?" Candy said.

"Naw bitch, I can't believe you topped him and I also can't believe his dick is that big on hard. Now come on, let's get the fuck out of here before we miss our flight. Its 9:45am...our flight takes off at 10:30am."

"Wait, before go you must swear to secrecy. Promise me, you won't tell a soul," Candy said holding out her pinky.

"Girl Scouts honor," Lexi said as they locked fingers and headed out the door.

I should've let this bitch oversleep, then it wouldn't be no wedding. What if she knew when she kisses him after they say 'I do', that she tasted my ass on his lips...

"Best friend, does Cane eat your ass like groceries?

"Naw, he's not really into that stuff."

"Could've fooled me," Lexi said. "Maybe he'll eat that mufucka tonight."

"Maybe," Candy replied as they stepped on the elevator. "Boy, was this gonna be one hell of a day."

CHAPTER 21

The Calm Before The Storm

"Today is the day my nigga...are you ready to sign your soul over to the devil. Not saying that Candy is the devil...she's actually an angel, but this is it; your last moments as a free man. How does it feel?" Yella asked Cane.

He got up got up out of the bed wearing nothing, but his boxers. They were completely lit last night after they left the strip club. Neither one of them were in shape to drive, so Yella bought two double-bed suites for the night at the Motel 6 across the street. One for him and Cane and one for Jere and Main Man. Candy's brother Kevin decided to sit this one out, which was a good thing, because he probaly woulda snitched anyway. He was a soft ass nigga. They invited him to come, but his bitch ass gon' call his girl back home to see how she felt about it. She told his ass that she didn't want him to go.

"I'm not selling my soul to the devil, I'm committing my life to the woman I love. Candy is the love of my life."

"Nigga if you woulda had balls enough to do it, maybe the love of your life would still be living," Cane said as he sat up on in his bed.

"Bitch ass nigga, don't speak on a subject you no little to nothing about. You petty as fuck for that comment nigga. If it wasn't yo special day nigga, we would be thumpin in this bitch right now," Yella said aggressively.

"I know my nigga, that was uncalled for and I do apologize. I'm just still a little upset my nigga. Not only did you put my life in danger, you put my little brothers in harms way. I told yo ass when we ran into Mercedes sister baby daddy yesterday at the liquor store to let that shit go, but yo ass wanna turn up with the man like we was totin pistols or somthin."

"That nigga up'd on us, don't you know we could all be dead right now if that cop had not pulled up?"

"Yea, you right bro. It's just sometimes when I'm off the liquor; I tend to let my anger get the best of me. I know I should've just let that shit go, but you heard some of that shit that came out of buddy mouth... I mean that man called me all kinda sick ass faggots, tal'm bout I'm out here killing mufuckas and how it was my fault Sadie was dead. That shit just made me so mad my nigga," Yella said as he paced back and forth.

"Yea, I feel you. But you have to look at it like this, we're in relationships with transgender women. That's often how we're viewed by society. If you know that most of what that nigga was sayin wasn't true, then why let him pull you out yo character," Cane asked.

"I don't even know. I guess it's the fact that I really miss Sadie so much bro. I still ain't never really grieved about it." Yella broke down crying.

Cane came to his side, "Let that shit out nigga," he said as he embraced his friend. Yella stood up after about three minutes of cryin.

"Enough of that shit. I ain't soft, I ain't no bitch. Real niggas don't cry. You ready to go do this wedding shit?"

"Nigga its 9:00 a.m. the wedding ain't til two. I'm going back to sleep until check out. The turn up last night was a little to turnt my nigga."

"My head still spinning," Cane said as he tucked his head under the cover.

"Yea, last night was epic. I didn't know that them Dallas Cabaret's bitches were freaks like that. It's amazing what a bitch will do for a lil change."

"I gave them hoes a thousand dollars to split if they left with us. That's two fifty a piece," Yella said.

"Money well spent," Cane said. "The bitch I was with...Strawberry? That bitch head game so savage I started to call the wedding off. Did you see how shorty was sucking my dick? She was over here going bananas on this mufucka."

"I heard yo ass over there cryin nigga, but that hoe Buttercup pussy was so wet nigga. I thought about trading Lexi in my nigga, cuz shorty was valid. We shoulda tag team, switched them bitches," Yella said getting up walkin to the bathroom.

Cane didn't reply to Yella last comment because it kinda pissed him off. Lexi was wastin her time with this bitch ass nigga who was incapable of loving her. Cane had feelings for Lexi. And as much as he tried to deny them, he knew what he felt was real and he also knew that she felt it too. His mind drifted back to the other night when he and Lexi snuck away for one last secret sex session. But this session wasn't anything like their sessions in the past.

This time the sex was filled with passion and love. He had even done things to her that he had never done. He ate her ass and even gave her head. Lexi was amazing in the bedroom. He couldn't believe he would have to say bye to all that. It was probably for the best. Besides, he couldn't keep doing that shit to Candy. He loved her too much to hurt her and Lexi deserved better. She deserved more than just the title of side chick. When he was inside her the other night, he told himself that if he wasn't getting married to Candy, he would wife her.

He laid there in bed fantasizing about her. His dick got hard at the thought of how he was plunging in and out of that tight wet ass of hers. He was even gettin turned on at the thought of suckin her dick. He just admired the way he had her whole body shaking as if she was going through convulsions when she reached her climax. That was something he hadn't even done for his bride-to-be. He started jacking himself off under the covers thinking of how Lexi saddled him like a horse and rode his dick. Just then there was a knock at the door.

"Ain't that bout a bitch," he said to himself. He was just about to nut. Yella answered it. It was Jeremiah and Jermaine. They ass was still excited about last night, they acted as if they had never had pussy before. Yella bought them their own room and two of the strippers entertained them for the night.

"Bro, we had the bitches eating each other pussy," Jere said.

"Yea and we switched," Main Man chimed in.

"Damn nigga, I think lil bro nem got us beat. Their night seemed a bit more entertaining," Yella said. "But, look everybody get dressed. Let's go get some breakfast. Waffle House for everyone, my treat."

"For the hoes too?" Jermaine asked.

"Man, hell naw! Y'all still got them bitches over there? Rule number one in the player's manual: You don't lay up with no bitch that's not yo woman. We sent our bitches packin after we bust a few of em," Yella said arrogantly.

"Nigga stop cappin. That bitch left after you fucked. She had to get back to them bad ass kids that kept callin while you was in that wet ass pussy. My bitch stayed till eight until she had to get ready for school. She's a medical assistant," Cane said arrogantly.

"Damn nigga, you ain't have to bust me out! Fuck that! Yo ass ain't gettin no breakfast nigga. You a op ass nigga," Yella said embarrassed. Everyone burst into laughter.

They went and ate, then headed over to Candy and Cane's crib to get ready. Yella just got off the phone with Lexi. She informed him that their flight landed. Her and the girls were heading straight over to the wedding chapel to start getting ready. Candy's mother and Big Mama was going meet them there.

"Everything was in motion," he looked over at Cane who seemed a bit nervous. He noticed how he kept squirming in his seat. Cane thought he noticed a black Chevy Tahoe with tented windows. He'd seen it following him since he left the hotel. He paid it no mind.

It escaped his thoughts when Candy texted him

and said *The time is approaching.* Strange choice of words he thought. *But, yes it is my queen* he replied and smiled.

CHAPTER 22

Speak Now or Forever Hold Your Peace

Candy stood in the mirror of her dressing room admiring herself. She really looked beautiful.

"Aww, best friend you really look amazing! I'm so happy for you," Lexi stated as she stepped behind her and placed a tiara on top of her head.

"Thanks love," Candy responded as they embraced each other.

"I love you Candy," she whispered in her ear.

"I love you too bitch, you already know that."

"Best friend, I need to talk to you," Lexi said in a whispered tone.

"About what?" Candy replied. "Can't it wait till after the wedding?"

"No, it has to be said now. I have to get this off my chest, but I need to know that no matter what, we will always be friends forever."

"Yea, no matter what...now what's up? You've been acting really weird all day. What's the tea bitch...what's bothering? You can talk me about anything I'm your best friend. That's what I'm here for." A tear rolled off Lexi's cheek.

"But this shit I'm about to tell you..." Lexi was cut off in the middle of her sentence by the best wedding planner in the industry, Mrs. Brenda Reynolds. She snapped her fingers as she busted in the dressing room, dramatic as hell.

"Alright, alright ladies it's showtime. We need every one in formation. The bride, I need to come with me," as she grabbed Candy by the arm. They disappeared into a back room. "Line up!" she yelled as the door closed.

"Now how the fuck am I gonna get this shit off my chest?" Lexi said to herself as she wiped away her tears. Her conscience was beginning to get the best of her. Maybe it's for the best. After all, this day meant more to Candy than anything in the world. She didn't want to ruin it. *Maybe it's for the best*, Lexi thought to herself.

"I wonder what that was all about?" Candy said to herself as she stepped onto the elevator. Lexi has been acting weird all day, so it must be a big thing.

Anyway, whatever it is, it was going to have to wait.

Today is my day, Candy thought to herself, *and I'm not going to let nothing, I mean nothing stand the way.* Lexi and her dilemma would have to wait. Over in the guy's dressing room everything seemed be going as planned. The only problem they were having was Jamal's little brother Jeremiah had a hangover. Cane was heated, but today was the biggest day of his life. His dumbass little brother was going to have to wait.

"Somebody get his ass some Tylenol and a ginger ale!" Cane yelled.

All the men were dressed. One of the Richland Hills wedding chapel workers came into the dressing room to inform them that they were ready to begin the ceremony.

The gentleman exited their dressing room and lined up in the hallway where the women were already waiting. Big Mama was at the front of the line wearing a purple dress with white flowers and a big white church hat. Behind her was Candy's mother. She was the fourth bridesmaid wearing a strapless lavender gown that draped the floor. She wore her shoulder length natural hair in Shirley Temple style wand curls. The twins wore the same exact dress and they were next in line behind their mother. The twins wore their hair pinned up French rolls. Good thing they got it done professionally at the shop in Miami, because it still looked fresh.

Following them was the Maid of Honor Lexi, the devious mistress herself. She wore a custom made Ferragamo lavender evening gown similar to the other dresses, but her gown crisscrossed across the chest and tied around the neck. The back was completely lace and it stopped in a V-shape at the small of her back. Lexi wore her hair in a long Brazilian sew-in with a Chinese cut bang. All the ladies looked impeccable.

The men lined up in the hallway opposite the women. At the front of the line was the handsome groom wearing an all-white Calvin Cline suit with a lavender tie, dark purple button up and purple and lavender Stacey Adams shoes. Following him was Candy's brother Kevin, wearing an all-black suit and tie, a lavender button up shirt with black and lavender shoes. Jere and Main Main wore the same thing. Jeremiah wore his shoulder length dreads pinned back in a fish tail similar to the rapper Wale. Last but not least was Yella, the best man. He wore a white Calvin Cline suit with lavender shirt, white tie and all white Stacy Adams. Everyone in the wedding party looked amazing.

It was time for the ceremony to begin. The Richland Hills Wedding Chapel was decorated with lavender and white flowers. There were four big chandeliers that hung from the ceiling. They drew your eyes down towards a winding staircase that started from a balcony above the sanctuary. There was an audience of about two hundred friends and family. Every one to Oscar Delanii and his wife to

Lexi's crazy cousin Jazz, plus a few more of their family members flew in that day to take part in the festivities.

The ordained minister took her place at the alter wearing an all-white robe. It was time to begin.

Tell me have you heard the story that took place not long ago about an angel up in heaven, they said she up and ran away from home, word is she had unfinished business so back on earth she had to flee well that is so elating because she's laying right her next to me...

The sounds of Jamie Foxx played through the speakers. Big Mama appeared with her handsome grandson on her arm. She and Cane slowly made their way down the aisle with all eyes on them. Cane slowly escorted Big Mama to her seat in the first pew and took his place at the altar. Kevin proceeded down the aisle with his mom, followed by Jermaine and Marisella, then Jeremiah and Marisol. Finally, the Maid of Honor and the best man, Yella and Lexi flawlessly strutted down the aisle and took their place at the altar. Just then the music fell silent. Suddenly, a trumpet sounded from the balcony above and a small girl appeared at the top of the stairs in a white dress.

"The bride is coming, the bride is coming!" she said as she walked down the stairs sprinkling white flowers on the ground. She walked around the back and up the aisle sprinkling flowers and when she found her seat, the trumpet stopped. There was a short silence and the minister handed Cane the mic. Nobody saw this coming, he was gonna sing to his wife as she walked down the aisle. The last time Big Mama heard him sing was at his mother's funeral.

The original plan was for Candy to walk down the aisle to Jamie Foxx's wedding song, but he wanted to surprise her. He hired a pianist to accompany him as he sang to the woman he loved.

Candy was reluctant to walk out because that was not the music she chose, but Mrs. Reynolds damn near pushed her out there saying, "That's your queue."

Candy stood at the top of the stairs and all eyes beheld her in awe. Then Cane began to sing. She tried her best to hold back the tears, but by the time she made it down the steps to take her father's arm, her eyes were misty.

"Well it's been 8 years and I can't hold back my tears because I'm just so happy I'm marrying an angel today. And as I take your hand, I'll pledge to be your man, I'll vow to love to hold to cherish and never disrespect the love we share..."

Candy made her was down the aisle. She radiated bright and beautiful with tears trickling down her cheeks. The train to her all-white strapless Ferragamo gown trailed the stairs behind her as she made it to the altar. Candy's dress was covered in iridescent stone to match her necklace and tiara. Her hair fell down her back in a long sleek 26 inch sew in. Her makeup was flawless with her eyes beat with a lavender eyeshadow with a dark purple cut crease. Candy truly looked like an angel right out of heaven.

"Dearly beloved, we are gathered here today to join this man and this woman in Holy matrimony. If there's anyone who can show just cause as to why this woman and this man should not be lawfully joined together in Holy Matrimony, speak now or forever hold your peace."

There was a brief moment of silence, when the doors of the chapel flew open.

"Wait!" a woman with a raspy voice said. "I do!" She was wearing a black pants suit with a veil covering face.

"Jamiya!" Candy yelled as the woman removed her veil. "What the hell is this about?"

CHAPTER 23

What's Done In The Dark Will Always Come To The Light

"I got something to say," Jamiya said removing her veil and revealing her face!

"Get the fuck out of here James!" Lexi said.

"Ain't nobody got time for yo shenanigans faggot!"

"No, I'm not going any where. It's about time that I expose your sorry ass for the no good trifflin fraud ass friend that you really are!" Jamiya said as she took a few steps closer.

"What the fuck is going on? Y'all are ruining my fuckin wedding!" Candy cried.

"Candy," Jamiya said with a look of seriousness on her face. "Are you sure you're prepared to share your life with a man who has been sleeping with your best friend behind your back?" Candy's face froze as she soaked in Jamiya's words.

"That's right, Lexi told me everything. She's been fucking him for months and she's secretly in love with him," Jamiya said as she crossed her arms across her chest.

The entire room fell silent. A couple people gave dramatic gasps, but all of them couldn't believe what they were hearing.

"You bitch, imma kill you," Lexi screamed.

Candy turned to Cane, "Is this true Jamal?"

Lexi grabbed Candy's wrist, "Best friend I can explain.

Candy snatched away, "Bitch get your filthy fuckin hands off of me! Imma deal with you later. Imma ask you again Jamal...is this true?" Candy asked as her mascara began to run down her face from the tears.

Cane dropped his head. He didn't know what to say, he was so ashamed and embarrassed. He was about to lose everything and he couldn't think of one word to say that could prevent what was about to happen.

"Your silence tells me everything I need to know," Candy said as she slapped the slob from

Cane's mouth. She turned to leave and Cane grabbed her arm. "Get off of me, I hate you!" she snatched away and ran for the exit.

"We got a runaway bride," Jamiya said in laughter as Cane, Lexi and Yella chased behind Candy. Everyone else stood around staring at each other at a complete loss for words. Everyone caught up to Candy in front of the chapel.

"How long, how long you been fuckin this bitch Jamal?"

"Candy I can explain," Lexi said.

"Bitch I don't even have words for you, save your explanation!" Candy screamed.

"I'd like to hear this explanation," Yella said. Lexi fell silent. "What are you waiting for bitch? Speak! Inquiring minds would like to know," Yella said stepping in front of Lexi.

Just then, high pitched squeals from tires were heard as the black Chevy Tahoe pulled up to the curb and began to let off rounds. *Blicka blicka blicka!* The rounds shattered the windows of the church and Lexi immediately hit the ground. Yella didn't have enough time to flinch, bullets tore through his chest. He was dead before he even hit the ground.

"Sleep tight don't the grave bugs bite!" someone

yelled from the truck as it sped away.

Lexi already at Yella's side, "Call an ambulance!" she screamed in between tears. "Somebody call a fuckin ambulance please!" Cane sheltered Candy with his body when the gun fire erupted, but what he didn't know was that she had already been hit. When he stood up, his white suit was covered in blood. He instantly fell to his knees.

"Candy, hold on everything gonna be fine...somebody help!" he screamed.

"Why Cane?" Candy said whispering in between breaths. She gasped for air as blood began coming out her mouth.

"I don't why baby, but I'm sorry. I'm so so sorry. If I could take it all back I would," Cane said as his tears flooded his eyes.

"I forgive..." Candy said as her eyes rolled in the back of her head. She couldn't even finish her sentence before her body fell limp. She was gone. Cane started screaming as he sat there with Candy's lifeless body in his arms.

"This isn't happening, this isn't happening," he kept telling himself. In shock, he sat there on the ground rocking Candy, cradling her head in his arms. Everyone from inside the chapel poured outside screaming. A couple people inside the church were hit. Cane's brother Jeremain was hit in the leg, one of Cane and Yella's coworkers in the arm. Neither one was life threatening. Candy's mom and sisters were in an uproar. Her mother ran up hitting Cane and screaming,

"This is all your fault!" Her husband picked her up and carried her away. Lexi stood up from beside Yella's lifeless body. She looked over to see everyone standing around Candy, who appeared to be dead as well. The first person she noticed was Jamiya standing in the crowd of onlookers. Shedding tears, she immediately attacked her like a wild animal. She grabbed Jamiya by the hair, yanking her to the ground. She punched her repeatedly over and over. Lexi pinned Jamiya's arms under her knees as she sat on her chest. She bashed her head against the pavement. Jamiya helplessly tried to get away, but was unsuccessful with every attempt. Completely caught up with everything going on nobody noticed the slaughter.

Candy's brother Kevin was the first one to notice. He picked Lexi up off Jamiya, but not before she could get a couple good kicks in. Before Kevin carried her away, the last kick came down forcefully and the heel of her stiletto went through Jamila's eye.

"Lexi, what have you done?" Kevin said lookin down at Jamiya's lifeless body. The sounds of sirens blared in the distance. You could tell they were quickly getting closer.

"I gotta get out of here," she said as she

snatched away from Kevin making a run for her car. Just as she hopped in and started the car, her cousin Jazzibell hopped in the passenger side. "Jazz get out! I just done some fucked up shit and I don't need you implicated...get out the car!"

"Yo blood, I'm ridin with you. Roll out!" Lexi didn't have time to debate; she dashed out the parking lot and headed in the opposite direction away from the sounds of the siren.

"I don't know where to go," Lexi said as she did a hundred down 75.

"First things, first, you gotta get out of town. They finna have every squad in Dallas lookin for this red Charger," Jazz said with a look of worry on her face.

"Where imma go, what am I gon' do?" Lexi started crying. "I fucked up Jazz, I really done fucked up now!"

"Just drive. We got enough gas to make it to Houston. My nigga Layit Down stay out there. I know he'a hide you out until we figure out our next move. Everything gon' be alright...I got you bitch, just drive." Lexi lit up a square and did the dash all the way to Houston.

"What the fuck did you do?" she kept saying to herself as she cried thinking about Candy and Yella.

CHAPTER 24

Who's Really To Blame

Lexi sat in the window of one of the bedrooms of Jazz's home boy, Layit Down crib.

It's been a week and a half since the wedding and her picture was on every news station in the country. She made America's Most Wanted. It was only a matter of time before her whole world came crashing down. Well, as far as she was concerned it already had. Lexi lost everything...her best friend, her man, her money and now she was about to lose her freedom. The clock was ticking and the only thing she needed to focus on was getting her affairs in order. She tried calling Oscar Delannii for three days now and every single call went unanswered. On this particular day, he just so happen to pick up.

"What do you want Lexi? You know I'm not supposed to be talking to you," he said angry and upset.

'That's no way to greet the love of your life

Oscar," Lexi said sarcastically into the phone.

"My wife is the love of my life. You're nothing...you're a psychotic lunatic! Anyway cut the crap Lexi! Why are you calling me? Half the state of Texas is looking for you," Oscar said into the phone.

"I need your help daddy," Lexi said seductively.

"I can't help you. This is one hell of a mess you done got yourself into Lexi. The only person that can help you right now is the good Lord himself," Oscar snapped back.

"Seriously Oscar, if you've ever loved me like you said you did...if I ever meant anything to you at all...do this one favor for me," Lexi said into the phone. She tried to hold back the tears.

She'd been extremely emotional since the wedding. All she did was drink, smoke and cry. She'd eaten only once or twice, because she just didn't have much of an appetite.

"What do you want Lexi? I'm not givin you any money," Oscar replied.

"No, I don't want your money. All I want you to do is take my case pro bono."

"I don't know if I can do that Lexi. I would have to discuss it with my wife first."

"Man fuck that bitch! Did you have to discuss it with her when you was laid up fuckin me, telling me how much you loved me? Did you discuss with her the fact that the same bitch I just caught a body on, you was fuckin in my house? Did you tell her that all this shit started because you fucked her...did you discuss that with her? And since y'all discussin shit all of a sudden, how about you discuss with the bitch how you've been still secretly seeing me once a month since she found out about us," Lexi snapped back.

"Or discuss how the dead bitch literally shitted on you, how about you discuss that with the bitch. You act like this bitch got a noose around your neck," Lexi said lying back on the bed.

"Where the fuck are your balls?"

"Look, don't try to flip this around on me. If putting the blame off on me is something you need to do to make yourself feel better to escape the reality of that fact that you were fuckin your now dead best friend's boyfriend behind her back for God knows how long...you do it, go right ahead. But I'll tell you what, I'll take the case and after that I'm washing my hands of you," Oscar said as he hung up in her ear.

Lexi broke down. Her life was crumbling around her and everything falling apart. Just then, there was a knock at the door.

"Go away," Lexi said.

The door opened and a short light skin dude with dreads and a goatee walked in.

"Hustle Man, didn't I say go away? I'm not in the mood." Hustle man was Layit Down's sidekick. They ran shit out in Houston on a drug tip. They sold everything from pills to powder and they was getting hella money. That was really the only reason Lexi felt comfortable there. Them niggas was gettin so much money, she didn't have to worry about them tryna turn her in for that reward money.

Her cousin Jazz stayed up there with her. Her and Layit Down was fuckin like wild animals for the past week. Jazz was tryna be Queen to his empire, but Layit Down liked to roll solo. They had been fuckin around for two years. They both had strong feelings for each other, but Layit Down just didn't want a wife or kids. He knew how dangerous his lifestyle was and he didn't wanna involve the ones he loved into this world. Jazz was lucky to have gotten this close to his operation.

"So yo ass just gon' sit up here in this room all day and feel sorry for yourself? Snap back into reality!" Hustle Man yelled. "What's done is done you can't re-do it. What you need to do is get up, get yo hair washed, yo ass too because you too pretty to be smellin like onions! And once you get yo'self together, let me show you a good time."

"I'm just not in the mood Hustle," Lexi said in a sad voice. She really did want to take him up on his offer. She also really did need to get out of that room, but he didn't know her tea. She wasn't tryna entertain no nigga who didn't know what she really was.

"How about this? I'm not taking no for an answer," he demanded.

"Hustle Man, now you know I can't leave this house. So what did you have in mind?"

"How about you come downstairs to my domain. I've cooked dinner and we can have few drinks and just unwind. I'm just tryna take your mind off everything that has been going on."

"Ok Hustle, dinner and a couple drinks. That's it now, get out! I have to get ready. I'll be down in an hour." Hustle Man wore a smile from ear to ear as he exited the room.

"Before I get dressed, let me try Cane one more time," she said to herself. Lexi called Cane everyday for over a week and he wouldn't accept or return any of her calls. Today, he finally picked up.

"What the fuck do you want man!" he yelled into the phone.

"Cane I just wanna talk."

"We ain't got shit to talk about!" he spat back.

"Cane, look we both played a part in this whole ordeal. You can't just blame me for what happened."

"I can blame you! If you woulda just kept yo dick suckin ass mouth closed, we wouldn't even be having this conversation right now! I'd probably just now be coming home from a wonderful honeymoon. Not sitting at home getting full on Jose Quervo, wishing I could have attended my wife's funeral!" Cane yelled in the phone.

"Wait, what do you mean wishing you could have attended?" Lexi asked.

"I mean just what the fuck I said! Her family had her body shipped back to Chicago and they had a private ceremony. They told me that I was not invited and it's all your fuckin fault Lexi!"

So Candy's funeral was today. Lexi burst into tears. Reality came crashing down, everything was finally beginning to feel so real.

"She gone, she's really gone and now I have to live the rest of my life with nothing! I betrayed her, we betrayed her! Cane believe it or not, this is just as much your fault as it is mine! I didn't put a gun to your head and make you fuck me. I didn't force you to like it. We knew what we were doing and we knew we was wrong! We didn't let it stop us, so we are both at fault here," Lexi cried.

"Ok, I can accept that. So what do you want...why are you calling me?" Cane replied.

"As you know I'm one of America's Most Wanted and it's only a matter of time before I'm caught. I can't trust any of my nothing ass family. Can I leave my treasured belongings to you in hopes that one day I can return to them and maybe to you?"

"Lexi you're wanted for first degree murder. That one day that you're hoping for ain't gonna be no time soon. But I'll do that for you and I'll take care of your things. As far as me and you though, that shit dead," Cane replied.

"Ok, I'm gone make some arrangements upon my return. When I get everything worked out, I'll call you when I get back to Dallas."

"Wait, when you get back? Where you at?" Cane asked.

"I can't tell you all that. You know that Cane. I'll be in touch. I love you," she said as she hung up the phone.

"I love you too," he said as the dial tone sang in his ear. She didn't even hear him, which was probably a good thing, he thought to himself. He picked up the phone a made a call.

"Hello Detective Zurcowski, she's made contact."

CHAPTER 25

The Element of Surprise

About an hour later, Lexi got out of bed, forced herself to get in the shower and do something with herself. Hustle Man was right, she did smell like a bag of onions. After getting dressed, Lexi stood in the bathroom standing in the mirror admiring herself. She forgot how good it felt to look good. Jazz picked her up a couple jogging suits from Pink. She decided to wear a burgundy and black crop top.

After she got dressed, she flat ironed her bundles and beat her face. She was finally beginning to feel like herself again. She walked downstairs and went into the sitting room in the back of the house. Layit Down and Jazz were kickin it.

As she approached the room's entrance, she heard *Sounds of Funk* blasting on the stereo...*Shol feels damn good to me when I'm pushin inside of you. Can't explain the way it feels all I wanna do is be with you.* Lexi walked in the room and was astonished at the sight before her eyes. Jazz was tooted. Face down, ass up, Layit Down was gripping her hips and slow stroking to the sound of the music. She had been watchin for a minute before they realized she was there. It wasn't until they changed position that they noticed her.

"Bitch get out!" Jazz yelled over the music.

"Naw, let her stay. I enjoy an audience," Layit Down said as he turned around to give her a full frontal view of his 10-inch pole.

"I'm cool, I've seen enough," Lexi replied as she turned to leave. "Damn, I see why the call him Layit Down," she said to herself.

Lexi made her way to the basement. When she walked down the steps, she was amazed at the sight. This was no ordinary basement. It was laced with plush white carpet wall to wall. It had a kitchen, a living room, dining room, two bedrooms and a bathroom. She stood at the bottom of the stairs and called Hustle Man's name. Hustle Man came from the kitchen wearing nothing but an apron and his boxers.

"Right on time beautiful, dinner is just about done."

"He walked over to where she stood and took her hand. He kissed it gently and guided her to the dining room. Hustle Man pulled out a chair for her and motioned for her to take a seat. He then disappeared back into the kitchen and returned with a bottle of red wine and two champagne glasses. He poured her a glass and handed it to her. He left again to continue his meal preparation.

After about ten minutes, he returned carrying two plates. He sat one in front of her.

"Dinner is served my Queen."

"This looks amazing Hustle," Lexi said as she looked down at the meal he prepared. He made T-bone steaks smothered with mushrooms, bell peppers and onions, loaded baked potatoes, and asparagus.

"You've really out done yourself," Lexi said to him with a look of admiration in her eyes.

"Yeah you didn't know a street nigga was capable of some gourmet shit like this, did you?" Hustle Man replied in his New Orleans accent.

"Naw, I didn't. This is not what I expected at all," Lexi replied. After they ate, they had a couple of more glasses of wine. Then Hustle Man stood up and took her hand.

"Would you join me on the sofa for some Netflix and chill?" he asked.

"Sure to the Netflix, I don't know about the chill," she said as she stood up from her seat. Hustle

Man was short compared to Lexi. He was only about five foot five to her five foot eight. Short men were a turn off for her, but he was a gentleman.

"That was worth some brownie points," she said to herself. They made their way into the living room and cuddled up on his big white comfy sectional. Hustle man turned on the 76-inch TV mounted on the wall and went to Netflix. He handed her the remote and said,

"Here beautiful, you choose the movie." Lexi decided on a movie called *Brotherly Luv* with Keke Palmer in it. Candy told her this movie was good and been begging her to watch it. She never took the time to sit down and do it.

About halfway through the movie, Hustle Man slid his arm around her and moved over a little closer.

Damn, he smelled so good, Lexi thought to herself. By the time they finished the movie, Lexi was in tears. Not just because the movie had a sad ending, but because reality set in. This was a movie her now dead best friend basically begged her to watch. This was filled with most of the things she dealt with for the past few months, disloyalty, lies, back stabbing and now death. Lexi broke down and couldn't stop the tears from flowing.

Hustle Man embraced her and layed her head on his chest. He held her as she wept. After her tears stopped, she felt his hand slowly make its way down her back side. Hustle Man caressed her ass and tried to slide his hands in her pants.

Lexi jumped up, "I knew this was too good to be true. So that's why you did all this, because you thought you was gonna get some pussy? Well I hate to rain on your parade, but you were gonna be disappointed when you found out that I don't have one." She didn't even give him a chance to reply. She grabbed her purse, made her way up the stairs and out the door. She was halfway down the driveway when she noticed Hustle Man running out of the house, telling her to wait. She kept driving.

Four hours later she made it back to Dallas. It was about 8:30 p.m. at night and it was beginning to get dark. Her first stop was at a storage place off 635. She talked to the owner and told him that she was gonna be away for a while, but she wanted to store away her belongings. She swiped the credit card Oscar didn't know she still had. The storage was paid up for five years. She knew there probably was an APB out on her red Charger, so she left it parked in the storage unit and took a cab home.

She stopped at Walmart and got a black hoodie to disguise herself. She also picked up some boxes, tape and a fifth of Hennessey. When she made it home, she put on Pandora and poured herself a glass and then she went to work. She had the entire house packed up within three hours. It was around midnight. She didn't wanna take the chance of paying a moving company to come move her shit into storage and one of them recognize her from the news. So she called someone she knew. She could trust her crackhead uncle Tyrone. He had a pickup truck and she knew he was always down to make some extra cash. She told him to bring a friend and come to her place. When he got there, she paid them two hundred dollars a piece to move everything into storage. It took them about two hours, four trips and it was done.

"That's why I like payin dope fiends. Cuz they gone get that shit done fast so they can hurry up and get high," Lexi said to herself. She looked at her phone. It was going on 3am. She went online and booked her a Megabus ticket to Mississippi where her mother lived. She took a cab across town to the Peachtree Apartments. It was 4am when she arrived at Cane's doorstep. At first she was hesitant to knock, but she built up the courage and just did it. She paid the cab driver to wait.

"Who is it?" Cane said from the other side of the door.

"It's me Cane," she said whispering timidly.

"Me who?" Cane replied.

"Lexi, it's me Lexi," she said this time while speaking a little louder. Cane opened the door with a look of disgust on his face.

"What are you doing here?" he asked.

"I'm here about what we discussed. Can I come in?"

He hesitated for a minute, then he stepped to the side. Lexi walked in the house. All she had with her was a suitcase. The apartment looked a mess. You can tell it was missing a woman's touch.

"Have a seat," he said. "Let me put on some clothes. She didn't notice that he was naked up until this point. He disappeared to the back. He was only gone about three minutes before he returned. It sounded like he was on the phone, but she figured maybe he was talkin to himself.

"So have you missed me?" she said when he returned.

"No, I haven't actually. I miss my wife, that's who I miss!" Cane snapped at her.

"Well I've missed you," she replied standing up to embrace him.

"Well do you know what else you can miss," he said as he brushed her off avoiding her embrace. "Me with the bullshit," he said. "You can miss me with the bullshit!" as he went to retrieve a beer from the fridge. "Why are you here?" he said with a look of disgust on his face.

"Well, you already know why I'm here, but I'm getting a vibe that I'm unwanted, so imma just leave." She stood up and placed the key on the table. "Just hang on to that key for me," she walked over and opened the door.

"Dallas Police Department, we have you surrounded. Come out with your hands up!"

CHAPTER 26

Facing Reality

I can't believe this bitch ass nigga set me up, Lexi thought to herself as she sat in a holding cell at the Dallas County Jail.

"I know he was upset, but I really can't believe he did me like this. I love Cane regardless of everything that we went through, regardless of all the lies, all the secrets, all the pain and hurt. I still love him! I just don't understand why he's so mad at me...like all of this is my fault. He played a part in this too. It ain't like I fucked myself, so if anything, the blood is on both of our hands.'

Just then the door to her cell popped open and a correction officer appeared in the doorway. "Damn he fine," Lexi thought to herself. "But he kinda of looks familiar."

"Ma'am, I need you to come with me. I have to take you to get fingerprinted and then transport you to homicide."

"Transport me for what?" Lexi asked.

"You would have to ask Zurcowski, the detective in charge of your case. I'm gonna get your fingerprints, then I'll get you down there to questioning."

"When will I get my phone call? I've been in this gotdamn holding cell for three hours!" Lexi snapped. "... and I need to call my lawyer."

The officer said nothing. "So you can take me for fingerprinting, but you can tell them bitch ass detectives they are going to have to wait until my lawyer gets here? I'm not talking to nobody without my lawyer present."

After her fingerprints were done, the officer placed shackles on her wrists and ankles. Then he spoke into his walkie-talkie, "Officer Campbell here transporting inmate to homicide."

"Campbell as in Calvin Campbell, Lake Highlands High School Class of 2008. I knew you looked familiar," Lexi said as stepped up in the van. Officer Campbell stopped her.

"I'm sorry, have we met?" he asked with a confused look on his face.

"You can say that," Lexi said and she glanced over her shoulder.

"Might I ask where?" He replied.

"I was a student tutor senior year of high school. I tutored you in physics."

"Oh wow, Alex is that you?" Officer Campbell said with a confused look on his face.

"It's Alexis now," Lexi replied. "Now about that phone call."

"Right, right...that phone call." Lexi could tell that Campbell was extremely uncomfortable after she revealed her true identity to him. She's going to use this to her advantage.

"Let me get you down to homicide first. I'll make sure they let you make your phone call," he said. "...seeing as though you've already asked to obtain a lawyer." It was a very short ten-minute drive before they made it to homicide. He kept his head straight the entire time trying to avoid making eye contact with Lexi. She loved when boys acted this way. That's how she knew they were curious.

Some fat white Roseanne lookin bitch was in charge over in the homicide building. She kept referring to Lexi as Sir.

"It's ma'am," Lexi snapped back every time.

"Well your file says male," the fat white lady spat back.

"But what does my appearance say?" Lexi replied with a sarcastic smirk on her face.

"Now are we done here? I believe I'm wanted for questioning?"

"Yeah, were finished here sir."

"Alright, that was your last time Roseanne. I'd like to speak to your supervisor."

"Ask the officer in your unit for a grievance," the officer replied. She cracked up laughing, revealing her coffee-stained teeth.

You won this time, but this isn't over, Lexi thought to herself.

After that circus act, Campbell took her to make her one phone call. She three attempts before she finally got an answer. *You have a collect call from, "It's me Lexi" an inmate at the jail to accept the charges, please press 1.*

"Oscar, I'm in jail. I need your help...they're holding me on a million-dollar bond. I don't have anyone else to call. I really need you daddy."

"Lexi when I agreed to take your case, bonding you out of jail wasn't a part of the plan. I don't just have a million dollars laying around. And if I withdrew that much money from the bank, my wife will be in an uproar."

"Please Oscar, just help me and after this promise I'll be out of your life for good."

"Okay Lexi, I'll do it. But, after this case is done and everything is over...I want you out of my life. I mean it!"

"Can you come now? They're about to question me."

"I'm on my way," Oscar said into the phone as he hung up. He posted her bail which was only ten percent of one million. He knew that because wouldn't have agreed on giving her a million dollars to get out of jail.

Lexi picked up the phone to dial another number.

"Inmates only receive one phone call," Campbell said as he grabbed the phone from her.

"Please just one more," Lexi said with a sad puppy dog look on her face.

"I'm going to get in big trouble for this, you know that right?" Campbell said as he looked into her eyes.

"Promise, it'll be worth it," Lexi said as she took the phone back from him. She dialed the next number. *You have a call from* "It's me, Lexi" *an inmate at the Dallas County Jail to accept the charges please press 1.*

"What do you want?" a raspy masculine voice spoke into the phone.

"So that's what it is, that's what we on now Cane?"

"What's done is done Lexi," Cane replied in a dry tone. You can tell he didn't want to have this conversation.

"You know what I don't get? How you can be just so upset with me like all of this is my fault? I never asked for any of this, I never meant to hurt my best friend. I never meant for her to lose her life. I never meant for none of this to happen…I didn't expect to fall in love with you. I didn't want any of it and I tried to pull away, but you kept pulling me back into this shit! Then you have the nerve to be upset, mad, and angry at me…constantly pointing the finger and putting blame on me. Cane, you're just as guilty as I am in this. It's as much your fault as it is mine. The blood is on both of our hands, so it's about time you faced reality baby. Cuz if I go down, I won't be going alone. Bitch you're going to suffer too one way or the other!" Lexi cried into the phone.

"I'm already suffering and as I said before, what's done is done. Goodbye Lexi." Cane said as he hung up the phone. Lexi was furious.

"I got to deal with this bitch. If he thinks he can

just ruin my life and move on with his, he got another thing coming! What's done is done! Naw, it ain't done yet...but it will be," Lexi thought to herself as she up hung the phone.

Next, Campbell took Lexi down for questioning. He left her sitting alone in a room staring at what appeared to be a window for well over an hour. Two detectives walked in the room. A woman and a man, they both looked familiar. She thinks she noticed or seen them before on the First 48. Just as they sat down Lexi said,

"Y'all ain't even got to get comfortable, I ain't got shit to say."

The female officer spoke first, "We just want to ask you a few questions about what happened that day at the wedding."

"Like I told you, I ain't got shit to say. You can talk to my lawyer... I plead the fifth," Lexi replied. Just then there was a knock at the door. Her counsel was here. Oscar Delani walked in.

"This line of questioning is over. Let's go Lex, your bond has been posted."

When they left the jail, they stopped at Jack and the Box to get Lexi something to eat.

"I don't understand how you eat this poison," Oscar said.

"Well everyone isn't fortunate enough to have their own personal chef like you, Mr. Delani."

"I've paid for a weeks stay at the Ramada Inn. I'll give you some money to hold you over. After that you're on your own."

"I can't thank you enough Oscar," Lexi replied.

When they arrived at the hotel, Lexi turned to him and said,

"Do you want to come up for a while, so we can discuss the case?

"I'll call you. We can discuss it over the phone. Your picture is all over the media and I can't afford to be seen with you right now," Oscar replied.

"I just want to thank you for everything that you've done for me. Just come up and let me show you how grateful I am." Oscar knew this was going to get him in the ass. He couldn't resist. He knew he shouldn't be alone with her. He parked the car anyway.

They went upstairs to the hotel room. Lexi has always been irresistible to Oscar. One last time he told himself as they walked into the room. Lexi ate her food on the ride, so when they got into the room, she wasted no time. She immediately stripped from her clothes and unbuckled his belt. She pulled his pants down to his ankles and started making love to him with her mouth. About five minutes into it he reached his climax. She swallowed every drop, then stood in front of him and said,

"I'm going to shower. You get comfortable and get ready for round two." When Lexi got out the shower Oscar was gone.

She powered on her phone, Hustle Man called thirty-seven times, left twenty-three voice mails and left fifty-two texts.

Damn was he persistent, she thought as she went to call him back. But all that came to a halt when an unknown number called her phone.

"Who is this?" she answered trying to disguise her voice.

"This is Officer Campbell. I'm sorry to bother, but I got your number from the system. I was hoping I could have a conversation with you."

"Sure, what do you want to talk about? She asked.

"No," he replied. "I'd rather speak in person."

"Ok, I'll text you the address now," she said and hung up. Before she could send the text there was a knock at the door. She opened it without asking who it was assuming it was Oscar. Expecially since he was the only one who knew where she was. But boy was she mistaken.

"Hustle Man, what are you do..." before she could even finish her sentence, he kissed her.

Here's A Sneak Peak into Part 2

Sex, Love, Lies, & Revenge

"Where am I? Why am I here? Why are these tubes in me? Where is Cane?" Candy screamed as she began unattaching herself from the hospital's monitors. Just then a nurse came in "Miss Rodriguez please calm down I assure you everything is fine. You've undergone some serious pain and trauma. You need your rest!" she stated as she stood next to candy's bed.

"What do you mean? I feel fine," Candy said as she went to stand from the bed and fell to her knees. The nurse rushed over to help her grabbing her arm.

"Let go of me I can get up on my own" she snapped snatching away from the nurse.

"Where is Cane? Why isn't he here? Why am I here?" She felt a pain in her side; she looked down at her right torso to see a bandage that had started bleeding. "What is this? What happened to me?" Candy screamed.

"Ma'am, you suffered from a gunshot wound to the Torso. You have also undergone short term memory loss. You've been in a coma for three weeks. You need your rest your lucky to be alive…"

The Girl from a Thousand Fathoms

David Gullen

Designed & typeset by Nellug

Cover art by Giles Meakin

The Girl from a Thousand Fathoms

To Gaie

Acknowledgements

Like many stories this one has its origin several years in the past. This particular one emerged from a short writing exercise during a working weekend with fellow members of my writers group. It is good to look back and remember that this story first emerged in fun, companionship, and friendship. We stayed in a house beside the sea; the beach was beautiful, the sea too dangerous to swim.

Several people deserve explicit thanks. Helen Callaghan, Andrew Wallace, and Gaie Sebold all read a late draft and gave exceptionally useful and thorough feedback; David Bezzina created the cover art for the original online edition; Giles Meakin created the cover art for this version; Sarah Ellender, mermaid-maker and friend; and last but not least Clare Kelly for her essential advice on formatting and layout.

Paul Fletcher, from the Sussex Police Authority, gave invaluable advice on police procedure and methods; Chris Harlow, and Mandy Griffiths were generous with their advice on accountancy; as was Päivi Vepsalainen on various matters of Finnish language and culture.

Finally, the staff of the Hangar café, Fairoaks Airport, where much of the first draft was written in my lunch hours.

Many other people deserve thanks too. You are all lovely. Mistakes, oversights and omissions are mine. Likewise, so are the good bits.

DG, 2020

Midnight

CLOSE TO MIDNIGHT a mermaid came ashore at the bustling resort town of Brighton on the south coast of England. Swimming strongly, she entered the half-mile of water between the town's two piers. The one to the east blazed with light, life, and fairground music. The other was a storm-battered and fire-wracked skeleton of bare girders, the post-apocalyptic roost for a thousand starlings.

Drifting on a lazy swell she listened to the surf push and suck at the shingle beach. The waters of the English Channel were cold but they lacked the chill of the distant Atlantic swells, and their wild dangers.

Weary from her days-long swim she coasted under the ruined west pier and looked up past the limpet-encrusted legs into clear night sky. She had made it, she had escaped and now she was free. A pang of intense sadness welled inside her. She was alone, but she was free.

Light from a quarter moon glinted on her bare skin as she knelt at the waterline. She hesitated and touched the shell-crusted purse on the kelp-string tied around her waist. It contained everything she possessed: her comb, a handful of pearls, a handful of octagonal gold coins.

No turning back. She reached across the collapsing wavelets and placed her hand palm down on the shingle beach. Her body formed a conduit between the elements of sea and land. She felt their power, the eternal tension. She spoke the shoreline words her mother taught her long ago:

David Gullen

This child of oceans is not changing sides,
Not abandoning one for the other.
I know my origin, gifts, and graces.

Land and sea, you agreed
We may cross your war grounds
In our own times of need.

I know, I am asking for a strange thing.
I do not expect you to understand
Now, let me walk as a child of the land.

The waters behind her flattened and the wind died. The mermaid shivered. Neither of these were calm things, they were the stillness of sudden attention, of great strength held in check.

Out of the flat water six heavy waves rolled towards the shore one by one. As they broke they pushed up the shingle into a platform of sea-built land. At the same time an angry wind came off the shore, tore spindrift from the wave tops and flung it away into the night.

This far, the wind said. This far, and no further.

No turning back. With her heart in her mouth the mermaid hauled herself onto the shingle mound.

A seventh wave came. Power thrummed up from the water through the skeleton of the old pier. A thousand starlings shrieked up into the night air as the sea surged forwards.

The wave roared across the platform and lifted the mermaid up. A staggering wind shoved back. The wave could not break. The mermaid hung inside the water behind a glassy salt-water wall, her long fair hair fanned about her.

Wind-snatched shingle flew off the beach, land hurled into the sea. Each stone slammed into the wave-wall and carved bubble-streaked trails deep into the water.

Her but not you, the land told the sea.

This far and no further.

You and your tricks.

The sea briefly held, but water like wind cannot stay still for long. The land-wind whirled and roared and shoved. The wave burst apart in spume and spray and crashed down to nothing.

Salt spray swirled, the wind died. A shimmering mist settled to reveal a barefoot woman dressed in a sky-blue blouse, a knee-length green skirt, a matching jacket. A pair of flat shoes lay at her feet beside a small shoulder bag. Strange things, she would get used to them.

Her own purse was already starting to dry and crack. She emptied the contents into the new one and saw the front was decorated with a cat face in silver sequins.

The Elements had kept their word, but the Land had a dry sense of humour and the Sea's was rather salty. Only later did it occur to her that the image was a warning.

She picked up the shoes and crossed the shared ground, the littoral that turn and turn about was land then sea. Further up the slope of the beach a scattered row of dried seaweed, scruffy feathers and frayed rope formed a ragged and wavy tide-line. She took a deep breath and stepped across.

Dry land.

Bright sounds from the other pier ebbed and surged on the night wind, the air tinged with the aromas of chip oil, candy floss, curry and beer.

Those gangs of mermen could not reach her here. Her old life was gone and along with it her old name. One night she had surfaced behind a South American cargo tramp. High on the stern was the ship's name, below it the country of registration. She liked what she saw and took it for herself. Now, for the first time in her life, she felt safe. She could fit in here. She must.

Up on the boardwalk she slipped on her shoes and climbed the wide concrete steps to the King's Road. She crossed the deserted neon-lit street and entered the winding lanes of Brighton town.

Some yards behind her a rather beautiful cat dropped soundlessly out of the shadows. Tail held high it trotted after her.

The Truth

THE SIGHT of Tim Wassiter's second ever client made him think that becoming a private investigator was one of his better moves.

She was young and she was beautiful. She walked straight through the door and spoke in a rich New England contralto. 'Mr Wassiter, my name is Dolores Vogler. I'm a marine biologist and I really need your help.'

Dolores wore her straight black hair cut to the line of her jaw. Her dress was the same carmine red as her shoes, low-cut and close-fit, the frilled hem just below her knees. On her head was a pillbox hat with a short veil of open black net and she held a red leather clutch bag in her hand. She stood on his worn old carpet like a rose in a rusty bucket. A worried rose in need of Tim's help.

These are clothes nobody wears any more, thought the part of Tim's mind that was still able to think. Especially not at half past two on a dull afternoon in the run-down office of Brighton's newest and most alternative private investigator.

You're being played, keep it cool.

Tim walked round his desk and gestured to one of his chairs. 'Please sit down. How may I help you?'

The cuffs of Tim's flower-patterned shirt were fastened by silver skull cuff-links, his black jeans were last year's, his shoes had seen better days. He needed a haircut.

Dolores Vogler took in his appearance with a single sweep of her eyes. She sat down and crossed her legs. One shoe dangled from her toes, her legs were bare. 'I need to find a missing automobile,' she purred.

'No problem. What sort of car, Ms Vogler?'

'A 1934 Airflow Chrysler Imperial Eight. Black, with Finnish plates.' She looked Tim straight in the eye. 'It's my husband's car.'

There it was.

Tim played it straight. 'Have you reported it to the police?'

'Of course, but we all know how busy they are.' She smiled and stood up. 'It's his favourite vehicle. He doesn't know it's missing yet and I'd love to be able to return it before he notices.'

He took out his notebook. 'Where did it go missing?'

Dolores moved to the edge of his desk and sat there with one long leg swinging as she trailed a red fingernail back and forth under the edge. Her skirt rode up. She watched Tim through her veil. 'Oh, in Brighton.'

'And when was that?'

'A few days ago.'

'Do you know the registration?'

'I can't remember.'

And there it was again.

Dolores extracted a tight roll of bank notes from her clutch bag and placed it on Tim's desk. She looked worried. 'I have to go now. Please find my husband's car quickly, Mr Wassiter.'

'A few more questions, Ms Vogler—'

She turned at the door, her red dress stretched flat across her shapely pelvis. Her smile was full of promise and brilliant perfect teeth. 'I really would be ever so grateful.'

Tim listened to Dolores' light footsteps on the stairs. As soon as he heard the door open and close he snatched up the money and went to the window. Down in the street, shoulders slung back, Dolores stalked towards a Mercedes S-class drophead, cream with white leather interior. An athletic brunette wearing long white boots and a short leather dress stood beside it with one foot on the chrome-trimmed running board. A platinum blonde sat behind the wheel.

Tim loosened his collar. Dolores Vogler was no more married than he was. What sort of a man had three mistresses and a car like that?

Dolores' floral perfume lingered in the air. As the surface notes faded a cloying undertone grew, syrup-sweet like over-ripe fruit. Tim opened the window. It was too strong, too definite, as if it were there to cover something up. Something rotten.

Down in the street the S-class sank down on its rear springs and surged away. He watched the car until it turned the corner. None of this was right and it wasn't real. Dolores had lied and Tim strongly suspected she did not care that he knew. Yet if that was the case why the distraction of the clothes and the coquetry? Unless that in itself was a double deception, a false diversion never intended to work, implying a deeper layer of chicanery.

It was far simpler to believe Dolores Vogler's wealth allowed her to behave like that all the time. Unless—

He could either speculate himself into a paranoid headache or just take the case and find out. One thing was certain, this sort of thing had never happened when he had been in uniform. Right now, right in front of him, was a cash up front case. In all probability it was a risky one, possibly even dangerous. He checked the money roll—a thousand pounds—and revised that to 'probably'. He didn't care, he couldn't afford to. A nagging voice said he should have written Dolores a receipt. He pushed it aside, finding a missing car wasn't difficult, cops did it all the time. This was his case and he was going to solve it.

Tim was still looking out of the window when he heard the slow stamp and clump of Mrs Woosencraft's wide-fit court shoes on the bare wood of the stairs. He pushed the money roll into his pocket and went to the door and called down.

'Hello Mrs W. How are you today?'

'*Prynhawn da*[1], Tim. Not so bad.'

Mrs Woosencraft was short, dumpy and stronger than she looked. Sometimes her corona of fine white hair was dyed pale pink, today it was powder blue. Her skirts were floral, her inevitable shawls hand-made.

A round metal tray covered by a kitchen towel sagged alarmingly in Mrs Woosencraft's hand. 'I've made you some Welsh cakes. They're still warm, too.'

Tim quickly took the tray before the cakes slid off. 'I'll put the kettle on.'

Mrs Woosencraft lived at number twenty-three in the middle of a Victorian terrace of seven houses further down the street. She often popped in on some little excuse or other. Tim didn't mind. She was lonely and it wasn't as if he had much else to do. At least, not until today.

Tim poured the tea, a mug for him, a bone china cup and saucer decorated with daffodils and violets for Mrs Woosencraft. He had bought it from one of the antique shops in the bustling Brighton Lanes.

Tim took one of the golden brown flat cakes and ate half the soft buttery thing in one bite. He nodded in appreciation. 'These are very tasty.'

'Not bad at all, though I say it who shouldn't.' Mrs Woosencraft's head came up, she sniffed the air and looked at the open window. 'As I came down the street I couldn't help but notice a lovely old car with three well-dressed young ladies in it. Such a pleasure to see such smartness, there are too many jeans and t-shirts these days. Call me old-fashioned but a nice girl shouldn't wear trousers. It's not proper.'

---

[1] *Good afternoon.*

Tim was certain Dolores Vogler would not fit into Mrs Woosencraft's definitions of 'nice' or 'proper' but he enjoyed listening to her lilting South-Wales accent. He liked her enough that he didn't mind her gentle nosiness or old-fashioned opinions. The cakes were good too.

'They were customers, Mrs W. Marine scientists.'

Mrs Woosencraft made no response. Tim raised his voice. 'I said they were customers. I've got a job.'

The wrinkles round Mrs Woosencraft's mouth deepened. 'Another job, is it? How lovely,' she said without any sign of pleasure. For a moment she sat very still. Then she reached out, her cup rattling in the saucer. 'Top that up for me, will you?'

Hurriedly Tim took her cup and poured more tea.

'Tell me, Tim. Has your Morse come back to you yet?'

'Not yet, Mrs W. At least the chickens are happier.'

Tim's cat Morse was mostly Turkish Van, white-bodied with ginger brow, ears, and tail. He was a friendly and capable cat and still occasionally kittenish after ten years. He'd been missing for weeks. Tim had looked and looked and missed him like hell.

'Cats are so vulnerable in the streets.'

'Morse isn't a vulnerable cat.' Tim said the word 'vulnerable' deliberately, hoping Mrs Woosencraft would say it again, in the way only little old ladies from Carmarthen could.

'Too many cats are disappearing.'

That was true. Tim ate another cake and waited for Mrs Woosencraft's inevitable question.

'Well, now you have a proper job I expect you'll have no time to look for my poor Un Deg Naw.'

It was true, he didn't need reminding. Work was work and he really needed it. 'I'll make time to look for your cat.' It wasn't entirely a lie. He felt a little glum. 'Mine too.'

Mrs Woosencraft gripped Tim's hand in her papery, arthritic fingers. 'She's Bengalese.'

'You told me before, remember?'

'Of course I remember,' she said sharply. 'I'm not daft, just worried. I know I've a lot of the blessed creatures. Too many some people say, just a mad old Welsh lady with nineteen cats, they say that too.' She held up her hand. 'No, I know they do. Too many for a little place in the middle of Brighton, but listen—I'm all alone and I need them all.' Her eyes grew watery, her smile brave. 'Every single one.'

Right that moment Tim thought she too looked a little vulnerable. Brighton was not always a friendly town.

'Little wretch that Un Deg Naw. Ruined my curtains climbing onto the pelmet. The Siamese copied her.' She tugged a hanky from the cuff of her cardigan and dabbed her eyes. A faint smell of lavender filled the air. 'She should be grateful I want her back at all.'

Mrs Woosencraft drank half her tea and announced she had to go. 'It will take me a while to get back on these legs. Finish the cakes, *bachgen*. I'll see myself out.'

Once again the office was empty. Tim looked at the gold lettering on the door:

TW Effectuation

~

Private Investigators

He squeezed the roll of notes with intense satisfaction. That's me, Tim Wassiter. And I have my first real case.

About time too, another part of him said.

Build it and they will come, the first part replied.

He'd used the severance money from the police to rent and equip his office. Furniture comprised a second-hand desk and two chairs, and a sagging settee nobody sat in. An ancient computer occupied the desk, the desk sat on a carpet just the right side of threadbare.

A second door opened onto a short corridor to his bedroom, shower and galley kitchen. The corridor ended at the bottom of a narrow staircase to the roof.

The Vogler case had come just in time. In just a few more weeks the cupboard would have been bare and he'd have to accept the standard casework of a PI: divorce, petty fraud and office theft, family intrigues. He'd turned cases like those down as he waited for the right kind to turn up. The kind of case where he could prove his theories of alternative detection.

Now he could afford to pay some bills and have some flyers printed. In the future lay expansion, larger premises, junior investigators, an efficient middle-aged secretary. Beyond that, perhaps, the Tim Wassiter Academy of Alternative Investigation.

Tim came back to earth in his shabby office. Before any of that, the case itself. He took out his notebook and wrote on a clean page:

The Vogler Case:
Dolores Vogler is a liar.
She's beautiful, stylish and probably very rich.
She's still a liar.

Babylon

LOW EVENING SUN shone through the glassless window of prince-priest Banipal's work room. Outside, the ochre mud-brick walls of ancient Babylon glowed golden orange across the city. At the end of a long and tiring day Banipal still worked at his bench, transcribing his notes from the reusable wax trays onto a stack of clay tablets.

Amending and expanding as he went, he pressed his stylus into the clay with painstaking care, filling tablet after tablet with dense cuneiform script.

Finally the task was done. Banipal wiped the stylus clean and laid out the tablets ready for the ovens. After firing the clay would be nearly indestructible. With good fortune his work would endure.

He rubbed his eyes and stretched. Although he was weary from the day his brain seethed with plans for tomorrow. The implications of his discoveries, what they might let him attempt and what might one day be possible years or even lifetimes from now, awed him. The universe was indeed a beautiful and wondrous place.

Hunger growled in his belly. By the length of the shadows he realised he was late for his evening meal again. Banipal washed his hands, face and shaven scalp and dried himself with a small towel. He left his room, descended the exterior steps and crossed the sun-warmed flagstones of the square to the open-fronted cook-house. The other prince-priests were already eating at the wooden tables. Conversation buzzed, a few raised their hands in greeting. It was the normal contented end to a normal day. Also as normal one of the bonded servants had put aside a bowl of dates, millet bread and goat cheese for Banipal.

Not in the mood for conversation he took his food back across the square and climbed up to the roof of his quarters. He sat on the low parapet with his legs dangling over the edge, nibbled a date and looked out across the city.

Directly below him lay the main quadrangle of Esagila, House of the Raised Head, the home of Marduk, patron deity of Babylon, and his consort.

Banipal had been in the quadrangle many times and seen the golden god statues, their attendant butler, hairdresser, baker and door-keeper, and the fearsome winged Kurubs guarding the inner portal. Like the vast majority of the populace he had never entered Marduk's temple. Only once had he glimpsed the interior and seen for himself what everyone knew—even the great cedar rafters were gilded.

Towering halfway to the sky beyond Esagila temple soared the enormous stepped ziggurat of Etemenanki, the broad Euphrates river flowing around its feet. Three hundred feet on each side, Etemenanki, the House of the Platform of Heaven and Earth, was visible for miles across the plain.

Banipal became lost in thought. Knowing how to measure the world, how could he measure the heavens?

That was how Banipal's great friend Ishkun found him as the golden edge of evening rose up the platforms and broad stairways of Etemenanki.

'Blessings of Enki fall upon you,' Ishkun said, his ready smile white above the tight black curls of his beard. He frowned as he saw Banipal's barely-eaten meal in the bowl. 'Oh, my friend, you are still eating. I would have come later, but I missed you.'

Banipal swung his legs over the parapet. 'Then stay. It's good to see you and I have had my fill.'

Ishkun made an expansive gesture. 'Eat! No need for formality between friends.'

This was an old conversation. Banipal's face was thin from lack of eating, not lack of food. 'Truly, I am full. What remains is for Marduk.'

Ishkun thought Marduk fed well enough as it was. How much fruit meat and bread did the Gods need?

'Let us walk through the city then. You're so thin I worry that if we stay up here a zephyr might waft you away. Then what would I do?'

Banipal laughed. 'You would do very well. And I'm sure Inanna's priestesses would be much happier not having to pretend to like me as much as they do you.'

Ishkun and Banipal walked down to the temple courtyard and out into the streets of the merchant quarter. As they passed through the temple gate Ishkun finally said what he had come to say.

'Banipal, I've just had a marvellous idea. Tomorrow let us go—'

'Not hunting, Ishkun, please.'

Banipal's eyes were fever bright, Ishkun could see the skull under his skin, his raw bones. He determined to stay cheerful. 'All right, I have a confession. Banipal, listen to me for this is the truth: I have transgressed.' He held up his hand before Banipal could speak, 'No, don't ask me what it is, it is far too embarrassing. The thing is I must hunt, and soon. A sacrifice for Marduk.'

Banipal nodded, smiling patiently. 'And whatever he does not want, we shall eat?'

'It had crossed my mind.' Ishkun clutched Banipal's arm as they ducked under the hanging fabrics of the merchant stalls. 'But listen, now I really have transgressed because I lied about the need to make sacrifice and in doing so I invoked Marduk's name. He surely heard me, so—'

'So your lie about transgression has become the transgression itself. A neat circular argument. That is very clever, I like it.'

Ishkun beamed. 'So you will come?'

'Not tomorrow, nor the day after. My work…' Banipal looked up at the great ziggurat, the summit still capped with the last of the sunlight. 'I am discovering too many wonderful things.'

'Think of what we could discover out in the wide world,' Ishkun protested. He loved his friend dearly despite, or possibly because of their differences. He simply wanted him to be happy, to put on a little weight. To not fade away through obsession. He was convinced that if he could only prise Banipal away from his studies he would relax and learn to enjoy life. 'We would hunt, race, feast, lie with women—' Ishkun saw how unconvinced Banipal was and took a deep breath. 'We could even go fishing.'

Banipal gave a great shout of laughter. Ishkun could not abide fishing. Hour after hour sitting on the river bank or floating on a reed raft. Meanwhile the implacable urge to get up, to do something, do anything, grew in him moment by boring moment. At his side Banipal would be perfectly content, lost in thought, lost in his beloved numbers and never minding if they caught sixty *qa* of carp or none at all. Taking up Ishkun on his offer was something Banipal simply could not do. That the offer was sincere broke his resolve.

'All right, I promise you,' Banipal said. 'The day after tomorrow I will ride with you in your chariot through Ishtar's gate and we will hunt and run, and bring back enough meat for Marduk to forgive you and feed Babylon for a year and a day.'

'We will, we will!' Ishkun cried, hugging his friend. 'And in return I will help you with your sticks and string and counting pebbles.'

'Then you are the better man,' Banipal said. 'Because I do very much enjoy hunting with you, my friend.'

'Very much?' Ishkun queried.'

'Quite enjoy,' Banipal admitted. 'Mostly.'

Ishkun had visited Banipal's poles and pebbles out on the plain and listened patiently to his friend's explanations of distance, measurement and angle. He looked at the neat rows of stones, the sets of pebbles grouped and arranged into further sets, and tried to understand. It made his head swim and if he persisted, sent him into a black mood for failing to see what was so obvious to Banipal.

'That's exactly how I feel when we're tracking game,' Banipal said. 'You point to plain signs and I see nothing.'

'But they're so obvious anyone—' Ishkun began, then raised his hands in apology. 'We both dream of great exploits. Yours take place between your ears.'

Banipal shook his head. 'Across the universe, Ishkun. The world is made of numbers. Just by knowing the days in a year, the seasons, the cycles of moon and sun, we know when the rains will come, in which season the rivers will flood, the nights the moon will be hidden by the spawn of Anu. All these things affect our lives and destiny. Numbers prove they are connected to one another.'

'Perhaps…'

'Think what might we discover if we measured the heartbeats in a man's life, the direction of a bird's flight? Our astrologers can tell us something of the future, if I can combine my discoveries with theirs we might find out so much more.'

Ishkun was troubled. 'Surely some things are too big to measure?'

'Such as?'

Ishkun gestured around him. 'The whole world.'

'Even that is almost in my grasp.'

Now Ishkun laughed. 'You could never have a rope long enough.'

'But I already have the rope.'

Ishkun listened to his friend's explanation of the varying distances between the top and bottom of vertical poles on a sphere. It was common knowledge the world was round: stars rose at different times in different places; the tops of distant mountains appeared before their bases.

'Some things the Gods do not mean us to know.'

'They test our worth.' Banipal looked steadily at Ishkun. 'If I could measure everything I would know everything. I could even make new things happen.'

This troubled Ishkun even more. After walking in silence for a while he reminded Banipal of the things he should bring for the hunt and departed.

Warning Signs

THAT NARROW FLIGHT of stairs behind Tim's office led to the roof. Once upon a time it might have been possible to see the sea from there. Now the view was blocked by the beachfront hotels.

A mug of breakfast tea in his hand, Tim sat with his back against the chimney stack. The early morning breeze felt fresh on his face. He looked out across the untidy aerial and satellite-dish strewn roofscape of the North Lanes and sipped his tea. Then he counted his chickens.

There were still three.

Brighton had its own share of urban foxes, with plenty of places for dens and hiding places in the local gardens. It would be an agile fox indeed that could make it up the fire escape ladder.

Tim's shadow crept across the flat roof as the sun rose. A few sheets flapped on washing lines hung between the stacks in the next street. The three chickens scratched and pecked in the sand of their enclosure.

Tim knew plenty about cats but less about chickens in general or these three in particular. He didn't know their breed, he hadn't given them names and he didn't want to. All he needed was to know how to look after them until their time came. Until they were needed for detection.

Cool excitement coiled in his stomach. Now he had taken the Vogler case the long-awaited opportunity to put magical theory to practical test was here.

He went into the enclosure, swept away their dirt, changed the water and put down fresh grain. He considered the tawny-feathered birds with mixed feelings. They knew nothing of their fate and had food, shelter, and safety. There were times in Tim's own life where he would have been content with no more than that.

The hens softly clucked and tipped their heads, quietly going about their business, oblivious to the fact that their owner intended to use them for methods of detection the police would never consider in a hundred years.

He was running low on feed. And he'd need a galvanised tray too. Something to collect the blood.

Back in the office he printed off a new missing cat sign for Morse. Old notices faded and people ignored them. The pet shop was happy to have signs in the window, there was already one there for Mrs Woosencraft's own missing cat.

Tim opened the file for Morse on his computer. Under a picture of his cat he had typed:

Missing Cat
White, with ginger ears and tail.
Breed: Turkish Van (mostly)
Name tag: 'Morse'

He hesitated, wondering if he should add something about Morse's quirky charm and idiosyncrasies, his love of water.

Morse's continuing absence brought a fresh pang. Days became weeks, the local Cats Protection League had no news and Morse's absence left a cat-shaped hole in Tim's world. Some cats went roving at certain times of the year but Morse was not like that. Tim checked his phone number was correct then printed the file and carefully slid it into a large envelope. Folded or rolled signs brought less attention. On the way out he closed the window and locked the door.

As he walked to the pet store he wondered if it was more than coincidence that both cats had disappeared within a few days of each other. Morse was only mostly one breed, but he had attractive, symmetrical markings. Mrs Woosencraft's cat was a pedigree Bengal. Could they both be cases of cat-napping? An international band of cat thieves stealing cats to order? Tim's mind wandered into more and more implausible theories and he walked into the pet shop barely aware of his surroundings.

'Hey, mind me!' a woman said sharply.

Tim found himself looking into the steady gaze of a pair of sea-green eyes level with his own.

She was young, broad-shouldered like a swimmer, trim at waist and hip. Her white blouse was crisp, her dark green skirt tight about the knee. A band of freckles ran across her nose and her untamed hair shone pale gold. She looked at him like he was some kind of idiot, put her hands on his shoulders with such reluctance it was obvious she didn't want to touch him, and moved him back. 'You're standing on my left thing.' She frowned and looked down at her shoe. 'My foot.'

Her accent was intriguing, definite but not immediately traceable, neither East-European nor American, not Australasian or South American.

'I'm sorry, I was in a dream,' Tim said.

'You're supposed to do that that in your sleep, not the pet shop.'

Tim held up his envelope. 'I was worrying about my cat. He's gone missing.'

'Hardly surprising if you dream while you're awake. Do people do that a lot around here?'

'I don't think so. Why?'

'Too many stray cats.'

'You've lost one too?'

She at Tim suspiciously. 'No. I don't trust… The real problem is, every time I open my door there's another one.'

'You shouldn't feed them.'

'Do I look like someone who feeds cats?'

She did not. She looked like someone who was—the words came to Tim unbidden—wild and fine, a free spirit, He so, so wanted to keep the conversation going. They were standing beside the fish tanks, he took a guess. 'Do you keep fish?'

'I miss them.' She looked at the guppies, neon tetras, catfish and angels. 'I had a mackerel called Tony.'

'If I had fish Morse would jump in the tank. He loves water.'

'Who's Morse?'

'My cat.'

She frowned again. 'I'm really not keen on cats.'

'They seem to know if you don't like them, then sit on you.'

'Is that why they hang around my place? They want to sit on me?'

'Maybe.'

She backed away. 'That's too strange. It's not what I want.'

'Cats are strange creatures.'

'Anything with legs is a bit weird.'

She sounded so serious Tim laughed 'Why do you say that?'

'You ask a lot of questions.'

'I'm sorry, I'm a PI, a private investigator.' He took a card from his wallet and held it out. 'I've just started out.'

She squinted at the card, moved it forwards and back.

'You've, um, got it…' Tim started.

She turned it the right way up. 'TW Effectuation.'

'TW, that's me, Tim Wassiter.'

'Foxy,' she said. 'That's my name. Foxy Bolivia.'

Tim held out his hand. 'Pleased to meet you.'

She didn't take it.

Hand out, Tim stood there with a mild out-of-body sensation. He recalled Dolores Vogler, darkly vivid and intriguing—and false. Whoever this suspicious and wary woman in her impractical pencil skirt was his instincts said she was authentically the exact person he saw in front of him.

The shopkeeper, a gangling young woman with loose-cropped purple hair, lip and nostril studs, and a nose that was slightly too long for her face, watched them like a bored goldfish.

Tim turned back to Foxy. 'I'm sorry about your shoe.'

She looked up from Tim's hand. 'My what?'

Tongue-tied, Tim gestured helplessly. 'Your foot.'

'Oh, that, yes, the foot thing.' She looked straight at Tim and he fell deep into her green eyes all over again.

'Your accent, is it from Barbados?' he said.

Her eyes went wide. 'You can tell that just from my voice?'

Tim squared his shoulders. 'I've had some training.'

'I lived near there when I was younger—' Her gaze hardened. 'I don't need to tell you anything.'

And she was gone, out through the door and away down the street.

The door jangled closed. Disappointed and surprised Tim told himself he needed to get used to these encounters. He was a PI, and Private Investigators tended to encounter beautiful and sometimes dangerous women. If he worked on his style, developed a sense of savoir-faire then maybe one of them… Maybe one of them would stick around. Maybe.

Such was his hope.

The most obvious thing in the world occurred to him: Foxy's home was full of stray cats, there was a good chance both Morse and Mrs Woosencraft's cat were there. The realisation was so obvious that it coming after she had left actually felt cruel. He ran out into the street and looked left and right but she was gone.

Tim hurried back into the shop. The purple-haired shop keeper looked at him with sardonic pity.

'Do you know where that woman lives?' Tim said.

'Jeez, no. This is a pet shop, not a pick-up—'

'We were just talking.'

'Yeah, I noticed. Look, it's OK, you find it where it is. Follow your heart—'

Tim stared at her. She shrugged, apologetic. 'I've never seen her before.'

Tim could have kicked himself. Disconsolate, he bought a large bag of bird feed, replaced the sign in the window, and headed home. Foxy Bolivia had been a lead and he'd blown it. More than a lead. She was not so much beautiful as unforgettable. He tried to stay positive, she had to be local or she would not have come into the shop. All was not lost. He was a PI. He'd use his skills and ask around. He would find her, find the cats, find someone who—

The thing he thought about most on his way home was, when she turned at the pet shop door, how the long waves of her golden hair hung down to the back of her knees.

Half way up the stairs with a 5-kilo bag of chicken feed under his arm and junk mail in his hand, Tim noticed the door to his office was open.

In his mind he eased up the stairs, back to the wall. Avoiding the loose tread three from the top he got the drop on the intruders with his trusty snub-nosed revolver. In reality all the treads of the ancient stairs creaked, popped and groaned. Stealth was an impossibility and Tim did not own an illegal handgun.

'I'll be right up,' Tim called.

After a brief silence the hurried sound of rustling papers was followed by a muffled thump and a curse.

'Hey!' Tim sprinted up the stairs and burst into his office. A beefy middle-aged man with close-cropped hair sprawled with feigned nonchalance in the chair beside Tim's desk. It was Troy Jarglebaum, Tim's ex-partner from his time in the police service. Troy wore his usual cheap rumpled navy-blue cop suit, a food-stained cop tie and incongruously shiny black lace-up cop shoes. A loose sheaf of papers hung in his hand, an A4 sized parcel sat on the floor.

Tim dropped the sack of bird seed by the door. 'Troy. I might have guessed it was you.'

'Tim, good to see you too.' Jarglebaum grinned massively and dropped the sheaf of papers onto the desk. 'The wind blew your papers all over the floor.'

'It must have been quite a breeze considering the window was shut.'

'I just closed it.'

'Good of you. So did I, before I went out.'

Tim dropped the junk mail in the wastebasket, walked round the desk and put the papers back in the open drawer. As he did he rested his hand on the top of the computer monitor. It was cold, at least Jarglebaum hadn't had the time or the gall to try and break into his electronic files.

'There's a knack to shutting this drawer, you need to push it from the left side or it sticks. Try to remember that next time. Also, my door was locked. That's breaking and entering.'

'Nothing's broken, pal.' Jarglebaum hauled himself to his feet. 'Look, we're getting off on the wrong foot. I just came over to see how my old partner in crime-solving was getting along. There was this box on the outside step so I thought I'd bring it up before it got stolen.'

Inwardly Tim seethed but there was little point trying to hustle Detective Sergeant Jarglebaum out of any room he didn't want to leave. Thirty years in the service had immunised him to all forms of coercion short of physical violence, which he was delighted to reciprocate. During those three decades his diet had been one of pasta, beer, curry, and pizza. Sometimes all in one meal. Troy Jarglebaum had acquired a physical inertia to match that of his career.

Tim summoned up a polite smile. 'OK Troy, thank you very much. So, how are you doing?'

'Onwards and upwards, Tim,' Troy said, smoothing his rumpled tie across his belly.

'Promotion? Congratulations, you've certainly had to wait long enough.'

A scowl passed over Jarglebaum's face like a cloud across a badly ploughed field. 'You chose a bad time to leave the boys in blue. Everything's changing. Technology, modernisation—'

'That must be exciting.'

Troy shrugged dismissively. 'I'm talking about bigger fish. Extra-mural opportunities, pal. Real ones.'

Tim shook his head, he'd heard it all before. Congenitally dissatisfied, Jarglebaum was always scheming, always able to explain previous failures in terms of other people's mistakes.

'You're finally leaving the police?'

'No way, kiddo. There's an indexed-linked pension with my name on it. It's smaller than your cock but I still want it.'

'What are these "opportunities", Troy?'

Jarglebaum paced the threadbare carpet then peered out the window. 'Freelance commissions, legal consultancy. I'm not allowed to say more due to client confidentiality.' He walked round to Tim's side of the desk and started pulling open drawers. 'Where's your whisky, son? I could use a drink. Every P.I. in the world has some cheap booze hidden in their files. A half-empty bottle and two chipped glasses—'

Tim pushed shut the drawers and moved between Jarglebaum and the desk. 'Sorry, Troy, I don't have any. How about a cup of tea?'

'Jesus, kid,' Jarglebaum said sadly. 'What sort of a PI are you?'

Tim straightened his shoulders. 'A new kind.'

Jarglebaum rolled his eyes. 'You're still into all that voodoo shit. Dowsing and reading tea leaves.'

'It's not shit, Troy. It works and you know it.'

Jarglebaum scowled again. 'Once, just once.'

'That woman found a missing child using just a map and a pendulum. I saw her do it, everyone in the incident room did, you too. We discovered a new method but the Chief Constable didn't like it so we turned our backs on something that can solve mysteries and pretended it didn't exist. Well, I'm not a cop any more so I'm going to learn how to do that. I'm going to do things differently.'

'Well, you were certainly a different kind of cop,' Jarglebaum grumbled. 'The kind that gave his partner the worst percentages in the service.'

Tim sighed inwardly. Here we go again with the blame game. 'That's all in the past, Troy.'

'Yeah, right.' Jarglebaum wiped his mouth with the back of his hand. 'You sure you haven't got a drink?'

'I'm sure.'

Jarglebaum's shoulders dropped. 'So what's in the box?'

Tim glanced at the label. 'Flyers for my business.'

'Good plan.'

'Thanks.'

'Let's have a look.'

'Sorry, my hands are dirty.'

'No problem.' Jarglebaum tore open the wrapper and pulled out the top sheet. He leaned back in the chair, one side of his mouth curling into a wider and wider smile as he read:

David Gullen

TW Effectuation
Private Investigators

Detection through Evidence & Intuition

~

Alternative & Traditional Methods

~

Drawing on years of Practical Constabulary Experience
And Spiritual Techniques Ancient & Modern
TW Effectuation will help you:

– Resolve Intriguing Mysteries
– Locate People in Time and Space
– Observe & Inform

~

The Evidence is Out There!
T.W. Effectuation will help you find it

'Sheesh.' Jarglebaum dropped the sheet on top of the parcel. 'OK, let's have it, what's your case load?'

Tim couldn't help himself, he held up two fingers. 'I have two current investigations.'

'Tim, that's great!' Troy seemed serious. 'No, kid, I mean it, I'm impressed.'

'Thanks,' Tim said cautiously.

Playfully Jarglebaum punched Tim's shoulder. 'Like I said, what have you got, kiddo?'

All at once Tim realised the trap and it was as if he had never left the police, had never escaped his partner's interrogative ridicule. 'Sorry, Troy,' he said. 'Client confidentiality.'

Laughter blew out of Jarglebaum's face like a gale. 'Let me guess. Divorce.'

'No.'

'Missing cat.'

'No.'

'Liar.' Jarglebaum crowed with satisfaction. 'Never lie to a cop unless you're a cop. Come on, don't you remember anything I taught you? Finding a missing cat, that's good, Tim, very good. Never underestimate the importance of little old ladies and community relations. What's the other one?'

All at once Tim just wanted to get it over with. Jarglebaum had come here to mock his dreams, so be it. 'A stolen car.'

'Stolen car.' Jarglebaum slowly nodded his head. 'What sort?'

Tim shook his head. 'I'm not going to tell you.'

Jarglebaum shadow-boxed the air between them. 'That's it, go it alone, plough your own furrow. Give it a go, then give me a call.'

'I've got it covered.'

'Sure you have, kid. The way you're going all us cops will be out of a job.' Snapping a card out of his breast pocket Jarglebaum tossed it onto the desk. 'Phone in when you get stuck.'

'Right.'

'I'm here to help.'

'OK.' It had always been easier to agree.

Pausing at the door Jarglebaum kicked the sack of chicken feed. 'This what they're paying you these days?' His mocking laughter followed his heavy footsteps all the way down the stairs.

Tim slumped back in his chair and stared at the flies flying their square circles under the ceiling light.

Why do they do that? he wondered. Come to that, how do they make right-angle turns in mid-air? Maybe they stop flapping one wing for a split second. Maybe they can just grab hold of the air and swing round like a kid on a lamppost.

It had been a strange and disappointing day. He'd found a lead and lost it, and the woman who had been that lead was someone he'd really have liked to have seen again. Worst of all Troy Jarglebaum had turned up like a bad penny and worked his energy-sapping black magic on Tim's self-esteem. Every encounter with Jarglebaum left him feeling useless, with a long fight back into the light.

Despite Jarglebaum's offer it was unlikely he could help. Stolen car reports were logged, filed and generally forgotten. Nobody actually went looking for them because there were more important things to do. Patrol cars had computerised license-recognition cameras, the cameras scanned passing vehicles and sounded an alarm when they made a match.

Then Tim remembered Dolores Vogler hadn't actually said the car was stolen, she had said it was missing. No wonder she had to come to him, the police would be interested in a missing person, never a missing car. Not only that, the car was not even UK registered.

Which meant that Troy actually had nothing to offer at all. He couldn't even find the registered owner. Tim sat up straight, filled with renewed energy and determination. 'Beaten you, Troy Jarglebaum,' he said to himself. 'I don't need you, and I never will.'

But how could a car go missing? It wasn't as if they had minds of their own or could drive themselves. Not yet anyway, and certainly not one made in 1934. Was Dolores

Vogler a scatterbrain who had simply forgotten where she'd parked? She hadn't given the impression she was that sort of person. More likely she'd let someone borrow it and he—it would have to be a he—had not brought it back.

Everything was connected. Philosophers, shamans, and mystics had known it for hundreds of years before physicists discovered it in new and scientific ways few people genuinely understood. Tim believed both ways were true, but how to make the connections himself?

Up on the roof the chickens lived out their days, but the moment lacked true significance and this was not the time for their blood and their lives. Perhaps the patterns the flies flew could be measured and overlaid on a map of Brighton. An intriguing idea but connections didn't work like that, there had to be a true link, something emotional, something physical. A piece of rust from the car's wing, a fleck of paint or chrome from the bumper. Even the police realised the value of these things except in Tim's opinion they were never used to their full potential and often just filed away in bags and boxes labelled 'Evidence'.

Under the lampshade the flies still flew their geometric designs.

'You poor things,' Tim told them. 'You don't even know what a car is, unless for you it's some kind of terrible monster to frighten your children at bedtimes.'

He imagined a row of tiny cots, each one occupied by a young fly, their blankets tucked up to their chins while they listened to stories of a metal nemesis roaring out of nowhere and squashing little flies across an invisible surface.

That was no good. Any empathic link he had was with the flies, not the car. Perhaps if he suspended a model of the Imperial under the lampshade…

Tim had no idea what a 1934 Airflow Chrysler Imperial Eight looked like, let alone Finnish registration plates. Now would be an excellent time to find out.

A few minutes searching the internet told Tim more than he ever needed or wanted to know about:

The manufacturing history of vintage Imperials.

The current availability of spares.

The history of individual cars.

Their current condition.

Their previous owners, where they lived, and reason for sale.

Their current owners and their partners (or former thereof).

Their state of health and where they liked to holiday.

The precocious achievements of their children.

The breed and temperament of their dogs. (Collectors of Imperials did not appear to be cat lovers).

How their dogs had ascended to doggy heaven, a place where the more intellectually challenged canines could presumably continue to chase large cars without resultant tragedy requiring the onwards sale of a much-loved Imperial the owner could no longer drive due to lingering memories of That Tragic Day.

All things considered, it was strangely fascinating.

Tim became lost in close-up pictures of the gloriously extravagant Virgil Exner designed tailfins from a '59 MY1 Convertible.

The office door creaked, a shadow passed in front of the desk. Tim looked up and saw a tall slim woman with a bun of platinum blonde hair and eyes of palest blue. Strikingly glamorous, she wore lipstick and nail varnish of nude pink, and a high-collared sleeveless cheongsam embroidered with blue, green and gold sea-serpents.

Behind her, a crop-headed brunette in a halter-necked red leather mini-dress, knee-high white boots and black fish-nets leaned nonchalantly against the doorjamb.

'Mr Wassiter.' The platinum blonde spoke with a clipped east-coast American accent. 'We've come about the car.'

These were the two other women in the Mercedes, and clearly the sort who would only be impressed by confidence and achievement. Tim knew if he let himself be distracted by their stunning, if slightly trashy get-up, he would never gain their respect or find out what they really wanted. He was being played again.

'1934 Airflow Chrysler Imperial Eight,' Tim said smoothly, keeping one eye on the computer screen. 'With aerodynamic styling, full steel body construction and custom bodywork by LeBaron, it is considered by many to be the most radically styled production car ever built.' He hazarded a knowing grin. 'After all, the single-piece curved windshield was an industry first.'

The platinum blonde returned a look of unsmiling appraisal. 'You're very well informed, Mr Wassiter.'

'That's not the half of it. The CW eight-seater weighed in at over 5,900 pounds, twenty feet from bumper to bumper with a wheelbase of 146.5".' Tim strolled round to the front of his desk, his smile was easy, his step confident. 'They were magnificent vehicles. In fact, I'd like one myself.'

'An unlikely ambition. Less than 2,500 Airflows were built, only a handful remain.'

'No matter. The '55 Newport is more my style.'

'The one we have employed you to find is still missing.'

'It's only been a day.' Tim thrust out his hand. 'Call me Tim.'

Her grip was dry, cold, and like a vice. Tim was forced to squeeze back and for a full ten seconds they smiled politely at each other and tried to crush each other's hands. Tim was losing, and just as his smile began to slide into a grimace of agony she laughed humourlessly and let go.

'I am Electra Vaughan.' She gestured to the woman standing in the doorway. 'This is Imelda Marchpane. We are good friends of Dolores Vogler.'

'Very good friends,' Imelda said, her American accent harder than Electra's. 'Great mansplaining just then.'

Tim surreptitiously massaged his aching hand. 'I saw you in the Mercedes.'

'Imelda likes to drive.'

'I love it.' Imelda bared her teeth in a silent snarl. 'Fast and hard.'

Disconcerted, Tim turned back to Electra. 'Your Imperial—'

Electra held Tim with her ice-cold gaze. 'Where is it?'

'I don't know.'

'Why not?'

'It's not that straightforward, Ms Vaughan.'

Electra took a step forward. 'Explain?'

'Well, for one thing Dolores said her husband's car was missing, not stolen.'

Electra and Imelda exchanged looks of cagey surprise.

'Dolores said that?' Electra said.

'Yes, she did. Having Finnish plates makes it harder—'

Electra spoke very slowly. 'Her *husband's* car?'

'Selfish, greedy,' Imelda hissed under her breath.

Tim cleared his throat. 'An ordinary car might simply have been dumped after a joy-ride, but the Imperial has probably been stolen to order. And this car is a valuable machine, isn't it?'

Electra and Imelda glared at Tim. He retreated behind his desk. 'It's not a case of putting up pictures on lampposts like you do for a missing cat.'

'Do you have a missing cat, Mr Wassiter?' Electra said sharply.

'I, ah— Yes, I do.'

'Missing but not stolen?'

Tim felt deeply confused. Electra swept forwards like a beautiful ghost. 'We want you to concentrate, Mr Wassiter. Focus exclusively on our case. No more cats. No more lampposts.'

Imelda unfolded her arms to reveal hands encased in fingerless black leather gloves. She gripped one side of the doorframe, tore it from the wall and tossed it onto the carpet in a scatter of plaster fragments. 'Exclusively.'

Now Tim was a little scared. Dolores had been exotic and alluring. Her two friends might be beautiful, Electra might radiate an aura of otherness, but being in the same room as Imelda felt like being in a cage with a tiger. She moved like a trained fighter and looked like someone who enjoyed hurting people.

'I'll talk to my other clients,' Tim said.

Imelda reached up and hung from the architrave. Wood shrieked and splintered as her weight tore it down. 'You do that. Or I will.'

The idea of Imelda Marchpane confronting little old Mrs Woosencraft sent shivers down Tim's spine.

'Money is not an issue, Mr Wassiter.' Electra placed another tight roll of notes on Tim's desk. 'What else do you need?'

Right now, Tim thought, I'd either like you out the office or a shotgun in my hands. Good grief, even Troy Jarglebaum would be a welcome sight. 'It would help if you had something that belongs to the owner, Mr…?'

'Dolores' husband?' Electra's face froze in a hard, white smile. 'Yes, I think we can provide you with that.'

Imelda lifted the hem of her red leather dress. A triangular fold of white material came into sight, held against her thigh by her stocking top.

Electra removed the fold of material and placed it in Tim's hand, the fabric still warm from Imelda's thigh.

'Don't let this out of your sight,' Electra said. She picked up one of Tim's flyers from the box on the desk, glanced at it and slipped it into her purse. 'We're interested in your methods, Mr Wassiter. You're out on the edge, we like that. Interesting things don't happen in the middle, they happen at edges, where things collide. You've got an open mind, we like that too. Frankly, it's what you're going to need.'

Imelda slipped her arm around Electra's slender waist, her fingers splayed across her hip. 'In fact the more open your mind the better it will be for us all.'

Tim placed the fold of material on the desk and sat down. He needed to. He wiped his brow, his heartbeat slowed, his breathing steadied. Insight often comes in moments of crisis. This is why PIs have a fifth of bourbon and two chipped glasses in the filing cabinet, he realised. It's for when your doorframe has just been hauled off the wall by a beautiful but wild girl in a red leather mini-dress and nothing but the sensation of raw spirits at the back of the throat will do.

He unfolded the material, an expensive silk handkerchief with a plain, over-sewn border. In one corner the monogram 'MK' had been embroidered in fine aquamarine thread. There was nothing else, no notes, ink stains or folds of paper tucked inside.

Tim rolled the new wad of money back and forth across the desk. He took off the rubber band, counted it, then added it to the other roll. Used tens and twenties, no sequence. Another thousand pounds. At least his cash pile had grown bigger. Those three women really wanted that car back.

He'd need to spend some of that getting the door fixed and, he decided, on a couple of shot glasses and some half-way decent scotch.

The rest would help compensate for the knowledge that once again Jarglebaum had been right. His ex-partner had only been in his office for a few minutes before pointing out a major flaw in Tim's lifestyle. Perhaps the overweight but highly observant detective really had just been looking for a drink all along.

And that's just what I need now, Tim decided. A couple of pints of decent beer in the Bat and Ball would help restore a sense of perspective.

Tim's ancient leather jacket hung on the hook on the wall. Wearing it to the pub had become a kind of ritual. He slipped it on and turned up the collar. He looked at the money roll on the desk. It was a lot of cash to carry around but it would be reckless to leave it in a room with an unlockable door and people like Troy Jarglebaum at large.

The monogrammed handkerchief still lay on his desk. Electra had warned him not to let it out of his sight and somehow Tim thought that she would know if he did. He carefully folded it into the jacket's inside pocket and distributed the money around the other pockets of both his jacket and jeans. Then he wedged the door shut as best he could, went downstairs, out the front door and up along Cheapside towards Ditchling Road and the pub.

Dark Waters

IN THE DEPTHS of the night Dolores tossed and turned in the grip of a lucid dream, a nightmare agony of fear and desire. More than a dream, it was a message from her lord under the ocean, Tuoni the life taker and life giver. It was a warning, a demand, a reminder that when they first met she had been dying…

…and now she dreamed she was dying again, struggling for breath in the stale freezing air of the crippled bathyscaphe. Miles down deep in the crushing dark, slumped in her chair before the ship's command console, she watched the lights of the emergency systems flicker from green to amber to red, and die.

Totally without power the lightless bathyscaphe canted to one side and sank down through unnaturally warm waters towards the ocean floor.

'Imelda? Electra?' Dolores gasped weakly in the pitch darkness. Her head pulsed with pain, the bitter cold. No matter how hard she tried she couldn't get her breath. Somewhere in the cabin were oxygen tanks, somewhere a torch. She fumbled with her harness with clumsy fingers. The skin on her knuckles tore on the edge of the simple release but her oxygen-deprived brain could not work out how to open it.

'Electra?'

'She's not moving.' Imelda's voice came ragged and faint.

'Is she…?' Dolores couldn't say the word. The thumping agony in her head surged and silent white noise flared behind her eyes. Electra, so bright, so quick to see new ideas, always the leader.

'Not yet. Won't be long. Not for any of us.' Imelda was never the one to prevaricate.

'Oxygen tanks?'

'Empty.'

She had forgotten. Hope had made her forget, had wanted her to try again. There was no hope.

'Imelda, I'm so scared.'

Imelda didn't speak for a moment. 'So am I, honey.'

'There's no way out, is there?'

Another pause. Even now she knew Imelda was calculating, thinking. Still hoping to beat the odds, still trying to do better than her best.

'Not this time,' Imelda finally replied. 'Whatever killed those mining drones has got us too.'

It had been exactly like that, just as if something had reached out and struck the valiant little submarine a series of blows, killing its systems one at a time: sensors, engines, computers, life support. They had felt it too, felt it come for them, a psychic pulse the failing instruments registered just before they died.

'What the fuck was that?' Electra cried as the dials swung and numbers scrolled. Then the main drive and manoeuvring motors stopped. All eight of them.

Around them in the dark ocean phosphorescent life surged and writhed in weird ecstasy.

Pain beat inside Dolores' head like a hammer. 'I'm so sorry,' she whispered. 'This is my fault. We wouldn't be here if it wasn't for me.'

This time Imelda did not reply.

The agony in her head intensified. Then, blessedly, it was gone. Dolores realised her chest had fallen still. She could feel her body just lying there, motionless, no longer breathing. This is what comes next, she thought. This is what it is like to travel beyond life and light, but no-one can be told. An immense sadness filled her. She wasn't ready to die, she didn't want to—

A strange grey light rose up around her and Dolores found she could see through the walls of the bathyscaphe as easily as through the round armoured windows. A dreary, flat vista stretched in every direction, cold and colourless. Far in the distance black plumes of superheated water boiled up from volcanic vents in the ocean floor.

Far beyond them something watched her, vast and curious. It reached out and bleak words flowed through her dying mind.

You feel your death. I watch you die. All things die. All toil in vain.

No!

You would rather live?

Yes!

Cleave to me. Be mine. Accept.

I—

You are dying.

No! Save me! Save us!

Accept.

I— I will.

Now.

Yes.

The sea-thing filled her mind. It became her mind. Dolores knew life from another life, another time.

At the same time, the intruder rummaged through her own memories. It too wanted to live and to know. It was huge and old, ancient beyond reckoning. It had slept through the ages and now it was awake it discovered it no longer remembered who or what it was.

All it knew was that once there had been a great labour, and that it had toiled alongside its brothers and sisters for their masters. When that that titanic work was done there had come not reward, only betrayal.

Close to the surface of Dolores' mind it discovered the stories Markus Koponen had told her on their long walks alone. Ancient legends from his northern culture, the deeds and names of heroes and Gods. Identity and meaning lay there. It found who it wanted to be.

There was a hell, Dolores learned, and Tuoni was its master. Her own guttering life endured at his will.

Hell was a place called Tuonela, the grey realm of the oceanic abyss. An endless plain of cold, grey silt, rent in two where the world heaved itself apart in a jagged rift ten thousand miles long. Its denizens were the blind shrimps and armoured worms who clustered around vents of boiling black water, and the enormous ten-legged crustaceans who chewed tunnels through the flesh of dead whales.

Under that soft silt Lord Tuoni slept, dreamless for millennia. Then, when new warmer waters bathed him, he dreamed.

It was still too cold for Tuoni to fully wake. He dreamed the fall. He dreamed the great betrayal again and again, the burial of his kind. This place should have been his grave, was the grave for his brothers and sisters. His creators had meant to destroy them. Now their time was long gone, creators and created. Only Tuoni remained.

A Lord defends his realm, as the sparse wreckage of mining robots and remote drones showed. A Lord also needs followers, a household.

'*I wake, yet I still dream,*' Tuoni roared in Dolores' head.

Compelled, Dolores cried out. 'The whole world warms, spring comes sooner, glaciers melt, ice sheets calve, winter recedes, ocean currents are changing.'

'*This will be my new world. I desire it.*'

'We fear it.'

'And so you came to my realm?'

'Yes.'

'At your old master's bidding.'

'Yes.' Unbidden memories filled Dolores' mind: Koponen excited at the rewards of deep-sea mining; Koponen cursing the loss of yet more equipment; Dolores persuading Electra and Imelda to accompany her in the bathyscaphe.

Something awful ransacked the contents of Dolores' mind, selecting this, discarding that. Lost within her own skull, Dolores witnessed her own rearrangement and discovered she could not miss what she no longer was.

'I dream he will fail,' Tuoni said.

Coming from within Dolores' own mind the words were irresistible, as if she thought them herself. 'We will stop him for you,' she said.

'For us.'

'My Lord.'

'I will reward you. I will remake you fit to dwell beside me when I rule.'

An iota of Tuoni's cold blood flowed within her veins, the promise of change to come.

I should not want this awful thing, Dolores thought. But I do. Oh, how I do.

'I release you,' Tuoni said.

Darkness. Pain.

Dolores' skull felt like it was being crushed in a vice.

Then she was back in the light, back in the bathyscaphe. Electra cradled Dolores head while Imelda pushed rhythmically on her chest. She opened her eyes and took a rattling breath.

Imelda wept and laughed. She kissed Dolores' cheek, kissed her brow, her mouth. Behind her eyes lay new knowledge.

The bathyscaphe was fully functioning, filled with sweet air, bright light, the steady drone of pumps and filters, the sweep of radar. External lights blazed into the oceanic night.

Dolores sat up. A quick look at the console showed they were rising, rising. Panic filled her, she was not who she was, she needed to prepare. This was too fast, too soon.

Electra's hand lay on her shoulder. 'We are here.'

Dolores looked into her friends' eyes and saw with a mix of relief and sorrow that Tuoni's thoughts also crawled inside their minds. She was not alone.

Imelda and Electra spoke together: 'Koponen sent us here.'

Dolores felt words form in her mouth. 'Tuoni says we must stop him.'

'Tuoni says by any means,' Imelda said.

'Tuoni—' Electra's beautiful mouth trembled, twisting, ugly. She bit down, bit through her own lip but still could not stop the words. Blood streamed from her mouth. 'Tuoni bid me seek his bride, the salt-water woman come to dry land.'

The three women exchanged looks of mutual, lustful, revulsion. Tuoni had altered them in body and mind. The shuddering horror in them was pity for who they had once been, the understanding that their changes were incomplete and one day they would cease to care.

They were three ships sailing into dark waters. Each day the shore-lights of sanity lay further behind.

Dolores wanted—ached—to give herself to Tuoni. Before that she must do his bidding on dry land. Only then could she sink down and live with him in his realm of Tuonela. Only then could she join with him in an awful coupling and have his seed crawl and bloat inside her.

Her own desires appalled her.

As the bathyscaphe rose towards the surface her terror diminished to anxiety, fading like the echo of a dying shriek. Her two best friends were with her, she felt a kind of fulfilment, an anticipation for the future she had never known before. All became well.

Dolores resumed her seat, fastened her belt and checked the ship's systems. The bathyscaphe trembled as she vented ballast from the tanks.

Electra's smile was wider than before, as if there were more teeth in her mouth. She wiped drying blood onto her sleeve. 'Let's go have some fun.'

Persistence

TIM WOKE SLOWLY, something was… not wrong, just different. Despite last night's beers it was not a hangover. Roped into an impromptu darts match he had stayed the entire evening. Half-asleep in the pre-dawn light he shifted his legs and felt a familiar and much missed weight across his feet.

Delight filled him. 'Morse! You utter rascal, where have you been?'

He reached for the light. It wasn't Morse.

A plump, black, green-eyed Manx cat sprawled at the bottom of the bed. Around its neck was a red leather collar with an enamelled red and gold Welsh dragon for a nametag. This member of the unusual tailless breed belonged to Mrs Woosencraft. The cat gave Tim a look of casual disregard then laid its head between its paws and went back to sleep.

'Oh no you don't.' Tim rolled out of bed and pulled on trousers and tee-shirt. 'Come on you lump, I don't know how you got in here but I know where you came from and you're going home.'

He scooped up the cat and it sagged artlessly in his hands. Tim hung it over one arm while he unhooked its claws from the blanket.

Out in the hallway Tim checked his watch: 5:30 am. With the excitement of thinking Morse had returned he was wide awake. He put the cat down on the floor, where it began to wash.

'I don't blame you coming up here,' Tim told it. 'Sharing your home with eighteen other cats can't be easy. Well, seventeen, what with one missing. Still, a one-nineteenth part of extra living space can't be very noticeable.'

The kettle boiled and Tim made the tea.

'Right, let's see which one you are.' He picked up the cat and it was content to sit on Tim's knee and be stroked. He turned the nametag over and saw 'Woosencraft' engraved there, her phone number was at the bottom, and in the centre, 'Pedwar'.

'Hello, Pedwar.' Tim scratched it behind the ears. Pedwar purred and pushed its head against Tim's fingers. Tim yawned, his early morning burst of energy had faded. 'It's time to take you home… In a minute…'

The sun was in his eyes when Tim woke again, feeling well rested and content. Pedwar was gone from his lap but unlike Morse, Tim knew exactly where he was.

Ten minutes later Tim rapped the heavy iron ring knocker on Mrs Woosencraft's front door. Pedwar hung comfortably in the crook of his other arm.

He knocked again and as he did the door slowly swung ajar. Instinctively Tim checked around the lock. The wood was intact, the paint undamaged, there was no sign of forced entry. Mrs Woosencraft liked to think she was capable but she was growing old and forgetful. He pushed the door open and stepped inside. A narrow hall ran straight ahead. Two closed doors were on the left, the stairs on the right.

'Mrs Woosencraft? It's Tim. Are you there?'

As soon as he stepped across the threshold Pedwar came alive in his arm, plumped to the floor and raced upstairs.

Apart from the certain fusty bouquet nineteen admittedly clean and well-behaved cats would bring to any small terraced house, the single word that best described Mrs Woosencraft's home was comfortable. Odours of baking, polish, and laundry filled the air.

Tim closed the front door behind him. He called out again. 'Mrs Woosencraft?'

She was not in the front room, a space surprisingly free of clutter. A carriage clock ticked in the centre of the mantelpiece, two large brass candlesticks flanked the fireplace, an aspidistra grew in a blue chamber pot in the centre of the bay window.

A narrow display cabinet in the near corner was filled with a menagerie of small glass animals, some elegant, some as grotesque as those from a medieval bestiary: a giraffe; a turtle; an oddly-shaped duck; and many more. A massive black oak dining table with heavy barley-sugar legs, clawed feet and a plain top occupied the centre of the room. The table was very old and showed it. One of the legs had split along the grain, the corners of the top were rounded and worn, the surface scratched and chipped from numerous incidents across numberless years. Yet like the rest of the room it was spotless, dust free, and shone with the deep gloss of decades of beeswax polish. Apart from a silver and blue-glass condiment set[2] its surface was bare.

The clatter of oven trays came from the kitchen at the back of the house. Tim realised with some relief that Mrs Woosencraft was baking.

'Hello, Mrs W. It's Tim.'

'*Bore da*[3],' she called back. 'Come on through.'

Tim went through to the back room. Every surface dripped cats. One sprawled on top of a decrepit upright piano and idly batted the hinged candle-holders to and fro. A knot of mixed varieties colonised the settee. Two black moggies with white feet circled each other round and round the fireguard. A young Siamese clung half-way up the green velvet curtains.

---

[2] *A full set, including a mustard pot and spoon, not one of those half-arsed modern things where the salt never comes out.*

[3] *Good morning.*

A winged armchair stood beside the fireside, front legs scratched to half their original width. Under the chair lay a tapestry bag filled with knitting-needles, yarn, crochet hooks and patterns.

Down in the kitchen was Mrs Woosencraft with a mixing bowl in her arm and flower-patterned apron over her sensible twin-set. Two more black cats loped and twined between her stockinged feet.

'I brought Pedwar back,' Tim said. 'I woke up and he was on the bed.'

'The little rascal! He's such a wanderer, gadding about all over.'

'Your front door was open, Mrs W.'

Mrs Woosencraft bent over the bowl, stirring vigorously. 'Oh, I don't think that was it. He'll just jump out of the window and over the fence.'

Tim folded his arms. 'It was open when I came in. Did you forget to shut it yesterday?' He felt protective towards this little old lady from Wales. She baked him cakes, she was alone, she might be old enough to be his grandmother but she was also his friend. 'Was it open all night?'

Mrs Woosencraft spooned the mix out of the bowl into a baking tray, pressing it into the corners. 'I'm baking some flapjacks. We can have a cup of tea while they do.' She slid the tray into the oven, slowly straightened up, pulled off her apron and handed it to Tim. 'Hang that on the back of the door would you.'

When he turned back she was leaning on her walking stick and looking straight at him.

'I'm perfectly safe in this house, *bachgen*. Nothing and nobody is going to come in here and trouble me.'

'That's much less likely if your front door is actually shut.'

Mrs Woosencraft herded him out of the kitchen. 'You've plenty to worry about without me. My cats are better than any lock. Go into the front room and I'll bring you a cuppa and something to nibble.'

Tim walked through the back room and into the hall. 'Not as good as a decent cylinder lock and two good bolts top and bottom. What can cats do against a full-grown—'

Out of nowhere a cat dashed under Tim's feet. Then another was there, heading in the other direction. Tim wobbled on one leg and tried to find somewhere to put his foot that didn't have a cat under it. He lost his balance and fell on his back through the doorway.

He looked up and saw a cat on the shelf over the door, nosing a heavy ornamental copper plate. The plate shunted forward and teetered on the edge. In his mind's eye Tim saw it drop edge first across the bridge of his nose.

The cat pulled back and the plate settled back into position. Tim sighed with relief but before he could move a river of felines hurtled across him into the hall.

'Agh!' Tim exclaimed as the cats streamed across him. 'Oof,' as a heavy paw drove into his stomach. 'Ouch!' as another tested its claws on his chest. 'Ptah!' as a third filled his mouth with fur.

'Did you say something?' Mrs Woosencraft called from the kitchen.

'Urgh. No, it doesn't matter.' Tim clambered to his feet, wiped his tongue on the back of his hand and tried not to think about where that tail had been. He peered through the banisters to the top of the stairs. Not a single cat was to be seen. He hurried into the front room while the coast was clear and sat at the table.

The steady tick of the carriage clock was soothing, and somehow timeless. The warm, enticing smell of fresh-baked flapjacks drifted from the kitchen. A moment later Tim heard the rattle of the tea-tray. Mrs Woosencraft appeared at the door, the tray tilting precariously in her hand.

'Let me,' Tim took the tray and put it on the table.

Mrs Woosencraft shuffled onto one of the chairs. 'Honey flapjacks,' she announced proudly, scrunching up her shoulders. 'It's a little early, but why not? Let's live dangerously!'

Morning sunlight diffused through the net curtains behind the aspidistra. Tim watched Mrs Woosencraft pour the tea through a strainer.

'Leaf is best,' she said. 'Those little bags don't give a good brew.'

Tim bit into the soft and moist block of honeyed oats, still warm from the oven. 'There's nothing dangerous about your cooking, Mrs W, except perhaps to my waistline.'

'Oh, just tuck in and enjoy them. You're thin as a rake. Enjoy your food.'

Memories of his tumble in the hall faded as he sipped tea from a cup with a handle too small to put his little finger through.

Mrs Woosencraft sat back in her chair. The comfortable silence grew less so. The busy tick-tick-tock of the carriage clock loomed loud. She cleared her throat. 'Tell me how you're getting on with that new job that's keeping you so busy.'

'Not much luck so far.' Tim washed the flapjack down with a mouthful of tea. 'It's missing, not stolen, and unreported too. An old Chrysler, probably worth a lot of money.'

Mrs Woosencraft's cup rattled in the saucer as she put it on the table. 'Well,' she said a little loudly. 'Don't look at me. I know a fair bit about mending tractors but that's it. Have you seen those three young ladies again?'

'Yes.' Tim winced at the memory. 'The other two are aren't as nice as Dolores.'

'Dolores. Such an exotic name. I'm just plain old Dorothy.'

'They're American.'

'Well, of course they are. That's why they've lost an American car.'

Tim put down his cup. 'It's not their car, it belongs to their boyfriend.'

'Their boyfriend?' Mrs Woosencraft's eyes grew round as saucers. 'You don't mean…?'

'That's right.'

'Oh, that's shock—king,' Mrs Woosencraft said, her Carmarthen accent grown strong. 'Shock—king.'

Tim wondered how he came to be drinking tea and gossiping like he was a little old lady himself. He helped himself to another flapjack.

Mrs Woosencraft shuffled her bottom on the chair. 'I can hardly believe it. They were too well turned out to be such— Hussies! What did they want this time?'

Tim savoured the moment. 'Actually, they brought me a clue.'

Mrs Woosencraft clapped her hands. 'A clue. Well don't keep me waiting, what is it?'

The handkerchief from Imelda Marchpane's stockinged thigh was a little rumpled but still neatly folded. Tim dropped it into Mrs Woosencraft's outstretched hand.

'Oh, that's lovely, that is.' Mrs Woosencraft unfolded the material onto the table.

'See the monogram,' Tim said. 'MK.'

Mrs Woosencraft went very still, her eyes fixed on the silk handkerchief. All colour drained from her face. Seconds passed and she remained motionless.

'Mrs W?'

Her left hand jerked, sending her teacup skittering across the table.

'Mrs W?' Tim jumped to his feet and took her hand. Her cold hand.

Dregs from the spilled cup pooled at the edge of the table and dripped onto the carpet.

'Ah…' Mrs Woosencraft's eyes swam back into focus. She looked up at Tim. 'Right then. Look, don't worry,' she said.

'It's just my angina.' She pointed vaguely towards the mantelpiece with a shaking hand. 'Yes, that's what it is. Fetch my pills. They're behind the clock.'

Tim fetched the small brown bottle and shook out a pill. Mrs Woosencraft washed it down with cold tea.

She massaged her left arm and gave Tim a lopsided smile. 'It's nothing to worry about, just pain from a tired old heart.'

'I was really worried,' Tim said.

Mrs Woosencraft grinned ghoulishly. 'Not as worried as me. Every time it happens you can't help thinking well, that's it for me. Sayonara, auf weidersehen, merci beaucoup, and adios Tonto. I'll be all right but I need to rest. It wears you out you see.' Mrs Woosencraft poked the monogrammed handkerchief with her tea spoon. 'Put that thing away before it gets dirty.'

Tim fetched a cloth from the kitchen and dried the spilt tea, tidied the things away and washed up. He took his time, he wanted to hang around as long as he could. As he was drying the crockery Mrs Woosencraft came through to the kitchen. She looked frail and exhausted.

'How are you feeling?'

'I'll do.' Mrs Woosencraft put her hand on the kitchen table and it was as if colour flowed up her arm and into her face. For an instant she looked younger. 'Thank you for tidying up, but off you go now. I'm going to bed. A good sleep and I'll be right as rain.'

Tim gently patted her shoulder. 'Look after yourself.'

Mrs Woosencraft squeezed his hand without much strength. 'Careful, boyo. There's nitro-glycerine in my pills. Read the label if you don't believe it. Hit me too hard and I might explode.'

Back in his office Tim ruminated on his problems. The easy one was deciding which of them was worst—the women in the red dresses. Disconcertingly assertive, they were unlike anybody he'd met before. Troy Jarglebaum would never have let Imelda break the door.

He always ended up comparing himself to Jarglebaum, a habit he'd tried to break many times.

He was starting to wish Dolores had never walked through his door.

And they're not assertive, a small voice in his head insisted. They're threatening, violent, strange and scary.

Next: Mrs Woosencraft, slowly going senile, and the missing cats.

Finally, the fact he had met someone with a room full of stray cats but didn't know where she was. And she was not just someone.

He paced backwards and forwards then took a wide step to one side and continued. If he was going to walk in circles, he should at least try to spread the wear.

It was time to prioritise. It was time to make a new list.

Tim took out pen and paper, smoothed the sheet, uncapped the pen and held it poised. He drew a line down the middle of the paper. Lists always worked when decisions were required. All you needed to do was write the choices to be made in the two columns, add them up and the column with the highest number was the right way to go.

A moment passed. Doubt clouded Tim's resolve. Perhaps a list wasn't the best way forward. He noticed the flies were back under the lampshade. They knew what they had to do and they got on with it. Jarglebaum would know what to do too. It might not be the right thing, but he always did something.

Tim had a flashback to his time with the police, stuck at his desk, unable to decide how to progress his case load. It wasn't the job that was at fault, leaving the police had solved nothing. He was still who he was, indecisive, a dreamer, someone who could not make up his mind.

Almost by itself Tim's hand moved across the paper and wrote:

Find the car.

Tim stared at the three words.

It would be the easiest thing in the world to call Jarglebaum. Troy would know people who knew people who knew. Already Tim could see his old partner's self-satisfied grin grow wider and wider as he listened to Tim's pleading.

You'd make me beg, you smug bastard, Tim thought.

No way, it was not going to happen. There were other people he could talk to, other options to try.

He spent the entire day making calls. People said you could not prove a negative but he felt he was coming close. No body shop had anything like the Chrysler in for repair, no garage for maintenance. The breakers yards responded with a laughing 'You what, mate?' and simply hung up. The owners club was a long shot that turned out to be too long when it quickly became obvious it was aimed not unreasonably at owners in the USA.

There was one last hope. Tim picked up the phone again and called the Brighton Council dumped-car hotline.

For an hour he endured piped music of mind-numbing yet foot-tapping inanity as he was passed from department to department in a great circle that eventually returned him to the person who originally answered his call. Finally he was connected to the right department where, after he convinced someone called 'Stu' that he did not want to report an abandoned vehicle, own one, or know a neighbour who had one, he discovered that nothing approaching the description of a large, old, black Chrysler had been included in the rusty hulks, burned-out chassis and stripped wrecks they had towed away in the past month.

'Nearest we got was a white Roller on the beach last year.'

'Really?'

'Straight up.'

'Where did it come from?'

'Some greengrocer in Billericay.'

On the verge of asking what happened to it Tim realised he did not actually care. He put the receiver back in the cradle and closed his eyes. He had a headache like a clamp across his temples, his left ear burned hot from being pressed flat against his head by hours of phone calls. He drank a glass of water and stared bleakly through the window. He had tried his best and he had achieved nothing. Troy Jarglebaum waited, a middle-aged nemesis in a nylon shirt.

When you were out of options you called the man. For Tim that man was Derek 'Persistent' Smith. Less fixer than walking encyclopaedia, more wild-card than ace of trumps, Smith was an unconventional and original man. Bright and observant in ways most people were not he could be both slow on the uptake and capable of vast leaps of intuition. Tim felt at ease with some forms of the unconventional and Smith was several of them. Thorough in his methods, Smith was nothing if not determined. Some might even say he was unstoppable. He had helped Tim before, there was a very good chance he could do so now.

Smith's loud voice came on the line. 'Greetings, earthling.'

'This is Tim Wassiter. I've some work if you're interested.'

'Is it a mystery?'

'Yes, it is.'

'Interested.'

'The usual place. Half an hour?'

'Agreed.'

The usual place was the Bat and Ball, exactly where Tim wanted to be. He shrugged into his old leather jacket and went to the pub.

'A motor car registered in Finland won't have a record with the Driver and Vehicle Licensing Authority.'

'I know.' Tim took a pull on his pint. With Smith patience was required.

Smith didn't talk, he boomed. His round, ruddy face beamed into the middle distance under copper-red curls tamed by a fortnightly short back and sides. His blue fleece was zipped up to his neck and under it, Tim knew, his tieless shirt would be buttoned to the collar. Smith's glass of orange juice sat neatly centred on the beer mat, he sat on his hands.

'The local DVLA office is at Mocatta House. Head office is in Swansea. From the train station take the number 36 bus—'

The locals at the Bat and Ball were used to Smith and accepted his loud voice, oblivious manner and seemingly endless well of trivia with good humour and protective affection. They gave him space.

'How much is the fare?' Tim said.

Persistent stopped in mid flow, smiled an angelic smile and proclaimed, 'I'm going to give you a bunch of fives.'

That didn't worry Tim one bit. 'Then you won't get paid.'

'I'll squish you flat and steal it away.'

'I didn't bring the money.'

'D'oh! You always say that.' Smith pulled his hand out from under his heavy buttocks and formed it into a mouth.

'He always says that,' the Hand repeated in higher-pitched voice.

'Smith, what do you know about cars?' Tim said.

'What sort of cars?'

'The Chrysler Imperial Eight Airflow.'

'He means an Airflow Chrysler Imperial Eight,' the Hand said.

'Put the hand away, Smith,' Tim said patiently.

'I can help,' the Hand said. 'Which year?'

'I'm serious.'

A frown creased Smith's smooth brow. 'Are we talking turkey?'

'Yes, we're talking turkey.'

Smith's face suffused with excited wonder. 'Goodbye,' he told the Hand and it disappeared beneath his backside.

'The year is 1934. Colour, black—'

'They're all black,' Smith said dismissively. 'Except the white ones.'

'Finnish plates.'

'It's got Finland plates.' Smith rocked happily on his hands, there was nothing he liked more than facts. 'It's black. It's from Finland, 1934. A missing vehicle, a mystery vehicle. Who shall find it for you?'

'I thought you might.'

'That's Good Thinking. I will do my very best.'

'That's right. You're good at this sort of thing.'

'I shall find it for you and then I will get paid—?' Smith looked expectantly at Tim.

'Fifty pounds a day.'

Smith beamed happily. 'Where is the car?'

Tim had to laugh. 'I don't know. It's a missing car, that's why I— ' He realised what Smith meant. 'Somewhere in Brighton.'

Smith blew out his cheeks in relief. 'Phew, that narrows it down.' He looked absently at his drink and said, 'I'm good at this sort of thing.' He drained the glass and strode from the pub leaving the door wide open.

Little Pests

Someone was ringing the doorbell and they were ringing it a lot. Long, sustained rings came interspersed with short finger-jabs. Sets of equal-length jangles stretched into a great, drawn-out clamouring, grew shorter and closer together before ceasing entirely. After a brief pause another manic pattern began.

'I'm coming,' Tim shouted. The ringing continued unabated. 'I'm coming.'

Nobody but nobody ever rang the doorbell. He'd forgotten it was there let alone that the thing still worked. It had to be kids or some hyper-active delivery person. It wouldn't be Smith, he always used the phone.

As he hurried down the stairs a sustained ring passed a sonic pain threshold and bored like a drill in his skull.

'Stop it!' Tim flung open the door. 'What the f—?'

'Hello!' Foxy cheerfully shouted above the sound of the bell. Dressed in a soft high-collared raspberry top, cream pencil skirt and shoes that seemed to consist of nothing but arching heels and ankle straps, she danced on her toes. 'I need a bell, let's go shopping.'

Tim stared in amazement, blinked, swallowed, then lifted her finger away from the bell. 'No. Believe me, you do not. Nor do your neighbours.'

Foxy's face fell. 'You're cross with me. You gave me your card and I came to see you. Now, without saying a word, apart from these words now, somehow I've upset you.'

'Most people just ring once or twice. Short rings.'

'I'll do that next time.' Foxy drew a finger across and down her chest. 'Cross my heart and hope to die.'

She looked so serious, Tim's irritation evaporated. 'Come on in. It's good to see you.'

'Really?'

'Yes, it really is.'

Tim stood to one side and Foxy stepped past him into the hall bringing a sea-fresh aroma with her.

At the top of the stairs Foxy was still apologetic. 'The button said 'Press', so I pressed it.'

'It really doesn't matter.'

'OK.' Foxy looked around Tim's second-hand furnished office with approval. 'So, this is where you hang out and do your detectiving.'

Tim considered the balding carpet, battered desk and faded paintwork. 'It's a start, I'm going to—'

'It's wonderful!' Foxy spun full circle. Her rotating heel bored a hole through the old carpet, the torn warp and weft gathered in a ball under her shoe.

'You like it?' Tim said, surprised and pleased.

'Do I ever. You must have worked so hard to get this look. It's so run down, authentic "shabby noir", just the right side of sleazy.'

Was that a compliment? Tim hoped so. 'I just threw a few things together.'

'I'm impressed.'

As she turned into profile Tim noticed her tummy had the slightest and to his mind delightful bump. It was a stomach that should be stroked, Tim fantasised, quite sure that if stomachs had opinions that was exactly what it would want. Stroked, or used as pillow after...

'What's wrong?' Foxy tugged down the hem of her top. 'Doesn't this go? I thought it was OK.'

'No, it's fine, I— Would you like some tea?'

'I don't like hot drinks.'

'Water?'

'Do I look dry?'

Not in the slightest, Tim thought, caught by the band of dusty freckles under her eyes. 'I'm just trying to help you relax.' He pointed to the chair. 'Please, sit down.'

'No thanks. It's not easy—' Foxy thought for a moment, '—in this skirt. But you're right, I'm all agitated. You noticed because you're a detective. You gave me your card and here I am, for your detective help.'

Disappointment fleetingly clouded Tim's mind. 'Is it the cats?'

'Oh, you're good, aren't you? First you notice I'm a bit stressed, then you guess it's the cats.'

'I used to be in the police but I wasn't very successful,' Tim said and immediately wondered why he confessed to that.

'Everyone knows the police are slow and stupid.'

Troy Jarglebaum's paunchy, jowled bulk loomed in Tim's mind. 'Not all of them. Some are clever and sly.'

'The police wouldn't help me. They just laughed and told me to keep my doors and windows shut. They're still all over the place. Somehow they keep getting in, they won't leave me alone.'

'The police?'

'The cats. One or two I can deal with, but there's too many. I'm running out of places to...' Foxy's hand went to her mouth. 'Where's your cat?'

'I don't know. He went missing a few days ago.'

'Oh goodness, what does he look like?'

'He's a Turkish Van, white with a ginger tail and ears.'

'I haven't seen one like that.'

'Thanks, anyway.'

'Well... That's a good thing, probably. Can you find out where they're coming from?'

'No,' Tim said. 'But I might be able to make them go away.'

'Good.' Foxy produced a semi-circular comb, an elaborate thing with mother-of-pearl scrollwork along the top like waves. She ran it through her hair three times, once to each side then down the middle. 'I'm ready. What's the plan?'

'The pet shop in the South Lanes. We can get some humane pest control.'

'That's what cats are, aren't they? Pests.' Foxy spoke with some venom.

'Not all of them,' Tim protested.

'Maybe not but they're starting to get to me.'

The White Ibex

'THERE, SEE? Stay low, keep quiet and watch her flight.'

Ishkun turned his friend so he could see the path of the bird. 'Doves fly straight to water. On the way back they take a more cautious path.'

This Banipal could see, this difference in behaviour he understood along with the need to stay downwind of quarry.

'I will make a hunter of you yet,' Ishkun said when they knelt beside a doe gazelle struck down by their arrows. Ishkun's arrow lay deep in its chest close to the heart, a near-perfect shot. Banipal's lay further back behind the ribs, a respectable strike.

'A killing blow,' Ishkun congratulated Banipal as he carefully cut the arrow free. 'She would have bled out within a few minutes from that alone.'

'I aimed for her heart, but she moved.'

'You must aim for where she will be when the arrow arrives, not where she stands when you fire.'

'I feared I would miss altogether and slay another tree.'

'You are not that bad,' Ishkun said. 'Accept my praise for a decent shot.'

Despite his protests Banipal was pleased with himself. This trip he was surprised to find himself enjoying the hunt almost as much as he enjoyed his friend's company. Ishkun was right, he would have slain this doe on his own, though it would have run for a while. Ishkun's own arrow, striking the doe a fleeting moment after Banipal's, had dropped the gazelle to its knees and saved them the chase.

At first the liquid black eyes and long lashes of these beautiful animals had summoned difficult emotions in Banipal's heart. Their first kill, less clean than this one, required Ishkun to sprint forwards and cut the kicking animal's throat. They had tracked it half the day and it had taken all of Ishkun's bantering good humour to maintain Banipal's enthusiasm through the long hours of heat and dust.

Thinking he saw reproach in the death-gaze Banipal knelt beside the creature, placed his hand over its face and closed the eyes.

Ishkun mistook Banipal's actions for piety. Chastened and impressed he had sacrificed that first beast to Ninurta and burnt it on a great pyre of brushwood they gathered over the rest of the day.

It seemed Ishkun's decision had been the correct one. Ninurta blessed the hunt and the following day they killed a yearling wild ox they separated from its herd.

With their beards salt-stained with sweat and arms red to the elbows after gutting the animal, Banipal sacrificed to Ea while Ishkun again made offering to Ninurta.

Some minutes later a young man from a local village appeared and offered them the hospitality of the guest-house in exchange for some of the meat.

Banipal and Ishkun exchanged a shared look of agreement.

'We gift you the entire animal,' Ishkun said.

The villager bowed, delighted. 'You are blessed.'

Ishkun made the sign of Ea. 'We are all blessed.'

That evening Ishkun and Banipal floated naked in a covered stone cistern inside the village's small temple complex, in reality a God-house shared by all the deities.

'This is the life,' Ishkun said. 'Mankind, with the blessings of the Gods, is born to hunt. There is little better than the company of friends.'

Two members of the sisterhood of Inanna entered the room, their heads covered by opaque grey veils, their bodies in white cotton robes. They stood at the door until Ishkun and Banipal knelt in the water and made Inanna's sign of The Shared Gifts. They returned the sign, knelt beside the cistern and began to comb and oil the men's hair. Beakers of beer were to hand, the tantalising smell of roasting ox drifted in from the oven pits outside.

Playfully Ishkun splashed water over the priestess beside him. Already wet from washing Ishkun's hair and beard, her white linen shift clung to her body, translucent with water.

The priestess gave a low laugh and filled a bowl of water from the cistern. She dumped it over Ishkun's head and pushed him under the surface.

He surged up, his face contorted with mock outrage, and seized her wrists. He pulled, she resisted, a gentle tug of war followed, one that she easily won. Ishkun released her and bowed in acknowledgment of her free will. In return she laid her palm on his brow. He knelt in the water and again made the sign. The priestess removed her shift but not her veil and stepped into the water beside him.

'I cannot fault you,' Banipal said quietly as he watched them join together. He drank deeply from the beer, still thirsty from the long, hot hunt. As he did his eyes met the gaze of the other priestess.

Banipal knew he lacked the boisterous charisma of his friend, and his own body was slighter and less heavily muscled. He had never considered himself handsome. None of these were reasons to refuse Inanna's gift, yet he felt shy. Banipal bowed, pressed his hands together and made the sign. The priestess stood still for a moment, then disrobed. Banipal marvelled at the sleek curves of her beauty, that he could be so blessed, that Inanna blessed his own body in return. Gifts to be shared. The veiled priestess stepped down into the water to join him. They held each for a moment while she studied his face through her veil. Then she embraced him. He was more than ready and she welcomed him. Together they joined in Inanna's holy embrace while Ishkun and the other priestess celebrated beside them.

Later that night Ishkun found Banipal sitting alone, pushing slivers of wood into a pomegranate.

Banipal held up the round fruit, turning it in the fire light. 'There is something I just don't see, my friend. Something here I cannot work out.'

'The world is much bigger than a pomegranate.' Ishkun took the fruit from Banipal. 'I wish I could help you, but my mind is unsuited to the task, tired or rested, drunk or sober. You will find it easier to think about this in the morning and I will be better able to listen.'

'You are right.' Banipal took back the pomegranate and tossed it into the fire.

'It will come to you one day, if it is meant to be.'

Banipal stared into the fire. 'Explain something to me, Ishkun. I know you love this life and I know trying to understand what I do frustrates you. Why, then, do you keep returning to it?'

'Ninurta is a wise God. Although he is Lord of War and delights in combat he wishes to be entertained by more than unskilled hacking and slaughter. To honour the Gods we must strive to be complete. I believe each one of us needs three challenges: one for the hands, another for the spirit, a third for the mind. Therefore, I hunt and make weapons, I bend my knee and my will to Ninurta, and I try to follow your numbers.'

'It is a good philosophy,' Banipal said, struck by Ishkun's wisdom.

'We are not always fated to succeed, but we must try.'

Banipal nodded with growing understanding. 'This has done me a deal of good, Ishkun. I hear the truth in what you say. This is a right life and from now on I shall not neglect it.' He filled two shallow bowls with the village's cloudy beer, handed one to Ishkun and raised the other in salute to his friend. 'Thank you for taking me away from the temple and my own fascinations.'

Ishkun touched his cup to Banipal's and they drank. 'You are welcome. Though I am also thinking you will soon wish to return to Esagila.'

Banipal heard the disappointment in Ishkun's voice and told a white lie. 'I am not ready yet. Let Ninurta decide when the hunt is over.'

In the morning Ishkun borrowed a pair of asses from the headman, promising to return them along with meat and hides in payment for their loan.

The days of the hunt passed, days of heat and weariness, frustration and laughter, stealth and sudden action. Banipal found himself less troubled by the eyes of the animals they killed. Reduced to hides and cuts of meat the beasts had no ability to haunt him. After each kill they would skin the animal, light a fire, cut the meat into strips and hang it to dry. Ishkun showed Banipal how to strip and prepare gut and sinew for their bows, and how to rub the ash of the fire into the flesh side of the skin, a crude tanning that would preserve them until they could be properly treated.

Boys from the village came to guard the meat, listen to the men's stories round the fire at night, and take the laden asses back to the village.

One day Banipal and Ishkun were on the trail of a magnificent white Ibex. They were a good hour behind their quarry when Banipal found his mind wandering.

'Ishkun, do you remember the cistern at that village temple?'

Ishkun grinned, 'How could I forget?'

'Did you not notice how the level rose as the priestesses entered the water?'

'Thinking back, I cannot in all honesty say that I did.'

'I've just realised something. If you measured the rise you would know how much space she occupied.'

Incredulous, Ishkun stared at his friend and roared with laughter. 'Truly, I shall never understand you.'

The trail was clear, they took after the ibex at an easy jog and began to gain on it. The wind shifted, the ibex caught their scent and began to run. Ishkun raised the pace and they settled into a fast trot he knew would wear the swift beast down.

Late in the afternoon they came to a stand of wild palm. High grasses and thorny acacia lay across their path. Thinking the ibex had gone to ground Ishkun lead them towards the palms. Suddenly he dropped to a crouch and motioned Banipal down beside him.

Swiftly Banipal knelt and gave Ishkun a questioning look.

Moving very slowly Ishkun unslung his bow and nocked an arrow. He nodded towards the tall grass a few yards ahead of them.

'Lion,' Ishkun mouthed.

Then Banipal saw it. A huge male, bloody muzzled, crouched over the body of the ibex. It watched them steadily and rumbled long and low in its throat.

'He thinks we're after his kill,' Ishkun whispered. 'Draw your bow.'

'Will he attack?'

'He's thinking about it.'

'What good will these demon-buggered arrows be?'

'None whatsoever unless you can put one in his eye.'

Banipal felt a dead weight in his belly. 'Marduk preserve us.'

Ishkun took a deep breath. 'I am going to stand. When I do, rise slowly with me.'

Smoothly Ishkun rose to his feet, keeping the tension on his bowstring. Banipal followed, silently cursing the trembling in his legs. Now he could see the lion clearly, see its back legs shuffling and its haunches twitching with tension. It glared at them, and lashed its tail.

Tipping back his head, Ishkun laughed lightly. His hand pressed on the small of Banipal's back and moved him along. 'Tell me about the cistern again.'

'What?'

Ishkun laughed again. 'We are going to walk slowly away. I am going to be amazed and fascinated by your tale. The lion will see we do not fear him. No, do not look at it.'

'All right,' Banipal said doubtfully.

'Now, begin.'

Slowly they walked away, Ishkun regularly exclaiming in wonderment at Banipal's revelations.

Illegal in Paraguay

'WHAT SORT of things don't cats like?' Foxy asked as they walked to the pet shop.

'They don't like being stared at.'

'I can't look at them all.'

'Lion droppings are good.'

'Aren't lions just enormous cats?' Foxy scowled. 'I don't want a pile of lion shit in my kitchen.'

It was a fair point.

Foxy stopped at the window of a jeweller's. 'This is the shop where I sold my pearls. They've got some nice stuff.'

The more esoteric shops in the Lanes changed hands frequently. Tim was unsurprised to discover the one that sold life-size wooden giraffes and chairs shaped liked giant hands had turned into one that sold pretty much anything as long as it was pink.

'You could try sprays and ultrasonic whistles.'

Foxy wrinkled her nose. 'Sprays make me sneeze.'

'The whistle thing then.'

'Won't it frighten the bats?'

'I don't know. What bats?'

'There might be bats. I just wouldn't want to upset them. I like things that fly, it's like they are swimming in the sky.'

Once in the pet shop Foxy was immediately distracted by the fish tanks. 'Lampreys and catfish, they're so cute.'

Catfish but not cats. Tim peered into the tank and wondered which fish was which. One was broad-bodied and brown-speckled with jaws fringed with tentacle-like feelers. The other was eel-like, a pallid grey creature with a jawless sucking 'O' for a mouth. Neither appealed.

Foxy watched him. 'You don't like them.'

'I— No, not really.'

'Why not?'

'They just don't look very nice.'

'Don't you listen to the nasty man,' Foxy whispered at the tank. She seized Tim's elbow and moved him away. 'That just shows what you know. Lampreys are very loyal. And catfish are… Well, catfish are useful. They eat—most things.'

Today the young shopkeeper wore lilac eye shadow and green hair teased into a wispy ball so light it surrounded her head like a dandelion clock.

'Wow, I like your hair,' Foxy said. 'Can I touch it?'

'Sure.' The girl leaned forward. Foxy gently brushed her fingers through wafts of hair.

'So soft,' Foxy whispered.

'I like girls and boys.'

'Boys grow up into big fat stupid lolloping men with horrible habits and oily skin.'

Tim found renewed interest in the Golden Orfe and Shubunkin. A small boy appeared at his side, stood on tip-toe to peer into the tank and prodded the glass with sticky fingers.

The shop girl gave Foxy a wry smile. 'Well, they only want one thing.'

'Tell me about it,' Foxy growled. 'Ten at a time.'

The young shopkeeper drew back from the counter round-eyed. The gentle plip, gurgle and hum of the pumps for a dozen aquaria the only sound in the shop.

Tim met the gaze of the boy's mother, her arms laden with guinea-pig food and bedding. Simultaneously they looked down at her young son then across to Foxy. The mother dropped her goods on the counter, groped in her purse and stacked a neat pile of coins beside the till. 'That's the right money,' she said in strangulated voice, grasped her son's wrist and marched him out of the shop. As the door closed the young lad said, 'Mummy, what did ten men want to do?'

The shop girl blinked at Foxy. 'What did you want again?'

Tim took his cue. 'A cat scarer.'

It took a few moments for her to adjust. 'Battery or mains?'

'Battery.'

'What's wrong with mains?' Foxy said.

'They're harder to fit,' Tim said.

'So?'

'I just thought—'

'What?' Foxy bridled. 'That I couldn't fit one?'

'Actually he's right,' the shop girl said. 'Battery is better.'

'I want mains.'

'You're sure?'

'Do I look unsure?'

The shop assistant handed it over. Foxy paid up.

'I can always—' Tim began.

Foxy's eyes flared. 'I can do it.'

Tim held up his hands. 'I never said you couldn't.'

'Just because I'm not from round here, just because things are different where I come from you think I'm incapable. Both of you.'

The shop girl turned to look at Tim. Governed by the laws of inertia and drag, her nimbus of green hair slowly followed. 'No we don't,' they said together.

'Fine.' Foxy backed away.

'Right,' Tim said.

'OK.'

'OK.'

Foxy flared her nostrils, turned, and marched from the shop. Tim and the shop girl admired Foxy's retreating form.

'Are you two…?' the girl began.

Tim's mouth twisted into an expression of equal parts relief and regret. 'No.'

Self-consciously casual, the girl fluffed up her hair. 'Women, eh?' She rolled her eyes. 'You can call me Gabby. This is my shop. Most people think I'm just the assistant, but actually I own it.'

'That's great,' Tim took a step towards the door.

Gabby jerked her thumb towards the door behind the counter. 'I, ah, need to get a new cat-scarer. Would you like a tour of the stock room? The light's faulty, but you don't look like you're scared of the dark.'

Tim stared at her. 'Excuse me,' he said and ran out of the shop.

The narrow lane was packed with students in jeans and flower-patterned shirts, dreadlocked skateboarders in death-metal tees, lanky street vendors, middle-aged tourists all in beige, ageing punks with purple mohicans, tattooed pamphleteers and Boho refugees. Despite her height and golden hair Foxy was nowhere to be seen

'Who is she, kid?' Troy Jarglebaum's familiar and unwelcome voice came from behind Tim 'What's her name?'

Spinning on his heel, Tim confronted Jarglebaum. 'Are you following me?'

As always, Jarglebaum stood too close. His too tight shirt gaped under a houndstooth jacket exposing a strip of hairy belly, yet despite his dishevelled appearance his black lace-up shoes were clean and polished.

'Course not, kiddo.' Jarglebaum's meaty face split into a broad grin, displaying pearly white blunt teeth with a wad of gum clenched between them. 'Deduction, plain and simple. Here comes old TJ perambulating in a northerly direction and minding his own business when a good-looking blonde with a superbly mobile derriere runs out the pet shop. Moments later a man comes out even faster, head swivelling like it's on gimbals. Common sense says they know each other. I suspect a mild altercation, perhaps even a lovers' tiff. Then I see it's my buddy Tim from the good old days.'

Buffeted, pushed and shoved by the milling crowd, Tim moved into Jarglebaum's lee. The big detective stood athwart the pavement yet somehow the crowd flowed around him.

Jarglebaum's teeth reminded Tim of gravestones. He doubted the man had ever considered his partnership with Tim to be the good old days.

Troy punched Tim's shoulder a little too hard to be playful. 'What did you say to her, kid? That girl of yours put on some turn of speed, tight skirt and all.'

'She's not my girl,' Tim realised the truth of it as he spoke. 'I was helping her out. She's another new client.' He may as well just say it, Jarglebaum would find out anyway. 'She has a problem with cats.'

Jarglebaum's leering expression softened to something approaching pity. Before Tim could react, Jarglebaum's arm draped itself over Tim's shoulder like a yoke.

'Timmy boy, you're a PI for Chrissakes. Give up helping out women with their cats. There's no mileage in it and no money. Missing cars, maybe, but get yourself back to basics. Divorce cases, follow some people around, maybe some business fraud. Put some of those little cameras and microphones inside some lampshades. You've got bills to pay and a reputation to think of.'

Jarglebaum's robust advice cut Tim's dreams down to size, his hopes of being a radically different sort of Private Investigator.

'Come on, son. Let me buy you a drink.'

Tim's shoulders dropped, his head hung low, the day was not living up to its promise. 'Tea,' he said. 'Tea would be nice.'

For once Jarglebaum let their different preferences for restorative drinks pass without comment. His heavy arm still across Tim's shoulder he steered them both up the narrow street using his bulk like an ice-breaker to open a path through the milling crowds to the nearest cafe.

Tim knew this was not Troy's kind of place. Not only was the open-fronted café staffed by art students and punk teenagers, it was also dry.

Three young waitresses stood in a lethargic clot behind the counter. Eventually one of them dragged herself over, jeans hanging from her pelvis, a tight black tee-shirt ridden up to expose a pale midriff with a pierced navel. 'Hi guys, what's it going to be?'

Tim ordered his tea. Troy scowled at the menu, sighed, and dropped it on the table. 'Coffee, black.'

The waitress stood back, hand on hip. 'You want decaff?'

'No love, I do not.'

The drinks arrived. Troy sipped his with grudging approval and studied the other customers: Bicycle couriers with long dreadlocks, skinny musicians, Goth girls, middle-aged vegetarians in red and blue anoraks.

Tim considered his ex-partner. Perhaps it was nothing more than coincidence that they had met but Jarglebaum had never been one to socialise without good cause and here he was doing it for the second time in a few days.

'So, then,' Jarglebaum said. 'What's the deal with this new client?'

Prepared for more criticism, Tim said, 'She's got some kind of plague of cats. Anyway, she says she doesn't own any and they keep bothering her.'

'Interesting. Your little old lady doesn't have enough cats, this girl's got too much pussy. Where does she live?'

'I don't know,' Tim confessed.

Jarglebaum shook his head in despair. 'Her name, kid. You must at least know her name.'

'Foxy. Foxy Bolivia.'

Jarglebaum's slabby cheeks quivered with emotion. 'You are shitting me.'

'That's her name.'

'You know that? I mean, you can prove it?'

Once again Tim felt outmanoeuvred. 'It's what she said.'

'Foxy Bolivia.'

'That's right.'

Jarglebaum's face twisted into a grotesque leer. 'Foxy Bolivia. As in the Bolivian Foxtrot, allegedly the most erotic thing a man and woman can do fully clothed, standing up in public, and not get arrested.'

'She's just a client.'

'Nuns have fainted.'

'I don't know her that well.'

'Illegal in Paraguay.'

'It's just her name, Troy.'

'You dog.'

'I've talked to her twice.'

Troy reached across the table and whacked Tim in the chest. 'You sly old dog!'

All at once Tim realised what was going on. This was why Jarglebaum had broken into his office. Not only could he not bear not knowing what Tim was up to, Jarglebaum couldn't stand the idea that Tim was better off without him, that he was making a go of it. That he was happy.

Tim leaned back in his seat with new confidence. 'You're jealous.'

'Don't be daft,' Jarglebaum watched the waitresses as they moved between the counter and tables. 'How are you getting on with that missing car?'

Tim described his encounters with Dolores Vogler, Electra Vaughan and Imelda Marchpane. Jarglebaum's face grew slack, his mouth unpleasantly moist.

'Where's that handkerchief now?' Jarglebaum said.

'In my pocket.'

Jarglebaum wiped his mouth on a paper napkin. 'Let's have a look.'

Troy unfolded the linen square, rubbed the embroidered border between his fingers, then lifted it to his face and breathed in. For one horrified moment Tim thought he was going to blow his nose. Then, with a flourish, Jarglebaum tucked it into his sleeve. 'M.K.' he said thoughtfully. 'You know who that is?'

'Not yet.'

Now it was Jarglebaum's turn to smile. 'Want some help?'

'Are you going to give that handkerchief back to me?'

Jarglebaum pushed back his chair and heaved himself up. Bent-legged, he winced and tugged at his groin.

Tim looked away. 'Do you have to do that?'

'It's not what you think,' Jarglebaum puffed. 'Damned thing rides up.'

'You're disgusting.'

'See you later, pal.'

Tim held out his hand. 'The handkerchief, Troy.'

'Sorry, chum. Old habits.' Jarglebaum winked and dropped the handkerchief onto the table. 'Take my advice and get your pussy problems out of the way. That car job is where the real action is, take my word.'

The Djinn

TIM RAKED the sand in the chicken run and gathered old grain, husks, droppings, feathers, straw and other detritus into a pile beside the door. Clustered in the opposite corner his three chickens huddled in consternation, unhappy with the interruption to their routine. Heads bobbing, each bird tried to hide behind the other two, resulting in a continual and futile gyration.

In short order he scooped the sweepings into a waste sack, changed the water, topped up the grain, and scattered a few lettuce leaves around. Lastly, he made an inspection of the whole structure, checking for broken wire, holes, and loose joints.

As he moved round the roof so did the chickens, keeping as far away from him as possible.

I know exactly how you feel, he thought watching the birds alternately huddle together and dash around in small circles. You just want to know what's going on, and whether it was something you did that made everything change.

He had upset Foxy when all he had been trying to do was help. Right now there was nothing he could do except hope she would realise that, and give him a call. Even if she didn't, he could still help her with her plague of cats. Yes, there were obstacles: he didn't know where she lived and she wasn't a client, but this was an opportunity to put theory into practice. He should be able to do something right here, inside his own office.

Over the years Tim had accumulated a sizeable collection of books on alternative beliefs, divination, magic and meditation. Brighton, with its strong new-age culture, was a perfect place for this with several specialist shops and a good second-hand market from disillusioned or impoverished past practitioners. He had restricted himself to the traditional and academic texts, unable to see the point in learning about fairies, mermaids and dragons, and other creatures that did not exist.

Carrying a selection of books to the desk, he leafed through them, looking for something to break a connection, make a sending, or cause a diversion. The first thing he found was a prayer from Haitian voodoo, an appeal to the Loa, the Mavoungou Mystères, asking them to find something better for an enemy to do. The prayer was subtle, sinister, and daunting. To use it he would need one of the chickens. Faced with that immediate prospect he realised he was not ready to take that step. The knife of his soul, to paraphrase one commentator on ancient rites, was not yet sharp. Neither, for that matter, were the ones in his kitchen. There had to be another way.

Soon books on Wicca, Futhark rune divination, lost secrets of Ogham and Wyrd, and the hermetic lore of the Kabala covered Tim's desk. He set to work, browsing indexes, tagging pages. After a while he got up and fetched more books.

The number of tagged pages grew along with the notes he was making. Wearily Tim rubbed his eyes and stretched his back. This was not as easy as he had hoped. When he'd bought these books he'd been thinking about how to discover things, not about how to change them. The tomes on Mo and Sho Mo, I Ching, the Nordic runes and Tarot were about divination, not alteration. Some were lavishly illustrated with photographs, paintings and reproductions of medieval woodcuts, while others like the Haitian voodoo and

Goidelic Wyrd were dense, archaic and poorly printed, and in the case of the Haitian book, contained large sections in nineteenth century colloquial French.

He went back for more books.

The shadows had moved across the room before Tim finally pushed the weighty tomes aside. His eyes swam, his head felt clogged. The more he read the more overwhelmed he felt by alternatives. In his mind the information had all started to blend together: The Pharaonic Book of the Dead with the Mayan winged serpents and Toltec jaguars; numerology with the Ptolemaic elements; modern Wicca with Ahura Mazda, Mithras, Confucianism and Tao.

He knew he was a dabbler, a dilettante and parvenu. Each one of these ways was worthy of a lifetime of study, not simply sets of instructions to cherry-pick favourite recipes from. They weren't cookbooks, they were systems of belief and ways of life.

Slumped forwards in his chair Tim rested his arms on top of the books, his head on his arms. What did you think you were doing? You've got nowhere, you haven't helped Foxy, you haven't found out how to banish the cats.

He settled his head more comfortably and closed his eyes.

Outside a motorbike droned past. Tim slipped into a light doze. The sounds of traffic and pedestrians faded away along with the feel of the books beneath him, his sense of location, the very aura of the room.

I'm asleep, Tim realised. This is odd. I know I'm asleep, and I know that I know.

Still able to sense his own body, he could feel how it lay and that it was content, but he felt no connection to it. He was drifting.

I've become detached from my soma, my physical self, Tim thought. I can wake up if I want, or go to sleep properly. Or, because it feels nice and peaceful, stay like this.

Slowly he became aware of change, a difference in the quality of the light permeating his eyelids, the texture and taste of the air he breathed. A low, gentle murmur came to his ears, a shuffling, rustling noise like cloth moving, or people breathing. It was in no way disconcerting. Tim concentrated on the sounds, trying to work out exactly what they were. Calmly he realised it must be because there was someone else in the room. As if to confirm it, there came a scuffing noise of a heel or a bare foot on stone.

On stone?

Tim opened his eyes.

While he had slept someone had redecorated his room, removing all the furniture, replacing the walls and windows with featureless bare stone and lighting the room with smoky oil lamps and tapers that filled the air with a miasma of animal grease. The decorator was still there, a thin man of middling height with a crooked nose and a beard like a tangle of grey wires. Barefoot and wearing a dirty toga with an unravelling red hem and a comically outsized golden turban, he stood in front of Tim with arms upraised. A pendant of woven gold wire hung by a thong round his neck. Suspended in the gold sparkled a single blue diamond the size of a wren's egg.

Behind him a dozen men and women occupied the rear half of the room. They must have been working hard because they were all asleep, lying on the packed dirt floor with their hands folded across their breasts, their feet towards Tim. The men wore simple breechclouts or sarongs, the women plain black ankle-length shifts that left their arms bare. Behind them stood a crude wooden door.

Belatedly, Tim realised that he was he was upright. Off balance, he staggered forwards.

'Aieee!' the turbaned man screeched. He raised his arms higher. 'Hold! You are compelled. Not one step further.'

'Ooh.' The apparently sleeping crowd behind him, shifted uneasily.

'I am Asklepios,' the man declaimed in a surprisingly deep voice. 'Opener of the dark doorway, seeker of truth, master of the indivisible three, five, and seven.' He took a breath, 'And also of the eleven.'

Slowly Tim became aware of the rancid odour of Asklepios and his cohorts. 'What are you doing in my room?'

Confusion briefly clouded Asklepios' brow. Glancing surreptitiously at a fragment of parchment concealed in his palm, he raised his arms again. 'I am Asklepios, philosopher of the crystal spheres, adept of the Eleventh Circle of Light. Discarnate soul, I command thee pronounce your true name.'

'Er… It's Tim.'

'Then know this, Eritstim, I have bound you to this place and to my will. You are my servant until your task is complete. Only then shall I grant you leave to depart.'

Looking down, Tim saw he was standing inside a circle gouged in the mud, the groove filled with an unpleasantly glistening dark stain he sincerely hoped was red wine. Small piles of wilting herbs lay outside the circle, interspersed with smouldering cones of incense.

'This is a really odd dream,' Tim said.

'Aaah.' The people lying on the floor were not as deeply asleep as Tim had thought. 'We are the dreamers.'

Tim shook his head. 'This is my dream.'

The room fell silent.

'Asklepios,' a worried voice hissed among the prone crowd. 'Are you sure this is the right one?'

Tim reached across the circle and picked up some of the herbs, eliciting a soft wail of dismay from Asklepios.

'Bay leaves and lavender. What are these for?'

Sweat broke out on Asklepios' brow. 'For protection and health, binding and summoning. Eritstim, I have passed your test of my knowledge. Now, heed the words of Asklepios, your master. I am Asklepios, traveller of the lands above and below. I have bound you once, bound you twice, bound you eleven times on pain of Hell's freezing fire and the eternal darkness that lies between the spheres.'

That was pretty good, Tim thought. Despite his unprepossessing clothes and silly turban, Asklepios delivered his lines with verve and power. 'I liked the way you said that. It was very convincing.'

'Thank you,' Asklepios' chest swelled, a trickle of sweat gleamed on his temple. 'You therefore acknowledge me as your master and I now bind you to utter only truths.'

'Sure, why not. It doesn't really matter, you're all going to vanish when I wake up.'

'Aiee.' A distressing keening came from the women in the group.

'Liar,' Asklepios cried, waving his small piece of parchment. 'Deceiver. I have followed the precepts. You are bound.'

'Not at all. This is my dream and I'm imagining you all.'

'Aieeee!' Now the men joined in the wailing.

The parchment dropping from Asklepios' trembling hand. 'Liar.'

'No. You see, I was reading about people like you and trying to see if there was anything useful you could do.'

'And was there?' Asklepios quavered.

'Not really, no.'

A skinny man naked except for a breechclout scuttled forwards on all fours and prostrated himself in front of Tim. 'Don't unmake us, mighty one. Don't undream us. Oh Lord, oh Master.'

It was the start of a rush. Moments later Asklepios was surrounded by men and women abasing themselves at Tim's feet.

'Save us from the unmaking.'

'Don't undream us, we implore thee.'

'We are your servants.'

'Mighty one, how may we serve you?'

Tim held up his hand. An expectant silence fell. 'Well, there is one thing.'

'Tell us, oh Master!' the throng cried.

'I have a plague of cats.'

Expectant faces looked up at Asklepios. A dozen trembling hands pushed him forwards.

'He can do it. He really can.'

Asklepios clutched his beard. 'Um… I think I can do that.' He thought for a moment. 'Yes, I am sure I can.'

'I'd really appreciate it.'

'Aieee!'

Emboldened, Asklepios managed a sickly smile and patted a few heads. He raised his hands. 'Now, go from this place, Eritstim. I dismiss thee. Begone and return, Eritstim. Get ye hence to whence ye came—'

'That's not really my name, you know,' Tim said, and stepped out of the circle.

Asklepios stared at Tim's foot and bleated in terror. He broke and ran but the crowd behind him broke first. Men and women surged screaming for the door. Behind them Asklepios clawed and fought to get past the skinny man. The man twisted free with extraordinary agility, picked up Asklepios and flung him bodily at Tim. 'Take him,' the man cried. 'Take Asklepios.'

Asklepios crashed into Tim and they fell back into the circle.

All the lamps went out.

Whatever it was that had been, it wasn't there any more.

Tim woke at his desk, straightened up and looked around. The sun had set, the room was filled with cool evening light. The world appeared two-dimensional, nothing looked quite as real as it should. Gradually the impression faded.

Tim rubbed his face, cotton-headed from the intensity of the dream. The dream had felt so real. Asklepios' screams still rang in his ears, the acrid reek of unwashed bodies filled his nostrils. The groggy feeling persisted, Tim gulped water from a glass. It was cold and refreshing but somehow didn't dispel the smell of body odour. Tim turned on the desk light.

Tim started forwards with an involuntary cry of astonishment. A pair of dirty, bare feet protruded beyond the desk. Still wearing his huge golden turban, Asklepios lay unconscious on the carpet.

Interesting

PERSISTENT SMITH stood across the road from the home of Clive Barnett, treasurer and founder member of the Brighton and Hove branch of the Chrysler Owners Club. He had an appointment, he was three and a half minutes early.

As he stood waiting, Barnett's front door opened and a small group of middle-aged men, their hands stuffed into the pockets of their khaki and camel-coloured coats, silently ambled away down the street. Pressure grew inside him, he forced himself to wait one more minute then crossed the road. His hand on the garden gate, Smith faltered, struggling with the need to solve the mystery of the car and the imminence of facing a stranger.

'This is Good Adventure,' he said out loud. 'And adventures include Tough Stuff.'

'We can do this,' The Hand said.

Encouraged, Smith took a deep breath and pushed open the gate.

The front door had no bell, no knocker. Smith raised his fist ready to pound on the wood. Before he could, the door was opened by a short man with floppy black hair, a Roman nose, and thick glasses. An outsize brown-buttoned cardigan hung from his shoulders, tartan slippers were on his feet. Clive Barnett gazed frankly up at Smith through bottle-bottom lenses and spoke in a nasal twang. 'Was that you shouting?'

Smith looked away. 'Maybe.'

'You'd better come in,' Barnett said quietly.

Smith stepped into the hall. 'I'm on a mystery car adventure.'

Barnett eased the door shut. 'There's not much happens round here and that's how I like it.'

Smith looked round the living room with admiration. From the TV aligned in the corner to the perfectly positioned settee and the alphabetically arranged collection of videos and DVDs, it was superbly neat.

'Sorry it's a mess, we've just had our AGM. My wife is on a late shift.'

'Your head looks like a number eight,' Smith said.

'My glasses make it look that way.' Barnett spoke in quiet and even tones. 'I have an important eye defect. Less than 1% of the Caucasian European population who require optical correction has the same prescription as I.'

'My eyes are perfect. And I'm quite tall.'

Barnett's hands trembled half way to his ears. 'Please don't shout.'

Smith didn't realise that he had. 'Sorry,' he whispered. 'Sorry.'

'It's all right. Come upstairs.'

Barnett used the front bedroom as a study. Pictures of Chryslers in identical thin gold frames lined the magnolia walls at shoulder height. A row of mirror-bright hubcaps hung above them. An enormous chrome fender spanned the chimney breast.

Barnett touched one of the pictures. 'This is mine. A 1959 New Yorker Deluxe Newport two-door convertible. I also have a 1964 300K hardtop, but it's in storage. This summer I intend to start renovating it. As you can imagine I shall have plenty to keep me out of mischief.' He looked away into the future and smiled to himself. 'I estimate I will be seventy-one years old when I finish.'

Smith was barely listening, for on the table was a small stack of exercise books and a card index. One of the books was open. Between the neatly hand-ruled columns spanning the double page were row upon row of data: numbers, dates, countries and names.

'This is interesting,' Barnett said. 'For the past three years and five months I've been cataloguing the ownership history of vintage Chryslers.'

Smith turned the pages, fascinated by the hand-written columns.

Clive Barnett gazed down at his work. 'Once you start it's hard to stop. I don't like leaving things half finished. When it's complete I might put it onto a computer but I don't like them much because it's annoying when they go wrong. Books don't break down or catch colds.'

'They can catch fire,' Smith said.

'451 degrees Fahrenheit,' they said at the same time.

'Do you have every single car?'

'No.' Barnett pushed his glasses up his nose. 'So far I've completed Britain, Northern Europe and Scandinavia. The Mediterranean countries don't have such good records, but ultimately I shall triumph. After that I'll do Japan. I'm saving North America to last.'

Excitement coiled inside Smith. 'Finland is in Scandinavia.'

'Correct.'

'What I want—' Smith hesitated. Sometimes he found it very hard to say exactly what it was he wanted. Sometimes he said he wanted something he didn't want at all, like an apple, and then he was stuck with it. 'What I want is in Finland.' Then he kicked himself, because it wasn't in Finland, it was from Finland.

'Model?'

'Airflow Imperial Eight.'

Barnett extracted one of the exercise books from the stack and flipped it open. 'Year?'

'1934.'

'Interesting choice.' Barnett turned the pages of the book and ran his finger down the columns. '2,450 were built in 1934. According to my records at least thirty two are currently registered in Scandinavia. Six in Norway, eight in Sweden, over eighteen in Finland. Registration number?'

'I don't know.'

'Chassis number?'

'I don't know.'

'Engine number?'

Smith's mouth sagged. 'I don't know.'

Barnett looked at Smith and blinked. 'Interesting.'

Smith didn't like not knowing, it made him feel useless. He already knew he was different, that was enough. 'Ask me a question I know the answer to, or I'll bash you flatter than a pancake.'

'You couldn't do that, it's not possible. You'd need a road-roller or a giant duck-press.'

'A— A what?'

'A duck-press.'

'And it's for—?' Smith couldn't say it. Instead, he locked his thumbs together and flapped his fingers like wings.

'Pressing ducks.'

'That's horrid.'

'Horrid and interesting.' Barnett blinked again. 'Colour?'

'The duck?'

'The car.'

'Black.'

'As you recall, there are at least eighteen of this make and model in Finland. All are black.'

Smith's face fell. 'Eighteen.'

'More than eighteen. There are definitely others.'

'How many?'

'That datum is not available.'

'No!' Smith cried in disappointment. And then the Hand was back, burrowing deep into his pocket wanting to help.

Barnett winced at Smith's outburst. 'Don't give up too soon. Examine the facts as we know them.' He put down the book and laid a ruler on the page alongside the column of current owners.

At first Smith was absorbed by Barnett's near-perfect handwriting, the symmetry of his 'O's, the parallel uprights of his 'H's and perfectly horizontal cross-bars on his 'T's and 'E's. Then he read down the columns where the ruler lay and laughed.

'You see what I mean,' Barnett said.

The Hand leaped from Smith's pocket. 'Oh yes we do,' it chirped. 'We see what you mean.'

Barnett looked from Smith's hand to the man himself and gave a curious little jerk of his head. Hair from his swept-over fringe flopped across his eye and he carefully patted it back in place. 'I'm thirsty. Would you like some juice?'

The Hand dove back into its pocket and emerged with half a pack of chocolate cookies. 'Swap?'

'Let's go downstairs.'

Down in the kitchen Barnett filled two tumblers with orange juice. Smith nodded in approval to see him leave a clear inch at the top.

Barnett drew Smith's attention to a pair of photographs on the wall. One was a round-faced man prematurely bald, the other a young woman in college robes. 'These are my children.' Barnett appeared to glow. 'My daughter has just graduated and my son is a mechanical engineer. He's married and I'm going to become a grandfather.'

To Smith's profound surprise he felt jealous. 'Er, well done.'

'Thank you. It is a source of great personal joy.'

The two men stood in silence and munched their cookies and drank juice. Barnett smacked his lips and placed the tumbler exactly in the centre of a coaster sporting a black and silver version of the Chrysler logo. Smith stacked his tumbler inside Barnett's.

For a moment both men stared at their feet.

'I think the set of all things not in a set excludes itself,' Barnett said.

'The 14:19 to Waterloo takes 1 hour 6 minutes. So does the 14:49. The 14:34 and the 15:04 take 1 hour 16 minutes,' Smith replied.

'Interesting.'

Barnett smiled at Smith, who found he didn't mind the pressure of his gaze. 'All the Chrysler Imperials in Finland are owned by one man.'

'Interesting.'

'Interesting.'

Toast

AT FIRST Tim did not want to touch Asklepios. For one thing, it wasn't every day that you woke up and found someone from your dreams unconscious on the floor. For another it was pretty obvious where the smell of unwashed humanity came from. He opened the windows, he tried to think about what had happened but couldn't get a grip on where to start.

To be pragmatic, Asklepios was in the way. Tim gingerly pushed his shoulder then shook him more and more vigorously until it was obvious the strange and smelly man was not simply asleep.

Finally he put his hands under Asklepios' rancid armpits and dragged him onto the settee. Asklepios still did not wake.

Tim went into the bathroom and washed his hands. As he soaped and rinsed he thought what a shock it must for an imaginary person to be yanked out of a dream into reality.

He thought about that a bit more.

To be blunt, how the hell did that work? People in dreams were from the imagination, they weren't real and they never, ever ended up on the office carpet. So, either Tim himself was still asleep or somehow he had gone mad.

Or it hadn't been a dream.

Tim went through the options. If he was still asleep then this was a particularly messed-up dream, but he would eventually wake up and everything would be OK.

If he was mad then Asklepios would turn out to be a sack of potatoes or the postman.

He hesitated over the third alternative. If it wasn't a dream and he hadn't suffered some sort of a breakdown then this was real. It was actually happening and he had to deal with it.

Deep inside he knew that this was the truth. A dream would have felt more convincing but less logical. Also, he didn't feel mad (although some people said that was in fact the first sign). He turned that idea around: did the world make about as much sense as it ever did apart from the recent arrival of a golden turbaned, toga wearing stranger with chronic body-odour and crumbs in his beard?

Yes, it did. All he could do was to accept the facts and worry about the reasons later.

Tim's head drooped. He jerked awake with a start, he really did not want to fall asleep on these books again. Somehow it had become very late, he was cold. He fetched a blanket and draped it over Asklepios, still deeply asleep on the old settee.

Dead on his feet. Tim went to his bedroom, wedged a chair under the door handle, dropped onto bed and fell asleep immediately. He woke in the middle of the night and crept back to his office in the dark, hoping Asklepios would be gone. The scrawny old man lay curled up on his side hugging his oversized gold turban like a teddy bear. He was snoring.

Tim went back to bed. An hour later he checked again. Asklepios was still there, still snoring, still smelly. He was there an hour after that too. When light from the rising sun began to brighten his bedroom he checked again. This time Asklepios was awake. He sat with his knees drawn up at one end of the settee, the blanket pulled up to his chin. He stared at Tim with round, fearful eyes. Then he hastily put on his turban, knelt on the carpet and bowed, touching his forehead to the floor. 'Master,' Asklepios croaked. 'Master.'

'Please don't do that,' Tim said. 'I'm not your master.'

'I am your servant.' Asklepios rose to his feet and bowed. 'Master.'

'I'd be much happier if you called me Tim.'

Asklepios raised his eyes. 'Tim is not your true name.'

'Not my full name.' Timothy Alan Wassiter, he couldn't help thinking it. His parent's lives had been conventional and unadventurous. They had worked, raised a son born late into their own lives, and now they had retired. For them excitement consisted of a weekend flutter at the local races and growing blue hydrangeas. Life was a kind of permanent late Sunday afternoon, whatever the day, time, or season.

They had been so pleased when Tim joined the police service after university, so very quietly disappointed when he had left. He knew there was nothing wrong with a life like theirs, it was what they had wanted and they had chosen it. He'd had to leave or he'd have stayed there forever. The police had been a mistake, a failure. At the time he thought that was what he'd wanted, he had been wrong.

'And now I realise neither was Eritstim.' Asklepios spoke with humble self-effacement.

'No.' Tim tried not to laugh, grateful for the interruption to his thoughts.

Asklepios gave a rueful smile. 'You are right to mock me, I should have known better. You teach me much wisdom with few words. I now realise why my other summonings failed.'

Of course. The realisation thrilled through Tim. This was neither dream nor delusion. Asklepios was a true sorcerer and what had happened was real magic. It was exactly what he had wanted from life—mysterious wonderful adventure. He just hadn't imagined it would be so—unwashed.

Tim grasped Asklepios' hands. 'And you, Asklepios. You are teaching me more than you can ever know.'

Once again Asklepios bowed. 'You humble me, Master.'

'I am praising you.'

Asklepios bowed lower.

Somehow it had all become very formal. Despite Asklepios' absurdly large turban, filthy toga and dirty bare feet, his manner and speech contained a self-conscious dignity.

Tim released Asklepios' hands. 'I'm sorry you ended up here. I don't know how it happened and I don't know how to get you home. I'm as amazed as you are and I've a hundred questions'

'Please, ask me.'

'Where are you from?'

'Marib, in Saba.' It was a place Tim had never heard of and Asklepios was not surprised. 'This is because I am from your future. I used my magic to contact great ones from the golden age.' He gave a grimace half-way between smile and apology. 'It worked.'

The future. Tim did his best to absorb the information. 'What happened to—to everything? To civilisation, to science?'

'The Golden Age ended in catastrophe. I do not know what this science is.'

'Then how can we understand each other?'

'I have a lesser Mare of Illumination bound to this bauble,' Asklepios indicated his blue diamond pendant. 'It brings me understanding.'

'May I see it?'

Asklepios shook his head. 'If I remove it, it will lose force. A single use remains.'

Tim saw the filigree mesh of the pendant was designed to hold seven diamonds in a half-moon curve but just one gem hung in the setting.

'How does it work?'

'You simply ask it for understanding. When I found it, it still held three gems. As I held it in my hand I wondered aloud, "What do you do?" A gem crumbled to dust, and I knew.'

'Can you teach me how to make one?'

'I am ashamed to say I do not know how. I found it in the tomb of a priest of an unknown God.'

Or a scientist, Tim thought. The last of her kind doing her best to preserve the knowledge of her doomed civilisation.

'You must stay here, as my guest. As long as you like.'

'You are most generous, but I would not wish to outstay my welcome. In truth, I would hope to return to my own land one day. My home, my family.'

Tim's heart went out to the strange, polite old man. 'That is all I meant. Stay just as long as it takes for us to work out how to send you home.'

'Oh, Master, then I am happy to accept,' Asklepios beamed, exposing a mouth of snaggled but healthy looking teeth. 'And I shall remove your plague of cats, though I do not see much evidence of them today.'

'It's for a friend, she lives elsewhere.'

'A woman, I understand.' Asklepios tapped the side of his nose. 'A lady friend of the female kind. I shall be extremely discreet.'

Asklepios looked so incongruous, so conspiratorial, so decidedly dodgy that Tim burst out laughing. After a moment Asklepios laughed too, a hesitant shoulder-shaking giggle that made his turban wobble.

'Would you like some breakfast?' Tim said.

'I am famished.'

'While I get it ready perhaps you would like to bathe.'

'Oh no, that is—' Asklepios caught the tension in Tim's shoulders, '—an act of generosity I could not easily refuse.'

'Master?' Asklepios called over the sound of the shower a few minutes later. 'EritsVeronica is not a true name either, is it?'

'No, it isn't,' Tim called back from the kitchen.

The shower stopped. A minute later Asklepios stood in the kitchen doorway with a towel wrapped round his waist and another across his shoulders. His grey hair was clean, his beard combed, he smelled of lavender.

'Master?'

Tim sighed patiently. 'Yes, Asklepios?'

'Neither is UmJohn.'

'No, Asklepios. One more thing, I am not your master. We're in this together, equal partners, so let's do our best to understand each other and be friends.'

'Thank you. I will not make these errors again.' Asklepios clasped his hands together. 'I would very much like us to become good friends.'

'I am sure we shall.' Tim handed him a slice of toast and marmalade. 'Have some breakfast.'

Asklepios looked at the toast, sniffed, bit, then looked again in amazement. 'What is this nectar of the Gods, this ambrosia?'

'Mrs Woosencraft's marmalade.'

From the look on Asklepios' face Tim knew the older man would be his slave forever.

Children

AT THE EDGE of a field in Southern England two men of similar height and build stood chest-deep in a crop of white-flowered oil-seed rape. One was the slender fair-haired Finn called Markus Koponen.

Koponen wore his signature white Stetson and an open collar. Accompanying him was Palmer, his chief financial officer. As always Palmer was perfectly turned out in a dark pinstripe three-piece, a white Oxford-weave shirt and black brogues. Today he wore a saffron-yellow tie.

Koponen spoke excellent English with a soft Scandinavian lilt: 'I appreciate we're spending more than we earn and faster than we planned. The question is, how long can we keep going?'

Palmer quoted a date from his report.

Koponen did straightforward sums in his head. 'That's long enough.'

'It could bankrupt you, Markus.'

'Nearly, or actually?'

For Palmer numbers had texture, colour, and shape. It made him brilliant. 'Nearly.'

'Sisu,' Koponen said quietly. 'Whatever it takes.'

His phone rang. He looked down at the screen. 'Dolores, my sweet.'

Koponen waited until Palmer had moved to a discreet distance away then said, 'Tell me, how is everything going with the car?' He listened attentively then said, 'Speed things up please. Bring it to resolution. How? Use your own judgement.' He listened again, when he replied his tone was gentle. 'Yes, of course I will see you tonight.'

The sun shone from a cool blue sky, a warm southerly breeze blew, warmer than usual for this time of year. Warmer, at least, than had been usual when he was a child. Koponen was fifty-eight years old and knew there was still an enormous amount to do. Problems came from nowhere, there was never enough money and always, always delay. Some days he felt time slipping through his fingers like a fistful of sand. Days like today.

And yet there was hope, and there was always the plan.

'I don't have a family.' Koponen spread his arms above the field of white flowers. 'These are my children.'

The First Time

'THERE'S A MAN from Finland who owns at least eighteen cars,' Persistent Smith informed his mother between mouthfuls of dry cereal.

'Then he must be very rich, dear.'

Smith had little interest in money, no burning desire to have lots of it. Even so, when you worked, you got paid. It was the rule. When he did get paid he gave it all to his mother. He had little idea how much he actually had, more than a hundred, less than a million. A little bit was useful but he knew from past experience a pocket full of money was like having a voice whispering in your ear, endless, driving. 'Spend me, spend me. I'm not doing any good down here in the dark.'

Violet Smith understood this very well. She took good care of her son's money in the hope that eventually he would want to manage it for himself. There was no reason why he couldn't, he liked numbers, enjoyed columns of figures, it was just that where money was concerned he didn't see the point. She put it aside so that one day, if her son ever wanted to set up on his own he would have something, a start. One day.

Her plan worked partly because she never told him exactly how much he had. Violet was not a deceptive person, lying did not come easy and made her feel deeply uncomfortable. She had, however, learned to dissemble.

'I think I'd like a car.'

Violet said nothing, although she had a clear idea about what was coming next.

'Mummy?' The word came drawn out.

'Yes, dear?'

'How much money do I have?'

'Not enough to buy a car.'

'How much more would I need?'

'Oh, I don't know. Anyway, you don't know how to drive.'

That was a good point. Smith folded his arms and sat back. 'Daddy could teach me.'

'He's too busy, dear.'

Smith frowned. 'Where is he now?'

'You know where he is. He's working.'

'When is he coming back?'

Violet kept her smile going. 'Later, after supper time.'

'I hardly ever see him.'

'Finish your breakfast.'

Smith munched away at his dry cereal and washed it down with mouthfuls of orange juice. He would not see his father tonight but this time it would not be for the usual reason that daddy was too tired and just wanted to watch his stupid goggle box. This time it would be because he, Persistent Smith, wouldn't be there. Smith thought about what he would need for the next part of his adventure, and as he did his eyes grew hooded and he smiled his secret smile. He pushed back the chair. 'Finished.'

Violet heard him clump upstairs, go into the bathroom, wander round between the bedrooms, then thunder back down the stairs.

'Going out,' Smith announced to the empty hall and zipped up his fleece.

His mother hurried from the kitchen. 'Where are you going?'

Smith looked up at the ceiling. 'On a big adventure.'

'Be careful, dear. Come back for tea.'

Smith opened the door, hesitated, turned back. 'Mummy?'

'Yes, dear?' Reaching out, Violet tucked a curl of hair behind her son's ear. For once he didn't pull back.

'Mummy,' he said slowly. 'I know I'm not like other people.'

Violet closed the zip on his fleece the final inch. 'Oh, I don't know. Normal people aren't that normal half the time.'

After he'd gone, shutting the door too hard like he always did, Violet cleared away breakfast, made herself a cup of tea and took it into the front room.

The old, familiar worry rose up inside her: what would happen when she and Albert were gone? She resisted the urge to look through the window and down the street.

She knew he had to learn, knew his adventures were just little things, trips to the railway station and the museum, but there were so many things he didn't notice, so many he did not understand.

This time, for this adventure, there was something Violet Smith herself would not notice for quite some time. As her son marched, skipped and occasionally hopped down the street with his water bottle in his hand, a notepad, pencil and sharpener in his right-hand fleece pocket and house keys in his left-hand trouser pocket, his other trouser pocket jingled with the loose change he had emptied out of his mother's purse. And zipped snugly into his inside left breast pocket were clean socks, fresh underpants, and his toothbrush.

A Tail Fin

THERE WERE two types of people: those who belonged in pet shops and those who didn't. Gabby looked at the pair of beautiful women walking towards her past the dog leads and bird feeders and instinctively knew these girls were not on the list.

In other circumstances she'd be quite interested in the spikey-haired brunette in the red leather dress, white boots and fishnets. Especially considering how she looked bending down beside the tank of Golden Orfe. But customers weren't supposed to dabble their fingers in the water. She had a sign.

That wasn't really the problem. The problem was the other woman because she freaked Gabby out. Her high-collared, sleeveless blue silk dress should not have gone with her sub-arctic complexion and platinum locks, yet it did. Her clothes, like her poise, had a below-zero, glacial self-possession. Like her complexion, her clothes were perfect. She was the one who did not belong in the shop, she should be in a palace, a temple. She was a goddess.

Gabby didn't realise her mouth was hanging open until the woman put a finger under her jaw and lifted. Gabby's teeth clicked together.

'Hello. My name is Electra. She's Imelda. We like your fishy little shop.'

Straightening up from the tank the brunette bared her teeth. 'Love it.'

'We're looking for a man,' Electra said, her eyes drawn towards two angelfish hovering face to face in the centre of their tank.

Freaked or not, Gabby still had a tongue in her head. 'Me too.'

Electra stood very still. 'Is that so?'

Gabby knew she'd made a mistake but didn't know what it was. 'Or a woman.'

'We're looking for a woman too.'

Imelda flipped the sign on the door to 'Closed' and slipped the bolt.

'Hang on, you can't do that.' Gabby moved out from behind the counter.

Electra stepped into her way, her sudden smile filled with teeth as iridescent as mother-of-pearl. 'She just did. Tell me about the man.'

'What man?'

'The one you're looking for.'

'There isn't any man. I haven't found him yet.'

Electra shook her head. 'Don't lie. We know he was here. And the woman. Tell us her name.'

The hell with personal space, Gabby wanted these two gone. 'You're right, we're closed. Leave the shop please, right now.'

Imelda leaned back on the door. 'We don't do "please".'

Gabby was scared now. They could have the shop as long as she could leave. She tried to push Electra out of the way but somehow her hands slid away and she stumbled into the hutches. Hamsters, guinea-pigs and rabbits scrambled in a whirl of thumping feet, scrabbling claws and leaping fur.

Somebody gripped her elbow: Imelda, the brunette. That close Gabby could smell the leather of her dress and something else, something sweet, yet old and rotten.

'Mind your pretty, fluffy hair,' Imelda said. 'It might get torn out.' The grip tightened. 'Come over here, I've got something to show you.'

It was the tank of Golden Orfe, and it was empty.

'What have you done? Where are they?'

Imelda let Gabby go, her grin even wider than Electra's. Her tongue flicked over her teeth, worrying at something. Her fingers pinched it free, held it out to show Gabby.

A tail fin.

Outrage broke through Gabby's fear. 'You sick fuck.'

'There's no need for that.' Electra was right behind her, body pressed against hers, hands on Gabby's hips, mouth breathing in her ear. 'We'll pay.'

Gabby turned fast, broke free of Electra's grip 'Damned right you will. And I want her out of my shop right now.' She kept the tremor in her body from her voice, she was proud of that.

Electra and Imelda exchanged a look, then Imelda unbolted the door and stood outside. Electra peeled notes off a roll, 'Tell me, how much do I owe you?'

Good grief, Gabby thought, it's not the money. Those poor fish, some people were just too weird to be real. What's wrong with them? What makes someone come into a pet shop and eat the animals? Then Gabby saw the thickness of the roll of notes Electra was holding and the business-woman inside her elbowed her morals aside.

'Two fifty.' The poor little things were only a couple of quid each, but this was compensation.

Electra kept putting notes down on the counter. 'Let's make it three. I really am sorry about my friend. She's going through a life-altering experience.'

Gabby considered the heap of notes and sighed. 'You're supposed to forgive other people's sins.'

'Are you?' Electra held out her hand and smiled her wide and dazzling smile. 'What's your name?'

'Gabby,' Gabby said. She took Electra's hand and was surprised at the strength of her grip.

'Well, Gabby, I don't think you've told me everything you know about that woman.' And Electra began to squeeze.

Eventually the roaring red darkness lifted from Gabby's mind. Whimpering with pain she cradled her hand and dragged herself along the floor until she reached the counter. Cold sweat bathed her scalp, her corona of lilac hair hung in rat's tails. Her hand hurt so much, a ball of pure pain. She didn't want to look but she had to see. She forced herself.

Dislocated knuckles jutted at grotesque angles, the back of her hand was a swollen purple bruise, the skin stretched so tight it glistened.

An accident, she told herself, I can tell the hospital it was an accident. One of the hutches slipped, I tried to grab it and the whole stack fell. Just an accident.

It turned out that Electra already knew quite a lot about the man. She wasn't really interested in him, she wanted to hear about the woman with the long golden-blonde hair. The more Gabby described her the more excited Electra became. Her questioning intensified. Gabby tried hard to remember but it took a long time before Electra was convinced she hadn't seen which direction the woman turned when she ran off.

'Next time it might be me, or it might be Imelda.' Electra kissed Gabby's tears. 'She's a proper little maiden of pain, that one. Shall I ask her to come in and you can ask her yourself? You can say, "Imelda, next time I want you to be the one to hurt me." She'd like that.'

By then Gabby was beyond words. Curled up against the wall, all she could do was wail and shake her head.

Then Imelda did come back into the shop. She showed Gabby just what she would do, as the sad little red-streaked heaps of fur she left in the rabbit hutches made very clear.

A Spell for Bez

ASKLEPIOS was a fast learner. Fascinated by the shower and the toilet, even the glass in the windows, he clapped his hands with delight as Tim demonstrated the light switch, the kettle and the toaster. Then he begged to be allowed to make himself some more toast and marmalade.

It wasn't long before he started to become a pest.

Asklepios leaned on the wall flicking the light switch on and off and on again.

'Please stop doing that.' Tim was trying to concentrate, trying to order his thoughts, prioritise tasks in what increasingly felt like a life that, while filled with wonders, was rapidly slipping out of control.

Asklepios bashfully strolled into the office, his hands clasped behind him. He wore a pair of Tim's jeans and trainers, an old sweatshirt hung loose on his thin frame.

He walked behind the desk where Tim sat and peered through the window, cooing like a dove at every car and bus that drove past. Then he gave a choking cry, grabbed Tim and pulled him round. 'How does he do that? Why does he not fall off?'

Tim watched the cyclist pedal down the street. 'It just takes practice. Look, if you want to help, why don't you feed my chickens?'

'Of course, my pleasure. Where is your farm?'

'On the roof.'

'I— Really?'

Tim showed the way and returned to his office.

Asklepios looked out over the roofscape and breathed the unfamiliar air filled with exotic fumes and strange sounds. The city was truly enormous. Despite his elevation he could see no end to it in any direction. To the south (he had always been good with bearings, it felt like the south) the buildings rose in great, blocky towers of ten or even an astonishing fifteen stories.

Despite its size the city was remarkably free of the stenches and reeks of his homeland. Under the human aromas of food, garbage, smoke, and the acrid reek of their marvellous machines was a sharper, more natural tang. Overhead birds cried. Asklepios looked up at the circling white gulls and knew he must be near to the sea.

With a sudden, intense pang he ached for his simple, mud brick home, his dark eyed mischievous grandchildren, the comfortable complexity of family life. The sun held little warmth here, the air was cool and damp, very different from the dry, fresh heat he was used to. Yet despite these differences in the world and the marvels he had seen both inside and outside Tim's home it was the cleanliness, the lack of familiar odours, that made him feel furthest from home.

Where am I, and when? Asklepios wondered with some anxiety. Will I ever see my family again?

The chickens were kept in a large cage of metal wire woven with marvellous regularity. They had plenty of grain and Asklepios realised this was simply make-work, Tim had wanted him out of the way. Very well, he accepted he was an unwanted nuisance causing his host considerable difficulty. Nevertheless, there were rules of hospitality and as a guest he would obey them.

He opened the cage, refreshed the water from a covered bucket and searched for eggs, finding only one. That wasn't surprising, he thought, with only three hens and no cock.

Tim might be keeping them for food but mostly likely they were for divination. It was a reassuring thought, his host was not so different after all and neither, perhaps, were the powers he controlled.

Tim had had explained how the lights, the jug that heated water, and the slotted box that toasted the bread worked. When Asklepios saw the plugs and sockets formed three connections he became excited. Tim opened up one of the plugs and showed him the three coloured wires.

Although there was much Asklepios had failed to grasp, it was clear the power was some form of life-energy. Red symbolising blood was balanced between the brown earth and the blue sky. Here once again was the indivisible three, simple yet powerful. Though why they considered the blue of the sky to be the neutral or passive phase was beyond him. Unlike the earth, where the dead were laid to rest, the sky was never still.

With the simple task he had been sent to do complete, Asklepios decided to stay on the roof a while longer. A good guest should always do more than he had been asked. This was an opportunity to contemplate the problem of the cats.

Animal banishments were simple things, used to protect the granaries from rats and mice and keep birds from new-sown fields. Asklepios had performed them many times. In the main cats were summoned rather than banished. For example the farmer's protection against birds invoked Bez, the feline spirit, to drive off avian Masgatha.

A simple reversal of the ritual should be effective. Asklepios looked at the chickens and a smile broke out on his face. Everything he needed was here, he could perform the ritual right now.

Wind-blown dirt had collected in the lee of the low parapet. Asklepios scrapped up a handful, dampened it with water from the bucket and fashioned a pellet with a crude muzzle and ears at one end. He placed it to one side and went back into the chicken run.

Two of the birds backed away into the corner but the third, intent on its dust bath, had not noticed him. 'Bird, lend me your spirit,' Asklepios said and snatched the chicken up by the neck.

The startled bird frantically beat its wings. Asklepios pulled a handful of speckled feathers from its breast. 'Bird, I hold your spirit.'

He released the chicken and it dropped to the ground and lay there with its wings spread.

Carefully keeping his fist bunched, Asklepios worked five feathers free of his grasp and pushed them into the mud pellet, four for legs and one for a tail.

'You are Bez,' he told the feather-legged effigy. 'I made you and hold you here.'

The wind gusted. One of the unused feathers danced and waved half-free of his grip. Asklepios dexterously pushed it back into his fist with his thumb. The wind-flurries proved he had powerful Masgatha's attention but she tested him. Letting her take a feather now would ruin the spell.

Asklepios cracked open his fist and worked the effigy of Bez down onto the feathers in his hand. All was prepared. He thrust his arm into the air.

'Masgatha of the upper sky. Hear me and listen, I am speaking to you. Look down, see me in this high place of sacrifice. See what I have for you. See, it is your enemy, Bez, trapped here in my hand. Take him, I give him to you. If this pleases you grant me this boon: where his kind gather, throw them down in confusion.'

Asklepios drew back his arm and flung the cat effigy as hard as he could. With great satisfaction he saw it arc high through the air and impact on a chimney pot three houses down the street. Loose feathers swirled up and away. Higher and higher.

This was all excellent. The effigy of Bez was marooned high off the ground, carried by the bird's spirit. Wherever the plague of cats was it would be defeated by something from the air. It would not be permanent for nothing ever was allowed to be. A few days, perhaps as much as a week, thus Masgatha would reward him for this small victory in her eternal war with Bez.

Almost as a reflex Asklepios analysed his actions, an act of self-criticism he had long ago learned was an essential part of his magic. That he now stood on the roof of a house in an unknown city told him he still had much to learn.

The simple ritual had worked well, his casting had clarity and purpose, a desire for something outside of himself. This was all good but it was also a mirror on his own past ambitions. He saw now how his earlier summonings had been selfish things to increase his prestige, a short-cut to knowledge he lacked the patience or resources to study for. The indivisible three he understood, and the five. Far more powerful and varied, seven was still not fully in his grasp. He had been a fool to attempt the eleventh way.

Yet the disaster of his attempt to bind 'Eritstim' was both blessing and curse. He laughed with embarrassment at his own ignorance and folly, thank the powers he had never succeeded in summoning a real djinn. He should be grateful to be alive, let alone find himself in a place where the opportunities to learn seemed boundless.

For despite all his mistakes, and although those summonings had not worked as he intended, they had still worked. In the last case it had worked magnificently and triumphantly for he had in effect summoned himself to another era of time. The thought made him weak at the knees. A small ember of pride flickered—he had created a new spell.

Or was he simply the latest foolish over-ambitious sorcerer to hurl himself across creation and vanish forever?

His old summoning ritual had worked each time, it was now just a question of refinement, of accuracy and focus. He could eliminate several factors: herb lore was common knowledge, the spoken words were from a universal compendium, goat's blood was goat's blood. What remained was the structure, the binding circle itself, the placement of the various items more than the items themselves. In many respects they were simply place-holders. His circles had not been perfect, the angles not aligned with precision. He felt it in his gut with absolute certainty that this was where he needed to improve. He had no idea how.

Down in the office Tim tried to prioritise: life; the missing car; Foxy… It was impossible, Asklepios occupied his thoughts completely. Until Asklepios' situation was resolved he wouldn't be able to deal with anything else. They had to talk, they needed to plan. Tim headed to the roof. When he opened the door to the stairs Asklepios was right there. He held out an egg. 'I found this.'

Tim took the egg. It was warm. 'Where?'

Asklepios hesitated. Was this another test? His new friend was such a curious mixture of knowledge and innocence it was hard to tell. 'Under a chicken.'

Tim left the egg in the kitchen and they returned to the office. 'Asklepios, I have to get on with my life and so do you. What are we going to do?'

Asklepios' face fell. 'You want to send me away.'

'Yes.' Tim paced left and right. 'No. Look, you're a real person and so am I, but I belong here and you don't. You summoned me while I slept and because you got my name wrong the circle was broken and you came back with me when I woke up.'

'That is also how I see it.'

'So, can't you just do it again?'

Asklepios hung his head. 'My friend, I cannot summon you because you are already here. I would summon someone else, and—'

'That would just make things worse.' Tim imagined the arrival of a second surprise guest. Keep that up and Brighton would be filled with an eclectic mix of time travellers. They'd fit right in.

'I don't know how to get you home, Asklepios.'

'I know. And neither do I.'

Nothing had changed but things felt better for having admitted it. Dressed in modern clothes, Asklepios seemed no more unusual than any other visitor.

Asklepios smiled hopefully. 'May I make some more toast?'

'Go for it.' Tim waved him away, anxious to get on with the things that needing doing. The problem of Asklepios' future would have to wait. First thing, the broken door. Tim recalled an advert for a local handyman on the free street maps that came through his letterbox.

The smell of toast drifted in from the kitchen. Just as he found the map he remembered Mrs Woosencraft. Tim sat stunned. Guilt consumed him. How could he have been so thoughtless? Yesterday she had been in terrible pain with angina, today he hadn't given her a thought. All the cakes she'd made him, the marmalade in which Asklepios took such delight, all her visits and small kindnesses over the past months. She had given him his first case and paid for it out of her pension. He had to visit her straight away.

Asklepios was in the kitchen with a half-eaten piece of toast in one hand. Two slices of bread sat ready in the toaster.

'I'm going out,' Tim told him. 'Stay here. Don't touch anything.'

Asklepios gave the toaster a disconsolate look.

'All right, you can touch that.'

'Thank you.'

Tim was already halfway towards the office door. 'I won't be long.'

He clattered down the stairs. The bottom door slammed. Asklepios stood alone in the silence. Whatever the matter was, Tim would no doubt explain on his return. Meanwhile he had little to do but wait.

Munching toast he wandered into the office. His eyes roved over the books on Tim's desk. The diagrams and pictures were fascinating, clearly these were esoteric volumes but the words were incomprehensible. He touched his pendant half-decided to use the final charge to gain understanding of the written words. He would be patient and ask Tim to explain the books when he returned.

The smell of burning toast came from the kitchen. Asklepios dashed down the hallway and flipped up the lever. Two blackened slices emerged, smoking gently. Asklepios scraped the charred surface and spread the toast thickly with marmalade. The jar was half empty, but there two more pots on the shelf. Unfortunately the bread was almost all gone.

Toast was nice enough, but as far as Asklepios was concerned it was simply an edible surface upon which to put marmalade. He reached a decision: as a guest it would be rude to consume all his host's bread. Therefore he must sacrifice enjoyment of toast and restrict himself to marmalade. Impressed with the power of his own logic, Asklepios scooped a large spoonful of marmalade from the pot and lifted it to his mouth.

Ffwch

TIM DETOURED past the local flower shop, bought a bunch of yellow and purple freesias and headed straight to Mrs Woosencraft's house. Once again the front door was off the latch. He pushed it open and went into the hall.

'Hello? Mrs W? It's me, Tim.'

The house was silent, and strangely so, for there was no thump and scurry of cat paws hurrying downstairs to see who the visitor was. Nor was there a rattle of crockery in the kitchen or the sound of a badly-tuned radio.

'I don't pay any attention to what they're on about,' Mrs W once told Tim as he adjusted the dial. 'It's the company, see?'

Tim listened to the silence. The steady tick of the clock on the mantle in the front room only emphasised the stillness of the rest of the house.

She had not gone shopping. The one concession Mrs Woosencraft made to security was to lock the front door whenever she went out. At the far end of the hall the doorway to the back room acquired the aura of the entrance to a mausoleum. A sweet waft of scent came from the freesias. Tim's imagination ran away with him: a pathetically motionless huddle under the blankets in the bedroom; stockinged feet among a scatter of baking trays behind the kitchen table. Bracing himself, he went into the back room.

Mrs Woosencraft sat in her upright chair. Her head was tipped back, her eyes were closed and her mouth hung open.

A tangle of knitting lay on floor, a cold cup of tea sat on the nest of tables.

Tim had seen death several times when he was with the police, it had never been someone he knew. The flowers in his hand felt like cruel anticipation. He took her hand in his, it was cool but not cold.

A low organic grumbling came from the nether regions of the chair, Mrs Woosencraft let out an impressively sustained fart. Her nose twitched, she lifted her head, closed her mouth and opened her eyes. Her gaze swivelled towards Tim. They looked at each other uncomfortably. Tim let go of her hand.

'Hello, Tim. Catch me having forty winks, did you?' Mrs Woosencraft said.

'I was worried. After yesterday I thought…'

'Oh, don't be so maudlin, I've a good few miles in me yet.' Mrs Woosencraft wrinkled her nose. 'Those cats and their digestion. I think it's all that meat. Let's get some fresh air in here.'

Mrs Woosencraft pushed herself out of the chair, took the step down into the kitchen with a roll of her hips and opened the kitchen door. 'It's brightening up and about time too. It's not like me to drop off during the day.' She spooned tea into the pot, filled the kettle and clanged it down on the hob. 'Time for a cuppa.'

Tim held out the freesias. 'I thought you'd like these.'

Mrs Woosencraft's eyes almost disappeared among the wrinkles as she smiled. 'Bless you, pet, I do. Let's get them into water.' She buried her face in the blooms. 'Freesias are my favourite, a little old fashioned but so am I. Let's be posh and put the tablecloth out for them.'

The cloth was old, heavy white linen hand-embroidered with violets, and roses in the corners. Tim helped her smooth it out. She put the vase on the table.

The sound of the kettle coming on was the only noise in the house. 'Where are the cats?'

'Oh, they're here and there, looking for this and that like cats do.'

'Mrs Woosencraft, your angina—'

She waved her hand dismissively. 'It comes and goes.'

'I was worried.'

'I know, and I'd rather you didn't. Now, tell me how things are going?'

'I haven't found out who MK is yet.'

Mrs Woosencraft became brisk. Cups and saucers clattered onto the table, teaspoons rattled, milk and sugar appeared in jug and bowl beside a plate of honey flapjacks. The kettle sang. She picked up the teapot, turned and knocked the pot against the corner of the oven. The spout detached itself from the pot with a musical clink and skittered across the worktop.

'Blast and bother, look what I've done now! I've had that pot for ages. We'll just have to have mugs and tea bags instead.'

Before long they were sitting at the table. One by one the cats appeared. Pedwar the Manx leapt onto the top of the dresser while others just seemed to materialise under the table.

'Any news of Morse?'

'No.' Tim picked up the broken teapot spout and turned it round in his fingers. 'I'm still looking for your cat too.'

Mrs Woosencraft patted Tim's hand. He seemed so despondent. She subtly adjusted the position of her mug in relation to the freesia jar and tried a little cantrip. 'In the last five years I've lost four cats, three came back, two are still with me so that just leaves the one. Now, tell me what happened since we last met.'

To his own surprise Tim found himself telling Mrs Woosencraft all about this girl with the long golden blonde hair and how she was so suspicious and distant. How she had needed help and he had tried to give it. That they had argued and for the life of him he couldn't work out why, or what he had done wrong.

'Of course you can't, and there's a perfectly simple explanation.'

'There is?'

'Yes, *bachgen*, and it's this: you've done nothing wrong. That's why you can't work it out, see?'

'Really?'

'She likes you, she just hasn't got used to the idea. Now tell me, when are you going to see her again?'

Tim's shoulders slumped. 'Never, probably. I don't know where she lives.'

'Well, that is a bit of a problem. Do you know where she works?'

'I don't even know what she does.'

'Never mind. I'm sure something will happen.'

Tim idly matched the broken spout to the pot. 'I don't know.'

Mrs Woosencraft took the spout from him. 'Here's something we can fix straight away.' She ducked under the sink, shooed an inquisitive cat away and emerged with an ancient and over-sized pot of contact glue with a crusted-over lid. She handed it to Tim. 'Uncrack that will you?'

Tim twisted off the lid. Pungent vapours emerged, the pot was filled with white glue like viscous cream. Mrs Woosencraft handed him an old wooden spoon. He used the handle to smear glue on the two sides of the break and left them to dry.

All the cats pricked up their ears and turned to look at the kitchen door.

An enormous bumblebee with a furry black body and orange bottom zoomed through the open door and circled the kitchen. Down on the floor cats danced on their hind legs and patted the air with their forepaws. Up on the dresser Pedwar followed the bee with rapt fascination.

Droning like a saw the bee battered against the window and swung back towards the flowers. Pecwar leapt off the dresser, landed on the tablecloth and swept the flowers and teapot towards the edge.

Mrs Woosencraft snatched the flower vase away to safety.

Tim grabbed the pot and spout.

'Glue!' They both darted forward. And they both stopped to let the other one go first.

Cat, tablecloth and glue pot tumbled onto the floor.

The bumblebee looped around the room then zoomed through the outside door. The drone of its wings faded into the distance.

Mrs Woosencraft gingerly lifted one edge of the tablecloth. Tim peered past her arm. A pair of feline eyes blinked up at them from a small cave dripping with white glue.

'*Ffwch*[4],' Mrs Woosencraft said with feeling. She turned to Tim. 'I'll deal with this best on my own, pet. Get yourself home.'

It took some persuading but finally Tim was out the house. Mrs Woosencraft looked down at her glue-covered cat and swore at length and with admirable creativity. Accidents like this should not happen in her house and she was not happy at all. They should not happen because she had effective protection against such chaotic mishap. Which meant somebody was deliberately dicking her around. And to do that they must be using magic.

---

[4] *Bother.*

Red-Handed Thief

ASKLEPIOS LAY on Tim's settee with the blanket pulled up to his chin and a glass of water on the carpet beside him. He mournfully rubbed his stomach. 'I believe I have a small indigestion.' He sipped water and suppressed a quiet belch. 'I hope to recover shortly.'

'You ate all the marmalade?'

'Just one pot.'

Tim wondered if his life was already beyond his ability to impose control.

Asklepios groaned and pulled the blanket over his head. 'I do apologise.'

'Forget it.' Tim knew Asklepios to be a man driven by passion rather than foresight. It explained both his stomach ache and how he ended up in Brighton.

Tim went to his desk, took out the handkerchief with the MK monogram and spread it on the desk.

Suddenly Asklepios flung back the blanket and sat up. His complexion was pale, pasty and tinged with green. Tim pointed mutely to the bathroom, Asklepios lurched to his feet and staggered away with his arms wrapped round his belly.

Feeling entirely unsympathetic, Tim waited for him to return. 'Feeling better?'

'Yes, thank you. I am sorry to be such a nuisance.'

Tim needed some space, some peace and quiet. 'Why don't you go for a walk? Fresh air will do you good.'

Asklepios was immediately enthusiastic. 'Oh yes indeed. I would like to see the wonders of your city very much.'

Tim gave him the free map, showed Asklepios his own street and circled it with his pen.

'Giving every alley and street its own name is a remarkable idea but for me it would only confuse.' Asklepios touched his enamelled pendant and pushed away the map. 'I can understand the spoken word, not the written. Do not be concerned, I have an excellent sense of direction. I shall walk to the sea and return before sunset.'

Tim gave Asklepios some coins from his pocket, a ten pound note from his wallet and explained their relative values.

Out on the pavement Asklepios took a deep, satisfied breath and looked around. 'I will see you later.'

To Asklepios the city was very fine. The streets were broad, the houses elegant and well-proportioned. He was even getting used to the strange vehicles these people rode in. Apart from the bitter smell they gave off they were marvellous things, rolling effortlessly along as fast as a galloping camel.

And the people. More specifically, the women. Some of them wore hardly anything at all, tops with no backs, skirts with no bottoms. Bare arms, yes, but bare legs too! Yet everyone appeared to accept their dress without comment and he quickly realised his stares drew hostile looks.

Lowering his gaze Asklepios determined to behave with more dignity. This was their way, he was the visitor and it was his responsibility to act according to the norms. He made his way downhill into a region of narrower streets packed with pedestrians and found himself in a kind of bazaar.

All the races were here. Mainly pale skinned, but also the brown black and yellow peoples. Everyone mingled together harmoniously, it was impossible to tell rich from poor. There were no grand processions, no ostentation, and only a few beggars.

This was further proof he was in the most ancient past. He had been brought to one of the great cities before the fall, when magic was commonplace and all men lived without rancour.

It just wasn't quite how he had imagined it.

These people were so wealthy and content they had no need to display their riches, no need to assert their station. It was confusing. The women wore earrings and necklaces of silver, the men bands and chains of gold, black beads or silver crosses, but they also seemed happy to dress in the simplest clothes, even torn and ragged ones.

A sudden pulse of happiness filled him. This was the time before the great rivalries, before jealousy and discontent threw mankind down and so much had been lost. It was the Golden Age, and he was part of it.

'Greetings,' Asklepios accosted a young man in a flowing black coat, long black hair and eye shadow.

'Hi, man.' The stranger walked on by.

'Hi, man,' Asklepios said to a broad-shouldered man with a black goatee and ponytail, wearing baggy trousers and a sleeveless striped vest.

'How's it hanging, ancient dude?'

The man raised his palm. Hesitantly Asklepios did the same. The man slapped his hand against Asklepios' palm and walked on.

Laughing with happiness, Asklepios walked through the lanes.

Out of the crowds emerged a young woman with fair skin, golden hair and eyes of green. A band of freckles dappled her cheeks. She was the most beautiful woman Asklepios had ever seen. He couldn't help himself. 'Blessings be upon thee, oh golden one.'

Before he could even squeak she had him pinned against a wall. 'Poseidon's hairy arse. How is it you know my tongue?'

Asklepios' smile slid off his face. 'Forgive me, golden one. I was enchanted by your beauty, I—'

The woman's green eyes burned with emotions closer to panic than anger. 'Don't talk to me like that. Answer my question. How can you speak my language?'

Instinctively Asklepios reached up to touch his pendant.

The woman grasped his fist, enfolding his hand and the pendant. 'This? What is it?'

'Let go!' Asklepios wrenched his hand free along with the pendant. The cord round his neck snapped. Desperate, he held the pendant tight.

A crowd quickly gathered around.

'What's the problem?' It was the bearded man who had earlier slapped Asklepios' palm in greeting.

'A misunderstanding, I—'

The man glowered at the two ends of the cord hanging from Asklepios' fist. 'What's that?'

'It's mine. I found it.'

The man was strong, he forced Asklepios' fist open and pulled the pendant from his grasp. He held Asklepios against the wall and showed the pendant to the woman. 'Is this yours?'

She gave Asklepios a quick look of guilt tinged with fear. 'I— Yes.'

He dropped it in her hand and she hurried away.

'No, it is mine!' Asklepios struggled helplessly in the man's grip. 'Please—'

The bearded man clenched his fist. 'You're lucky I don't—'

The pendant's magic faded, the rest of his speech was gibberish. All around the crowd babbled excitedly. Several people held up small multi-coloured tablets. Something distracted the beaded man and he loosened his hold.

Asklepios took his chance, twisted free and fled through the crowd.

A narrow alley opened nearby, he dodged into it, ran through another busy lane, turned left and right, sometimes uphill, sometimes down. The angry shouts behind him faded. All around came words he did not understand, and hands pushing and clutching. Weeping with fear and the injustice of his treatment, he ran on.

Perfect Cover

TROY JARGLEBAUM'S card lay on Tim's desk front and centre. Tim looked at it with the same affection he would have for his own tombstone. His hand hovered over the phone. He picked the receiver up, put it down, drummed his fingers on the desk and paced the room.

'Damn it.' Tim dropped into his chair. 'Morse, where are you? I need some non-critical company.'

Tim had been an unorthodox policeman but Morse was a standard-issue cat. Food was equally likely to be sniffed at or eaten, the occasional small rodent was presented for admiration, he was a past master of the 'wrong side of the door' game and he hunted and killed old paper bags with enthusiasm. He also sat on Tim's lap, purred like a small motorbike and magically erased all stress from his soul.

The phone was on the desk, Jarglebaum's card beside it. Something had to be done. Tim either needed to call Troy Jarglebaum, endure the mockery and accept his help, or come up with some brilliant right-brained intuition.

He covered his right eye and tried conceptualising his problems as different coloured polyhedrons, medieval armies, and finally as mushrooms pushing up paving stones. No radical insights arrived.

He forced himself to make the call. To his vast relief Troy was away from his desk. The voice mail tone beeped. Tim said, 'Troy, it's Tim. I could use some advice. Call me.' He hung up. It was a lot easier to ask a machine for help than Troy Jarglebaum.

Even so, he hoped Troy called before Imelda and Electra returned and he had nothing to tell them.

As if on cue, the doorbell rang, a single firm ring of assurance and self-possession. Tim went down the stairs cracked open the door and peered through the gap.

There she was, in an open necked blouse, a short jacket and a grass green hip-hugging skirt.

Tim's heart gave a jump. 'Foxy.'

She looked at him through the gap. 'What's the matter?'

'I thought you might be someone else.'

'Are you hiding?'

Tim pushed the door wide. 'Me? Nah. Come in.'

Tim led the way. Foxy paused at the splintered frame, went to touch it then jerked her hand away. 'You should mend that.'

He was so pleased to see her. He did his best to be professional. 'How can I help you, Ms Bolivia?'

Foxy folded her arms. 'The cats.'

'Well, I'm sorry about that. I haven't had much time and after you walked out of the shop I thought—'

'They've gone.'

'They have? All of them?'

'Every single one.'

'Oh. OK. Good.'

Foxy's eyes narrowed. 'How did you do it?'

'I don't—'

'Don't give me that stuff about professional secrets, I want to know.'

'Didn't you fit the cat scarer?'

'The cats went first.'

'It didn't work?'

'I don't know. Yesterday the cats were still there. This morning they were gone.'

Something didn't add up. 'When did you fit the scarer?'
Foxy shifted evasively. 'The day I bought it.'
'Then you did it, not me.'
'No. I—' Foxy hesitated. 'Promise you won't laugh?'
'OK.'
'I forgot to turn it on.'
He couldn't help himself.

Tim looked up at the cracked ceiling. The little flies were back under the shade. Three of them, alternately cruising their square circles and indulging in brief, dizzyingly fast dogfights.

The carpet was actually quite comfortable.

He wondered why he was lying on it. And why the side of his jaw hurt.

Foxy knelt beside him, her eyes filled with worry and guilt. 'I'm so sorry. Are you all right? I honestly didn't mean to hit you—'

It all flooded back. He had laughed, Foxy's fist floated towards him, the room tipped onto its side.

'—so hard.'

Tim sat up. He worked his jaw. It was actually still quite funny. 'You forgot—'

Foxy raised a warning finger.

'All right, I promise.'

Tim put his back against the settee. Foxy sat beside him, her legs tucked under her. It seemed easier to stay on the ragged old carpet than get up. He found himself telling Foxy about his work, his time in the police. How he had his big idea.

'There was a missing child. Days went by and we were getting nowhere. Then this woman phoned in, she said she was clairvoyant and could help. And the Inspector went for it, he invited her in and she became part of the team. We found the child, it was her who did it too. I knew then that we could solve crimes by combining old ways with new.'

Foxy considered Tim's words. 'Is that what you did for me?'

If Tim wanted Foxy to be more than just a client he would have to trust her. What better time than now to tell her about the amazing, magical and more than a little scary events that had happened to him?

'I tried, but it was too difficult. I wasn't properly prepared. I didn't do anything that could have worked. I fell asleep, I—' Tim took a breath. 'I had a dream, it sounds impossible—'

Foxy leaned close. 'Try me.'

Tim related the events as best as he could, ending with Asklepios' appearance in his room. Foxy appeared completely unfazed by the revelations.

'Some things are waiting to happen. If you don't believe, they can't flow.'

A strange thrill ran through Tim. 'An eerie thought.'

'Where is Asklepios now?' Foxy said.

'He went for a walk.'

Foxy's mouth twisted. 'What does he look like?'

'About fifty and quite thin, scrawny really. Straggly hair and beard, a bit of a nose. I gave him some of my clothes, they were pretty baggy on him.'

Foxy became still.

'I'm amazed you believe me,' Tim said.

'It's not as hard as you might think.'

Foxy moved the conversation on to inconsequential things. Somehow this let them discover more about each other. The sun moved across the window, Tim let down the blinds and fetched a bottle of red wine and two glasses from the kitchen.

'Wine is really such a good idea, don't you think?' Foxy said. 'I never drank it before I came to Brighton.'

'How come?'

'Too… difficult.' Foxy went still for a moment then shivered her shoulders and raised her glass. 'Cheers.'

Tim clinked his glass against hers. They both drank.

'Now, tell me what you've been doing to find that car.'

Tim gave a brief summary of his lack of progress.

'Well, there's your mistake,' Foxy said. 'You've been acting like an ordinary copper, making phone calls and doing interviews. In your head you're still pounding the beat. Mine was an unusual case and you solved it in a very strange way. If you're serious about being alternative you've got to start acting a little weirder.'

She was right. This was not only her challenge to him, it was his own challenge to himself. 'Right.' He knocked back his drink. 'All right.'

'So, what's the plan, Mr Detective?'

Tim didn't have any clear ideas. 'Let's try divining, it's how the missing boy was found.'

He took the map down from the desk and spread it on the floor. Foxy became enthusiastic. 'Put the ruler over the edge of the desk and stand the wine bottle on the other end. Hang the pen from the ruler.'

It was makeshift, but looked like it might do the job. Foxy and Tim crouched beside the map and watched the ballpoint pen swing across the paper.

Tim studied the construction critically. 'The pen's not hanging straight. The string's too thick.'

'Use one of my hairs.' Foxy teased out a strand.

'I'll get my scissors.'

Foxy was emphatic. 'No way. I never ever cut my hair.' She wound a hair around her finger, tugged it free and handed it to Tim.

It lay across his palm like a yard of spun gold.

'Now you can cut it,' Foxy said.

Tim found he didn't want to. He tied the pen to the hair and the hair to the ruler, looping the excess around the bottle. The pen hung absolutely vertical and steady as a nail.

'Now what?' Foxy said.

Tim prodded the pen with his finger and it swung in a wobbling, chaotic ellipse. 'Concentrate. Think about the car.'

Heads together, they intently watched the pen move over the map.

Slowly the motion of the pen steadied to a pendulum swing. Slowly the arc reduced, oddly less on one side than the other. Silence potent with anticipation filled the room. It was happening, something was actually happening.

The pen came to a halt, not hanging vertically but unnaturally, impossibly, to one side. Foxy and Tim looked at each other, their faces inches apart.

'Tim, it's—'

'Yes.' Tim was lost in the deep green pool of her gold-lashed eyes, the scent of her breath filled his mind with glass-green, foam-flecked waves and wind-torn skies—

A loud hand-clap followed by Troy Jarglebaum's cynical laughter sent Tim leaping to his feet shocked half out of his skin. Beside him Foxy swept to her feet in a single smooth movement.

Jarglebaum could move quieter than a spider wearing socks. The office door was still be broken but the front door had a lock on it. A damned good one.

Furious, Tim confronted Jarglebaum. 'Troy, damn you, how did you get in?'

'I've got to admire your technique, son.' Troy grinned and continued his slow handclap. 'It's unique, damned unique.' He jerked his thumb down the stairs. 'How did I get in? The door, kiddo.'

'You're using skeleton keys.'

Troy tapped the side of his lumpy nose. 'It's an idea, Ace. I couldn't possibly comment. Why am I here, I hear you ask?

You called, remember? I got your message and here I am, the answer to your prayers.'

His eyes swept Foxy from tip to toe. 'Ms Bolivia, I presume.'

All that Foxy could manage was a nervous smile. The overweight detective both repelled and fascinated her with his beefy neck and solid stomach, gaping shirt and black tasselled slip-ons.

Jarglebaum looked down at the map and the slowly swinging pen. 'Oh, this is good. The Ace Patent Car Locator and Bird-pulling device.' He winked at Foxy. 'Looks as if one half of it is working properly.'

Tim clenched his fists. 'Troy, I don't care why you're here, just go home.'

Troy grinned. 'I could help deliver those leaflets.'

'I don't need your help,' Tim said.

'Oh, I think you do, Ace. I think you do.'

Foxy found her voice. 'His name is Tim.'

Jarglebaum's eyes fell on her like shards of cold flint. 'I know that, love. Good old Tim Wassiter who never solved a case. Tim and Yours Truly, the partnership with the lowest clean-up rate since records began. That's why we called him Ace. So, Miss Foxy Bolivia, please allow me to introduce you to Tim Wassiter, a.k.a. Ace Timewaster.'

'You're a nasty, bitter man.'

'No, love. It was all a joke. Coppering's just a job to me. We were having a laugh, weren't we Tim?'

Tim felt primeval: he wanted to knee Jarglebaum in the groin, bash his face in and kick him down the stairs. He didn't often get angry, but when he did, he felt it down to his bones. He growled and took a step forward.

Troy held up his hands, grinning. 'Not in front of the lady, son. It's undignified.' He spied the bottle on the desk. 'Finally, a proper drink in the office.'

He lifted the bottle. Ruler, pen and string tumbled to the floor as he eyed the two inches of wine in the bottom. 'Skol.' Troy poured the wine down his throat and thumped the empty bottle down on the desk. 'Well, this has been lovely but duty calls.' Once more his eyes roved across Foxy like envious hands. He straightened into a clumsy salute. 'Evening, all.'

And he was gone.

'I'll kill him,' Tim fumed.

'He's not worth it.'

'I mean it. I'm going to kick his teeth in.'

Foxy stood in front of him and held his shoulders. 'No, you're not. He's bigger than you. He's a better fighter.'

'Oh, thanks.'

'Well, I'm sorry to say it but he is. He's also half lard. He's smug and he thinks he's special. Men like that are common as mud and they're all jerks.'

Tim was taken back by her vehemence.

Foxy laughed grimly. 'I'm right. You'll see.'

He knew it too. Tim released a long slow breath and let the anger flow through him and away. He could live with this. After all, Foxy was not only on his side, she was right here at his side. 'All right. So, let's finish this divining.'

Foxy looked down at the map. A look of awe spread across her face. 'I don't think we have to.'

The ruler lay where it had fallen, the strand of hair strewn in loops across the carpet. The biro stood point down in the map, stuck into the carpet like a little spear.

Tim carefully tugged the pen out of the paper and examined the hole. 'Trafalgar Lane, between Kemp and Tidy Streets. It's all office buildings.'

'And under the offices?'

Tim snapped his fingers and grinned. 'Car parks.'

Foxy brimmed with excitement. 'When do we take a look?'

He wanted her to come. He thought about Electra Vaughan. 'It might be dangerous.'

'We're only going to walk down a street and look for a car.'

'Any other vehicle and I'd agree. I'm serious, Foxy.'

'Then you're going to need a lookout. Isn't that what people do on a stake-out?'

'We're not going to stake anything out. We're just going to take a walk down a road, remember?'

'Then it won't be dangerous. Besides, I'll be the perfect cover.'

Of course. If you want to avoid attention there's nothing like walking down a street with an amazingly attractive woman with hair second only to Rapunzel.

A second set of thoughts grabbed him by the throat and tried to shake some sense into him. What are you doing trying to put her off? Stop being an idiot. 'A pair of jeans might be more practical.'

'This girl does not wear trousers.'

'This evening, about six. Most people will have left work and it will still be light. I'll meet you at the end of Trafalgar.'

'Great.' Foxy's eyes danced with excitement. Picking up the strand of hair she wrapped it round her finger then slipped it in her bag. 'Don't want to make a mess,' she said when she saw Tim watching. 'See you there.'

Tim felt like he might levitate. 'See you there.'

Kemp Street

'LOG ME IN PLEASE,' Persistent Smith boomed as he took a seat in the internet café. 'I don't like that bit.'

The chubby young man with a peach-fuzz beard smirked as he leant over the keyboard. His fingers rattling across the keys. 'There you go, mate,' he said and waddled back behind the counter.

Persistent Smith didn't mind computers but he didn't like the internet one little bit. He didn't like the way it was so disorganised, so higgledy-piggledy. You could never tell what you were going to find. Or rather, you could, and it was rude. In fact it was more than rude, so much more that it needed a whole new word to describe it. Smith didn't know what that word was but it was extremely rude and the temptation to look was hard to resist. His mother would not have approved. 'Oh Derek,' he could hear her say. 'That was not Good Looking.' He was not entirely sure she was right.

Smith sucked at his water bottle. The internet was very naughty and he was determined not to be diverted, not to take even a quick little peek at whatever. He typed in the name Clive Barnett had given him:

Markus Koponen.

He sucked anxiously on the bottle again and discovered it was empty. He asked the man behind the counter for a refill, returned to his seat and began to read the search results.

They quickly became very interesting.

Some time later he typed 'Kylma Kala'. Soon after that he startled the other customers with a great guffaw of laughter. Shuffling his bottom on the seat, Smith extracted the pen and pad from his fleece and carefully copied down an address.

A shadow fell across the screen. 'All right, mate?' The café assistant peered suspiciously at the screen, bemused that anyone might find multinational company information so hilarious.

'Finished now, thank you!' Smith clicked the window closed and logged off. 'Finished, haha. Finished with the Finnish.'

Despite his fascination with timetables Smith disliked public transport and walked whenever he could. It gave him an excellent sense of direction, shoes that needed frequent re-heeling, and knowledge of the streets of Brighton that any taxi driver would have sold their soul for.

It didn't take long to walk to Kemp Street and find the right office block. Smith carried on past and looked back. Even if there were no armed guards, attack dogs, laser-droids or air-tight blast doors, a building like that would at least have a receptionist.

Receptionists asked questions, they looked at you and everything. Smith would rather confront laser-droids.

Low in his belly an uncomfortable pressure grew.

Smith knew he only had one chance to bluff his way in. If it didn't work the first time he was bound to be recognised if he tried again. One of the many things Persistent Smith knew was that he was no Master of Disguise.

He paced up and down at the corner of the street, anxiously sucked on the nozzle of his water bottle and considered his options:

1. Pretend to be making a delivery.
2. Pretend to be there for an interview.
3. Pretend to be a meter man.
4. Rush in. Shout 'Look at that!' Point outside, then hide.
5. Sneak in on hands and knees.

The water bottle was empty again. Smith slipped it back in his fleece.

The pressure in his body continued to grow. Smith realised he rather urgently needed the toilet. He gave a small whimper of frustration. This was not Good Planning and Foresight.

Pressing his knees together Smith waddled towards the building. The pressure grew to an insistent agony. Idea! Smith galumphed knock-kneed along the pavement, lolloped up the building stairs, pushed through the revolving door and staggered across the marbled foyer.

'Can I use your toilet?'

The reception desk was deserted.

A wide, grey-panelled foyer lay ahead. Stick-man and stick-woman signs were on the doors to one side, lift doors on the other. Smith hurried into the men's room.

None of the urinals were occupied. Moving to the far end, Smith did what he had to do, huffing and puffing with relief. As he stood there a dark-haired man dressed in dark trousers and white shirt, tie and jacket entered and stood at the next but one place[5].

Smith noted the breast-pocket badge and epaulets. This was the security guard. He stayed where he was as the man washed his hands and left the rest room. He stifled a giggle. By sheer luck and, he had to admit, even more luck, he was inside the building.

---

[5] *Urinal occupancy follows fixed rules: Adjacent urinals are never used until every alternate one is taken. Only then will the intervening ones be used. It's a bit like electrons filling atomic orbits.*

He washed his own hands and checked his watch. It was late afternoon, people would be leaving soon, he didn't have much time. He eased open the door and peered down the corridor. The uniformed man was sitting behind the reception desk swivelling on his chair smiling and talking into his mobile phone. The lift on the opposite wall pinged, the doors slid open and half a dozen staff emerged. Smith crossed smartly into the lift and pressed the button for the highest floor. The doors hissed shut and he was whisked upwards.

The Eunuch

ROBBED, humiliated and threatened Asklepios wandered through Brighton heedless of direction. His fists involuntarily clenched and unclenched, impotent anger burned his insides. That woman had seen the pendant for what it was. Somehow she had manipulated events so he looked like a thief. He replayed the encounter in his mind again and again but could not work out where things had slid out of control. For some reason the young man had believed the golden-haired woman in preference to Asklepios.

Asklepios sighed deeply and his anger drained from him. Of course the man would believe a pretty woman in preference to a scrawny old man. He would have done the same himself because in most cases he would have been right to do so.

He had always thought of himself as a lucky man and he realised with bone-dry amusement that he was lucky now. In his own time he would have been fortunate to keep his hand.

His flight had brought him to a broad plaza, a rich merchants' quarter. The shops were grander than those in the narrow bazaar he had fled, the goods looked expensive and the people around him were better dressed.

Gulls wheeled and cried overhead. The far end of the plaza was open, the sky clear and blue. Asklepios realised the sea was only a few hundred paces away.

In the opposite direction a short street ended in a high white wall and an intriguing white onion dome. The architecture was elaborate but the style was familiar. A small crowd milled by the entrance, Asklepios' heart surged, it must be a temple or the palace of a local caliph. He could ask for help.

A shaven-headed man sat behind a kiosk, most probably a palace eunuch. The people ahead of him paid the eunuch a donation, Asklepios dug in his pocket for the money Tim had given him and offered it all. The eunuch made some questioning comment. Asklepios grinned and offered his hand again. A sly look came into the eunuch's eyes, he divided the money between a compartmented box and his own pocket and waved Asklepios on.

An hour later Asklepios emerged from another door dazzled and amazed. Even the caliphs from his own time would be hard pressed to match such magnificence. Delicate stone columns supported fluted, onion-dome minarets, friezes of perforated stone flanked magnificent doors. Each room was more incredible than the rest and culminated in the awe-inspiring opulence of the dragon room.

Back out on the street Asklepios wandered towards the sea in a daze. The building was a pavilion fit for a prince or a god, but there was no lord and no deity. As far as he could determine the palace had been built for no other reason than that it could be built. His head spun, he simply did not understand. These people had wealth yet some dressed in rags, thieves were allowed to run away, and they built with such magnificence. What kind of people were they?

He was penniless and completely lost. Crowds thronged around him. Strange traffic flowed along the road. He had never felt so alone.

Alive but Sleeping

THERE SHE WAS. Tim saw Foxy in the early evening light. There was something different about her and after a moment he realised she wore her hair over her shoulder in a great golden plait. It was her sole concession to practicality for she still wore her tight knee-length skirt, green jacket and heels.

Tim considered his own ensemble: blue jeans, a faded maroon cotton shirt and old leather jacket. He tried to imagine himself in a variety of more stylish outfits. A Saville Row brown and mustard three-piece gave way to a zoot-suit and homburg, then a leather trench coat, high boots and monocle. He discarded them all, this was who he was and he had no inbuilt desire or indeed talent to wear clothes other than the ones he felt comfortable in. Also, accessories were problematic. A trench coat and monocle demanded a half-track armoured staff car with uniformed driver and motorcycle outriders. Considering the turning-circle, parking in Brighton would be a nightmare.

'Hi,' Foxy said, arriving with a small jump and a bright smile.

They looked at each other for a moment.

'Well, here I am,' Foxy said. 'What do we do now?'

Tim's guess about the number of people who would be around at this time of day was wrong. The sky was overcast but the streets still thronged with people walking home, waiting for buses or gathering in animated groups before heading off for an early drink.

'Take a walk and have a casual look around,' Tim said. 'And try not to be noticed.'

'OK. How about this?' Foxy slipped her arm through his. 'Two friends out for a walk.'

It was worth it just for this, Tim decided.

'What's up?' Foxy said.

'It feels strange to be here just because a pen made a hole in a map.'

'That's down to you. When I first came here I didn't think men were good for much of anything, but you're not like those guys, you've got some real talents.'

'Foxy, where exactly did you come from?'

'A place where all the men are fat, lecherous bores. Just like that Troy Jarglebaum.' Foxy briefly hugged his arm. 'You wouldn't fit in at all.'

They walked in silence for a moment then Tim said, 'One or more of these buildings will have a car park. We'll check them as we walk past.'

'What does the car look like?'

Tim told her.

Foxy nodded. 'Big, old and black.'

'Big, old, black, and beautiful,' Tim said.

'Only ships can be beautiful. Other machines are just things.'

'This car will prove you wrong.'

'We'll see.'

The first car park was at ground level under a concrete cube of a building on concrete stilts. Foxy and Tim strolled past. All the cars were modern ones.

The next car park was in the basement of a large and featureless office block. A concrete ramp descended from the street and ended in a metal roll-door. A security camera on the wall covered the approach. As they passed by the door clanked up, a car exited up the ramp and the door rolled down behind it.

It was going to be difficult to get in there unnoticed. Although there were long glassless windows at pavement level they were only about eighteen inches high.

'Let's try further on,' Tim said.

By the time they reached the end of Trafalgar Lane the commuter crowds had thinned to a few lone individuals. The rest of the office buildings either had no parking at all or open lots where it was easy to see all the vehicles. There was nothing that looked like the Imperial.

Tim looked doubtfully back at the basement car park. 'If the car's anywhere, it's in there.'

Overhead the clouds lowered, flinty grey. A cool wind started and moments later a few fat drops of rain spattered the pavement.

Foxy slipped her arm free from Tim's. 'Keep an eye out, I'm going to take a look.'

A stronger gust of wind blew a flurry of rain and litter down the road. Foxy crossed to the other side. Tim looked up and down the road, saw it was deserted and hurried across to join her.

Foxy dropped to her knees beside one of the long low openings and peered through.

Tim looked left and right. A lone man exited a doorway, raised his umbrella and hurried away.

Foxy pulled her head back. 'It's too gloomy, I can't see anything.' She shrugged out of her jacket, lay flat on her stomach and wriggled in past her shoulders.

'I can see seven, eight cars, more further back. My body's blocking the light.' She slid a little further in then went still.

Tim crouched beside her. 'Foxy, are you all right?'

'Yes,' came the muffled reply. 'My eyes are getting used to the light.' More of Foxy disappeared into the low gap. 'The floor's not that far down. I think I could… Eeek!'

Before Tim could move she vanished. All except for a single aqua-blue mid-heel pump. The street was still empty.

Tim lay flat on the pavement and called into the gap. 'Foxy, are you all right?'

After a moment he heard her moving, then a low laugh. Foxy's fingers wiggled at the lip of the sill 'I'm fine. Where's my shoe?'

'Here.' Tim dropped it down, along with her jacket.

'Nobody's here, it's very quiet. I think everyone has gone home.'

It looked like there was just enough room. Tim took off his own jacket and pushed it into the gap. 'I'm coming down.'

He wriggled in head-first and saw the floor was about five feet below him. He swung his legs round and dropped down.

Foxy was right there, her eyes bright, her smile mischievous. She swung her jacket over her shoulder. 'This is fun.'

The cold air smelled of damp concrete and exhaust fumes. Tim looked around anxiously. If they were caught it would not look good, they'd have few excuses. Once again he'd be forced to ask Troy Jarglebaum for help. 'Let's keep the noise down.'

Dim light seeped in from the street behind them. Further back scattered pools of illumination came from widely-spaced wall lights. To their right the steel shutter closed off the exit ramp. In the far corner a green 'Exit' sign glowed above a door. Most of the parking bays were empty, a few dim silhouettes of vehicles showed here and there.

Foxy's heels echoed off the walls as they walked forwards. A small green hatchback emerged from the gloom, a large saloon straddled two bays further back. A couple of the wall lights were out, Tim walked through a pool of darkness and found it empty.

'Well, at least we…' Tim began and the words died in his mouth.

'What?' Foxy said, then, 'Oh.'

In the furthest corner of the garage was an alcove wide enough for three cars. A glint of reflected light shone from the centre bay. Tim took a step closer, then another. A twin rail front fender with chrome over-riders gleamed, above it a tall grill fronted a high, black bonnet.

Tim and Foxy walked slowly forwards, the scuff and click of their shoes on the dusty concrete the only sound.

Twin headlight cones, white-wall tyres, chrome hub caps. Glistening black bodywork deep and dark as midnight water. The glorious, grand sweep of the front wheel arches and running boards revealed themselves as they approached.

Foxy stood still. 'You were right, it is beautiful, like it's alive. Alive, but sleeping.'

'Single-piece curved windshield,' Tim whispered. 'Wind-tunnel designed streamlining. Both firsts. Chrysler was the first company to realise that cars were, up until that point, essentially built back to front.' Unbidden his hand reached out to touch the liquid black paintwork.

'Don't.' Foxy's hand was on his arm. 'You'll leave prints.'

'Have you done this before?'

Foxy's eyes glittered in the quiet gloom. 'No, but I wish I had.'

Seeing her standing in the half-light beside the Airflow the thought came to Tim that she was a woman from another time, another world.

Foxy shifted under his gaze. 'What is it?'

'We did it, Foxy. We found the car.' He could hardly believe it himself. 'The divining worked.'

Suspension creaked softly as Foxy stood on the running board and peered through the side window. 'Empty. It's so clean it could be new.'

Tim took a long admiring look at deep-buttoned red leather upholstery, carpets, chrome fittings and walnut trim on the dash. Then he made his way round the back. 'She's definitely the one. There's an old FN badge on the rear fender.'

Foxy offered Tim a tissue. 'Try the boot.'

'This is better.' Tim removed the handkerchief with the 'MK' monogram from his jacket. 'It belongs to the owner.'

Foxy studied the embroidered material as it lay in his hand. 'I don't like it,' she said. 'Use my tissue.'

'It's just a handkerchief.' Tim wrapped it round the handle. With a soft clunk the boot opened, a dim bulb lit the interior.

The boot was lined with a plush burgundy carpet. A cardboard stationary box sat to one side. Taking up most of the space beside it, a large hessian sack bulged with something bulky and heavy.

Tim looked down at the sack with cold dread. Foxy's hand crept into his. Gratefully he held it tight.

'What do you think it is?' Foxy whispered, her eyes as round as saucers.

'I don't want to know.'

'I know what you mean. I want to close the lid and walk away, forget we ever saw it.'

'We can't.'

'I know that too.'

Gingerly Tim reached into the boot and prodded the sack. He pushed it again, harder. 'I don't think it's a body.'

'Are you sure?'

Tim swallowed. 'Fairly sure. Also—the smell.'

'What do you mean?'

'There isn't one.'

'You need to take a look.'

'Me?'

'Yes, you.'

'Right,' Tim said.

'Well, go on then.'

Tim squared his shoulders. He took a moment to memorise how the sack lay, then opened the neck and looked inside. Relief flooded through him. 'Oh, thank goodness.'

'What— What is it?' Foxy asked.

'I don't know. It looks like a bit like coal, a bit like black, knobbly potatoes.' Tim reached into the sack and extracted a dark, round lump a little smaller than his own fist, a squat and bumpy ovoid heavier than stone. The knobbled surface was smooth in some places, pitted elsewhere.

Foxy took it and turned it in her hand, puzzled. 'That's very strange. I'm sure I've seen this before.'

Tim took it back and slipped it into his pocket. 'Let's see what's in the box.'

As he lifted the lid the stairwell door banged open. Footsteps moved crisply across the car park.

Foxy and Tim crouched down. The boot light shone on their faces. Tim reached up and eased the boot lid down. The strange lump lay cold and heavy in his pocket. Whatever it was, what reason could there be for a sack of it lying in the boot of such a beautiful old machine?

A sluggish starter motor churned, an engine burst into life. Transmission whined briefly as the vehicle moved across the car park. The metal roll-door noisily clattered up on its chains, the car drove up the ramp and the door rattled down again.

'We should go,' Tim said.

'Wait.' Foxy pulled some printed sheets from the box and quickly looked them over. 'They're all the same. OK, let's go.'

Tim replace the box lid and refolded the top of the sack as best as he could remember. The boot closed with a soft clunk, the light went out.

Back where they had come in Foxy slipped off her shoes, reached through the gap and put them on the pavement.

'Here'. Tim cupped his hands and made a step. Foxy stepped up into his hands, her foot warm, muscular and strong. He took her weight, she slipped neatly through the gap.

'Come on,' Foxy had her shoes back on. All Tim could see of her was her feet and ankles. 'I'll help you.'

Tim put his hands on the sill, jumped up, and fell back. The skylight was too narrow, he couldn't get enough leverage to push himself through. He tried hooking up one leg but it was too high. He lost his grip and fell hard onto the concrete.

'You all right?' Foxy peered through the gap.

'Yes, but I don't think I can get out.'

'Try again.'

Tim jumped again. Foxy grabbed his collar and pulled. His head and shoulders emerged through the gap. Foxy pulled again. Tim swung a leg up, wriggled, twisted and rolled. Scraped and dusty, he was through. Tim stood up and brushed himself down. He looked at Foxy's broad, yet feminine shoulders with renewed respect. 'You're pretty strong.'

Foxy dusted off her hands. 'I do a bit of swimming.'

Trafalgar Lane was deserted. Wind gusted fitfully, a tattered white plastic bag spiralled into the air then rolled along the street. While they had been underground the sky had darkened, Thunder rumbled over the hills of Ditchling beacon.

Foxy gazed at Tim, suddenly serious. 'We did it, Ace. We found the car.'

'We did.' Tim was more than half amazed himself. He thought back to the pen and map, Foxy's unquestioning support. His life was changing for the better and she was the reason. 'I couldn't have done it without you.'

'Thanks.' Foxy smiled. Hesitantly she lifted her hand. 'You've got a smudge on your chin.'

'So have you. On your nose.'

He reached out. Foxy bobbed her head and ducked away. She produced a tissue from somewhere and dabbed the smudge away. Her comb appeared in her hand and with three strokes, left, right, and down middle her plait fell apart and her hair rearranged itself into cascades of loose, bouncing curls.

Self-conscious at his own scruffiness Tim ran his fingers through his hair. A few drops of rain spattered down. Tim took a chance. 'Let's go for a drink.'

'Sure,' Foxy said, then froze. 'Damn. My jacket.'

'I gave it to you,' Tim said.

Foxy looked down into the car park. 'I must have left it in there. Dammit, I can't remember—'

'What's in it?'

'Nothing. It's just a jacket.'

'I'll fetch it,' Tim said.

'No, don't bother.' Foxy looked up at the darkening sky. 'Let's go for that drink.'

'I don't think we should.'

'Oh, yes, I see what you mean.'

'Wait here and help me back up.' Tim lay flat and swung his legs back into the gap.

With a rumble of thunder, the heavens opened. Foxy shrieked as a deluge of rain poured down drenching everything.

'Don't worry,' Tim shouted over the thunder, 'It won't last.'

'I love it!' Foxy cried.

Tim looked back and saw her in the middle of the road with her head thrown back and arms wide.

'You'll get soaked!'

'I don't care.'

Then she looked down at herself and gave a panicked cry. Saturated by the rain her blouse was near transparent. Her arms covered her chest, she turned away. 'I have to go.'

'No, wait, your jacket,' Tim cried. He rolled to his feet, slipped on the wet pavement and barked his shin on the kerb. He clutched it in agony. 'Wait, Foxy. I can't get out on my own.'

But she was running.

'Wait.' Tim rubbed his leg, trying to hop and run at the same time.

Foxy turned the corner.

The rain stopped as suddenly as it had started. Dark clouds parted and the evening sun shone down, the air filled with the oddly pleasant smell of wet pavements.

'Foxy.' Tim called. He ran to the end of the street. 'Foxy.' It was no good, she had gone.

Rainwater dripped off the end of Tim's nose and trickled down the inside of his collar. The elation he felt at finding the car vanished. Despondently he began to make his way home.

Then he slowed as he remembered something and the spring returned to his step. Foxy Bolivia had called him 'Ace' and she'd said it like she meant it. It was a good feeling.

Adoration & Terror

One floor from the top the lift halted. The doors opened and Smith looked out onto an open-plan office. Right in front of him several office workers, young and old, male and female, waited for the lift. Horrified at the thought of them all squeezing into the lift with him, Smith stepped out. The office workers piled in. As the doors closed a middle-aged woman with permed hair said, 'Oh, it's going up.'

Smith looked around. The office ran the length and breadth of the building, the work space divided into cubicles by chest-high partitions. Doors opened on a stairwell at the far end, windows formed the walls on either side. Smith stood in an open space in front of the lifts. A water cooler stood between two vending machines. Smith thumbed the button to recall the lift then refilled his water bottle from the cooler.

Low conversation came from behind a partition, a man and woman talking. Smith listened attentively.

'Still working, Heidi?' the man said.

The woman sighed. 'I'm getting there, Mr Abercrombie. Some of the accounts just won't balance.'

'How long——?'

'Another day if it goes well. If not…' The woman's voice tailed off. Smith liked her voice, it made him think of smooth things like velvet and double cream.

'Heidi, this is very important. Can you stay on a bit?'

'I suppose so.'

'I'm so sorry. You have plans.'

'No, Mr Abercrombie, not this evening I can do another hour or two.'

'Thank you very much. I won't forget it.'

Smith's fingers were wet, his bottle was overflowing. He put the bottle away and ineffectually rubbed his foot over the damp spot on the carpet.

The lift pinged, the doors opened to reveal a stocky man of middling height in a blue boiler suit and paint-spattered boots. He had untidy greying hair, two days' stubble on his seamed and friendly face and a pencil behind his ear. A battered yellow metal toolbox rested beside him on the floor.

'All right, Lofty?' The workman beamed. 'Get out too early did you?'

'No,' Smith lied and immediately felt guilty. 'Yes. Maybe.'

Smith entered the lift. The workman peered up at him. 'This your first day?'

Smith nodded.

'Thought so. Tell you what, you stick with me. I'll show you round and you can give me a hand. How about that?'

Smith nodded again, wondering how this had happened.

'Smashing. Right, I'm Ralf, Mr Tuppence if you want to be formal.'

The lifts at the top floor opened into an enclosed foyer. Smith followed Ralf through a pair of doors and discovered the rest of the floor was a single open space without partitions and cubicles. It was occupied by a small army of carpenters, plasterers, electricians and fitters.

There were step ladders, trestle tables, rolls of carpet, stacks of boxes, reels of electric flex, two scaffolding towers, sections of air-conditioning ducts, a pyramid of paint cans, a double row of bubble-wrapped chairs. Right in the centre dust sheets covered an enormous table.

It was organised chaos and there was noise, lots of noise.

Some of that noise came from power tools, saws and hammers. The rest of the racket was shouting from the workmen swarming across the room. Smith wasn't sure exactly how many there were because they kept moving around, climbing the towers, disappearing into gaps in the floor, peering into the ceiling void, carrying things from place to place, jumping up and down and clutching a thumb and swearing, or wandering about with a mug of tea and laughing at the state of some half-finished job.

The workmen up the ladders shouted to the ones on the floor, the ones on the floor shouted at the ones in the floor void. The ones in the floor void probably shouted too, but nobody could hear them. The only time any of them stopped moving was when they leaned against something and watched everyone else with a superior air.

'Here you go, matey,' Ralf said, offering Smith a mug of tea. Not knowing what else to do, Smith took it although the level of liquid was far higher than looked safe.

Ralf pulled a rumpled scrap of paper from his back pocket and studied it intently, his lips moving as he read. 'Finalise partition in front of rest rooms. That's the gents to you and me. Righty-ho and off we go.' Ralf scurried away through the room swinging his yellow toolbox. Smith followed, carefully carrying his mug. It seemed there was little choice, much like the times his mother decided he need a bath or a haircut. He was being organised. This time he didn't mind. It looked like fun.

The room was fascinating. Patterns were forming, things were happening. Stuff was being put together and occasionally, accompanied by muttering, shaking of heads and rolling of eyes, taken apart again. And always shouting. Lots of shouting.

Smith decided he loved it.

'Oi, matey!' Ralf shouted at Smith. 'Pop your mug on the floor and cop hold of this.' He offered Smith the end of a long piece of two-by-four. 'That's it, hold it steady.' Ralf ran a tape measure along the wood, licked his pencil and made a mark. He measured again. 'Lovely.'

'Lovely,' Smith bellowed.

Ralf gave him a look then laughed. 'Measure twice, cut once, that's the trick. Come along, can't stand here all day.'

Time passed. Ralf measured, sawed, tenoned, bevelled, drilled and screwed. Cold and empty tea mugs were replaced with brim-full hot ones. Smith tried a sip and found it was strong, hot and very, very sweet. 'I like tea.'

'Pukka, this is, matey,' Ralf agreed.

In no time the partition was up with plaster board screwed to one side while the electricians added fittings to the other.

Ralf yelled across the room. 'Oi! Bert, what's left?'

A pot-bellied, slope-shouldered man in a check shirt, braces and jeans pointed to a stack of two-foot-square aluminium grills with his mug. 'You could stick those somewhere useful.'

'Yeah, and I could think of somewhere,' Ralf guffawed. He turned to Smith. 'Fit them into those air vents down by the bottom of them walls.'

Smith worked his way round the room. It was easy, the grills were light and just clipped on.

'That's us done, Lofty.' Ralf drained his mug. 'Quick wash up, down the tavern for a swift one, then pick up a fish supper on the way home for me and the missus.'

'Blimey,' Ralf tapped the washroom sign as he went through the door. 'This is for both men and women.'

'That's a bit modern,' the man behind him said. He looked round nervously to make sure no females had secretly joined the end of the queue.

'It's how they do things in Finland,' Ralf pronounced sagely. 'I've heard they're all Scandinavian over there.'

The entire room had been transformed. The carpet was down, the chairs unwrapped and placed around the uncovered table. All the ducting had been fitted into the overhead void, the scaffolding towers were parked against one wall beside a heap of dust sheets.

'Still here matey? Don't forget to clean up.' Ralf exited the washroom, hands scrubbed, his spikey grey hair slicked back.

'Righty-ho, pukka, cheers!' Smith walked into the washroom just as the last of the other workers pushed out past him.

With the exception of a waste bin overflowing with used paper towels the workers had left the room spotless. Toilet cubicles stood along one side, white enamelled basins and mirrors along the other. At the end of the room three windowless doors opened onto shower cubicles.

Smith's head hummed with the sights and sounds of the evening. Sawing wood, banging in the nails. Bang, bang BANG! Tea, piping hot and sweet. And all the shouting, with nobody going hush or shush, nobody telling him to keep his voice down.

For the first time in several hours he thought about what he should do next. He filled one of the basins with warm water. He was tired and very hungry. He stood motionless for a moment with his hands in the water then washed and dried his face and hands and went back into the main room.

The side walls were glass from waist-height to ceiling and black with night. Smith looked down on the streets of Brighton. Lines of traffic moved along the neon-lit roads, parallel ribbons of lights, one red and one white. A maroon and cream double-decker bus halted at a stop. Condensation from his breath clouded the glass as he counted the passengers embarking and disembarking. Five people off and eight on. Interesting.

He began to calculate how many stops it would take before the bus was full, but to do that he needed to know how many people were on the bus to start with. Assume none. No, if it were none then five people could not get off. Assume five.

He drew the calculations in his breath on the window. His tummy rumbled, he was starving.

He wiped away the sums with his sleeve. Come on, he told himself, this needs some Good Thinking.

Getting in was lucky. If he went home now he wouldn't be able to come back. This adventure was a real one, not dangerous but far too exciting for it to end now. He would have to hide, but where? The floor below was open-plan. Assume the other floors were the same. There would be no Good Hiding there

Smith took in the great empty space around him. Hide under the table? No, that was silly, even with the sheets over it he was bound to be spotted. He considered the suspended ceiling, still incomplete and with gaps through to the void beyond. The scaffolding towers would give easy access but the roof tiles would not take his weight. Then an idea came to him that made him laugh and clap his hands. It would work but first he would need supplies.

Down at the vending machine Smith used the money he'd taken from his mother's purse to buy chocolate, crisps, and bourbon biscuits. He was busily stashing everything down the front of his fleece when a mellow female voice behind him said, 'So you had to work late too?'

It was Heidi. Smith felt desperately awkward and big and acutely conscious of the crisp packets poking out the top of his fleece.

Heidi was neither short nor tall and possessed what Smith's mother called the fuller figure. Her straight, shoulder-length hair was a rich glossy red. She wore an ankle-length blue-black skirt and a long-sleeved black woollen top that Smith couldn't help noticing was filled with female bosom. Chins were two, her eyes grey-green. Her bottom lip and left nostril were pierced with small silver rings. For the first time in his life Smith experienced the simultaneous emotions of adoration and terror.

He beamed inanely. 'Yes indeed. Correct. Carry on.'

'I thought I was the only one,' Heidi sighed. 'I've only been here a couple of weeks, I'm not sure I like it. Mr Abercrombie keeps asking me to work late.' She whispered conspiratorially, 'I don't think he's got a first name.'

Abercrombie. Useful information. She was really close. Smith's anxiety grew, he felt the Hand stir. It wanted to come out but Smith didn't want it to. He wanted to talk to Heidi or run away. Ideally, both. He clenched his fist, took a step back and bumped into the vending machine.

'Are you new too?' Heidi said.

'Yes, today.' Smith winced at the sudden, high pitch of his voice. His face ached from grinning, he blew out his cheeks. 'Started today.'

Heidi held out her hand. 'Welcome to Kylma Kala. I'm Heidi Tollund.'

Trapped. Her nails were the same deep blue as her skirt. Seeing no other option Smith shook her hand. Her grip was firm, her skin cool. 'Measure twice, cut once,' he blurted and stuffed his hand back into his pocket.

That was me, the Hand protested in Smith's mind. I can get you out of here.

Heidi gave a good-natured laugh. 'That's good advice. What's your name?'

Argh, she was good at this. 'Derek.'

Hand, the Hand grumbled. I'm the Hand.

'Well, Derek, I'm going to finish up and get the hell out of here.'

'Get the hell—' A trickle of sweat ran down the back of Smith's neck. 'Pukka plan.'

Heidi stepped away. 'Nice meeting you, Derek.' She waved with her fingers. 'See you around.'

Smith fled to the lift and thumbed the button for the top floor. The doors slid open, he tumbled inside and slumped against the wall as the doors closed behind him.

The Hand came out, swung round and stared Smith in the eye. 'Lucky escape,' the Hand said.

'Yes.' Smith wasn't sure who had escaped from whom.

Back on the top floor Smith cleaned his teeth and topped-up his water bottle in the washroom. He pulled a dust sheet from the pile and carried it to one of the ventilation grills he'd fitted earlier. He unclipped the grill and squirmed feet first into the vent and pulled the dust sheet in behind him.

Smith lifted the grill back into position and snapped it closed. He backed into a wider space, it was a tight squeeze but there was room to turn. Oblong ducting ran left and right, wider than it was high. Dim light spilled in at intervals from the wall vents. Smith squirmed down the ducting on his elbows, the metal thrumming and bonging as he went. Midway between two grills was a safe and cosy spot. He wriggled out of his fleece and arranged his chocolate, biscuits and crisps in a neat row along one wall. His toothbrush, water bottle, torch, notebook and pen went along the other. He shook out the sheet and kicked it down over his legs, folded his fleece for a pillow, laid his head down and shut his eyes.

For a few minutes he could not sleep. What an adventure this was! Had anyone ever done anything so daring? Not himself certainly. Smith had discovered he was a daring man indeed. The ducting was cosy, secure and safe. There was food in the machines, toilets and washbasins, water, and safe places to hide. He could live here almost indefinitely.

He yawned and snuggled into his fleece. Sleep claimed him as he thought about Heidi, how nice her voice sounded, and how she had little dimples across the backs of her knuckles.

The Fool in Time

LITTLE BOXES with black glass eyes were attached to the corners of buildings. Some were motionless and some could move. Every now and then one would turn and follow Asklepios. He didn't like that one bit.

He had walked back inland to try and find his bearings. It was no good, his sense of direction had deserted him. North felt like south, west was east. Whenever he felt like he was going the right way he ended up in a part of the city he had never seen before.

Now he was light-headed with hunger and thirst. When he saw a passer-by drop unwanted items into a bin Asklepios swallowed his pride and sat in a nearby shop doorway. A man threw away what looked like a bottle half full of water. Asklepios went to retrieve it. He heard a voice, a hand touched his shoulder. He turned, head down, ready to face more anger, ready to run. It was a young woman in a purple headscarf and a multi-coloured dress. In her outstretched hand were a few coins.

Asklepios' heart nearly broke. He cupped his hands and she tipped in the coins. 'A thousand blessings on you and your family.' His voice cracked with emotion. The woman smiled in incomprehension and turned away.

By showing his coins to a stallholder and pointing at his goods Asklepios was able to buy a bag of nuts and dried fruit. He sat on some nearby steps, ate a handful and felt a little better. It was humiliating but he would be able to survive scavenging and begging. He continued to wander. The window of a shop caught his attention. It displayed several objects he recognised and valued. Pens and styli, paper and ink, and measuring instruments made of the flexible transparent substance that was so common here. One instrument was a simple rule, though marked with superb precision and regularity. Another was a variation of the set square, a triangular section of a rectangle, again with each side exactly marked and divided.

It was the third item that caught his eye, a half circle with numbered lines radiating out to the edge. Lost in thought, Asklepios pressed his nose against the window and stared. Drawing a perfect circle was easy, requiring nothing more than stick, twine and chalk. It was the angles, the proportionality, the placement of the items around the circle that was the weakness in his summonings. Scaled up, this instrument was exactly what he needed.

He had to have it.

The shopkeeper, a lanky stooped man with slicked-over hair, eyed Asklepios suspiciously as he entered the shop. Smiling pleasantly, Asklepios strolled between the shelves, inspecting various items. The shopkeeper served another customer, Asklepios innocuously returned to the front of the shop. His heart pounded, his hands were damp, he had never stolen anything in his adult life. What if the eye-boxes followed him? What might they call down? No matter, he had to take the risk. He reached into the window display and snatched up the protractor and other instruments.

'Hey!' The shopkeeper erupted out from behind the counter.

Asklepios fled through the door and away into the streets, his three prizes clutched in his hand. He dashed across a busy road, turned into a side street and slowed, joining in with the other pedestrians. He risked a look behind him. There was no sight or sound of pursuit. He sighed with relief. Foolish, so foolish, but he had what he wanted and it had been worth it.

Moving with the crowds he found himself on the promenade overlooking the sea. Here was another marvel—a small town built on a platform of hundreds of legs out over the sea. An enormous mirrored ball slowly turned on one of the roofs. Far to his right lay the colossal wreck of another such town. No doubt there had been a war and one town had been victorious.

Asklepios descended to the beach, sat on the shingle and stared out to sea. The fact that he was alone and the sun was setting barely registered. When it was dark and he was shivering with cold he finally broke from his reverie. The town over the sea blazed with light and brash music. Behind him the city on the land was also brightly illuminated.

He needed somewhere to sleep, somewhere he would not be found. He trudged across the shingle towards the ruined sea town.

The sand against the road wall was still warm from the sun. He curled up there, sheltered from the wind under the rusting pylons of the ruin. How could there have been war when there was peace in the city, when so many races lived together? Something else must have happened.

All day he had walked through a city of riches. The night lamps stood atop metal posts in every street, the marvellous vehicles were built from the same material. This ruin he crouched under contained more iron than he had ever dreamed existed, yet nobody bothered to reclaim it.

How could such plenty, such knowledge and power have been lost? With growing certainty Asklepios decided he must be in the future, not the past. He looked down at the stolen instruments in his hand and felt very foolish. He had been wrong about so very many things.

A night wind blew. The lights of ships moved far out across the dark water. Hugging his knees Asklepios looked out to sea awed by the immensity of time.

Hardball

Early that evening at the Princess Royal Hospital Troy Jarglebaum studied the mass of direction signs with a sullen heart.

Crap jobs, he thought unhappily. I'm still getting all the crap jobs.

Once upon a time it had been lack of experience. Now Jarglebaum knew it was his age and the fact he was still a Detective Sergeant.

He had realised several years ago that he was never going to make Detective Inspector. At first, so he told himself, it was because he was a renegade. A free spirit and innovative thinker whose left-of-field methods rubbed the senior officers up the wrong way. Later he convinced himself being partnered with Tim was the reason.

Resentment knotted his guts as he trudged into the hospital. Jarglebaum was a good cop, clever and resourceful, tough and gifted with insight. The one thing he never understood was that it hadn't been the lack of results that had been the problem, it was how he had dealt with them.

Over time Troy came to see himself as unlucky, a plodder, an old-time cop, the guy who always arrived a moment too late, the man who missed the vital clue. Slowly he had stopped believing in himself.

He'd lost his coppering mojo, but now he'd had a break, the one he'd always deserved. Now he was moonlighting for Koponen his luck was going to change. The Finn had a hard business nose, a real player. More importantly he valued Troy's experience and police contacts. Jarglebaum was going to ride to a better life clinging to Koponen's coat-tails.

Meanwhile there was still coppering to do.

There she was, in a bed in the middle of the ward. Some youngster, her hair like candyfloss, her eyes red-rimmed and bloodshot. Right hand and arm plastered to the elbow. Just another kid who thought they were God's gift suddenly getting a nasty comeuppance and discovering that the whole world wasn't there purely for their own convenience.

Jarglebaum pulled out his notebook. Once he'd got this out the way he could go home, get down the boozer and pour this evening's quota of beer and cheap scotch down his neck.

'D.S. Jarglebaum.' Troy flashed his badge and sat down beside the bed. 'I'm sincerely sorry for what you have been through. How are you feeling, madam?'

'I'm OK.' Gabby vaguely waved her good arm. 'They gave me some stuff. It doesn't hurt any more but my head's on a go-slow.'

'If you feel up to it I need to ask you some questions.'

'Sure. Ask away, Mr Police-detective-man-person-son.'

Great. Troy flipped open his notebook and licked his pencil.

'Hey, you guys still do that,' Gabby said.

'OK,' Jarglebaum said, trying to appear interested, 'Let's start with your full name.'

'Gabby. I mean Gabriella.'

'Full name?'

'Sorry, head full of cotton-wool…'

Half an hour later Jarglebaum sat heavily on the wall at the bus stop. He tugged open his collar and groped for his hip flask.

Sometimes you needed a drink just to get your teeth unclenched.

Christ, that poor young woman had just been trying to earn a living and some freak sickos had fucked her up. So what that she had weird hair and probably a load of pointless modern affectations like vegetarianism and decaffeinated tree-hugging. She was just doing her best to get by. Cute too, in an unconventional way. Skinny, though skinny was OK, and also kind of beaky. Jarglebaum was old enough to acknowledge some of his own quirks. For reasons he'd never bothered to fathom a decent-sized schnozzle pressed several of his buttons.

The cheap whisky scorched Jarglebaum's gums as he sluiced it between his teeth. He'd been wrong about Gabby. He'd taken one look and jumped to conclusions and it was the wrong thing to do. That was his bad, an old man's habit, not the behaviour of a cop. He was meant to help people not dismiss them out of hand. It didn't make him feel good about himself. Jarglebaum took another drink then firmly put the flask away.

Hell, he'd make it up, he promised himself. He'd come back and see how she was doing, bring her some grapes, that kind of thing.

'Goddammit,' he growled and ground his fist into his palm.

The three scruffy young men standing beside him at the bus stop looked at him askance and took a step away. Jarglebaum had been so lost in thought he hadn't noticed them arrive.

'Sorry guys.' Jarglebaum held up his hands, taking in their unkempt but uniform appearance. Dressed in black drainpipe jeans, sleeveless vests, studded belts and torn jackets, the three looked back at him through the near-identical asymmetric haircuts.

They looked pretty disreputable, probably drug dealers. He didn't want any trouble. 'Just come from the hospital.'

'Sorry to hear that, dude,' the tallest, gangliest one said. 'You need a mobile you can borrow mine.'

Taken aback, Jarglebaum got to his feet. 'Thanks, I'm OK, really. It's not personal, I've been to see an assault victim, a young woman. She got messed up for no reason and it made me mad.'

'There are some shitty people in this world, man.'

Jarglebaum couldn't help but agree.

'You a social worker?'

Jarglebaum gave a dry laugh. 'I'm a cop.'

The three seemed unfazed by the revelation.

'That's cool job.'

'Helping people, solving crimes.'

They seemed sincere.

Jarglebaum felt disassociated.

I don't get this world any more, he thought, or it doesn't get me. I look at people and I can't work out who they are.

The thing was, it was worse than that. A lot of the whisky Jarglebaum swilled had been for himself. Despite the strong painkillers Gabby had given clear and accurate descriptions. Jarglebaum had a damned good idea who was responsible. Hell, no, he knew exactly who had crushed Gabby's hand and killed those innocent little animals.

He knew.

When he started moonlighting for Koponen he'd known the Finn played hardball and that had been all right. What successful entrepreneur didn't cut corners and pull the occasional fast move? That was the very reason he'd hired Jarglebaum. Unfamiliar with English law Koponen needed to know what he could bend and what he couldn't break, just how finely those corners could be cut before the law got interested. Koponen was all right but those three women of his were something else. Koponen didn't see it but he needed to be told. It wasn't going to be easy, the Finn doted on his mistresses, especially Dolores.

Exactly what had he got himself mixed up in? Jarglebaum fought off a wave of futility and self-doubt. Back in the old days he always knew which side he was on.

'You OK?' The young men looked concerned.

'Yeah. Yeah, I'm fine. So tell me, what do you guys do?'

'We're a band, modern jazz. Petersen and Brubeck up to Washington, those dudes.'

'I love jazz,' Jarglebaum exclaimed. 'You know Esbjorn Svensson?'

'Awesome.'

'Could never do what he did.'

A surge of goodwill filled Jarglebaum. He stuck out his hand. 'Pleasure to meet you guys.'

'Likewise, dude, likewise.'

That Word Again

TIM STRIPPED OFF his saturated leather jacket and hung it over the back of his office chair, where it began to drip on the carpet.

Why did life never run in straight lines? Maybe if it did more people would be able live without frustration and anxiety. Hadn't the evening been a success? Through the agency of something far beyond coincidence and luck he had found the car. In that light it was his dream come true: detection the way he wanted, using his own methods. And with the addition of an attractive and mysterious young woman as his accomplice. So why did he feel so low?

Whatever had made Foxy run off, he hadn't done anything wrong. He needed to believe that. Something had happened and when she was ready she'd come back and tell him. He had to believe that too.

He fetched an old newspaper to catch the drips under the jacket then sat heavily in the chair. If he hadn't done anything wrong, what had he done that was right? It didn't feel like much. Jarglebaum had picked up the bottle, the pen had fallen on the map. Foxy had found the car.

Maybe it had all just been coincidence after all.

A defiant little light burned inside Tim's head. What if these things were happening all the time? What if these clues were scattered all around and magic was no more than seeing what was hidden in plain sight? Ritual simply created moments that helped you see what was already there.

At least he'd have Dolores and Electra off his back. He'd found the car and earned their money. No more threats, no more rearrangement of the architrave.

The flaw in that line of reasoning was that Imelda probably didn't need a reason.

The phone rang.

'Hey. It's me,' Foxy said.

Relief flooded Tim, he forgot all about his doubts and worries. 'Hey. What happened, Foxy? Why did you run?'

'It was… Well, it wasn't you, it was the rain. I was getting soaked.'

Tim heard seagulls faintly calling. 'Where are you?'

'Walking along the beach road. The sea is up, the waves wild and grey. I can taste the salt on the west wind.'

He wished he was there. 'Thanks for helping me.'

He heard the catch in her breath. 'I'd do it again.'

'You mean that?'

'Sure.'

'I don't know when. That was the only real case I had and now we've found the car, it's over.' Belatedly he realised how much that sounded like a brush off. 'But there's something else is going on and I want to discover what that is.'

'That sounds mysterious.'

'It's odd. Dolores, the woman who employed me, never said the car was stolen, just missing. She also told me it was her husband's car. The two things I do know about her are that she's a liar, and she paid me a lot of money to find the car.'

'Enough for you to not ask too many questions?'

'I think that was the idea.'

'That garage isn't easy to get into with that automatic door.'

'So the person who left it there works in the building. I can find out who the owner is.'

'And there's that sack of rocks in the boot. They bother me, there's something about them, I'm sure I've seen them somewhere. We should find out what they are too.'

There was that word again: We. 'What was on those papers you took?' Tim said.

'Advertising about farming and plants,' Foxy said. 'I'll bring them round.'

'Now?'

'In the morning.'

He kept the disappointment from his voice. 'See you then.'

It was only after he put the phone down that Tim remembered that Asklepios had been gone for hours.

Tension

Violet and Albert Smith looked up and down the street through the bay window of their front room. The sun had set and the street lights were on. A few stars twinkled in the gaps between the rain clouds. It was well past their normal bed time.

'I don't know where he's gone.' Violet defensively folded her arms.

Albert jingled the keys in his pockets. 'You should have made him tell you.'

'Oh, Albert, you know I can't do that. If Derek doesn't want to tell you something he just won't. It's always been difficult. Now he's grown up half the time I don't know what to do.'

Keys jingling, Albert stared silently out the window.

'If you were around a bit more…'

'It's not my fault the boy's the way he is. I do have to work.'

A gap grew in the conversation, a distance that had grown familiar over time and reluctantly been accepted by them both. They had all the advice and help anyone could want while Derek grew up. People said they were being too protective, too smothering, but he was their son. Now he was grown, now that it was too late and they all lay in a bed of their own making, all they had left was doubt, and guilt, and wordless blame. It was easier to pretend everything was fine. Except that now it wasn't.

Violet tentatively took her husband's hand. 'That's not what I meant, Albert.'

Albert stood stiffly for a moment, then unfroze. His arm went around her shoulder. 'I know, my love. And I didn't mean to snap.'

'I'm sorry.'

'So am I.'

Holding each other was like a balm. The tension between them faded, and was gone. For a while.

'What do you think we should we do?'

Albert considered. 'I think we should call the police.'

Worry

MRS WOOSENCRAFT was not as young as she used to be but when it came to wrestling cats she was still up there with the greats. Her technique combined soothing words, dexterity, strong wrists, and cold deception.

It's not easy to fool cats. They might not be as smart as you[6] but they're not daft either.

Over the years Mrs Woosencraft had come to believe the insouciant élan cats so effortlessly projected was little more than a cover for paranoia, suspicion, and anxiety. That said, the average cat also possessed distinctly unaverage levels of self-esteem and would try to maintain a worldly indifference to potential unpleasantness for as long as felinely possible. Especially if it thought another cat was watching.

Her standard opening move was a big hug, soothing words, ear-scritches and slow movements. All these encouraged even the most wary cat to believe the sink full of warm soapy water it was being carried towards had absolutely nothing to do with its own immediate future. Part of the wrestler's art was allowing cats to deceive themselves. That, a firm and gentle grip, a stout coat and a pair of canvas gardening gloves.

The Way of Wrestling Cats[7] can be summarised in two maxims:

Win the match before it begins.

---

[6] *Debateable.*

[7] *Moggy-Do*

Really. Win the match before it begins.

Once you were locked into a tussle not only had you lost, but so had your jumper.

Mrs Woosencraft demonstrated her mastery with Pedwar. A balletic turn towards the sink resulted in Pedwar's expected lunge for freedom. A reverse turn used the power of the animal's own leap and she simply steered the cat through the air into the suds. Presented with total defeat and the weight of her hand on its neck it sulked.

Another thing about cats is that they look a lot smaller when they are wet. Considering the risks Mrs Woosencraft never felt any need to be magnanimous in victory. Laughing at soggy cats was one of life's guilty pleasures. Right now she would take anything positive out of this disaster.

'Out you come.' Mrs Woosencraft lifted Pedwar out of the water and wrapped him in a towel warmed on the oven rail.

Pedwar yowled plaintively. Even his little stub of tail managed to appear forlorn. He gave Mrs Woosencraft a look that said 'I trusted you,' and sneezed. Three or four cats peered round the door from the safety of the sitting room, curious, worried, relieved it wasn't them.

'Poor little poppet,' Mrs Woosencraft chuckled. 'You shouldn't chase bees round my glue pot.'

Regaining a little poise, Pedwar suffered himself to be patted dry. Especially under the chin.

Glue still matted Pedwar's back and flanks. One ear appeared stuck down but he shook his head and it came free with a soft 'plap'.

Pedwar trod the towel down and curled up. He watched Mrs Woosencraft with eyes filled with reproach.

'What are we going to do with you? Brushing's no good, so it's either leave it or cut it.'

Pedwar gave a few tentative licks at his matted fur, then pulled at it with his teeth.

'Right, then. I don't want you swallowing that stuff, so scissors it is. I'll be as careful as anything, don't you worry.'

Mrs Woosencraft's brow furrowed as she snipped away at the clumps of glue-ruined fur. It was a dratted inconvenience. Respect where it was due, however. Whoever had done this had known exactly what they were doing.

The thing about having nineteen cats, about using them to find the things and people nobody else could, was that they all needed to be in the right place at the right time. That in itself was only slightly less than impossible but the indivisible nineteen was a powerful tool. With Un Deg Naw missing and Pedwar thoroughly discombobulated it was socding hopeless. Seventeen? There was no way she could do what she was trying with seventeen.

The glue had formed a layer on top of the fur. By cutting carefully Mrs Woosencraft found she could snip away just the ends of the hairs.

She thought about the bumblebee, stopped snipping fur and looked at the freesias Tim had brought her and counted nine aromatic, blossomy sprigs. Pedwar gave another plaintive yowl and she returned to her barbering until it was done.

'A bit scruffy, but you'll do. Off you go and try and be a bit more careful.'

Pedwar dropped off the table and trotted up the kitchen steps. The cats at the door trooped after him and although he did not acknowledge them his body language somehow became smug.

'And you lot be careful too,' Mrs Woosencraft scolded. 'We've got a job to do and there can't be any more distraction. Food on the plates, this is. We all need the work.'

She gave her attention back to the flowers. Nine pretty sprigs. Add herself, Tim, Pedwar, and the bee, and that made a very interesting number. Everything coming together in the right place at the right time wasn't easy. Who could have done that? Who had the knowledge? And most importantly, why?

Ever since that slow Thursday afternoon when old Ethel Godwinsson said 'Oh,' like she had just remembered something nice, sat back in her armchair and died, anything she had left to learn about the magic of Deg Naw Wyth was going to stay unlearned. Ever since Mrs Woosencraft had taken up her quest to find others like herself and been drawn, first to the big smoke, then south and south again down to the sea and been recruited by her foreign employer. Nothing like this had ever happened before.

I didn't bloody well think there was anyone left, she thought.

It was good to know, and a worry too. A worry and a challenge. And it had to have been deliberate because it was just too sodding inconvenient to be chance. Of all the things Mrs Woosencraft believed in, coincidence was not among them.

Someone was out there and they'd had a go. So be it, she was more than capable of having a pop back. They had come at her through the air, she would return the compliment with interest.

Mrs Woosencraft set to work. If she had her way somebody was going to go on a long and unexpected journey.

Complicity

DOLORES was changing. Her dreams told her so, her thoughts, her desires. All three frightened and excited her in equal measure. As time went by it became harder and harder for her to tell the difference.

Of the three of them Dolores was the most prone to such conflicts of emotion. Imelda relished confrontation, met aggression with aggression and walked open-armed and smiling towards a fight. Electra was too rational, too cerebral to let fear touch her. 'The physical responses to fear and excitement are the same,' she once told Dolores. 'So choose to be excited.'

Ever since they met at college in New England the three women had done everything together. Each acknowledged the other's differences and different needs, a trio without conflict, without jealousy. They never lied. If one of them wanted something or someone they just said. Koponen had been perfect, a man whose ego and appetites were large enough for them all, whose wealth, ambition, and generosity gave them the freedom to indulge their own dreams of exploring the world's oceans, of seeing it all. To know it and understand.

But Koponen was not like them. Over time the flattery to his masculinity of having three beautiful, intellectual and passionate mistresses gave way to a deeper attachment to Dolores.

The three women remained content. Imelda and Electra occasionally joined with Koponen in erotic experiment while Dolores used her greater influence to get them all directorships in Koponen's company. It was a tax efficient way for Koponen to give them money.

Then something else changed, something that had never happened before. After all, three may be indivisible but four can be divided in several ways. Typically Dolores was the last to realise. It took Electra to tell her why.

Koponen had been raging at the loss of another deep-sea drone. He thumped the table with his fist and fulminated at the incompetence of his marine engineers.

'It's not their fault,' Electra said.

'I know.' Koponen slumped back in his chair and petulantly flicked his pen spinning across the desk. 'They are good people, skilful and experienced, and I am being unfair. Once more there is delay and expense and I am frustrated. Perkele! We are getting nowhere. There is no mining, no revenues, and still we do not know why.'

'Send someone down to take a look.'

Koponen waved the suggestion away. 'It is too deep. The bathyscaphe would be near the limit of safety.'

'There are better models.'

'Yes, yes,' Koponen clenched his fist. 'More delay, more cost. These vessels cost millions, what choice do I have?'

Without understanding why Dolores felt words rise up in her mouth. 'We'll go.'

Koponen shook his head. 'No, my dear, it is far too dangerous.'

'Markus, listen. We're qualified and we're experienced. We can find out what's wrong and restart the mining operation. Let us go and save all that time and money.'

We? Electra and Imelda were speechless with astonishment. We?

'What the fuck did you say that for?' Imelda said when the three were alone.

Dolores couldn't see the problem. 'Markus is in trouble, we can help him. After all he's done for us, how can we do nothing?'

'Easily. It's fucking dangerous.'

Dolores shook her head. 'This is what we've been trained to do.'

'Not at ninety-eight percent of operational limits. Why couldn't you keep your mouth shut?'

'Because she's in love with him,' Electra said.

'What?' Imelda laughed in disbelief. 'Is that really true?'

To her immense surprise Dolores discovered she couldn't deny it.

For a while they tried acting as though nothing had changed. That was why, in the end, they agreed to the dive. By the time they returned to the surface everything was different.

Now Dolores lay beside Koponen in his bed, naked under the covers. Even here, safe and secure in Markus's arms her belly trembled with nerves at what would soon happen to her, Imelda, and Electra. In the past there had always been the thrill of complicity, of watching Electra and Imelda and wondering what they were going to do next. She was the passive one but it was her who had set them on this wildest of paths.

Am I mad? Dolores thought. I yearn for Tuoni, I love Markus yet conspire against him.

In one sense it didn't matter because it was too late. Tuoni waited in her dreams, more than dreams for Electra and Imelda were there too. Yet whatever that creature really was he was no more lord of the underworld than she was his daughter, Kivutar. Not yet. They were just stories plucked out of her mind from the myths and legends Koponen loved to tell. Stories that would, over time, become true.

Koponen stirred beside her and woke. Dolores rolled against him and kissed his mouth. She ran her hand down across his chest and stomach and took hold of his sex.

'Tell me about Loviatar,' Dolores breathed into his mouth.

Koponen lay still for a moment then said:

'Old Lowyatar, that wicked witch,

Eyeless daughter of Lord Tuoni.

The ugliest of her father's children.

Of all hell's women, the very worst.'

His recitation faltered as Dolores caressed him, ceasing entirely when she pulled him onto her.

Koponen's presence, his certainty, their sex, had always been reassuring. She needed that now more than ever. Tuoni's kingdom under the Atlantic was not the dreary hell Tuonela, Electra could never be Loviatar, she was too beautiful for that fate. Whatever happened none of them could truly become those monstrous myth-women.

Yet a worm of doubt still gnawed.

Markus looked down at her. 'What's wrong?'

'Nothing.' She moved her hips and felt him move deliciously inside her. 'I love you.'

It's Not Stealing

'No, madam, I'm a detective. We don't always use marked police cars. Sometimes we need to blend in.'

Violet studied the beefy detective seated on one of their dining room chairs. A cup of her instant coffee cooled on the table beside him. He'd refused the offer of something stronger. Violet had offered in the hope he would say, "Not while I'm on duty" and had not been disappointed. His refusal left the distinct impression it was not what he would have preferred.

In all other respects the officer conformed to her preconceptions: he was overweight, his collar was tight and his tie was loose, his black shoes were well polished and at least size twelve. These signs, plus the way he scribbled in his small notebook, convinced her that he was a genuine officer and not one of those 'bogus constables' she had read about in the local paper.

'I've never seen a badge before,' Violet said, handing it back to the detective. 'I wouldn't know if it's real or not.'

'I can ask for uniformed officers to attend if you prefer, madam.'

'I'm sure it will be all right,' Albert said.

The detective sat forwards, his paunch rested on his knees. He licked his pencil again. 'Has Derek done this before?'

'Oh no, never. He's a good boy really.'

'How old is he, Mrs Smith?'

'Thirty-two, Inspector.'

'Detective Sergeant, ma'am.' The officer looked up from his notebook. 'He still lives with you?'

'Yes.' Violet felt her voice grow tight, she gave a short high-pitched cough. 'You see, Derek is a teeny bit special. He can't look after himself very well. The doctors say he's got—'

Albert broke in loudly. 'Derek's brain is wired up a little differently from you and I, Detective Sergeant. The doctors have lots of clever-sounding theories but they don't know why he's like he is or what to do. He's an intelligent lad and given the right encouragement he's perfectly capable of taking care of himself.'

'I understand, sir. Has he been in trouble before?'

'Never. He's not delinquent, he just sees the world differently.'

The policeman wrote again in his notepad.

The conversation turned to what Derek had been wearing: his blue fleece, he always wore his blue fleece; that he liked buses and trains but he didn't like travelling on them; the money he'd taken from Violet's purse.

'Do you have a photograph?'

Violet stood up smartly. 'Yes, I have one ready for you.'

The officer put it in his pocket without looking and pushed himself to his feet. 'Derek will go on the missing persons register. Because of his—differences I'll flag him as a vulnerable person. Try not to worry too much. People disappear all the time, often they do it on purpose and most of them come home. Forty eight thousand people were reporting missing last year. Forty seven thousand nine hundred and seventy two of them turned up safe and sound within a week. Here's my card. If he returns, or you think of anything, call me.'

'Thank you,' Albert said.

'Thank you very much indeed.' Violet felt very reassured.

Albert showed the officer out. Violet put the kettle on. Albert was by the window when she brought the tray through. They sat down together.

'I didn't know he took money from your bag,' Albert said.

'He's been doing it for ages. It's not stealing.'

'Well, I didn't know.'

Violet took Albert's hand. 'He never takes much.'

Albert sat in his chair, the one best lined up for watching the television. 'Forty eight thousand is a big number. Do you think he made it up?'

Violet blew gently on her tea. 'I expect some people disappear more than once. It's a habit.'

'Did he mean country-wide or just this county?'

'I don't know, dear.'

Albert gave a non-committal grunt. 'I didn't think much of that policeman at first. Bit of a slob, but he seemed to know his business.'

Violet picked up the card. 'D.S. Troy Janglebaum', she read. 'I wonder where his parents came from.'

The Ziggurat

WHERE THE HELL was Asklepios? It was dark and late and he had not come back from his walk. Tim chided himself, he should never have let that irritating yet likeable man go out on his own.

His leather jacket was still damp, he put it on anyway and walked to the end of the street and stood at the corner. Amber street lights illuminated a road with sparse traffic, fewer pedestrians and a lone cyclist.

There was little more he could do unless he wanted to spend the entire night walking the streets. Brighton was a reasonably safe town. Little harm was likely to come to Asklepios unless he was very unlucky. He would have a far better chance of finding him in daylight.

Tim returned home. Worried, he stayed up for another hour in the hope of hearing a knock on the door. He read a book, his eyes drooped, he dropped the book and jerked awake. This was achieving nothing. He took himself to bed, briefly lay in the dark making plans to locate Asklepios before he fell asleep…

…and found himself alone in a broad and deserted avenue of black-leaved trees. A blustery wind surged in the high branches. He looked up at the clouds billowing in the night sky and instinctively knew he could fly.

Tim took three steps and sprang into the air. Strong winds shoved him steadily out to sea. Far over the heaving water enormous clouds piled up in a roiling black mass. Lightning flashed soundlessly inside the clouds. Frightened by the sea-storm, he fought his way back to land against the relentless winds.

Brighton lay quiet and dark, a monochrome city of elaborate empty houses and windswept streets lit by a sparse scatter of streetlights.

Out at sea the storm clouds flattened into a titanic anvil-shaped thunderhead and spread towards the coast.

He looked for landmarks, there was nothing he recognised. Dream Brighton architecture was grand and uniform, every building a Palladian mansion. He rose higher, battling the wind, hanging close to the coast. The Royal Pavilion must be here, that white onion-domed folly was its own dream even in the waking world.

Irresistible gusts flung him towards some enormous trees. He caught hold and clambered into the swaying branches. The trees were stupendously high. Far below and far away he saw the white domes of the Pavilion among the black buildings of the dark city. A glimmering silver thread ran from the building. He pushed out into the air and the sea-gale flung him down towards the needle-sharp tips of the white domes. Tim kicked and struggled, he dropped into calm air in the lee of the Pavilion. The silver thread shimmered through the night, he followed it past palatial beachfront hotels into an alley that narrowed and narrowed so the beetling walls of rough black stone scraped claustrophobically against his body. Then he was free again and soared high over the shingle beach.

Monstrous waves crashed on the shore, pebbles sucked and roared in the surf. The silver thread ran on. Far down the beach a light flared. Tim swept towards it. A windswept figure stood among the tangled ruins of the west pier: Asklepios, lost and alone in the dream lands. He saw Tim and raised his arms.

This is my dream, Tim thought as he swept down, gathered Asklepios in his arms and rose into the sky. *I can take him home.*

The mist brightened then cleared. Tim hung over a narrow, dusty street flanked by whitewashed walls set with high, tapering archways. The air was warm and dry, spiced with heat, mint, and orange blossom.

Yes. Asklepios reached out happily. *Thank you.*

The mists rolled back, cloying, smothering. Blinded and disoriented, Tim felt a hostile third presence. It buffeted them, dragged and shoved them this way and that. Dislocation followed, Tim fought to hold his position. Then, once again there was bright sunshine and balmy air, a magnificent walled city of towering ziggurats. A throng of olive-skinned men and women in pleated white robes strolled along a broad paved way.

Tim had brought Asklepios home. He released him. Goodbye. Farewell.

No! Wait, Master! Asklepios cried, but he was falling, the scene fading into the mist.

Tim floated peacefully, the dream diminished. He stirred, awoke briefly in his own bed, and slept again.

Some Evil Force

THIS WAS NOT home. Aghast, Asklepios looked about him. Filling the sky, a titanic stepped pyramid of stone and brick rose three hundred feet into the air. Between it and himself a massive brick archway spanned a paved street wide enough for an army to march down. Enormous statues of five-legged lions with eagle wings and bearded human heads flanked the archway.

Trumpets blared, a squad of spear-men emerged from the archway. Bare-chested, in knee length pleated linen kilts and leather sandals, each carried a bronze tipped spear. Behind them a man with plaited black beard and dressed in a robe of quilted gold rode a gilded chariot pulled by two asses. He wielded a golden staff, a heavy scimitar hung at his hip, a dozen javelins stood in a rack beside him.

A young woman with a babe in arms looked Asklepios up and down and moved away. His blue jeans and t-shirt attracted unwelcome attention. A man carrying a rush basket full of dates confronted him, questioning and suspicious in a language Asklepios had never heard before.

Terrified, smiling blandly, Asklepios backed away on quaking knees. The man repeated his question and raised his voice.

Down the street came a great shout. As one the spear-men slammed the butts of their spears on the ground. The warrior in the chariot pointed his gilded staff directly at Asklepios.

The thronged street fell silent.

Moaning with fear Asklepios tottered backwards. The date seller reached for him. Terror gave Asklepios strength. He knocked the man's hand away, turned, and ran for his life.

Shouts came behind him, the sound of many running feet. Asklepios took a side turn to the left, another to the right. He burst out into a broad way lined with stalls of date and oil merchants, basket-weavers, cloth-sellers, bakers and jewellers. Another alley beckoned across the way. Asklepios dodged into it.

Washing hung on lines above his head. Asklepios snatched down a white linen sheet, hurried around a corner and found himself in a dead end with a solid wooden door set into the wall

His left hand hurt abominably. He still had the stolen measuring instruments and clutched them so ferociously tight the bevelled edges had cut his palm. He relaxed his grip, a little blood flowed and he fought down a mad giggle of hysterical laughter.

A tumult of excited voices swelled in the market. Asklepios froze, paralyzed with fear. The voices died away, Asklepios carefully put the instruments aside and rubbed his face with trembling hands. He had a moment to himself, he must not waste it.

Hastily he kicked off his trainers, rolled up his trouser legs and stripped off the t-shirt. Then he folded the linen sheet he had stolen into rough pleats and tied it around his waist, a simple version of the garment many of the local men wore. None of the men he had seen were bare-headed. He bit through the seams of the t-shirt with his teeth, tore it into strips and folded and tied a rough turban.

His skin was as dark as the city folk. His crude disguise would have to do. He picked up the instruments and took a shuddering lonely breath. He would learn, he would survive. He calmed his breath and returned down the alley barefoot into the marketplace.

He found a place to sit, far enough away from the stalls that the owners would not think him a thief, close enough to watch and learn. Everything about this city was deeply strange, from the gigantic stepped temples and mud-brick walls, where each brick was stamped with identical insignia, to the mannered way people walked and the warrior in the golden chariot. Only the earthy human aromas of the market were familiar.

He had been so close! Master Tim had found him with his dream-magic and carried him home. He had smelled the orange blossom and almost been able to touch the pink plaster walls. Almost. Then some evil force had cast them aside, perhaps the work of some great djinn he had crossed. If only he had never tried summoning them. He was cursed and would never find his way home. Despondency filled him and he wept.

A Bad Idea

'GOOD MORNING, gentlemen, ladies.' The man's voice had a lilting accent and was quietly authoritative. Drowsing in the air conditioning vent, Persistent Smith came awake instantly. He listened to the soft bumps and thuds of furniture as people seated themselves around the big table in the top-floor room.

'I apologise for the partial facilities,' the man continued. 'The new boardroom will not be complete for a few more days but we do have power, networks and, ah yes, environmental control.'

A gentle breeze stirred Smith's hair as a cool, steady wind blew through the ducts. Smith lay still, the events of the previous day thronged in his mind: sneaking in, Ralf and the builders, Heidi, the mission itself. Excitement coiled within him, the Hand emerged and looked Smith in the eye. 'Let's take a look.'

Smith packed his toothbrush, torch, notebook and water bottle into the correct pockets then elbowed his way towards the nearest vent. When he arrived all he could see were legs: black wooden table legs, metal chair legs, and the legs of the humans sitting on them.

'Item one, mining operations, progress in the past twenty-four hours,' the man said.

'No change in status, Mr Koponen,' a woman replied. Her tone was authoritative, definite. 'We dispatched another of the new drones at dawn. Once again we lost contact at a depth of approximately one point eight miles.'

Smith gasped and bit his lip. Markus Koponen! The man who owned all the Chrysler Imperials in Finland.

'Surface weather?'

'Continuing fair for at least another thirty-six hours. The *Iron Herring* remains at anchor above the mid-Atlantic ridge.'

'An endless waste of time, money, and resources.' Koponen sighed heavily. 'We will cease operations and resume only if— No, when we find her. We have to find her, we must.'

Smith wanted to see Koponen. He wormed his way along to the next vent but could still only see legs. He remembered the suspended ducting in the ceiling void. 'Let's go,' he whispered to the Hand.

At the far end of the room the ducting sloped steeply upwards. Smith started up, but as soon as his feet left the flat he slid back. The angle was too steep, the metal too smooth. Wriggling and twisting, he rolled onto his back. His knee knocked one wall, his elbow banged on the other. The thin metal bonged and wabbled like a mutant gong. Smith damped the noise with his hands and the noise subsided. He and the Hand exchanged a worried look.

Koponen's voice came from the room. 'The environmental system has some teething problems. Let's move on to better news—the harvest is in and transhipment to the docks will be complete tomorrow.'

Flat on his back, with his feet pushing against the floor and palms pulling against the roof, Smith worked his way up the slope slowly and quietly.

The ducting ran across the roof in three parallel arms. Smith crawled into the first one. Immediately the ducting began to sway in its suspension rods. He waited for the motion to cease then moved cautiously forwards. The view from the first vent was poor, he continued to the next and could look down on the table. On the far side a paunchy middle-aged man sprawled in his chair, a black-haired woman in a low-cut red dress sat beside him.

Directly below Smith was a man wearing a white Stetson, his face concealed by the brim. Two more women sat on his left, the hair of one nearest to him was as white as the hat.

The man in the hat passed round sheets of paper. 'This summarises projected mean yield per hectare, non-crop biomass above and below the soil level, petal cover as a percentage of area, total field albedo, nitrogen and CO2 capture, and so on.'

Now Smith could match the voice to the hat. He was right above Markus Koponen, if only he could see his face. Smith took out his pencil and pad ready to take notes.

The woman with black hair began to smoke an electric cigarette.

The paunchy man beside her scowled. 'Do you mind?'

'Not in the slightest.' She tipped her head back and blew smoke into the air. 'Markus, those yields are remarkable.'

'Thank you. I am very pleased.'

Smith gazed down the front of her low-cut top transfixed by the sight of her breathing.

'It's a trap.' Valiantly the Hand covered his eyes.

Smith jerked back, banged his head against the ducting and dropped his pencil. Metallic booms, pops, and creaks filled the air. Panicked, Smith scuttled backward. The swaying increased. With a bang like a gunshot one of the support rods sheared. Directly in front of Smith a joint in the ducting split open. Helplessly he watched the pencil roll through the gap and drop onto the suspended ceiling.

This was not safe! He hurriedly retreated.

Down below, the paunchy man laughed humourlessly. 'That sounds like more than a teething problem. It's not the only one you've got, believe me.'

Koponen spoke tersely into the desk phone. 'I don't care if it's your day off, the system sounds like a dustbin full of spanners. Perkele! You're the building manager, get out here and manage.'

He banged down the receiver. 'Apparently he's sending somebody called Ralf. Time presses, what is next?'

The white-blonde woman beside Koponen said, 'Wassiter's still looking for the cat.'

Koponen shrugged. 'It always was a long shot.'

Wassiter? Smith's heart raced. They were talking about Tim. Had he misheard? Were they really talking about a cat and not a car? He needed to write things down but the pencil was Missing In Action. He would have to remember.

'I can help,' the Hand said. 'I'll remember for you.'

'Be quiet,' Smith hissed.

'But I can do Good Re—'

Smith forced his fingers open. The Hand vanished, its voice faded to an echo. Smith listened to the conversation below.

'Wassiter's keen,' Electra said. 'He's put missing cat posters on half the lampposts in Brighton.'

'Mr Jarglebaum, what about the car?'

A cat and a car. Smith had heard correctly. He paid close attention.

'He's doing better with that.' Jarglebaum tipped a lady's green jacket out of a black plastic bag. 'I found this in the car park.'

'That's not his.'

'Obviously. He's got some help. I've met her and she's as ditzy as he is. In her case it doesn't matter, she's a real looker.'

'Do you know how they found it?'

Jarglebaum grimaced. 'They'll tell you it was magic, divination with a map and a pen. Wassiter's a dreamer, she's filled the part of his head that isn't already stuffed with nonsense with her own rubbish.'

Koponen put his hat on the table, revealing thinning blond hair. 'You underestimate Tim Wassiter. He's an unusual man—'

'You've got that right.'

'—and this proves what I suspected. He has real talent and we were right to choose him.'

Jarglebaum folded his arms behind his head. 'It's your money. I think they got lucky. You'll be surprised how much detective work comes down to getting the breaks.'

'I'm sure you know.'

Jarglebaum pushed the green jacket across the table. 'Any of you ladies want this?'

'Not my colour,' Electra said.

The body-language of the black-haired woman made it clear something about the jacket intrigued her. Smith was not surprised when she said, 'I'll take it.'

Jarglebaum stuffed the jacket back into the bag and pushed it across the table.

'Thank you, Mr Jarglebaum,' Koponen said. 'That is all for today.'

Jarglebaum took a breath. 'Mr Koponen, I need a word.'

'What about?'

Jarglebaum looked at the three women. 'It's private.'

'Don't mind us,' Imelda said.

'Sorry to disappoint, but I do.'

Koponen studied his watch. 'All right. Ten minutes once we're finished. What else do we know?'

'She's definitely here,' Electra said.

Koponen spread his hands. 'Of course she is. The missing cat proves it.'

'I mean she's been seen. In a pet shop. I talked to the shopkeeper.'

Now who were they talking about, Smith wondered. And why had the fat man Jarglebaum gone so still?

'You're sure it was her?' Koponen said.

'We had a very thorough conversation.'

'Did you get her credit card receipt?'

'She paid cash.'

Koponen slapped the table. 'So close! You must find her. Everything depends on this. Everything. Forget about the car, it's served its purpose. Use your electronic equipment. Do what you must.'

'Our pleasure, Markus.'

The three women departed and Koponen and Jarglebaum were alone.

Now he had his moment Jarglebaum found himself reluctant to start. This wasn't going to be easy. He braced himself. 'Electra and Imelda are doing things you need to know about.'

'What things?'

'The sort that could get you a lot of very bad publicity.'

Koponen doodled geometric shapes on his notepad. 'My girls have been through a lot and it has changed them. They're no longer carefree, I know that. Post-traumatic stress is a well-known phenomenon. I make allowances, so must you.'

Koponen looked up. Jarglebaum saw a degree of vulnerability he never suspected was there. 'I don't like it, Mr Jarglebaum. I accept it and do my best to help them. I don't like it because their problems are a direct result of something I once asked them to do.'

Then Jarglebaum told Koponen about his interview with Gabrielle at the hospital. He didn't mention her name, or the type of shop. As he talked Koponen embellished his doodles with overlapping squares and triangles, straight lines and spirals.

'Electra and Imelda,' Koponen said when Jarglebaum finished. 'What about Dolores?'

'She wasn't involved.'

'She's a good friend.'

Jarglebaum shifted awkwardly. 'Sure.'

'We live in a litigious world, Mr Jarglebaum. Everyone has an eye on the main chance. How did that shop assistant first describe her accident?'

'She said some boxes had fallen.'

'Then she changed her mind.'

'Yes.'

'I don't doubt Electra and Imelda asked her some questions, I don't doubt they may have raised their voices. But do you not think that having realised her last customers were obviously wealthy, this low-paid shop girl might try a little blackmail?'

Jarglebaum believed in keeping his powder dry. 'She was the owner.'

Koponen stopped drawing. 'Many people would rather pay up than see their names in the papers.'

'I saw the X-rays and the doctor's notes. She made the first story up because she was frightened.'

'Can you prove any of this?'

Jarglebaum's shoulders sagged. 'No, I can't. Look, Mr Koponen, Electra—'

'Is with me, Mr Jarglebaum. So are Dolores and Imelda.'

'I know that, sir, I—'

'You don't have a partner do you?'

'Married twice, didn't work out.' Jarglebaum tried a disarming grin, 'Look, boss, you took me on because I know the law. I know what you can bend and what you can't break. And one thing you can't do is go around breaking people. Keep that up and you risk a whole world of unwelcome attention.'

'If that's what happened.'

Koponen's words hung in the air. Jarglebaum felt himself becoming angry. He had something else to say and he was going to say it. It might be a bad idea, it might even cost him this lucrative job. He couldn't help it, he tried not to shout and didn't quite succeed. 'There's another reason. You shouldn't hurt people. You shouldn't smash their hands to make them tell you what you want to know.'

The silence after his outburst was deafening. Koponen studied his doodles and nodded his head. Finally he said, 'I hear you.'

Jarglebaum had said his piece. He stood up and walked to the door.

'One more thing,' Koponen said.

Jarglebaum stopped walking but did not turn.

'None of this leaves the room.'

Jarglebaum walked on. It seemed he'd kept his job. He was no longer sure that he cared.

Dolores reached the lifts well before Electra and Imelda and was already inside one when they arrived. 'I'm going shopping. See you later.' She gave them a little wave as the doors closed.

An unpleasant popping sound came from Imelda's hands as she cracked her knuckles.

Electra pressed the button to call the other lift. 'Does that hurt?'

'She's such a bitch,' Imelda said.

'She thinks she's so special.'

'Just because she and Koponen—' Imelda scowled. 'It's not fair.'

Electra tossed her head. 'I don't care.'

'Nor do I.'

'We have Tuoni.'

'And he has us.'

At night Tuoni, lord of the drowned underworld, called to them as they slept. When he fully woke they would join him in an embrace far more intimate than any they had ever shared with Koponen.

Imelda met Electra's pale-eyed gaze and smiled. 'He has Dolores too. She needs reminding.'

The Zone

IN THE SAME way most of the mass of an iceberg lay unseen below the surface, so did the greater meaning of the front room of number 23. The mantle clock, condiment set, aspidistra and candles were eye-catching in their own ways but it was their relative positions that were the main business of the room.

Mrs Woosencraft gladly shared the rest of her home with the cats but no four-footed creatures ever entered her front room. They were curious all right, all cats are. Every now and then an inquisitive furry face peered through the door, one paw hesitantly poised above the threshold. The paw never descended, they never went in.

The room wasn't a temple, nothing in it was sacrosanct or sacred, there was no mystic anti-feline radiance. It was just the place Mrs Woosencraft practiced the one thing that most exercised her intellect and to a significant extent defined her—the magic that allowed itself to be known quite wrongly as Deg Naw Wyth.

In that sense the room actually was Mrs Woosencraft. When the cats looked in, she looked back. Like young children at the threshold of an adult's private room they hung at the doorway, lost their nerve and quietly slipped away.

When Mrs Woosencraft first came to Brighton the glass animals in the display case felt more important. Rulers, set-square, protractor, and significant amounts of time had all been used to place them exactly as she felt they needed to be, in their relative positions and the alignments of their gaze.

She came to realise that all that careful arrangement was prevarication, a delay that could be better spent actually getting on with what needed to be done.

Also, the one that was supposed to be a duck but looked like nothing that had ever quacked kept falling over.

'It's just a lot of fiddling about,' Ethel Godwinsson once said. 'The only good it can do is help you focus. You may as well bake a cake or have a poo.'

The clock needed winding once a week, the aspidistra liked having its leaves wiped with a damp rag. They and the candlesticks drew down focus, centred and balanced the room. The angles between them were exactly right. It was all she needed and she knew it. Today, however, with sunlight slanting through the windows, she prevaricated with her glass animals. She turned the red octopus and the deer, adjusted the stance of the giraffe and balanced the almost but not quite a duck.

The dachshund came from Bangor, the pelican from Solva. The glass fly, perhaps the strangest beast in her glass menagerie, come from Prague, a present from one of Ethel's nephews.

Ethel Godwinsson had passed on. Her bungalow was sold to developers and that was that. Mrs Woosencraft might be the last practitioner of the craft but she hadn't given up hope. With the wisdom of luminaries such as Keith, Heegner and Cataldi to draw upon and the affinity of her cats for a certain type of oceanic person there was still every chance she would find what she had come to Brighton to look for. More to the point—who.

Losing her cat, had been a major set-back. Cats did disappear every now and then. They were nosey and they weren't as clever as they thought they were. Surprise led to panic, panic to flight, and flight to well, unfortunate encounters. Wherever Un Deg Naw had ended up she hoped the silly thing was happy.

Her absence had forced Mrs Woosencraft to 'borrow' a replacement so she had nineteen cats again.

That 'borrowing' brought a pang of guilt whenever she saw the original owner.

A disappearing cat was one thing, the bumblebee quite another. Some person with power had stepped in, rattled her cage and literally buzzed off again. She'd paid them back tit-for-tat, but still didn't know the who or the why. It was high time she took a deeper look into what was going on.

Pen and paper, slide rule, compass, log tables, pencil sharpener and rubber lay ready. Mrs Woosencraft took her place at the black oak table and became the final component in the alignments of angle and distance in the room. She sat quietly, listened to the steady tick of the clock and harmonised herself with the symmetry of the room. Focus arrived, she was in the moment that had no name, where consequence could be seen before action, an answer known before the question, the effect before the cause. It was the place Ethel Godwinsson called 'The Zone'. She set to work on the calculations for her spell.

It was late afternoon by the time she had finished. When she'd considered the results they felt like some kind of melodramatic joke:

Two groups of four travel together.
A journey across water.
Monsters in the deep.
Danger.
Death.

Tonight We'll Dream

DOLORES KNEW something was wrong as soon as she was home. There was a vibe, a coldness that wasn't cool, a subsonic tension pervaded the room.

This room, like its occupants, was elegant and spare. A picture window looked out over the Brighton coastline. Two white leather settees flanked a glass-topped coffee table. A large fish tank, water and weed-filled but otherwise empty, occupied a recess in the wall. Above the tank were three unusual photographs:

The deep-sea exploration vessel *Iron Herring* with her bathyscaphe deployed on the crane;

The bathyscaphe submerged in sunlit, shallow water;

Deep-sea fumaroles along the mid-Atlantic ridge.

Imelda stood by the window, Electra sat with her legs tucked up on one of the settees. Dolores threw her coat and the green jacket onto the bed. 'What's wrong?'

Imelda turned from the window. 'We've been thinking.'

Electra patted the settee. 'Come and sit down.'

'All right.' Dolores sat beside Electra. They'd had their spats, she wasn't concerned. The three of them had been together since they'd discovered their common interests at that exclusive New England college. They had barely legal adventures, they got their kicks from taking risks, they were brilliant at oceanography. They bonded in their souls.

Now they were going to change. Yes, she had been the cause, but they would still be together. Things were bound to be different in a different world.

Electra smiled her icicle smile. 'We've been worried.'

'Worried you'd forgotten,' Imelda said. 'You've been spending so much time with him.'

For Dolores it was simple. 'I like Markus. He likes me. We like doing things together.'

'We noticed.' Imelda cracked her knuckles, one after the other. Pop, pop, pop.

Electra put her hand on Dolores' knee. 'Koponen won't change.'

'I know.' Dolores' eyes showed regret. 'He's done so much for us.'

'He nearly got us killed,' Imelda snapped.

'Not on purpose.'

'And Jarglebaum knows more than he's letting on.'

That was definitely true. Fat cop, yes. Stupid cop? Not in the slightest.

'The time will come when they will both need to be stopped,' Electra said. 'That time is very soon.'

Dolores' eyes widened. 'Stop Markus's plans, you mean.'

Imelda's nails dug into the leather of the settee. 'That too.'

'I—' Dolores began.

Electra lifted Dolores' chin with a finger. 'When that time comes Imelda and I need to know you won't hesitate.'

Suddenly Dolores understood the anxiety in her friends' hearts. 'You think I'd not come?' she exclaimed. 'You think I'd let you travel that wild path alone?'

Electra's flawless, ice-blue eyes shifted uncomfortably.

Imelda chewed her thumbnail. 'We've been worried.'

Dolores took Electra's hand in her own, reached for Imelda and pulled her close. 'I have dreamed the same dream as you. I have heard the voice of the sleeper. Ever since that day down in the deep we have a common destiny. Yes, I fear it, but I want it too. With you—' Her heart fluttered, she heard the words before she spoke them and knew she must be mad. 'With you at my side I would rejoice.'

'I want to have the nice dream again but you're never here,' Imelda said.

'Then I promise I will be tonight,' Dolores said. 'We will make a dark place and lie and dream of what will be. The three of us together.'

'Welcome back.'

'I never left,' Dolores said, then gasped as Imelda gripped her upper arm hard enough to bruise.

Angry tears sparkling in Imelda's eyes. 'You'll stay and never leave.'

'I can't.'

'I say you will,' Imelda said, squeezed her arm even harder.

Dolores tried and failed to break Imelda's grip. 'You're hurting me.'

'I know. Is it nice?'

Electra reached across Dolores, gripped Imelda's little finger and lifted. The finger dislocated with a sharp click, Imelda yelped and let go.

'Dolores is right,' Electra said. 'We don't work for Koponen anymore but he needs to think we do. She should go to him and find things out.'

Dolores solemnly nodded. 'I will do that.'

'Find out everything. Stay with him—until we swim in warmer waters.'

Imelda tugged at her little finger with her teeth. 'Tell us everything. Tell us THAT too!'

'Everything?' Dolores smiled.

'We want to know,' Electra said.

'We're jealous,' Imelda said.

Dolores hugged them both. 'Don't be. Not tonight. Tonight we'll have the Sleeper. Tonight we'll dream.'

'I'm hungry.' Imelda glanced at the fish tank. 'Let's go out. You talk, we'll listen.'

Dolores looked at the tank. Air bubbled up through the water, weed waved in the slow current. 'It's empty. Again.'

'I— yes, well,' Imelda grinned bashfully.

'Come on then. The sushi bar?'

'There's a new one up in the North Lanes,' Electra said.

'What's wrong with the usual place?' Dolores said.

'Imelda's banned.'

Dolores laughed. 'So there are things you need to tell me too.'

'Wait.' Imelda held out her hand.

The three of them studied her dislocated finger. Imelda gripped it, pulled out and down. The finger snapped back into place with a nasty, wet clack.

Imelda splayed her fingers, made a fist and nodded. 'All right, let's go.'

Electra kissed Imelda's cheek. 'Did that hurt?'

His Secret Heart

OVER THE COURSE of the day Persistent Smith and the Hand explored their new home inside the ducting. Smith slid from floor to floor down the slopes and elbowed up the ramps. The layout wasn't what he expected. He'd imagined each floor would be self-contained but he discovered servo-operated doors that closed or opened sections of ducting to redirect airflow within and between floors.

The Hand peered round a corner and pulled back. 'All clear.'

Those doors meant the tunnels kept changing. In fact there were two sets of ducts, one for warm air rising, the other for cold air descending. The doors routed the air streams, shunting the columns of air to where they were needed. That was a problem, for what had been a right turn on the way down might be a straight tunnel on the way back. Easy to spot when they were open, the doors were nearly invisible when closed. Smith resorted to rapping on sets of panels until he found the one that moved.

The constantly reconfiguring maze was disconcerting but Smith decided he liked it. It was a pattern that changed and he was inside it.

The Hand waited for Smith at the next corner.

'Are you sure it's safe?' Smith said.

'Absotively posolutely' the Hand replied. 'Follow me.'

'Not so loud,' Smith whispered. 'Pygmy head hunters live in these tunnels. They've been tracking us for days.'

The Hand looked at him in open-mouthed dismay, peered cautiously over Smith's shoulder, then snaked between his legs and looked down through a vent into a room of office workers. 'What about the prisoners?'

'There's nothing we can do for them.'

Once again an opening had closed. It would have been useful to make a map or mark the doors If only he had not dropped the pencil. Smith rapped on the panels, searching for the one that moved.

'Hurry!' the Hand said. 'The guards have heard us.'

Smith looked down through a vent and saw a puzzled face, a hand reaching for the telephone.

One of the panels moved. He pushed it and found an up-ramp.

'Come on,' Smith wormed through and pushed the flap shut with his feet. 'If we can make it to the next floor we'll be safe.'

At the top of the ramp he rested. Smith was a big fellow, a fact not helped by his preferred diet of crisps, biscuits, chocolate and fruit juice. Crawling through tunnels little wider than himself was hard work. He drank from his water bottle, squeezed the packet of bourbon biscuits, then decided to eat the crisps. Crushed by his own body weight the contents were reduced to crumbles. Tipping them into his mouth, Smith chewed, swallowed and drank more water.

Even the Hand seemed tired. 'What now?'

'Good question. Food is running out, water is low, and the pencil is M.I.A.'

'Tim found the car,' the Hand helpfully reminded Smith. 'Jarglebaum told Koponen.'

Which meant there was no need to stay here. It had been a Good Mission with Good Exploring but now it was over.

Except he didn't want to leave. Here he was, all on his own, with nobody to tell him it when to eat, sleep, or brush his teeth. Who else could say they'd spent a night hiding in an air conditioning system? And he'd met Heidi. As he recalled his conversation with her, Smith looked down at the Hand and felt oddly foolish. He'd like to see her again.

'What's up?' the Hand said.

'Just thinking.'

A few things still puzzled him. Why would anyone hire someone to look for a car when they already knew where it was? Who was the girl they were looking for? What had either to do with the ship and the harvest? Why were they looking for a cat? There was no clear pattern but there had to be one somewhere underneath. That was what was really interesting.

'We'll stay one more night,' he told the Hand. 'Listen in at the morning meeting and discover more stuff.'

He'd be quieter this time. Nothing would break, no pencils would go Missing in Action. This evening he'd get more food from the machine. In his secret heart he hoped Heidi would be working late again.

Between Her Toes

THE ROOM was dark, the air humid and close. Dolores, Imelda and Electra lay completely under the covers. Dolores' legs made short, kicking motions. Inky blackness was all around as they sank deeper and deeper. The probing beams of the bathyscaphe showed nothing at all.

Imelda sat in the pilot's chair, her hands rested lightly on the control joysticks, her eyes scanned the camera screens, gauges and dials. She steepened the angle of descent and they sank lower.

Beside her Electra monitored her own set of instruments, her face serene with concentration and underlit by slowly phasing green and yellow lights.

Dolores' own telemetry showed current flow, temperature, dissolved oxygen and salinity, and the state of their life support systems. She watched and waited. The familiar change in the reading came and a moment later she felt the bathyscaphe's trim adjust as Imelda swung the craft down and down towards the warmer water.

A psychic pulse swept through them like a searchlight—Tuoni. The three women exchanged looks of nervous anticipation. Imelda pushed the throttles open all the way. Outside, interference patterns from the ship's lights flickered green and pink along the beating cilia of comb jellies.

Electra shut down her monitoring. 'We don't need this.' She touched her belly. 'I feel him.'

'You really are here, aren't you?' Dolores' mouth was dry. 'This isn't just my dream.'

Imelda reached for Dolores' hand. 'We're really here.'

The thought of encountering Tuoni alone awed them. Together it was something they could do.

Silent, dark and unchanging, the silty grey realm of Tuonela stretched endlessly below them, vaster than continents, ancient before life crawled onto dry land.

Buckles snapped open, restraint webbing whirred back into its housing as Imelda freed herself from the pilot's chair. She turned a key on the overhead console and flicked a row of metal toggles. One by one systems shut down. Engines stilled, lights dimmed, air scrubbers fell silent. The bathyscaphe drifted two miles below the surface of the Atlantic ocean.

Under the dim red maintenance light Imelda's face glowed with the same ecstatic trepidation Dolores felt thumping in her own chest.

Tuoni's mind, his desires, swept through them again.

Madness.

Electra spun the wheel of the hatch lock. She put her hand on the release lever and broke the seal.

Needle thin jets of water harder than steel carved into the decking, driven by three hundred atmospheres of pressure.

Intrigued, Dolores held her hand under the jet. Skin and flesh sloughed away down to the bone. She watched her ruined flesh re-knit, the new skin hard and pliant and filled with knives.

'Let us join him,' Electra said, and pushed impossibly up against the titanic pressure on the hatch.

Black, boiling concussion crushed them.

Tuoni gathered them to himself. He slid into their minds and bodies.

Bring her to me. Bring me my wife, my sea-bride.

Yes!

You too shall bear my children.
Yes!

Afterwards they crawled exhausted from the bed and clung to each other, sweat-drenched and unable to frame Tuoni's awful rapture into human words. Such desires.

Dolores fell back, her mouth open in a silent howl of ecstasy and despair. Tuoni still seeped through her mind, dregs of the ocean ebbed within her. She buried her face in the bedclothes.

And recoiled. Something on her bed had been touched by the sea. Alarmed, Dolores groped for the light.

'What?' Electra croaked.

Dolores held up the green jacket. 'This. It's hers.'

Each time Tuoni came to them a little more of his essence remained. Electra and Imelda held the green jacket and gasped. They felt it too. It was hers, she was here. Wassiter knew where she was.

In the morning light Electra found Dolores sitting on the bathroom stool, her stockings pooled forgotten on the floor. Together they looked at the webs of skin growing between her toes.

Off Limits

TIM SAT against the parapet wall and watched his chickens. One sat down, fluffed its feathers and began a dust bath. The second stood and watched, black eyes bright. The third continued raking through the litter with one foot, head tilted as it studied the disturbed ground with one eye.

Slowly he became convinced the birds' behaviour in his presence contained an element of self-consciousness.

Could I do it? he wondered. Could I actually take one out, get a knife and—

The images of blood, flying feathers and frantic struggling were very vivid. There were also the insides to consider.

No matter how soft and feathery chickens were on the outside, they had slippery, and no doubt smelly insides. Tim considered the practical realities of divining with entrails. If he was going to use the chickens for the reason he'd bought them, he would of necessity become familiar with those insides while they were still warm and steaming.

He would have to rummage.

Tim looked into nowhere, lost in an avian Heart of Darkness. Blithely, the birds continued to bathe, peck or simply stare. In the back of his mind he grew aware of light footsteps clanging on metal steps.

A shadow moved across the sun.

'What are their names?' Foxy said.

'Foxy?' Tim jumped to his feet. 'Where did you come from?'

'Up the fire escape.'

Tim regarded her habitual tight knee-length skirt and narrow heels and tried to imagine her climbing the perforated metal steps. 'But how?'

Foxy beamed. 'Impressed, huh? I rang the bell and when you didn't come I counted the front doors, walked round the back and counted the ladders. Simple detective work. Even a man could do it.'

Foxy registered Tim's hurt look. 'I meant a man back from where I come from. Not you, obviously, because you are an actual real detective. One of those useless short-armed, oily—' She unclenched her fists. 'Anyway, you live here so you don't need to calculate which is your back door. Also a detective, which you are, would instinctively know… I'm babbling aren't I? Hi there. Good morning.'

Tim wondered how he would manage on the fire-escape in high-heeled sandals, his knees constrained by a narrow, knee-hugging skirt. The image froze, panned back and rotated through 180 degrees. He forced it from his mind and looked again at Foxy, her carefree smile, freckled nose and startling green eyes. Today her golden hair was again in a long plait, draped over one shoulder of a cream cable-knit sweater that made him think of salt wind, seaweed, outboard engines and choppy water breaking over half-submerged rocks.

Foxy noticed him staring at her sweater. 'Do you like it? I love this wool stuff, it's so soft. It comes from sheep, did you know that? They've got four legs and eat grass.'

The sweater clung in a distracting way, enhancing the gentle roundness of her tummy. It was actually quite sexy.

'It's good to see you, Foxy,' Tim said.

'You too.'

Tongue-tied, Tim felt his face freeze into a half-smile. Say something, he thought, but repartee had deserted him in his hour of need.

Foxy pointed to the bowl at Tim's feet. 'What's that?'

'Breakfast.'

'Aren't you meant to put milk in it?'

'It's for the chickens.'

'What are they called?' Foxy said.

'I don't know. Nothing. I haven't given them names.'

'What about their own names?'

Tim laughed. 'They haven't told me.'

Foxy crouched down and regarded the three birds. The one bathing paused, tipped its head on one side, wriggled and fanned its wings in the dirt.

'This one's called Dusty,' Foxy said.

'It's having a dust bath.'

'Of course, they want us to know their names so they're giving us clues. What about the one with white feathers on its breast?'

'Patch?' Tim hazarded.

'Correct! And the last one?'

The third bird had retreated to the far corner of the coop where it watched them, head jerking to its own internal rhythms.

'I think it's shy,' Tim said.

'Then that's its name, Shy. There, that was easy, now you know their names you can start to build a relationship.'

Tim looked at the birds. All three watched him with one bright black eye. Shy took a step forwards, then another. 'Let's go downstairs,' Tim said.

'I had this crazy idea,' he said when they reached his office. 'I heard a joke and it made me think. Foxy, have you heard about voodoo acupuncture?'

'No.'

'You don't have to go.'

Foxy looked at him.

'That's the joke,' Tim said.

'Right.'

'The joke's not important. It was a difficult time, I'd just left the police. I was unhappy and wondering what to do with myself. It was the idea in the joke that was important, that I could do things in a new way.'

He took a deep breath. 'I always wanted to be a policeman, Foxy. It just turned out I wasn't a very good one. Jarglebaum was right, our clean-up rate was the worst in the service, the worst on record. I wanted to solve crimes and help people but I wanted to do it my way. I wanted to use intuition, connectedness, and the things the police service call "alternative methods".

'All the evidence is out there, everything you need to solve a crime is just lying around waiting to be discovered. What if you could just go straight there? What if you tried something new, like voodoo, like divining, and use it to catch wicked people doing naughty things?'

'Is that why they sacked you?'

That hurt. Tim winced as he recalled his final assessment, the suggestion that he should reconsider his future. Consider it very carefully and then leave, preferably today. He could even take all his holiday. They were very polite, sympathetic even. Budgets were being cut, redundancies were coming and retention of the staff was very important. The right staff. So please would he take the redundancy, fuck off and leave policing to the professionals. Thank you for listening.

He hung his head. 'They were right. In the end I didn't want to be a police detective enough to give up my ideas and do things their way. I'd end up like Troy Jarglebaum. That joke was just a joke but it gave me a direction, it opened my eyes. The chickens were part of it.'

'How, exactly?'

Tim told her.

'Warm blood,' Foxy murmured dreamily. She blinked and looked at Tim. 'So, you really do believe in magic?'

'I believe there's more than just what's in front of our eyes. That pen stuck in the map and led us to the car but it didn't happen the way I thought it would. Somehow Jarglebaum messed it up and made it work at the same time.'

'Sheer chance?'

'I can't believe that's all it was.'

'Perhaps the situation needed a catalyst.'

'Last night something else happened too.'

Foxy leaned closer. 'What?'

'Asklepios, I—'

Explanation would take forever, Tim kept it brief. 'I dreamed I took him home.'

'Have you seen him since?'

'No. Foxy, it could have just been a dream, but it felt—'

'Right?'

'Real.'

Foxy took it all in her stride. 'You know, I don't think those chickens can help you. You should let them go.'

'I don't think they'd do very well on their own.'

'They're birds, they can fly.'

'I don't know much about chickens but I do know flying is not one of their strong points.'

'You should give them the option. Anything with real power would want a lot more than half a pint of bird blood.'

A good point.

'I don't think I could do it anyway.'

'And I don't think it would work. That sort of ritual needs an anchor to the world, a myth-bond, a weave of belonging in time and place.'

The drone of a hoover came up through the floor. Dust drifted in the window light. Nothing had changed, yet something was different. A stillness came into the air as if something had entered the room and was listening.

'You sound like you know.'

Foxy hesitated. 'Just things my mother used to say.' She opened her bag and extracted some papers. 'Anyway, I brought you these.'

They were the sheets from the box in the boot of the car, glossy promotional flyers with a picture of rolling farmland, fields full of a tall, white flowered crop under a clear blue sky.

'Growth, yield, profit,' Tim read. 'A new variety of long-flowering Canola (oil-seed rape). Increased yield with reduced fertiliser, an engineered cross with leguminous species.'

He dropped the sheet on his desk. 'A sales brochure for some new crop variety. If I was an arable farmer I might care. I might even like that it's got white petals instead of yellow, but what's this got to do with anything?'

'What's the name of the company?'

Tim read the banner. 'Kylma Kala. I'll see what I can find out.'

'I'll make some more tea.'

Foxy returned to find Tim in front of his computer. He tilted the screen towards Foxy. 'Kylma Kala: a privately-owned engineering, bio-tech and exploration company with registered offices in Finland. UK headquarters are 10–18 Kemp Street, Brighton. They're into everything: ship building, deep-sea mineral extraction, agriculture, crop breeding, environmental systems, it goes on.'

'Wow. Good work, Tim.'

'That's not all. Kemp Street backs on to Trafalgar Lane. The Chrysler was in the Kylma Kala car park.'

'Wow even more.'

'I'm not finished. In fact, I'm not sure I'm even started.' Tim pulled the handkerchief Imelda had given him from his pocket and spread it on the table. 'The people who hired me to find the car gave me this.' Tim tapped the embroidered MK monogram with his finger. 'Guess who the owner of Kylma Kala is? A man with a personal fortune of over four billion pounds. Markus Koponen.'

Foxy seemed lost for words.

'Wow?' Tim suggested.

'Maximum wow.'

'Why would someone hire me to find a car that was in his own car park?'

'How do you know it was him?'

Tim flourished the handkerchief. 'This.'

'They could have stolen it.'

'I have the feeling they knew exactly where it was.' A wave of gratitude washed through Tim. 'Thanks for helping me, Foxy. I couldn't have done any of this without you.'

Foxy's self-possession faltered for a moment.

Tim screwed up his nerve. 'Let me have your phone number.'

'Yes, of course.' Foxy wrote on his desk pad.

With the blinds down the room was cool and shadowy. So close to Foxy Tim could smell her crisp, clean ozone perfume. Despite her city shoes and smart tailored clothes, she was an outdoors girl. And something else too, glimpsed for the first time just a few minutes ago, a cooler, more considered personality under the surface. A clue to her past.

Foxy straightened up, her hip bumped his and there they were, face to face. It seemed natural for Tim's arm to go around her waist. After all, she'd just done the same with him.

'What about the sack in the boot?' Foxy said softly.

'Maybe—' Tim cleared his throat. 'Ah, maybe it's fertilizer.'

Foxy moved a little closer. 'How will you find out?'

'I can ask around.'

A faint scratching came from the top of the stairs leading to the roof. Tim decided to ignore it.

Foxy shifted her leg. 'Are you comfortable?'

'Not really.'

They shuffled a bit, came together, hip against hip. Up on the stairs the scratching escalated to scrabbling.

'That's better.' Foxy's hand lay his shoulder, lighter than a gull on a wave.

There were gold flecks in the green of Foxy's eyes. Tim saw her lashes were so pale they were white. He breathed in. Foxy did too. Tim felt her chest push against his. Tim pulled Foxy close. Foxy's lips parted, she closed her eyes. Her rounded belly pressed against his stomach. It was bigger than a few days ago, he was certain. He stepped back from their embrace.

'What's wrong?'

'Foxy. Are you—? I mean, do you have a—' Tim didn't know how to ask such a delicate, such a personal question. 'What I mean is, are you—?'

Wings clattering, trailing a plume of dust like a bomber with a wing on fire, Dusty the chicken burst into the room. She swerved around the ceiling light and ricocheted off the wall in a cloud of feathers. In desperation she attempted an emergency landing on the desk. Paper flew in all directions as she flew off the end and into the blinds.

Several minutes later Dusty was safely back inside the cage no worse for wear.

Tim snapped the lock on the chicken run closed and rubbed the scratches on his hands.

'Well, you're safe,' he told the chickens. 'I don't know what I'm going to do with you, but it's not going to be anything bad.'

Foxy was right, his half-baked ideas about voodoo acupuncture were just that. If he was serious about being some kind of new-age detective solving crimes the way he wanted to, then he needed to be serious about what he believed in and what he wanted to achieve.

Foxy left, promising to call. Tim heard her clatter down the stairs to the front door as he took Dusty back to the roof.

The doorbell rang a series of short bursts as Foxy said goodbye.

The rings made Tim smile but it was bitter-sweet. Foxy was the most adjectival woman he had ever met: beautiful, intriguing, funny, wise, intelligent, and mysterious, but she was also off limits. She'd have to stay that way until he knew more. Foxy wasn't putting on weight, she was pregnant, and that changed everything.

Mr Man

TIM TRIED to lose himself in work. On the surface the car job had been a good deal, well paid and ultimately easy work and he still had most of the money. Although he had no way of contacting Dolores, he was sure she or one of the others would call on him soon.

He was equally certain that if they didn't visit for a few more days he wouldn't mind. Perhaps he should keep an eye on the car in case it was moved. He could let down one of the tyres, though he'd need Foxy's help to get out of the car park.

Before that, the door frame needed repairing and Persistent Smith needed calling off. If no other work turned up there were all those leaflets to distribute.

He found a reputable carpenter and called the office number. The carpenter's wife took a message. 'He's very busy, dear. No, I don't know when he'll be back. Yes, you are on his list. Tara, pet, someone's at the door.'

Next, Tim called Persistent Smith's home. When there was no answer he decided to walk over and put a note through the door. Perhaps he would get lucky and see a missing cat or two on the way.

He glanced wistfully at the door bell as he went out, his finger drifted over the button. He shrugged, smiled. The sun was shining, it was a nice day, he'd been indoors too long.

As he walked he thought about Morse, that playful, partially competent and strangely water-loving cat who had been his inconstant companion and unwitting provider of emotional support for the past five years. It came as a shock to realise that he wasn't missing his cat quite as much as he had a few days ago.

The Smiths lived in a street of box-like semi-detached houses. Several stood behind high privet hedges, others had turned their front gardens into parking bays for sports hatchbacks with fat exhausts, over-sized people carriers, or rusting classics up on bricks and down on their shocks.

Some might say the Smith's front garden was a relic from a golden age, others that it was living testament to the abuses of plant breeding.

Beds of purple pansies, pink button daisies and orange marigolds surrounded a perfect diamond of dandelion-free lawn. The flower bed between the path and drive was a strip forest of shoulder-high lemon-yellow and blood-red dahlias.

The front door was of imitation white wood and frosted glass. The doorbell button said 'Press', just like his own.

Tim pressed it.

Westminster chimes dongled serenely inside the house. Nobody came. Tim tried again.

There was still no answer. He slipped his note through the letterbox, returned down the garden path and out onto the street.

'Coo-ee! Mr Man,' a woman called behind him.

Tim turned and saw Violet Smith hurrying towards him. The sun shone but she had dressed for winter. Emerald green bobbles danced on her hand-knitted woolly hat, her purple coat was buttoned up to the collar. A wicker shopping trolley bounced behind her.

'Hello Mrs Smith,' Tim said. 'It's Tim Wassiter, we've met before. You remember Derek sometimes works for me.'

Violet Smith's knuckles were white against the trolley handle. 'Have you seen him? Do you know where he is?'

'No, I haven't. What's happened?'

'Oh dear.' Violet seemed to deflate. Small to begin with, she looked like a strong breeze would blow her away. 'I had hoped…' Her eyes filled with tears. 'I thought…'

'Let's go inside.' Tim put his arm round her shoulders and steered her up the garden path.

Violet led the way into the hall. Tim carried the trolley over the threshold. Violet pulled a hanky out of the cuff of her coat, dabbed her eyes and blew her nose. 'Look at me going all unnecessary. I must look a proper mess.'

'You look fine. Now, tell me about Derek.'

Violet clasped her hands together. 'He's missing. We've had to call the police.'

Ekad's Justice

BANIPAL VISITED his nephew at the site of his home in the 'new city' on the western bank of the Euphrates. He admired the size of the plot of land then sat under an awning with his nephew and his wife and shared mint tea. After a mutual exchange of pleasantries his nephew asked him to oversee the dedication and blessing of the foundations of the house on a date yet to be decided by the family astrologer.

Ever since the Processional Way had been extended across the great bridge spanning the Holy River, new residential areas on the west bank had become highly desirable. Not only were they close to the temple quarters, they took advantage of the clean north-west winds before they blew through the old city.

A prosperous merchant, Banipal's nephew had decided to exhibit his success by building a large and expensive property. Anxious to have the blessings of both Marduk and Tammuz, who would both have altars in his new home, and the river god Ekad, whose waters he would cross every day, he planned a lavish series of dedications and sacrifices. As a close blood relative, Banipal could be trusted to make the arrangements with integrity and at a reasonable cost.

For Banipal, only recently returned from his hunting trip with Ishkun, it was a time-consuming nuisance. Nevertheless, it was a family matter and he was obliged to accept with good grace.

As he returned home over the bridge he came across a small but vociferous crowd surrounding two men hard against the parapet wall. Banipal went to the back of the crowd to see what was going on.

One man, plump and angry, was clearly a local merchant. The other was a bush-bearded foreigner well past his prime, undernourished and unkempt. He was restrained by two men holding his upper arms. The old man did not struggle, rather, he was listless and resigned. Banipal was intrigued to see that under a ragged and dirty linen skirt he wore leggings dyed a rich and unusual blue.

'What's going on?' Banipal asked one of the other men, a narrow faced young scribe missing his top front teeth.

The scribe took in Banipal's priestly robes. 'Holy one, the merchant claims this old one stole dates from his stall.'

'Were there any witnesses?'

'Apparently not, but the merchant's friends attest to his honesty.'

'What does the stranger say?'

The scribe grinned. 'That's the trouble. He lacks our tongue as well as coin.'

The problem was clear. Accused of a crime, the stranger was unable to defend himself or pay a fine.

'To be honest,' the scribe continued, 'He didn't have any dates on him either.'

This no longer felt fair. Banipal pushed his way to the centre of the crowd. 'A moment, if you please.'

Seeing his temple robes, the merchant dipped his head respectfully. 'Your servant, and the Gods'.'

'I understand you accuse this foreigner of the theft of some dates?' Banipal said.

'From my stall, yes.'

'But he has no dates on him.'

'Admittedly, but I definitely saw him take them.'

'How did this happen?'

'The starveling was loitering so I kept an eye on him. I turned away for a moment, he grabbed the dates and ran.'

'I also understand there were no witnesses.'

The merchant stuck out his chin. 'It is true nobody else saw this. If my word is in doubt, first let me say I have no reason to persecute a stranger. Second, my friends will vouchsafe my integrity.'

Several voices chorused agreement.

Banipal looked over the parapet at the deep, fast-flowing water forty feet below. 'In the absence of witnesses it would be a gracious gesture to not bind his limbs.'

'It will be as you suggest,' the merchant said. 'Let it not be said I am a vindictive man.'

'Marduk guide us all.' Banipal raised his hands, bowed and stepped back. He looked at the foreigner with some sympathy. The man was alone and frightened. Probably he had been a victim of an earlier robbery himself and now was penniless, homeless and hungry.

Nevertheless, all was as it should be. The immutable laws, carved on a stele of black rock in the market squares of every city in the land, were being followed.

The merchant addressed the foreigner, mainly for the benefit of the crowd. 'Go now, to Ekad's justice.'

The two labourers hoisted the foreigner on to the top of the parapet. The crowd fell silent. Unresisting, the stranger looked wretchedly down at the river.

Then Banipal noticed the measuring instruments clenched in the foreigner's hand. They were made of sheets of transparent crystal.

'Wait!' Banipal cried.

It was too late. The labourers had already pushed the bearded stranger and he was gone into the river.

A Friendly Visit

NEVER BEFORE had Mrs Woosencraft been concerned about leaving the front door on the latch. As she looked at the three women in her tiny front garden she wondered if Tim hadn't been right to worry. Her feelings of trepidation grew when she saw their car, a cream drop-head Mercedes. These were the women who had visited Tim a few days ago. Close up they didn't look very nice at all.

However you looked at them they looked like trouble. All three looked like cruel little girls all grown up. It wasn't that they didn't care about being noticed, they flaunted it.

The one in front, with her spiky hair, white boots and fish-nets showed too much leg for her age, and was full of that cocksure aggression people these days called 'attitude'. Beside her the platinum blonde radiated a glacial, intellectual cruelty Mrs Woosencraft found quite disturbing. Behind them a darkly voluptuous woman tugged down the hem of her jacket and smiled.

You're almost normal, Mrs Woosencraft thought. Almost. The one who likes to watch and pretends that if she doesn't join in she's not involved.

Out on the street Mrs Woosencraft would have been vulnerable. In her own house, surrounded by her collections, her possessions and her paraphernalia, she was much safer. The white boots of the spiky-haired one who had pushed open the door and rung the bell were still outside the threshold. That proved a couple of things at least.

Mrs Woosencraft put on her best quavery old-lady voice. 'Hello dearies. How may I help you?'

The one with spikey hair bared her teeth. 'Go and put the kettle on, little old lady, or whatever it is you do. We've come from Koponen. He wants to know what's going on.'

Mrs Woosencraft held her ground. 'And you are?'

'Imelda Marchpane.'

Mrs Woosencraft peered myopically and let her head wobble. 'What a lovely name. Why don't you come through and sit down. I've just baked a nice seed cake.'

Imelda stepped into the hall. There was a sudden scrabble of cats racing upstairs and the rattle of the kitchen door flap as others fled into the garden.

Mrs Woosencraft led the way into her suddenly quiet house. Her age-seamed mouth pursed, her eyes narrowed. Concealed by her body her fingers touched tip to tip, constantly moving, tapping together. Under her breath she was counting, counting, counting. One, two, three. Five, seven, eleven—

'Make yourselves comfy.' Mrs Woosencraft called as she bustled in the kitchen. 'Tea all round?'

Imelda leaned in the doorway. 'Where's your whisky?'

'I don't believe in the strong stuff. I can do you a sweet sherry if you'd rather.'

The kettle boiled, Mrs Woosencraft set out the tea things on a tray and brought it through.

Imelda blocked the way. 'Mind you don't slip on those flagstones and break your hip.'

'Don't you worry, dear. I'm quite safe in what is, after all, my home. Now, step aside and let me pass.'

Smiling thinly Imelda stepped aside.

The platinum blonde sat in Mrs Woosencraft's personal armchair. Straight-backed, feet together, one hand on each arm, somehow she seemed regal. The chair's threadbare wings, cat-scratched legs and aged antimacassar had become an ancient throne.

'Shall I be mother?' Mrs Woosencraft balanced the tray of cups, plates, cake and teapot on the small table.

'I'm Electra.' The woman in Mrs Woosencraft's chair held out her slim, pale hand.

Unbidden, Mrs Woosencraft's own hand lifted. With a conscious effort she turned it aside and took hold of the teapot. 'One lump or two? Surely not three. Five—'

'I'm sweet enough.'

Mrs Woosencraft looked into her pale blue eyes and saw a glimmer of respect. She turned to the black-haired woman. What can I get you, Miss—?'

'It's Dolores. White and no sugar, thank you.'

'And some seed cake?'

'Thank you.'

Cup, teapot and strainer chinked together. 'I hope you don't mind odd cups and plates. It's all that's left,' Mrs Woosencraft said.

'I think they're pretty.'

'Charmed.' Mrs Woosencraft sat on the piano stool and folded her hands in her lap. 'Now, drink your tea and tell me what you want.'

'Koponen wants to know where she is,' Electra said.

'I don't know.'

'Why not?'

'The missing cat. Mr Wassiter was looking but he tells me he's been very busy looking for your car instead.'

'Nice Mr Wassiter.' All three women smiled wide, bright smiles. 'We think you should try harder.'

'I need nineteen cats and one is—'

'Missing?'

The room darkened as a cloud moved across the sun. A scuffing sound came from under Electra's chair. A scruffy

Manx cat with bald spots on its fur stuck out its head and said 'Miaow'.

Scat, Pedwar. Scat! Mrs Woosencraft thought as hard as she could.

Pedwar broke for the kitchen door, baulked as Imelda blocked its path and tried to go back under the chair.

Electra scooped it up by the scruff of its neck. 'What's wrong with this one? It looks like it's got mange.'

'Just a little accident.'

'What happened to its tail, did you use scissors?'

'It's a Manx, they're born like that.'

'It's a mess. Let me put it out of its misery.' Imelda said. 'If your spell's broken what's the difference?'

One of her hands encircled its neck, the other pulled at the patchy fur. Pedwar yowled and squirmed then fell still as she tightened her grip.

Mrs Woosencraft improvised a simple release cantrip. 'I see three nice ladies who aren't used to cats. I think I'm the only one of the five of us who knows what he wants.'

Twisting his head, Pedwar bit down on Electra's fingertip. Electra gasped and let got. Pedwar dropped off her lap and ran under the piano stool behind Mrs Woosencraft's legs.

Electra held up her finger. 'It bit me.'

Dolores leaned forward and gasped. 'Right through the nail.'

Electra inspected her finger. A fat drop of ruby blood welled from the hole in her nail then broke. A red rivulet ran down Electra's arm, vivid against her white skin.

Imelda bent over Electra's hand and swallowed her finger. Dolores wriggled and shifted her legs on the settee beside Mrs Woosencraft.

Enough was enough. It was time for some real magic. Mrs Woosencraft scooped up Pedwar and stood. 'There are at least eleven things to remember about cats. One, they have seven lives; two, Pedwar has five left; three, five of—'

'You can stop that. Right now.' Electra's voice was hard as old ice but held a brittle, nervous edge.

The air vibrated with energy from the part-cast spell. 'How about another cuppa?'

Electra gave her a smile cold enough to freeze oxygen. 'Stop buggering us about, old lady.'

'And you,' Mrs Woosencraft drew herself up to her full five foot nothing, '*Paid a ffwcio da fi yn fy nhy'n Lunan.*' [8]

'This is just a friendly visit. We all want the same thing.'

'Remind an old lady what that is, exactly.'

'Find her. Find her fast. We're tired of waiting.'

'We don't want to have to come back,' Imelda said.

Dolores touched Mrs Woosencraft's arm. 'Please, you really wouldn't like that.'

'I'd like it,' Imelda said.

'I'm glad we understand each other a little better.' Electra stood a foot taller than Mrs Woosencraft. She looked down at Pedwar, who bared his teeth and hissed.

'Do you want to bite me again, nasty cat?' Electra held out her hand. 'Here you are.'

Pedwar sank his teeth into Electra's palm. Electra closed her eyes and shuddered. 'Well, this is nice, but I don't have all day.'

Pedwar opened his mouth and spat.

Imelda sauntered out through the front door.

'Thank you for the tea,' Dolores said.

Electra held out her hand. Pedwar hissed and she laughed coldly. 'Be a good little old lady and do your job.'

As soon as they were gone Mrs Woosencraft shut the front door. Then she bolted it.

'Well done, you brave, foolish little cat,' she said and hugged Pedwar tight.

---

[8] *Don't push you luck in my home. (Or something like that.)*

The encounter had exhausted her. She returned to the back room, sat on the settee, pursed her lips at the undrunk cups of tea and scowled at her favourite armchair. She didn't fancy sitting in it just now, not until she'd purified it with something powerful, something from at least the seventeenth path. Pedwar settled onto her lap and she absently stroked him. It would have to wait for when she had more energy and focus.

Poor Tim. What have I got you into? As if I haven't treated you badly enough anyway. What a foolish, selfish old lady I have become.

One by one her other cats crept back down the stairs or in through the cat flap. Some jumped up to sit beside her, others lay at her feet. Pedwar began to purr. Mrs Woosencraft closed her eyes.

Once again the room was full of cats. Some slept, others groomed themselves. The Siamese licked each other's fur. Mrs Woosencraft's hand slipped from Pedwar and she began to snore.

Consultants

DOWN IN the control room of the Kylma Kala offices Ralf Tuppence scratched his head with a 12mm socket wrench and scowled at the environmental management display.

'I don't understand it,' he said. 'We installed it, we tested it, we got it signed off. Now it don't bleedin' work.'

Ralf's companion was a big lad with a crew-cut, bulging pectorals and sleeve-straining biceps. He pointed at the display with a large finger. 'There's a blockage, Mr Tuppence. Up there.'

'Well spotted, Tiny. Fetch the step-ladder and we'll take a look. And call me Ralf, I'm not the foreman.'

'Yes, Mr Ralf.'

Tired from his exploration of the building, Smith had retired to his nest of sheets in the ducting of the top floor. The bang and rattle of ventilation grilles being removed alerted him just in time. He grabbed his fleece and squirmed up into the roof void.

Ralf tugged on his braces. 'Right, lad, what are we here for?'

Tiny frowned. 'Fix the air-con?'

'Bang on, except these days we'd say "malfunction identification and remedy" instead of "fix".'

'Do we still say "air-con"?'

'What we have here is an atmosphere management and control system incorporating absolute filters for particulate allergens, optimised temperature and humidity via regenerative heat pumps and electronic gateways managed by artificially intelligenced computers.'

'Blimey.'

'Indeed. We've come a long way from opening a window.'

'What's wrong with it?'

'Good question. Short answer, dunno. Long answer? Haven't a clue. What we do know is that with all these noises and what-have-you, the computer saying some gates are opening when they should be shut, Mr Koponen wants it sorted out pronto. Hence this tidy piece of overtime.'

Smith decided the best thing to do would be to absent himself to another part of the building. He backed away, his boot thumped into the rear wall and an echoing boom rolled down the ducting and out of the conference room vents.

'Get that ladder, Tiny,' Ralf said.

By the time they were set up Smith was long gone, elbowing through the ducting to the opposite side of the room. In his haste he knocked a side panel.

Ralf and Tiny looked at the new source of noise.

'That came from over there, Mr Ralf.'

'Yes, lad.'

Tiny hugged himself. 'It's moving around, Mr Ralf, like an animal.'

'It's echoes from different vents,' Ralf said at the top of the ladder. He pushed up a ceiling tile and peered into the roof void. 'Looks like some bolts have pulled free and a seam's gone. Put your foot on the bottom step, I'm going up.'

Tiny's eyes grew round. 'Be careful, it might be up there.'

'Don't be daft, big lad like you.'

Standing on the topmost step, Ralf reached into the void. 'Looks like somebody left a pencil up here. Got it. Right, let's take a look over the other side.'

Smith backed away. Then the Hand was there, it fixed him straight in the eye and said, 'They've captured the pencil. Stay here and we'll be next.'

They scooted down to the next floor. Tiny's voice floated after them through the vents. 'It IS an animal, Mr Ralf. There's something alive in there.'

The Hand insisted Smith slow down. Just one more down ramp and they would be safe.

'Excellent work, soldier.' the Hand said as they reached the bottom.

'Sir, thank you, sir!' Smith attempted a salute and whacked his funny-bone.

'Aooarghaharhar!'

Two floors above, Ralf and Tiny listened to the hollow booms and eerie hooting. A shiver ran up Ralf's spine. He took the heavy rubber mallet from his toolbox, the weight reassuring in his hand. Things hit by a mallet stayed hit. 'Come along, lad.'

Tiny's eyes were as large as gobstoppers. 'It almost sounds human, Mr Ralf.'

'Don't be daft.'

Tiny didn't move.

'Look at the size of you. What have you got to be scared of?'

'I don't know, Mr Ralf. That's the thing.'

Ralf grabbed the lapels of Tiny's boiler suit. 'Look, I know this is your first evenin' and I know it's a bit weird, but remember this: we are Building Maintenance Engineers and we get the job done.'

'It's me imagination, Mr Ralf. I read a lot of science fiction.'

'You're my apprentice. You ain't got an imagination till I send you to stores to fetch one.'

'No, Mr Ralf.'

'Take this.' Ralf held out the mallet and Tiny took it.

'Now, come along.' Ralf strode away down the empty corridor.

Tiny anxiously twisted the mallet in his hands. With a soft, rubbery pop the head came off. 'Er—' He stashed the parts in his pockets then hurried after Ralf.

Always ahead of them, Smith headed down through the office levels, the post room, the canteen, and finally reception on the ground floor. There he discovered a hatch in the ducting floor, which opened to reveal a vertical tube set with rungs. He descended and discovered the car park.

Deep in the shadows at the back he found a black Airflow Chrysler Imperial Eight with Finnish plates.

Smith had never been afraid of the dark, it was just the same as daytime with the lights off. Where otherwise perfectly sensible grown-ups tried to convince themselves there was nothing there but didn't quite believe it, Smith knew the only scary things in the dark were the things from his imagination. They made it fun to be scared and when the fun was over they went away.

Crouched in the cool, dank gloom beside the Chrysler, Persistent Smith brimmed with quiet satisfaction. The pattern that ran from Tim Wassiter through himself to Clive Barnett, the computer, this building, and the car, was complete. He had earned his fee.

Faint, perplexed voices came from the ventilation duct. Smith grinned, unzipped and zipped his fleece then clambered back into the air conditioning.

An hour later, hot, dirty and tired, Ralf and Tiny staggered into the top floor conference room.

'I don't think I can do any more stairs, Mr Ralf.'

'Me neither, lad.' Ralf wiped his face with his hanky. 'I think I'll skip the running club tonight.'

'It's doing me crust in, Mr Ralf. We've been on every floor, right down to the basement and back. Just when we get close it moves away. What are we going to do?'

Ralf's stubble rasped as he rubbed his jaw. It was a good question. His eyes settled on the remote control on the conference table and held down the buttons. 'Let's try flushing the system.'

High overhead came the ascending whirr of great fans spinning faster and faster. The gentle breeze from the air vents grew to a roar. Freezing air blasted from the vents, loose papers blew round the room and frost-ferns crawled across the windows. Ralf and Tiny shook with cold. Ralf reset the controls. As the wind noise died down something big and soft thumped against the back of one of the grills.

Mist from Ralf's breath plumed in the cold air. 'Take a look at that, Tiny.'

Tiny removed the grill and extracted yard after yard of tangled dust sheet.

The two men looked down at the rumpled heap of material with the pride of Neolithic hunters beside a downed elk.

'We done it, Mr Ralf! That's the problem. It's been blowing round the whole building with you and me chasing after it.'

Ralf prodded the sheet with the toe of his boot. 'What muppet left that in there, do you think?'

'Wasn't me.'

'Never said it was.'

'It wasn't an animal after all, Mr Ralf.'

'No lad, it wasn't.'

The two men acknowledged the fact with slow nods. Both felt a relief neither would ever fully acknowledge.

'After all this mucking about I reckon we can call ourselves Consultants.'

'You reckon?'

'Absolutely. Now, let's pack up and get down the chip shop.'

Up in the roof void Smith's tummy rumbled. He and the Hand grinned down at the two men and quietly laughed.

Smith blew on his fingers, the air had been freezing but his fleece had kept him warm.

'It saved your life,' the Hand said. 'Mine too.'

It had been fun, but Smith was tired. He remembered his long bath times back home, along with the glass of cold milk and biscuits that followed, so much better than a shower with a dust sheet for a towel.

Heidi might be working late again. A strange excitement burned in his chest. Before he left the building he'd clean himself up, get some food and see if she was there.

The Hand rolled its head. 'So, we're going to see her again.'

An unfamiliar mood came over Smith. He turned the Hand into a fist, splayed his fingers and rubbed his palms together.

'No,' Smith said. 'Just me.'

Crud

THE ONE THING that hadn't been on Tim's to-do list was identification of the potato-shaped lump from the sack in the boot of the Imperial. He rinsed it under the tap and it sat on the kitchen draining board, cold and dense and uninformative.

Tim knew who he needed to call, he just didn't want to. Finally, reluctantly, he went into his office, picked up the phone and dialled.

For once Troy Jarglebaum played it straight. 'Tim, I'm glad you've called. Where are you?'

'At home.'

'Stay there. I'm coming over.'

A few minutes later Troy pulled up in an unmarked, dark blue saloon. Tim opened the front door. 'Come on up.'

Jarglebaum's tread sounded heavy on the stairs. He paused on the landing and studied the broken frame. 'Things are going on, Tim. Missing people. Odd stuff. Strange things, strange even for coppers.'

His serious tone made Tim feel off-balance. Today Jarglebaum was not the bluff, overconfident person he was used to. He looked and sounded worried.

'Do you want a drink?' Tim gestured towards the filing cabinet.

Jarglebaum wiped his mouth. 'To be honest, yes, I do.'

Tim opened the drawer and fetched out the quarter-bottle and tooth glasses with a strange sense of déjà vu. He had just taken another step along the road to becoming a true PI. Today it was the police who wanted something and he was the one they had come to.

Jarglebaum knocked back the drink and bared his teeth. 'Christ, what is this?'

'It says whisky on the label.'

'How much did you pay for it?'

'Not a lot.'

'Do my guts a favour and put your rates up.' Jarglebaum poured himself another two fingers. 'You know Derek Smith?'

'Yes, and I know he's missing. Is that why you're here?'

Jarglebaum looked impressed. 'How do you know?'

'I spoke to his mother. He was doing some work for me. The job was over, I wanted to let him know.'

'That job being?'

'The missing car.'

'You found it?'

'Yes.'

Once again Jarglebaum managed to amaze Tim. 'Kylma Kala. Markus Koponen.'

'You know him?'

Jarglebaum drank half his whisky. 'We're acquainted.'

That was less of a surprise, Jarglebaum seemed to know everyone. Tim was almost pleased to see a flash of the old attitude. 'How long has Derek been missing?'

'Not long. The guy seems to be a bit of a fruit-bat. His mother said he was "special".'

'He's a friend.'

'OK. Well, don't worry, he's probably fine. Most missing persons turn up right as rain.'

'Troy, is this official?' Tim asked.

'No.' Jarglebaum polished off his second drink and put the glass down. 'There's some heavy stuff in Brighton right now. People are getting hurt. There was this girl in a pet shop got her hand crushed. Christ on a bike, Tim, they killed the animals.'

Tim tried to keep the shock out of his voice. 'This is something to do with the car?'

Jarglebaum hesitated. Tim pointed to the bottle. 'Another?'

'Not bloody likely. That last shot gave me heartburn.'

'Troy, there's something you can help me with.'

Much to Tim's surprise Jarglebaum didn't crow. 'What is it?'

Tim fetched the potato-sized lump of rock from the draining board. 'I need to know what this is.'

'It looks like a lump of crud.'

'Yes, but what is it made of?'

'Where did you find it?'

'In a sack in the boot of the car.'

Jarglebaum raised his eyes then hefted the rock and put it down. 'Tim, I know you don't think much of police procedure and maybe all this mumbo-jumbo you're into works, but for once just try thinking this through. Think about where you found it and the bigger picture. Get it all down on paper, make some notes and use your noggin. Maybe you can work it all out for yourself. It might be better that way.'

Tim was disappointed, Jarglebaum usually took such pleasure in showing off how well-informed he was. Now he was… Was Jarglebaum actually trying to protect him?

'I get you don't want to tell me, but do you actually know?'

'Haven't a clue.' Jarglebaum looked steadily at Tim. 'Yeah, well, I've got to go.' He paused at the broken door frame. 'And just how did this happen?'

'A dissatisfied customer.'

'I hope he's paying for it.'

'She. Yes, she is.'

'You get this fixed. That's official advice so you'd better take it. You're a chump but I wouldn't like anything on my…

What's the word, that thing I never use?' Troy grinned, slapped Tim on the shoulder and stomped down the stairs.

Alone in his office Tim considered everything Troy had told him. And everything he hadn't. Jarglebaum liked to give the impression he knew a lot more than he was prepared to tell. Sometimes it was bluff but usually he actually did. Whatever Jarglebaum knew now it concerned him enough to warn Tim. He hadn't come to warn him off, quite the opposite, he'd encouraged Tim to carry on. Which meant Jarglebaum was involved in a way that constrained him.

That was hard to believe. Jarglebaum was a bully, a chauvinist and a hard drinker, but never a crook. Whatever was going on it involved the car, Markus Koponen, and that lump of rock, and it wasn't over yet.

He thought about Imelda and the door frame. With cold certainty he knew the woman Jarglebaum said had been hurt was Gabby with the pink hair. She'd suffered because of him, what could they think she knew that he didn't? His eye came to rest on the whisky bottle and the two glasses, one dirty, one clean. He hadn't wanted a drink while Troy was here but he did now.

The raw spirits burned like gasoline. Troy was right once again: the whisky was atrocious.

Too Much Too Soon

SMITH WAS on his knees peering under the vending machine when he heard Heidi's voice.

'Hello again. Lost something?'

Embarrassingly aware that she could see his bottom Smith hastily clambered to his feet. 'I didn't have quite enough. There's always some change under the machines.'

Today Heidi wore a long, black skirt, a deep green top, and an open black waistcoat embroidered with silver thread and little mirrors. This was something else Smith knew other people liked to do, wear different clothes every day.

'Any luck?'

Smith held out his hand. 'Two pounds twenty-three pence and a pencil.'

'Not bad. What are you going to get?'

'Chocolate.'

'Excellent plan.'

Smith fed the machine. Snacks rumbled out of the slots into the tray and he stuffed them into his pockets. 'Now I need water,' he said, holding up his bottle.

'The cooler's empty.'

Smith didn't much like fizzy drinks. He checked his money, selected the orangeade, the least-worst choice.

Heidi was looking at him.

He looked at her. She looked back. The urge to say something grew inside him, became an imperative, but what to say? He couldn't think of anything, so he stuffed his hands in his pockets and grinned.

'Well, here we are again,' Heidi said.

Smith kept grinning and looked around. Every desk in the open-plan office was covered in scattered sheets of paper, with more strewn across the floor.

'This place is a mess,' Smith said.

'Tell me about it. The air conditioning went crazy, like a hurricane. I'm meant to be working on the trial balance but it's taken me this long just to find everything again. Everyone's going to go mad in the morning.'

Even though he hadn't caused the mess, Smith felt guilty. Unbidden, the Hand popped out of Smith's pocket. 'Crazy!' it said. 'Yeah, baby!'

Mortified, Smith grabbed the Hand and wrestled it back into his pocket. 'Go away!' he cried. 'Never come back.'

Heidi, Smith noticed, covered her mouth when she laughed.

'Sorry,' Smith said, stony faced. 'It won't happen again.'

'It's OK,' Heidi said between giggles. 'That was unexpected.'

'I can help tidy up.'

'I've found what I need, the rest can wait.' Heidi sighed. 'I could use some help with the accounts. The trial balance won't, and I can't see why. You know anything about spreadsheets?'

'Maybe.'

Heidi flashed him a smile. 'Come and have a look.'

Feeling very grown-up, Smith did just that.

The spreadsheets were a revelation. Smith immediately saw how you could make lists with rows and columns. Cross-reference, add, divide, and take away. If this, then that. It was what computers were for and it was brilliant.

'Wow,' Smith said. 'This is cool.'

'It's a living.'

Smith scanned the sheet, totalling in his head. He flipped back and forth through the sheets. When he saw it he laughed. Yes, that was it, numbers could be funny. Someone was playing a trick. His fingertip mashed against the screen. 'There.'

Heidi sat back in her chair and considered. 'You're right,' she said finally. 'Thanks. Thanks a lot.'

Heidi called up more reports, cross-referenced between the worksheets on her screen and the print-outs. 'I don't understand the way Appropriations and the Suspense account have been set up. And so many cash receipts and contra entries, it's confusing.'

Smith didn't know about any of that, but patterns were fascinating. He leaned closer. His shoulder pressed against Heidi's, but he didn't notice as he muttered under his breath and ran his finger down the columns.

Now he knew about the trick he could follow it, see how the numbers flowed, divided and curved back on themselves. Then, when a few of the columns fed off into nowhere the ones that looped and doubled up concealed the loss. Almost.

'There's more,' he said, and showed her.

Heidi looked at him open-mouthed in astonishment. 'How did you do that?'

Suddenly, exquisitely, conscious of their touching shoulders, Smith moved away. 'It's easy.'

Heidi shook her head. 'No. It really isn't.' She followed through where he led her and picked up on something he had missed. They traced it back and it was huge. When they had finished she wasn't smiling.

Heidi spoke in a soft, conspiratorial whisper that made Smith feel excited. 'I've got to report this.'

He rubbed his knees in happiness. 'We're on an Adventure!'

'Yeah. Adventures in Accounting. Just the sort of jolly fun that gets you sacked.'

'Aargh,' the Hand said. 'We're doomed.'

'Who are you really?' Heidi laughed. 'And why are you here?'

'My name is Derek Smith, sometimes called Persistent. I'm looking for a car.'

'Have you found it?'

'Yes.'

'Where was it?'

'In the car park.'

Heidi clapped her hands in delight. 'Of course. Where else?'

Smith didn't understand why she found everything he said funny. Go with it, he told himself, half out of breath. This is the best adventure yet.

'So you're not some kind of auditor?'

The Hand wanted to join in. Smith stuffed both hands into his pockets. 'Nope.'

'How come you're so good with numbers? I mean, you really are very good.'

Smith had never thought about it. It was an excellent question. She kept coming up with them. 'Numbers make patterns. When the numbers are right the patterns feel nice.'

Heidi ran her hand through her hair. 'Look, I've absolutely got to deal with this right now. How about going for a drink afterwards? Say half an hour?'

It was too much too soon. Panic welled up inside him. Talking, even looking, was OK, but going out? With a girl, in public. People might see. And then they'd know. 'I— No, I can't.'

'Oh. All right.' She looked so disappointed.

Smith had the most brilliant idea of his life. It was so good it rooted him to the spot. 'Tomorrow! What about tomorrow?'

'You're sure?'

Smith took a deep breath. 'Yes. I'm sure. I want to, I'd like it. Definitely. Indubitably. Absolutely.'

'All right, then. It's a date.' Heidi fanned herself with her hand. 'I mean, we have an appointment. For a drink.'

'Yes. Great. Got to go. See you then.'

Heidi gave a small wave. 'See you tomorrow.'

Smith arrived at the lifts with no knowledge of how he got there. His finger hovered over the 'Down' button. If he left the building how would he get back in? He grinned and pressed the 'Up' button instead. He'd spend another day in the tunnels. His toothbrush was tucked in its usual pocket, his fleece bulged with chocolate, biscuits and crisps and he had more drink. He'd be fine, and this time he'd lie low and play no games. Tomorrow evening he'd meet Heidi and they would Go Out For A Drink.

The lift arrived, the doors slid open. Smith stepped in and pressed the button for the top floor. He felt calm and excited at the same time.

'Now you've done it,' the Hand said.

'Who asked you?' Smith replied.

Don't Be Afraid

'MR WASSITER?'

A stocky man with cropped greying hair and dressed in dungarees and tough workman's boots stood at the front door. He held a tray of carpenter's tools in one hand, a folding workbench leaned on the wall.

'Mr Tuppence? Come on up.'

'That's me, squire. Call me Ralf. Come to fix your door.'

Ralf slung the workbench over his shoulder, hefted his tool box and ran up the stairs. 'Good bit of exercise, stairs,' he said reaching the top. 'Surprising how fit you can keep yourself in your daily life if you keep your eyes open.'

'Tea?' Builders lived on tea.

'Now you're talking. Earl Grey if you've got it. In a mug, three sugars and a splash of milk.'

When Tim returned, Ralf had his workbench set up and was inspecting the broken frame. 'Your architrave is solid but the side post will have to come out. A bit of plastering and a lick of paint and Bob's your uncle. Who did this then? Angry customer? I'd have given him what for. Blokes that behave like that deserve a punch on the nose.'

'Actually, it was a woman,' Tim said.

'Crikey, what's the world coming to?' Ralf brightened as he noticed the mugs of tea and looked significantly at the filing cabinets. 'Cheers, mate. I don't suppose you've got anything to put in this have you? It's just that I'd heard you private dicks always have a bottle in the bottom drawer, for when you get beaten up and so on.'

'It's the cheap stuff.'

'Cor,' Ralf said. 'It's actually true.'

A few minutes later Ralf nipped out for a trip to the timber yard. The room felt very quiet after his incessant stream of chatter. Tim tried to order his thoughts and decided to make a new list:

1. Dolores Vogler
2. The MK monogrammed handkerchief
3. Markus Koponen, owner of Kylma Kala
4. An Airflow Chrysler Imperial Eight
5. Some round lumps of rock, origin and composition unknown
6. Pamphlets about crops

He thought for a moment, then added:

7. Persistent Smith is missing
8. Troy Jarglebaum's warning

He read it through. Everything on the list was connected. As a generalised statement it cohered with his own philosophy, with this particular list intuition said it was especially true and the connections were direct and explicit.

He had no idea what most of them were.

The car belonged to Markus Koponen, that was obvious. He drew a loop that joined them together. The car was parked where he worked, therefore he knew where it was.

The seductive Dolores Vogler and her scary friends knew who owned the car because they had Koponen's handkerchief. Dolores might have lied about him being her husband but it was a safe assumption Dolores knew exactly where the car was when she hired him to find it. More loops crossed the page.

This made no sense. Therefore, there had to be another reason. And how did the contents of the boot, Troy's visit, and Smith's disappearance fit in?

Tim shivered. "Disappeared" was a word with a wide range of causes and outcomes.

The flies patrolled under the lampshade. Long-distance cruises broken with brief, whirligig dogfights. They fulfilled their destinies with a sense of commitment and purpose. Or were they simply going around in circles?

Tim's reverie was broken by the sound of voices and footsteps on the staircase.

'Yes, Miss,' Ralf said. 'He's up in his office. Mind your step as you go. The door's off and my tools are out. Wouldn't want to put a ladder in them tights.'

The woman's voice was East-coast American and instantly recognisable. Tim tore off the top sheet of his desk pad, folded it and slipped it into a drawer.

'Stockings are they, Miss? Yes, oh, I can see they are.' Ralf appeared at the top of the stairs red-faced.

'Hello Miss Vogler,' Tim said. 'Why don't you come in?'

Dolores wore her black hair swept over to one side under a wide-brimmed summer hat. The hat, like her open-collared jacket and panelled skirt, was midnight blue.

She stalked across the room like it was a catwalk, deposited her small triangular handbag beside the chair, and sat down. Tim was disconcerted to see Imelda follow Dolores into the room, a carrier bag in her hand. Behind them, speechless, Ralf stood holding his spirit level.

Imelda ran her finger along the level. 'Do you know how to use that? Or would you like me to show you where it goes?'

'I, er… I got some more stuff in the van.' Ralf hurried away down the stairs.

Dolores crossed her legs.

Tim put his back to the desk. 'I've found the car.'

'Excellent. Where is it?'

Tim told her. Dolores and Imelda exchanged looks of exaggerated surprise.

'I have a question,' Tim said.

Hands folded in her lap, Dolores studied Tim with her dark eyes.

'Why pay me to find a car when you already know where it is?'

'Is that what we did, Mr Wassiter?'

'I think so.'

'Why would we do that?'

'That's my question.'

Imelda pushed herself off the wall. 'Perhaps it was a test to find out how good Tim Wassiter is at his job. Little Tim. Timmy.'

'How did I do?'

'So many questions, Mr Wassiter. I've got one of my own.' Imelda tossed him the bag.

Inside was the jacket Foxy had left in the car park.

'You had some help,' Imelda said. 'We want to meet.'

Tim felt very cold. He folded his arms to stop his hands shaking. 'I'm afraid that won't be possible.'

'Don't be afraid,' Imelda said.

'And anything's possible,' Dolores said. 'Show him.'

Imelda rolled her shoulders and cracked her knuckles. 'My pleasure.'

Tim backed round the desk. 'Hang on, it doesn't have to come to this.'

'I meant show him the money,' Dolores said.

Dolores left her chair and perched on the edge of Tim's desk, one leg swinging, her shoe dangling from her toes.

Imelda planted her booted foot on the edge of the desk. Her short, red leather dress rode high on her thigh revealing a money roll in her stocking top. Imelda removed it, peeled off fifty pound notes one after the other and let them fall to the floor.

Dolores stroked the edge of the desk with her fingers. 'Come around here, Mr Wassiter. We don't bite.'

Imelda laughed. 'She doesn't.'

'Blimey!' Ralf stood at the top of the stairs with gobstopper eyes on Imelda's barely concealed posterior. He hurriedly looked away. 'Excuse me.'

Imelda tucked the money roll back into her stocking, crossed the room and pressed her heel down on the steel toecap of Ralf's boot. 'Don't you know it's rude to stare?'

'Ow.' Ralf clutched his booted foot.

Dolores slid off the desk and smoothed her skirt. 'Arrange a meeting with your associate. If you're right about the car you'll know how to contact us. If you're wrong, then, oh dear, Imelda will have to visit again.'

Imelda casually bent one of Ralf's screwdrivers into a 'U' shape.

'Do you mind?' Ralf said through gritted teeth. 'They're vintage Pozidrives.'

Dolores and Imelda left. Ralf sat on the floor and unlaced his boot.

Tim watched through the windows as the cream Mercedes drove away and let out a sigh of relief. Once more Dolores Vogler had sat on his desk and left a pile of high denomination banknotes. On her first visit she had been beautiful and seductive, her narrow-waisted, full hipped figure summoned up rarely used words like pulchritude as she approached and callipygous as she departed. Now that seduction had been replaced with crude threats.

Tim steadied his shaking hand. All things considered they were very effective threats, though when he thought about it neither Dolores or Imelda had actually threatened anything at all. It was the way they didn't say things that was so effective, the way Imelda had casually bent Ralf's screwdriver in half.

'I can't get me boot off!' Ralf said. 'I got a run tonight.'

'Heavy people,' Tim said, half to himself.

'You're telling me.' Ralf finally wrenched his foot free and massaged his toes.

And there was Foxy's green jacket. Thank all the gods they didn't know where she was. He had to warn her. He reached for the phone then decided he didn't want to make the call with Ralf in the room.

'I'm sorry about your screwdriver, Mr Tuppence,' Tim said.

'That's not really the problem, it's me foot. I can't work without proper safety equipment. I promised the missus.'

Ralf and Tim regarded the dented steel toecap and Ralf's surprisingly clean sock.

Ralf wiggled his toes. 'I'll have to come back tomorrow.'

Tim gathered up the money and gave two notes to Ralf. 'For the boots.'

'Thanks.' Ralf looked Tim up and down. 'No way I could do your job. You must be a lot tougher than you look.'

The moment Ralf left Tim picked up the phone. He let it ring. Finally Foxy answered.

'It's me, Tim. Foxy, listen. Some people came here with the jacket you lost in the car park. They want to talk to you.'

'Well, that's good. I can say thank you.'

'I don't think so. They're not nice people.' His heart was in his mouth. 'It's my fault you're caught up in this. I'm sorry—'

Dolores had sat on his desk again. The same edge, the same place, something she seemed to make a habit of. The way she ran her fingers under the edge of the desk…

They had played him for the fool he was. All the seduction and threats and stocking-tops had been moves so obvious he hadn't seen them for what they were. Damn it.

Foxy's voice came down the line: 'Hello? Are you still there?'

'I've just realised something. I can't say any more now. It's important that we meet.'

'OK. Why don't you come over?'

'Yes, but don't tell me your address now, send me a text.'

The line went quiet. She's processing all this, Tim thought. She's smart and she's fast.

'All right,' Foxy said. 'I'll do that now.'

Tim ended the call then knelt in front of the desk. It didn't take long before his fingers found a flat, pea-sized object set in the angle between the desktop and the leg.

He prised the little metallic disk free. Anger filled him. Troy Jarglebaum would not have fallen for this.

Tim checked the rest of the desk, the chairs and under the rug. He dismantled the phone. There was nothing. If there was another bug he wouldn't find it without a scanner.

His email pinged as Foxy's note arrived. He memorised her address then deleted and erased the email.

It was time to go. A few hundred pounds still lay on the carpet. Tim grabbed the money and distributed it through the pockets of his old leather jacket.

He froze. Slowly he extracted the handkerchief with the heavily embroidered MK monogram and spread it on the desk. He stared at it sourly. So he was a fool, but a bigger fool didn't learn from past mistakes.

He fetched a craft knife and a pair of fine-nosed pliers from his tool drawer and carefully scratched through the embroidery thread with the knife tip. Then he teased the cut threads apart with the pliers. Set into the pillar of the letter K was a narrow metal tube. A delicate aerial connected to it curled through the M. Tim smiled with grim satisfaction. Those women knew where he'd been all the time, it was how they had known he'd found the car.

He removed the tracker from the handkerchief and put it in an old envelope. For a long moment he thought about what to do with the desk bug, then snatched it up and flushed it down the toilet.

He picked up Foxy's green jacket and went out. A few minutes later he was on the local bus. He took out the envelope holding the transmitter and pushed it down the side of the seat. After riding the bus for two more stops he disembarked, crossed the road and caught the bus going in the other direction.

A Lonely End

THE FOREIGN THIEF fell into the turgid river like a stone and vanished. Banipal, the merchant and the young scribe hurried across the bridge to the downstream parapet and watched the surging river for signs of life.

Banipal had begun to believe Ekad had judged the man and found him guilty when the scribe pointed far out across the rolling brown water.

'There.'

He followed the man's arm and saw a bearded face briefly clear the water. A hand clutched at the air then fell back. The body emerged, face down and drifting soddenly with the current.

Grim faced, the merchant and scribe turned away. Alone, Banipal squinted into the sun and watched the body, now a black silhouette, drift past the reedy bank beneath the temples of Esagila quarter where Banipal himself lived and studied. Justice had been served yet Banipal felt pity for the foreign man. It was a lonely end, and far from home, with nobody to save his body from the fish and crocodiles in the marshlands downstream.

Banipal knew he had been a reluctant servant of Marduk today, only grudgingly visiting his nephew to accept a task he regarded as little more than a chore. To chide him, great Marduk brought him to Ekad's bridge at the right moment to witness the lonely foreigner's fate. The fate of a man abandoned by his gods, yet who held instruments of measurement and scale. The message was obvious.

Out of respect for the unknown life chosen to deliver that message Banipal decided to bear witness to the body until it had drifted from sight.

After a while he wondered if it was false movement from the reflected sunlight or if the man was in fact trying to swim. Banipal made a fist and peered through the gap between first and second finger. The restricted view cut out glare and focused attention, a hunter's trick Ishkun had taught him.

He saw a half-drowned man struggle with the last of his strength towards the far bank. If he survived he would come ashore beneath the walls of the House of the Raised Head, Marduk's own temple.

Enlightenment came to Banipal like a thunderbolt. Marduk had brought him and the foreigner together for a greater purpose. This was no message—it was a test.

'Make way!' Banipal cried, and ran across the bridge like the wind.

The Price

ELECTRA SAT on the white leather settee, a portable console on her lap. 'The one on the desk has stopped sending.'

'Wassiter's not a complete dunce,' Dolores said.

'Not completely.' Electra returned to studying the console. The screen displayed a street map and showed a small red blip crawled along one of the roads. 'It looks like he's found the one in the handkerchief as well.'

'Where is it?'

Electra indicated the pulsing dot. 'On the 79 bus route along the Ditchling Road.'

'So he's on the bus,' Imelda said.

'Not when the third one is over here.' Electra pressed a key, the map jerked sideways to display another blip moving more slowly along another road.

'He dumped it,' Dolores exclaimed. 'I spent all day embroidering that.'

'That's almost clever.' Imelda studied the location of the slower moving dot then kissed Electra on the top of her head. 'We should go.'

'He's on foot.'

'Let's go!' Imelda jumped with impatience. 'This is it. It's starting to happen, we're going to do it.'

Electra folded down the console screen. 'You're right. Koponen's ship is about to sail. Warm currents are flowing. The Dreamer will wake.'

Imelda's eyes glowed. 'I will be Vammatar.'

'I will be Loviatar,' Electra said.

Turning towards Dolores, the two women held out their arms. 'And you will be Kivutar.'

Butterflies danced in Dolores' stomach as she stepped into their embrace. 'And she—?'

'She will be Kipu-Tytto. She will become Tuoni's bride and pay the price.'

Evasion and Deceit

Foxy lived in a first-floor apartment of a new-build tucked down one of the narrow roads between the main town and beach. She kept the interior minimally furnished, and lush with potted plants. A floor-to-ceiling picture window occupied one end of the living space, a banana plant unrolled its banner leaves to one side, a fibrous-trunked tree fern unfurled a cluster of black-stemmed fronds on the other. A flowering vine covered the back wall, globular clusters of waxy, star-shaped flowers hung among the jade-green leaves.

Instead of armchairs and sofas Foxy used outsize bean-bags and enormous cushions heaped either side of a low driftwood table.

It was also very noisy. Tim looked through the picture window down onto half a dozen light industrial units around a broad concrete apron. A white van was getting an engine tune-up while four men loaded a flat-bed truck with scaffolding pipes. Everyone else's jobs appeared to consist of shouting, dropping things, and not answering the phone.

'So this is where I hang out,' Foxy said. 'What do you think?'

'It's a bit of a racket.'

Foxy pulled the window shut. 'What?'

'Don't you mind the noise?'

'Oh no. There's always something going on, things to watch, something to listen to.' Foxy grew wistful. 'It's quite musical really, a bit like home.'

Today Foxy wore an open-necked white blouse with tight cuffs and a sky-blue cotton skirt with green darts. Her hair was loose and her feet were bare.

The crash of scaffolding poles, rattle of pulley chains, and the hoot of van horns didn't strike Tim as even slightly melodic. Had Foxy been born in a breaker's yard? Perhaps she was tone deaf. There were far more important things to discuss. Tim held out her jacket.

'Thanks.' Foxy swirled the jacket away into her bedroom. Tim glimpsed a room bathed in turquoise light filtered through drawn curtains, a sand-gold bedspread, a wardrobe of clothes.

'These people—' Tim began.

'Would you like something to drink?' Foxy disappeared into the kitchen.

Tim followed. 'Foxy, these people, it's important.'

'It's just that when I came to yours you mentioned a drink so I thought…'

'No. Thank you. Listen to me, Foxy. There are some people looking for you, three women. They bugged my room. They're dangerous.'

Foxy's happy smile faltered. 'You're serious?'

'Yes, I am.'

It was another one of those moments. Eye contact was involved. So was heartbeat and proximity. Pheromones almost certainly played a role. The cupboard door behind Foxy's head drifted open. Despite himself Tim looked inside. The shelves were bare except for three tins of squid in its own ink.

'We've got some things to talk about,' Tim said.

Foxy looked down at her feet and wiggled her toes. 'Yes, I suppose we do.'

'Then let's sit down and talk.'

They went back into the main room.

A cat, a rather beautiful Bengal, sat on the floor washing its paws.

Tim stared in astonishment. 'That's Mrs Woosencraft's cat. What a piece of luck—'

'Damned pests!' Foxy cried.

'It's all right, I—'

'Y'b'hyzn't Ism!' Foxy screeched (or at least that's what Tim thought she said).

'Y'b'hqrfh'd Esm!

B'n'ahd Asm!'

Out of nowhere a crashing torrent of water knocked the cat off its feet and washed it into the corner beneath the tree fern.

Just as suddenly the water was gone. Odours of salt water, seaweed and dead crabs filled the room. The echo of a gull's cry faded and was gone.

Beached in the corner the cat cowered, a drenched and shivering fur-ball of soggy self-pity.

'Sorry,' Foxy growled. 'Couldn't help myself.'

Open mouthed, Tim looked at Foxy, the cat, and back to Foxy. 'How did you do that?'

'I… filled a bucket.'

Tim scanned the room. 'Where's the bucket?'

'Under the sink.' Foxy stretched. 'That felt good. You can have your cat, I feel better now.'

'It's not my cat, it's my neighbour's, Mrs Woosencraft.'

Except it wasn't. The colours of its coat were running, its muzzle whitening. Colour dripped from its fur into a pool of black water. A more familiar cat was revealed.

'Morse?' Tim whispered in disbelief.

Even for Morse that had been too much water too soon. His shoulders hunched in wet misery, he looked up at Tim and gave a piteously faint miaow.

Morse? The ground felt unsteady under Tim's feet. Reality itself slipped and shifted. Of all the things that had happened recently this was the most utterly weird. His brain struggled to keep up, failed, and began to flounder. 'That's my cat. What the—? How the—?' He turned to Foxy. 'Whut—?'

'Do all cats do that?' Foxy said.

It seemed a reasonable question. Tim had no answers, only questions of his own. 'Can I borrow a towel?'

A few minutes later Tim held Morse wrapped cosily in a warm towel. 'Where did that water really come from?

'I needed it. It came.'

That didn't make much sense. Tim scratched Morse behind the ear. The cat looked at him with one eye then burrowed down into the towels. 'I don't think he recognises me.'

'Well, you didn't recognise him. You thought he was Un-whatsisname.'

'That was because—'

'If I was painted a different colour you'd still know who I was.'

'Yes, but—'

Foxy triumphantly snapped her fingers. 'There's your proof. Can't trust a cat. Let's put it outside.'

'He's my cat.' Tim checked again, there was still no sense of recognition from Morse. 'I think.'

'I don't like cats.' Foxy paced the room. 'Just not keen. Can't be trusted, it's as simple as that.'

Tim persuaded Foxy to sit down. The huge bean bags were low and comfortable. It was difficult to be agitated on a bean bag.

Tim told Foxy about Mrs Woosencraft, how she'd hired him to find her missing cat. Foxy was vehemently suspicious:

'It has to be her. She sent all those cats. She did something to this one, affected its mind to make it think it was hers.'

It sounded outlandish, but he'd seen it for himself. Morse had been dyed to look like Un Deg Naw. Tim still felt a vague duty to defend Mrs Woosencraft. 'She's got angina.'

'So?'

'So why would she do it?'

'You mean why do the thing that she obviously has done?'

'Well, yes.'

Foxy leaned forward. 'Because she's a witch. It's the only explanation.'

'A what? She's a little old lady who lives down my road.'

'Definitely a witch. The ones who live next door are the worst.'

'She bakes cakes and brings them round.'

Foxy gestured expansively. 'How easily she lured you into her web of lies.'

'She's a very good cook.'

'Tim, she kidnapped your cat and dyed it.'

There was that.

'Even if she is a witch it doesn't explain why she would do that and…' Tim struggled with the idea. 'And hypnotise it.'

'To find me.'

'And dye it to look like her own missing cat…'

'To find me, Tim.'

'Then pay me to find it.'

Foxy took hold of Tim's ears and turned his face towards hers. 'So she could find me.'

'Find you?'

'Yes.'

'Why?'

Foxy glared at Morse, now fast asleep in the towel. 'Go and ask her.'

Foxy was right. All he had to do was turn up on her doorstep with Morse and see what she had to say. In his mind the silhouette of a little old lady raised a long knife over her head while musicians sawed jaggedly on their violins.

It still sounded mad. 'She has a lot of cats, but that doesn't mean she's crazy.'

'I don't think she is,' Foxy said. 'I think she's very clever. Witches usually are.'

'But how? I mean, and why?'

'It's how people like her try to find—' Foxy hesitated. 'People like me.'

There it was again, that mysterious reference. Confused, puzzled, more than a little weirded out, and still with no idea where all that water had come from, Tim became annoyed. He stood up with Morse wrapped in the towel in his arms.

'And just what does that mean, Foxy? Where exactly are you from? There's a whole load of stuff going on: cars that aren't missing, dangerous women in red dresses, a sack of odd rocks, dyed and hypnotised cats, my friend has vanished, and now you want me to believe Mrs Woosencraft is a witch. Maybe she is, but what has any of this got to do with you? Or me? And why involve Morse? What's he done to deserve this? It's like everyone's got something to hide except for me and my cat.'

Foxy faced him. Tim had never seen her so serious.

'Tim, do you trust me?'

'I, well, yes. Mostly.'

'As much as yesterday?'

Tim matched her doubtful smile. 'Not quite so much, no.'

Foxy reached out, hesitated, then drew back. 'I came here to get away from some people, some men. My home is a mess, people are desperate. I just wanted to be left alone. Trust? Well, it's the same for me.'

'Where is your home?'

She was on the verge of telling him then changed her mind. 'Go and talk to your little old lady. Listen to what she has to say.'

'And then what?'

'Then I promise I'll answer all your questions. You'll see it all matches up and perhaps you'll find it easier to believe me.' Foxy opened the door. 'I'm glad you found your cat, but I'm gladder you're taking it away. You can keep the towel.'

Tim pulled open the door. As he did something glittered diamond-bright behind the coats hanging on the back of the door. Nothing could be left to chance today. He moved the coats aside and exclaimed in disbelief. Hanging on one of the hooks was Asklepios' pendant.

'Where did you get this?' Tim took the pendant and shook it at Foxy. 'I don't believe it. When I told you about Asklepios and my dream you already knew.'

Foxy shifted uncomfortably. 'Tim, I am so sorry.'

'He needed this. No wonder he couldn't find his way back to me. Why did you take it?'

'He— He spoke to me. In my own language. I was scared—'

'Do you know what this is? Yes, of course you do, that's why you took it.'

'I didn't know he was your friend.'

More evasion, more deceit. Tim no longer knew what to think about Foxy Bolivia. He stuffed the pendant into his jacket, walked out and slammed the door behind him.

His head full of quandary Tim marched down the street with Morse wrapped in a dye-stained towel.

Gods, he thought, the more you know the less you understand.

The pendant in his hand was worth a small fortune. What it potentially could do was worth far more. He hung it over his neck and tucked it inside his shirt.

Even accepting that everything was connected, this was so strange he simply could not join the links together in his mind. The pattern was so big it was like the dragon of creation and you could not see it all at once. Was his mind too small to encompass it? If that's the case he hoped that when he did discover the whole truth it would not burn too bright.

Right now discovering the whole truth was what he was determined to do.

Snug inside the towel Morse stretched, looked up at Tim and yawned.

'At least I've got you back.' Tim scratched Morse between the ears. 'Kind of.'

If there was one thing he had learned today it was that you can't trust anyone.

He scratched some more and Morse purred like a tiny sewing machine.

'So you remember that, do you?'

Despite Foxy's evasiveness and her theft of Asklepios' pendant, her suggestion he talk to Mrs Woosencraft was a good one. Tim had thought of the old lady as a friend, she owed him an explanation for her bizarre treatment of Morse. Once he'd got the truth from her he would decide about seeing Foxy again. Maybe.

Lost in his own thoughts, he didn't notice the cream Mercedes convertible parked in the evening shadows at the corner of a side street. Soon after he walked away the car's sidelights came on, the engine burbled into life and the vehicle slid around the corner.

The walk did Tim some good. By the time he climbed the stairs to his home his mind was clear and calm, he was ready to do what needed to be done. Soon Morse was asleep on his usual blanket after a special supper of sardines. It was good to have the old thing back, more than good, there was an aspect of him that now felt complete again. Morse, however, was not the same. Tim had hoped familiar surroundings might have made a difference, but although Morse responded to affection he felt like a completely different animal. It became obvious when Tim took a shower. Morse appeared at the bathroom door, ears back, curious but suspicious of the falling water. He refused to come closer. That more than anything upset Tim. Then it made him angry.

He called Mrs Woosencraft. After a few rings she answered in the old-fashioned way: 'Five two four two eight seven. Mrs Woosencraft speaking.'

'Hello, this is Tim Wassiter.'

'Hello *bachgen*. Lovely to hear from you.'

Tim kept his tone conversational. 'I've got some news about Un Deg Naw.'

'Oh goodness, tell me.'

Tim discovered the vengeful satisfaction of lying to someone he once thought of as a friend. 'I've found her.'

For a breath the line was utterly silent. Then Mrs Woosencraft said. 'Oh, that's lovely, that is. What good news.'

'You'll be pleased to know she's fine.'

'I meant to ask, I was so surprised.'

'I thought I'd bring her round tomorrow morning.'

'As soon as you like. I'm an early riser, getting on a bit and don't need as much sleep as I—'

'About eight then?'

'That would be lovely. I'll bake a Madeira.'

Tim hung up the phone and sat back. Tension drained from him. He was back in control and tomorrow morning he'd find things out. Tomorrow he'd start to put things right. He was motivated, he was justified. This was what it felt like to be a true detective.

Bigger Fish

THE SOUND of voices woke Smith. By now he was used to his situation and lay still until he was fully alert.

One voice droned in flat monotones about revenues, projections, credit and debit. Another voice interrupted, that of the man in the white hat, Markus Koponen.

'Well done, Imelda. Where is she?'

'In the Mercedes with Dolores and Electra.'

Another voice broke in, the fat man called Jarglebaum. 'She'd better be in one piece.'

'Of course she is.'

'There's no "of course" with you three.'

'Enough,' Koponen ordered. 'What about our young detective?'

Imelda gave a humourless bark of laughter. 'Wassiter is as ignorant and confused as the day he was born.'

Smith extracted his notepad and the pencil he had found under the vending machine.

'The *Sea Cucumber* is loaded and ready to sail. We'll pay off our old friend on the way out of Brighton. Mr Jarglebaum will drive me in the Imperial.'

'How about Dolores drives and I take the Mercedes?' Jarglebaum said.

'I want you with me. Any other questions? Very well, let's go to work.'

Smith's initial excitement grew into something akin to panic. They had fooled Tim, tricked, hoodwinked and bamboozled him. And now they were leaving. He had to find out where they were going, but how?

The answer was obvious. If only there was enough time. Smith thrust himself along the duct towards the down ramp.

Koponen listened infuriated to the hollow booms and thuds coming from the air conditioning. This was sheer incompetence. This time heads would roll.

The phone was already in his hand. He checked the time then slammed the receiver down. Sacking a useless middle-manager would have to wait. Today there were bigger fish to catch.

A few minutes later the shutters to the basement car park clanked up and the cream Mercedes pulled out onto Trafalgar Lane. Behind it rolled the enormous Airflow Chrysler Imperial Eight, the 4.9 litre engine quietly throbbing and black paint gleaming, and with Jarglebaum at the wheel.

Seated diagonally opposite Jarglebaum on the rear seat Koponen checked his watch again and allowed himself a satisfied smile. Despite difficulty, delay and expense, everything had worked out.

The world would never be the same again.

Curled up in the darkness of the capacious boot between a sack full of lumpy rocks and a cardboard box of agricultural brochures, Persistent Smith rode along with them.

The Scholar

CAKED IN stinking river mud the foreigner knelt among the rushes and retched up significant quantities of the Euphrates.

Beside him Banipal was equally wet and filthy. His body and clothes were saturated and reeked abominably, his sandals were somewhere at the bottom of the Holy River.

Too exhausted to move or speak, Banipal flopped beside the man he had just rescued. The scrawny foreigner looked uncomprehendingly at him. Drool and snot hung from his nose and mouth. He wiped his face with his hand then he too fell to the ground and curled into a loose ball.

'You are safe.' Banipal put his hand on the man's shoulder. The stranger flinched, Banipal dragged himself onto his knees. The man beside him looked half-dead. Perhaps even after all his efforts he would still die. Out in the river there had been a long awful moment when he had thought they were both gone. He pushed the memory aside. The Gods would decide, all he could do was try.

He cleared a tangle of hair from the man's eyes and wiped his face with a relatively clean corner of his robe.

'You are safe,' Banipal repeated. Pressing his palms together he bowed his head to the foreigner. 'You are safe.'

The stranger understood his tone if not the words, for he gave a weary smile.

They sat in silence for several minutes, dripping and reeking on the black mud among last season's rotted vegetation and this year's new growth. Banipal watched the river flow and wondered just what the Gods intended. The stranger coughed, turned aside and was quietly sick.

When he was done Banipal stood and held out his hand.

The stranger took his hand and unsteadily came to his feet.

Banipal touched his own chest and smiled. 'Banipal,' he said. 'Banipal.'

The foreigner looked back up the river towards the bridge and shuddered. Then he touched his own chest and bowed. 'Asklepios.'

Banipal gestured towards the upper bank where a flight of stone steps led to the walls of Esagila. Together they slogged through the mud towards the steps.

'Where do you think he is from?' Ishkun was more intrigued by his friend's fascination with the stranger than the man himself.

Asklepios sat silently beside Banipal in his rescuer's warmest robes. The three of them shared a meal of dates, cheese, bread, and water.

'I have no idea,' Banipal said. 'We have no common language, nothing at all.'

Ishkun reached across the table and squeezed Asklepios' shoulder. 'You look none the worse for your little swim. Marduk favours you.'

Asklepios smiled, spread his hands to show appreciation of the food and clothes, then bowed towards Banipal. Ishkun listened carefully to his speech. Despite having travelled widely he could make no sense of it. He had tried the languages he knew and Asklepios apologetically shook his head at each one.

'He seems grateful enough,' Ishkun observed. 'And so he should, he owes you his life.'

'And having saved it, I am now responsible for him,' Banipal said. 'Though you must share some of the blame, if you hadn't taught me the trick of looking through a fist I would never have spotted him in the river.'

Ishkun was delighted. 'I will make a hunter of you yet. What are your plans for this fellow?'

Banipal explained that when he first saw Asklepios he had been holding measuring instruments. 'He is a scholar, I want to find out what he knows.'

'How do you know he hadn't stolen them? He was taken as a thief after all.'

'They were made of a strange material. He must have brought them with him.'

'And they were lost in the river?'

'Yes.'

Left to his own devices, Asklepios amused himself by arranging date stones into rows and groups.

'You see?' Banipal laughed. 'He is just like me.'

When he realised he was the centre of attention Asklepios smiled bashfully. Encouraged by Banipal's gestures he laid two date stones next to each other, then three, a wider gap, then six.

'He cannot even count,' Ishkun crowed. 'I can do better than that.'

'No, he is multiplying not adding.' Banipal made his own sum, multiplying three by three.

In turn Asklepios attempted three by six. But now he did not have enough stones. He took a whole date from the bowl, touched it to his fingers and thumbs on both hands and placed it beside eight stones.

'Yes,' Banipal clapped his hands. 'I knew it.'

Ishkun shook his head in despair. 'Ninurta preserve me, I will never catch anything if I have to bring you both hunting.'

Legs

For once Mrs Woosencraft's front door was firmly locked. Tim lifted the iron knocker and banged three times. Inside the cat box Morse gave a plaintive cry.

Mrs Woosencraft opened the door almost immediately. '*Bore da*,' she said. 'Come on in and take your jacket off. I can't wait to hear where you found her.'

Tim followed her down the hall past the quiet dining room with its ticking clock and into the back room. Two cats peered down at him on the stairs, another trotted in from kitchen.

Mrs Woosencraft rubbed her hands. 'Let's have a look at her.'

Tim put the cat box onto the settee. He opened the lid, lifted Morse into his arms and faced Mrs Woosencraft.

'Oh,' she said as her face fell. 'Bugger.'

Tim felt not one ounce of sympathy. 'What's going on, Mrs Woosencraft?'

Mrs Woosencraft dropped into her chair. 'A good question, *bachgen*. And well put.'

Tim narrowed his eyes. 'I don't want you to call me that anymore. I thought we were friends. I was wrong.'

Mrs Woosencraft looked embarrassed, almost ashamed. 'Let me put the kettle on. A cup of tea and a scone from the oven.'

It sounded nice but Tim hardened his heart. 'You kidnapped my cat, Mrs Woosencraft. I don't think that is too strong a word for it. You kidnapped him and dyed him. Not only did you make him look like your cat, but you did something to him so he thought he was her too. That's not kind, it's not nice, it's certainly not what friends do. I'm still not sure if he's back to normal.'

Mrs Woosencraft peered intently at Morse and her eyes widened. 'He's Morse, all right. Somebody undid it all, somebody who knew a thing or two. Take it from me.'

'He doesn't seem the same to me.'

'He's just got a few things to think about.'

'So would I if I'd been hypnotised into thinking I was female.'

Mrs Woosencraft winced. 'I don't blame you for being angry. I'm sorry and I mean it, but I had my reasons. Selfish ones maybe, but important just the same.'

'Try me.'

'I worry that you wouldn't believe me.'

'That's what Foxy said. You'll have to try harder.'

Mrs Woosencraft's mouth hung open. 'Was it her who fixed Morse?'

'If you mean did she drench him in freezing cold salt water, then yes.'

A hopeful look flickered across Mrs Woosencraft's face. 'Are you sure you don't want a drink? I know it's early but personally I could use a large sherry. About half a pint.'

Perhaps alcohol would make her more talkative. 'Make it a proper one.'

'Then I'll get the scotch.'

Whisky for breakfast. Bring it on.

Mrs Woosencraft felt both shamed and elated. Yes, she'd done everything Tim had accused her of, she'd abused his friendship and more. But Morse had found her!

She had never truly believed such a complex spell would work. Nevertheless, she had to take the chance. Back in

Wales the numbers had been so clear, they said this was what she should do, that this was the best place to search. She had never actually thought it would happen. Not now, not at her age.

Used properly the power, the strength of Deg Naw Wyth was unfailing. And she had used it properly. A lifetime of practice had ensured that. There was always room for doubt, sometimes the answer you got wasn't quite the one to the question you asked. And that usually meant you hadn't asked the question you thought you had.[9]

'I think Morse will be happier back in his box,' Mrs Woosencraft said as she fetched the drinks. She was right, given the chance he eagerly climbed back in, curled up and promptly fell asleep.

Mrs Woosencraft poured sherry for herself and a surprisingly good peaty Islay for Tim. Lifting her own glass, she took a deep swallow. Tim cut the scotch with a little water.

'Tell me about the woman who found Morse,' Mrs Woosencraft said.

Tim shook his head. 'No. You owe me. You answer my questions first.' He knocked the whisky back, banged the glass on the table and leaned forward. 'So, Mrs Woosencraft. Dorothy. *Bachgen.* What the fuck is going on?'

Tim expected his language to shock the old lady but he was disappointed. Mrs Woosencraft finished her sherry and refilled both glasses. Her grey eyes glittered as she said, 'I'm a witch, see.' She wiggled her fingers at Tim. 'I can do magic.'

Then it was Dorothy Woosencraft's turn to be disappointed. Tim had had no breakfast, that double measure of high quality scotch surged through his stomach wall and into his bloodstream like water poured over sand.

---

[9] *This is very like cooking. All recipes work perfectly; it's just that sometimes you're just not baking what you think you are.*

'So you're a witch. Well, I've done some divining and do you know what? It worked. Not how I expected, but thinking about it I didn't really know what to expect. I've always believed there was more to the world than the things we can see. In fact that's how I try to solve crime. It's why I left the police.

'Foxy was right about you. An old lady living on her own, a house full of cats, and you're not scared to leave the front door open. What does surprise me is that I never noticed. Was that one of your spells? Another part of your sinister deception?'

Mrs Woosencraft looked genuinely hurt. 'I am not sinister. I make biscuits.'

'You have to admit you show some of the symptoms.'

Mrs Woosencraft didn't much like being told she had symptoms either but now wasn't the time to be taking offence. She didn't have the right. She tried to stay focused. 'My turn. Tell me about this Foxy.'

'She's the woman who found your cat. My cat. Morse.'

'Foxy's her real name?'

'Foxy Bolivia, yes.'

Now Mrs Woosencraft did look surprised. 'You mean as in the Bolivian Foxtrot? The naughtiest thing you can do standing up in public—'

'Without getting arrested, yes, yes. I'm surprised you know that.'

'It may have been a while ago, but I was young once. And I was married at a time when people knew how to dance properly.'

'Maybe I'll take some lessons.'

'Not with her, Tim. I don't think she could manage the footwork.' Mrs Woosencraft reached for Tim's hand. 'Tell me you haven't kissed her?'

Tim pulled his fingers from her papery grip. 'What are you talking about?'

'She's a mermaid.'

Tim gave her a long, steady look, then burst out laughing. 'You're a witch and she's a mermaid. Is this what this is all about? You think she's a mermaid? You really do.'

'I said you wouldn't believe me.'

'She's a woman. She's got legs.'

'You've seen them?'

'Yes.'

'In trousers?'

Tim's silence was enough.

'I thought not. Narrow skirts, nice shoes, long hair, combs it a lot.'

'Plenty of women are like that.'

'I've studied this type pretty thoroughly, believe me. My search has been long, and until now, fruitless.'

'Then you'll also know she's pregnant.'

Mrs Woosencraft's sherry glass slipped through her fingers and smashed on the stone floor. 'Drat. Never mind. Tim, listen, this is important. I came to Brighton to find a mermaid but I couldn't use my magic to find her directly because they have their own magic, Deep Magic. It's very old and very strong. To catch a mermaid on dry land you have to fish for them with cats. The way I do it you need exactly nineteen. Nineteen is indivisible, see? One of the numbers that can't be broken. I was getting somewhere until Un Deg Naw disappeared. I needed another cat, I was running out of time—'

There was a knock on the door. Mrs Woosencraft ignored it. 'My cats found the mermaid but then I lost the cat that found her, Morse. Except Morse was now, shall we say, disguised as my cat. It was obvious to me what was going on. Find the cat, find the mermaid. That's where you came in, Tim. You must tell me where she—'

The knock came again.

'I'll get it,' Tim said, happy to interrupt a monologue that belonged in a room with deep-buttoned walls.

He opened the front door to be confronted by Dolores Vogler.

'Dolores, what are you doing here?'

'Hello, Mr Wassiter. What an unexpected surprise,' Dolores said. 'I'm looking for someone called Dorothy Woosencraft.'

Tim felt light-headed. 'This is where she lives.'

Dolores sniffed the air in front of Tim's face. 'Have you been drinking?'

'All things considered, no more than absolutely necessary.'

Mrs Woosencraft pushed past Tim. 'You again. What do you want?'

Dolores turned to Tim in bemusement. 'I don't know what she means.'

'Oh, you dirty little fibber,' Mrs Woosencraft said.

Dolores' eyes narrowed. 'If you weren't so old—'

'You wouldn't dare!'

Tim took hold of Dolores arm and whispered, 'She's not having a very good day. She thinks one of my friends is a mermaid.'

'There's nothing wrong with me or my ears,' Mrs Woosencraft snapped. 'If I say she's a mermaid it's because she bloody well is, not because I've gone soft in the head.'

A man Tim did not recognise walked up to the door. He was in late middle age and dressed in pale blue slacks, a charcoal jacket and collarless shirt, and rather incongruously a white Stetson. He held out his hand. 'Mr Wassiter, an unexpected surprise. We meet at last, I am Markus Koponen.'

Tim didn't feel like shaking hands. 'I found your car.'

Koponen gave him a brilliant smile. 'Indeed you did. I am using it today. You have also done something which is difficult to put a true value on. As for the real nature of your friend, why don't you ask her yourself? Ms Bolivia is travelling with us in my Mercedes.'

Parked in the street Tim saw the beautiful and imposing Airflow Imperial Eight. In front of it was the low-slung cream Mercedes. There were three figures inside, all female. The driver and one of the rear-seat passengers wore red. The other had a head of hair so golden it shone. It could only be Foxy.

At some unknown impulse she turned. Her face was pale. She saw Tim and raised her hand.

Koponen extracted a thin white envelope from his jacket's inside breast pocket and handed it to Mrs Woosencraft. 'Payment in full, with my thanks.'

Mrs Woosencraft took it quickly and wordlessly. Koponen checked his watch. 'It's time we were off. I have a ship to catch.' He studied Tim thoughtfully. 'Mr Wassiter, I think you should accompany us.'

'No, thanks.' Tim gathered himself, ready to shove past Koponen and run.

Koponen's hand slipped smoothly into his hip pocket. The material jutted forward in exactly the way it would if the hand held a gun. Tim subsided and watched Koponen warily.

'I see you've noticed how serious I am. We'll ride together in the Chrysler.'

Dolores slipped her arm through Tim's. 'I'll walk you there.'

'Don't go,' Mrs Woosencraft exclaimed. 'None of you. I've seen it, a journey across water into danger.'

'Really?' Markus Koponen said, startled. 'Through your magic?'

'Two groups of four people travel towards their doom.'

'Then I can reassure you because there are only three people in the Imperial. Much as I respect your gifts, this time you are mistaken.'

As Tim climbed into the back of the Imperial he had another surprise: Troy Jarglebaum sat at the wheel.

'Troy,' Tim said. 'What the hell are you doing here?'

Jarglebaum gripped the wheel. 'I sub-contract. Get in the car, kid. Time and tide, we're on a schedule.'

'Troy, help me. Koponen's got a gun.'

'What?' Jarglebaum's head snapped round. He took in Koponen's pose with his hand in his jacket pocket in an instant. His big jaw worked, his tombstone teeth showed in a helpless grin. 'Oh, that's good.' He wiped a tear from his eye. 'Everything's OK, Tim. Koponen's not going to shoot anyone, trust me.'

Tim slid warily across the rear seat behind Jarglebaum. Koponen climbed in and pulled the door shut with a soft clunk. The cars swept away.

Mrs Woosencraft looked down at the white envelope in her hand and found her tongue. 'I didn't do it for the money, Tim,' she called out in a quavering shout. 'It wasn't just for the money.'

The cars turned at the end of the road and were gone.

'I'll look after Morse for you,' she whispered. 'I'll take good care of him. See if I don't.'

The Good Guys

THE INTERIOR of the Chrysler Imperial was spacious and silent, the high-backed seats upholstered in oxblood leather, the air faintly scented with hide wax. Polished walnut panels trimmed the doors, side pillars and arm rests, the bright work was silver rather than chrome. The steady murmur of the powerful engine came from the front of the car, a faint whisper of rushing air from the windows.

'I come from Finland, Mr Wassiter,' Koponen said. 'I enjoy summers but the world is warming too much and too fast. I have reengineered this car to run on Canola oil, my fuel supply is carbon-neutral and allows me to run a big-engined car with a clear conscience.'

'Oil-seed rape,' Tim said as he remembered the brochure from the boot of this very car. 'You've developed a high-yield variety.'

Koponen placed his Stetson on the seat between them. 'You've made a connection but that's not the full story. The high yield is the carrot to attract the farmers, and believe me they are being attracted in high numbers. My first commercial scale seed crop has been harvested and is ready to ship to the U.S.A. It will be sold to thousands of farms and planted across hundreds of thousands of hectares.'

'Is that where we're going?'

'To the United States? Only part of the way. As Mr Jarglebaum said, we have a ship to catch. That ship is the *Sea Cucumber*. She is waiting for us at Southampton water. From there we'll rendezvous with my research vessel in the mid-Atlantic.' Koponen looked out the window at the scenery speeding past. 'I plan to save the world, Mr Wassiter. Plans of that scale cost a huge amount of money. I've an immense fortune but I'm spending it fast. I don't begrudge a single penny but I'm going to need a lot more.'

Koponen's eyes glittered with excitement. 'Soon *doloresvogle*r, my white-flowered variety of oil-seed rape, will not only slow global warming, it will make me a lot of money too.'

They reached the roundabout underneath the coast road flyover. Jarglebaum followed the Mercedes as it powered around the curve and up the west-bound ramp.

A few miles later brake lights began to flare. Jarglebaum slowed the Imperial. 'Road works ahead, Mr Koponen.'

'Ah, this country. It's wonderful, but sometimes it is frustrating.' Koponen impatiently tapped his fingers on the armrest, picked his hat up by the brim and turned it in his hands like a wheel. 'Climate change, Mr Wassiter. Wave height in the North Atlantic is increasing as winds strengthen, the tropics have more frequent and more powerful hurricanes. Ice caps and glaciers are melting, sea level will rise ten, maybe twenty metres. A slow disaster of our own making. Governments are not doing enough, I decided to step in.'

He's mad, Tim though. A self-deluded megalomaniac justifying any means to an admittedly worthy end.

Koponen watched him with wry amusement. 'Whatever you may think of me I am one of the good guys. We've designed air conditioning that uses passive heat exchangers and solar fans that generate all of their own electrical power. Use them and we could shut down entire power stations.'

Tim sat uncomfortably in the corner. 'This isn't about air conditioning.'

Koponen flourished his Stetson. 'And this hat isn't just vanity. It's a symbol, a constant reminder of what my priorities need to be. Wherever I go I'm reflecting a little bit of the sun's heat away from the earth back into space.'

'What about the roof of the car?'

Koponen laughed. 'A fair point. There is also something called style, Mr Wassiter. Unfortunately high albedo black paint appears to be an impossible contradiction, don't think I haven't tried. Just imagine if one tenth of the world's population wore white hats outdoors. That's over 750 million people. With a conservative estimate of 9 hats to the square metre, that's almost 8,500 hectares of reflective surface, an area greater than Bermuda.'

'That doesn't sound like much,' Tim said.

'No, it isn't.' Koponen slapped his hat down on his knee and scowled. 'No, it isn't at all.'

They were through the road works. Jarglebaum sent the car surging through the traffic.

A surreal calm came over Tim. In his mind he compiled a list of items that defined his own life:

He had been kidnapped at gunpoint by an insane foreign businessman.

His neighbour was a witch who hypnotised cats and thought his friend was a mermaid.

Almost everyone he knew, including his former police partner, worked for the crazy billionaire.

He himself apparently had the ability to travel through time and space in his dreams.

'Are you all right, Mr Wassiter?' Koponen said. 'You were talking to yourself.'

'I was wondering if I was mad and the last few days had been a psychotic delusion.'

'As far as I am concerned this is all very real. This is my life.'

The interior of the Imperial was cool to the point of chilly, Tim turned up his collar. Koponen had spoken freely but he hadn't explained why Foxy was with him. Tim knew there was little he could do unless he could get the gun away from Koponen. He had to keep Koponen talking. With the Finn in a verbose mood it was a good opportunity to get some more answers.

'This is all to do with the flowers, isn't it?' Tim hazarded.

'Well done. Farmers will plant my crop because the plants are engineered to be nitrogen fixing, give higher yields and a better oil/protein balance. More profit, less cost, less fertiliser and less nitrate pollution. There is every reason to grow my Canola and none not to. Cost and yield is why farmers will buy my seeds, the environmental benefits will cut the ground out from under the feet of the GM protestors.'

Tim was grudgingly impressed. It all made good sense. He said so.

'A means to an end, Mr Wassiter. The real reason I want my new crop planted is because the flowers are white and they bloom for an additional three weeks White flowers, Mr Wassiter, my plants have white flowers. This is the first crop designed for a high albedo. Three years from now it will be growing in vast acreages, half a million hectares in Great Britain alone. Farmers grow wealthy, higher yield means less deforestation, I earn enough money to finance the next phase of my project. Most importantly, the white flowers will reflect sunlight and cool the world.'

Flecks of spittle grew in the corners of Koponen's mouth. He wiped them away. 'Change through positive incentive. Forcing change by punishing people with taxation is self-defeating. Governments don't understand. They want to control people; I want to set them free!'

Tim had limited experience with ranting megalomania. He tried flattery. 'That's brilliant. I'm convinced. Mr Koponen, you're a genius.' It actually was very clever

Koponen basked in Tim's praise. 'Enlightened self-interest, the new model for the free market.'

'So what has Foxy to do with this?'

Koponen blinked. 'Nothing at all. She's part of my Atlantic scheme, another thing entirely.'

Tim thought about her alone in the Mercedes with Dolores, Electra and Imelda. 'She'd better be all right at the end of the journey.'

Koponen stiffened. 'She will be absolutely fine.'

Tim saw Jarglebaum watching from the corner of his eye in the rear-view mirror. He's as worried as me, Tim realised. And he tried to warn me earlier. He felt a little reassured, at least in this they were on the same side.

'What I don't understand is why you hired me to find your car. You already knew where it was.'

'An excuse to keep an eye on you. Mrs Woosencraft worked for me but she was having problems and I was becoming concerned about her personal agenda. When I discovered she had hired you to find her cat, doing exactly what I needed someone to do, I decided to keep tabs on you.'

'The desk bug and the embroidered handkerchief,' Tim said.

'Exactly. Ms Bolivia's jacket was a helpful bonus.'

Of course. Tim could have kicked himself, they had bugged that too.

And to get all this done Koponen had used the oldest trick in the book: exotic women tantalising his baser male instincts, keeping him further off-balance with touches of violence. It was galling to realise how easily he had fallen for it.

'My initial assessment of you has been vindicated—you're a focus. No great talent yourself but things happen around you. If not, how else would you have become involved at all?'

Now was not the time to mention Asklepios and his dreams, Tim decided. He would let Koponen underestimate him for as long as possible.

'It is the strength of your desires,' Koponen continued. 'Your dreams for how the world should be as opposed to what you fear it actually is, something the two of us share.' Koponen pressed his palms together as if in prayer. 'In that we are not really so different.'

A muffled snort came from the front of the car. Troy Jarglebaum's shoulders shook as he tried to suppress his laughter.

'Ignore him, he doesn't see the world like us,' Koponen said. 'You managed to find something without even looking for it. That in itself is a rare gift and one I would like to use again. The car was simply an excuse to introduce some surveillance. You weren't supposed to find the car, you were meant to find the cat.'

Responsibility

TIME PASSED. Persistent Smith lay in the dark of the capacious and surprisingly comfortable boot and listened to the muffled male voices coming from the passenger compartment. He didn't hear it all but some of what he heard fit in with what he already knew and the rest he simply accepted as true.

Then the voices fell silent. Into that space an awful thought intruded: Heidi. Smith's mouth hung open in an agony of silent dismay. Heidi. They were supposed to meet, he'd let her down, abandoned her. She'd— What would she think of him? Smith had a very good idea. This was Bad, very bad. Bad Thinking, Bad Dating. Bad Lifestyle Choices.

The Hand came out, he couldn't help it. Frantically Smith silently pinched his lips together. The Hand studied him with an expression of profound disappointment and Smith knew he had let everyone down badly.

This level of worry and guilt was exhausting. Smith groped for his drink bottle then stayed his hand. He knew he drank when he was nervous, drinking too much here would be worse than a poor choice, it could be disastrous.

He listened to the sounds of the vehicle. The steady powerful beat of the engine, the thrum of exhaust and rush of tyres on the road formed a soothing harmony. Every now and then the car swung gently to one side and back again as it overtook slower traffic or negotiated a bend. Smith closed his eyes. What was done was done, there was nothing he could do to change it and it was his responsibility to put it right. All he could do was hope it was possible, and try.

Changes in the motion of the car woke him. They had slowed, the vehicle moved more actively now, turning, braking, and accelerating. The passengers were talking again, but their voices were indistinct. Outside there were sounds of other vehicles: cars, motorcycles and buses. Once the car was stopped for several seconds and Smith heard the beep-beep-beep of a pedestrian crossing. They were in another town. Wherever they were going it felt like they were getting close.

Very thirsty now, Smith opened his bottle of orangeade. Guilt-ridden thoughts of Heidi returned, orangeade sprayed into his face. He jerked back and knocked his head on the boot lid.

The car lurched from side to side, then steadied. Smith loosened the cap more slowly. The gas hissed out steadily. He lay back and sipped his drink.

Relax

'WE'RE JUST about on time.' Koponen fretfully checked his watch. The journey had taken far longer than he had hoped. Although they could still leave on a falling tide he had wanted to leave on the rise, it somehow felt right. Now the sun was setting, and thankfully the dense evening urban traffic of Southampton flowed smoothly.

They were nearly there. Koponen settled back, letting himself relax for the first time that day.

A muffled bang came from the rear of the car.

'What was that?' Koponen exclaimed. 'We hit something.'

'Relax,' Jarglebaum said. 'There was nothing, I'd have seen it. It's probably your stuff settling in the boot.'

'I felt it. There was a bump. Keep your eyes on the road.' Koponen slumped back, then started forward in alarm. 'Now I can hear hissing. I was right, you hit something. We have a puncture.'

'I can hear it too,' Tim said.

Jarglebaum swung the wheel back and forth. 'The car's handling fine. This babe is a dream to drive.' He caught Koponen's glare and turned forward to hide his smirk. 'Look, if it is a puncture it's a slow one. There's just a couple of miles to go and we've got a spare. Even if we need to change the wheel we'll only lose a few minutes. I'm sure Tim will be happy to help, won't you buddy?'

'Not with my back.'

'What's wrong with your back?' Koponen was suddenly sympathetic. 'I've had problems, I know how it feels. No-one believes you.'

'There's nothing wrong with his back,' Jarglebaum called out. 'He's lying.'

'There should have been plenty of time,' Koponen muttered. 'Those road works—'

'Nothing to do with me, I'm just the driver,' Jarglebaum said. 'Relax. I'll get you there.'

Only Chocolate

HEIDI HAD worked hard all day, she had even skipped lunch, though in truth she felt too excited to eat. Now her long day was over and she sat at her workstation and ran a final check on the last non-correcting audit she had run. It was really just something to do while she waited for Derek Smith.

Apart from her the office was empty. Even the light in Mr Abercrombie's office was off.

She smiled to herself as she remembered all the funny things Derek did and said, and how he argued with his talking hand. It was going to be fun to spend time with him. She could do with some fun.

She also needed to thank him and tell him about all the intriguing events that had happened as a result of his help. When she'd shown Abercrombie it had taken him a while to see it. When he did, he went very quiet and very pale. Paler than normal even for him, a man who seemed to have lived his entire life under office lighting.

Abercrombie cleared his throat. 'Have you mentioned this to anyone?'

'No.' Heidi decided there was no need to mention Derek.

Abercrombie picked up her phone and dialled a number. 'Mr Palmer, this is Abercrombie. I'm sorry to disturb you, sir. I'm with Ms Tollund. She's discovered something I think you should see for yourself.'

Heidi had never met the Chief Financial Officer before. She'd only ever seen Palmer's name on the organisation chart. Right at the top beside Markus Kononen.

Now she was really worried. Two weeks into a new job and her boss and her boss's boss were coming to see her. This was not good at all.[10]

Palmer and Abercrombie dressed like chalk and cheese. The younger Abercrombie kept his hair cropped short and wore narrow, black suits. He thought this gave him a sober, dynamic air, but actually made him look generic.

Palmer's bold liquorice pinstripe contrasted with his lemon-yellow shirt and pink tie. His jet-black hair was collar length and his fringe tended to flop over his eyes.

In his youth Palmer played the same game as Abercrombie and discovered it got you nowhere. You had to learn to be yourself, a rule just as true for accountants as for anyone. One day Abercrombie would work it out and Palmer would promote him.

'What seems to be the problem?' Palmer said affably. To Heidi's mind a slight overbite made his smile disconcertingly toothy.

Abercrombie leaned in close, whispering. His long, raw fingers stabbed at Heidi's screen, sketching out columns and totals.

Palmer rested his chin on his thumb. 'That's really rather clever. Tell me, Ms Tollund, did you elucidate this yourself?'

'Er, yes. Am I in trouble, Mr Palmer?'

'Quite the opposite, I salute you. However, I will now as Chief Financial Officer formally ask you not to talk about this to anyone except me.' Palmer beamed genially at Heidi, who found herself smiling back.

____

[10] *You can tell how badly things are going by the number of managers standing behind you at your desk. One is bad. Two is twice as bad as one, three are twice as bad as two, etc.*

'Yes, of course,' Heidi said. 'Can I ask who Vogler, Marchpane, and—'

'You don't need to know that,' Abercrombie broke in.

'It's all right, Robert. I'm sure someone as bright as Ms Tollund could find out if she wanted. Vogler, Marchpane, and Vaughan are non-executive directors. You could think of them rather like Ministers Without Portfolio appointed by Mr Koponen himself. I'm sure he'd be interested in these, ah— inconsistencies.' Palmer beamed at Heidi again. 'But don't forget, not a word. And jolly well done.'

Now it was dark outside and Heidi was wondered where Derek had got to. She also wondered which floor he worked on. He'd never said and she had just assumed he was new like her and in need of a friend. Maybe it would turn out that's all they would be, just friends, someone to chat with and share a joke. That would be all right, though she thought this time, maybe…

She waited a while longer.

And a while more.

She felt a little sad and told herself it was just the emotional intensity of the day.

Heidi shut down her workstation, picked up her handbag, turned off the remaining lights and walked through to the lifts. As she passed the vending machines she half expected to see Smith there, on his knees and looking for change. She stood there, not really thinking about anything. Then she summoned the lift and went home, a journey brightened only by the chocolate counter at the late-night store.

Cheap Tricks

TROY WAS right, the Imperial arrived at the docks without incident. He walked around the car and peremptorily kicked each tyre. 'They're fine.'

'Check the spare, please, and bring the sack from the boot,' Koponen said.

Tim stepped out onto the Southampton docks. The evening air felt warm compared to the chill of the Chrysler's interior. Twenty yards away Foxy stood beside the Mercedes with Imelda Marchpane close beside her.

Who knew how those devious and aggressive women had been treating Foxy? He had to help her and to do that he needed to get away. This might be his last chance before embarkation.

He looked around for a customs officer or security guard, anyone. The docks were deserted. Grey and yellow painted gantries and cranes loomed silently against the evening sky in the empty spaces between high stacks of shipping containers. Cargo ships lay tied up at berth all along the quay. Most were in darkness but the one nearest to them, a medium-sized vessel with a rust-stained white superstructure, showed a few lights.

Troy Jarglebaum swung up the lid of the Imperial's boot.

'Boo!' Persistent Smith shouted up at him.

'Jesus!' Jarglebaum jumped back, actually stepping out of one of his shoes. 'My God, it's you.'

Jarglebaum's shout brought Markus Koponen and Tim hurrying round.

Smith waved his empty bottle. 'Can I use your toilet?'

Markus Koponen paled under his white hat. 'Who the devil are you?'

Jarglebaum danced on one foot as he pulled on his shoe. 'I don't bloody believe it. This is Derek Smith, missing person. I interviewed his parents yesterday.'

His finger stabbed down at the grinning Smith. 'Stay right where you are, pal.' Jarglebaum reached into the boot and hauled out the sack.

Koponen slammed the boot lid shut and turned on Jarglebaum. 'What the hell is he doing in my trunk?'

Jarglebaum bridled right back. 'I haven't a bloody clue. I don't go around locking people in car boots.'

'Then let me make it very clear to you, Mr Jarglebaum, neither do I.'

Jarglebaum pointed at the boot. 'You just did.'

'That's different.'

'So what's he doing in there?'

Nice technique Troy, Tim thought, as astonished by Smith's presence as anyone. Jarglebaum had neatly turned the conversation round. Now it was him who was questioning Koponen.

Koponen grew exasperated. 'I told you. I don't know!'

'It's your car. You keep it locked in your car park.'

'Yes, but who is he?' Koponen said.

'He works for me,' Tim said.

'What?' Koponen exclaimed.

Jarglebaum simply laughed.

'He works for me. When Dolores hired me to look for the car I hired him to help.'

Koponen exhaled in relief. 'I take my hat off to you, Mr Wassiter. I really do. What resource, what enterprise.'

'That guy in the boot is a fruitcake.' Jarglebaum tapped the side of his head. 'You know, firing on three cylinders. Or five.'

'And yet he not only found my car, he ended up inside it without our knowledge.'

'Yeah, right. So what are we going to do with him?'

Koponen came to a decision. 'I'm not going to take him with us, and we can't let him go. He'll have to stay where he is.'

'Jesus, aren't you even going to let the poor guy take a leak?' Jarglebaum said.

Koponen waved away the question. 'There's no time. I notice he has a bottle, he can use that. I've arranged for the cars to be collected tomorrow morning. Leave the keys in the tailpipe. I'll tell the drivers what to expect. They can drive Mr Smith back to Brighton and buy him breakfast.'

Cold and beautiful, Electra Vaughan made her way from the Mercedes towards Markus Koponen. The uneven surface of concrete-patched old stone and new tarmac was no obstacle to her high, elegant heels. Both Koponen and Jarglebaum assessed her languorous walk.

It's now, or never, Tim decided. He hesitated, torn between making a dash for it, taking his chances against Koponen and his gun, or staying with Foxy. He was confident of being able to outrun the men, but the muscular and athletic Imelda was another matter. An encounter with her alone in the empty docklands was not a pleasant prospect. Tim steeled himself, he had to try. All he could hope for was enough of a head start to evade her.

Heavy hands gripped his shoulders. 'Hold on, son,' Troy Jarglebaum said. 'Where do you think you're going?'

'Get your hands off me.' Tim ducked out from under Jarglebaum's grip.

Jarglebaum took a step back and tugged down his jacket. 'Mr Koponen would be disappointed if I let you go now.'

Tim knew he was outclassed. Troy Jarglebaum was a bruiser, an old-style cop, perfectly happy to use his fists and his physical bulk if the situation required. Right now Tim wanted nothing more than to bury his own fist deep in his old partner's smug, jowly, middle-aged face.

Troy dropped into a half-crouch, balanced on the balls of his feet, arms splayed. 'Cool it, chum,' he laughed. 'This is Troy Jarglebaum remember? Your old pal.'

'What are you doing with these people, Troy? You're an intelligent man, despite everything I do believe that. Koponen's turned you into hired muscle.'

Jarglebaum beckoned Tim closer. 'It's not that easy, mate,' he whispered. 'The police service has been good to me but I'm not getting any younger. It's time to move on.'

'To this?'

Somehow Jarglebaum looked bashful. 'Look, there's this girl. I met her on a case, she's younger than me but we get along. I admit it, I'm sweet on her. Me, can you imagine it? Well, it's true. Koponen's all right, he's very concerned with the environment. An employer like that can impress the younger generation and he pays well.'

'I'm happy for you, Troy, really I am,' Tim said bitterly. 'But right over there is my friend and she's being held against her will by that same OK guy who, I might also point out, also kidnapped me at gunpoint and locked another of my friends in the boot of his car.'

'Excuse me.' Markus Koponen turned away from Electra. 'I do apologise for that deception, Mr Wassiter. As I'm sure Mr Jarglebaum will confirm, I do not even own a gun.' Koponen stuck his finger into his pocket and aimed it at Tim. 'Nothing but a cheap trick copied from the cinema. I simply wanted to speed things up and acted on impulse. I really was quite surprised when it worked. Guns and people form a deadly kind of synergy and I will have nothing to do with it.'

'What about Foxy?'

'My girls talked to Ms Bolivia and she has agreed to come along. Dolores and Imelda are helping her aboard as we speak. I hope you will allow Electra to do the same for you.'

'Foxy, you don't have to do this,' Tim called out.

Preceded by Dolores and with Imelda behind her, Foxy was already halfway up the gangplank and gave no reply.

Electra's arm slipped through Tim's, her other hand gripped his elbow like a vice. 'Shall we, Mr Wassiter?'

'For God's sake, Troy, help me. You're a cop!' Tim cried.

Jarglebaum couldn't meet his eye. 'Part-time, semi-retired. It's more of a consultancy these days.'

'I'll see you in my cabin in a few minutes,' Koponen called out as Electra led Tim away. 'Welcome aboard the *Sea Cucumber.*'

With Foxy aboard Tim had no option and allowed Electra to steer him towards the gangplank.

One hundred and eighty metres long, *Sea Cucumber* had a three-storey superstructure at the rear and cargo cranes fore and aft of the main hold. As Tim stepped aboard the ship shuddered as the engine rumbled into life. A steady stream of rust-orange bilge water slopped from the stern into the harbour. Four crew members, swarthy, muscular men in dark trousers and jackets, unhitched the heavy hawsers from the dockside bollards at the bows and stern.

Down on the dock Troy Jarglebaum slung the sack over his shoulder and faced Markus Koponen. 'This is my advice: Imelda should not be left alone with Foxy Bolivia.'

'We agreed that subject was closed. Ms Bolivia will be fine. Now, get on board and do your job.'

Fat Table

'HE'S A GENIUS, an avatar of Ea filled with His wisdom,' Banipal exclaimed.

Asklepios followed the conversation between Banipal and Ishkun with difficulty. The two men had been kind to him and they were clearly friends. Since Banipal had rescued him he had learned a substantial number of words and discovered he was in Babylon before the fall, that it was a city of magnificence, of stunning wealth, governed by kings who seemed determined to be wise, courageous and just. Everything they did, their daily lives, their politics and war, were governed by their worship of gilded statues that, as far as Asklepios could determine, were not mere representations of divinity but the actual Gods themselves.

Ishkun was less impressed. 'He is a skinny old man who knows barely sixty words of our tongue. Wise? Perhaps he is, but he is no divine messenger. He did not descend from heaven on the back of a Kurub, you pulled him from the Euphrates like the half-drowned she-goat he smelled of at the time.'

Nevertheless, Ishkun had been considerate, content to sit with Asklepios and teach him new words, carefully repeating them when Asklepios forgot or made mistakes. He had to admit the foreigner was a fast learner who was also civilised, polite and grateful.

Banipal smiled patiently. 'You do not understand, beloved friend. We converse with numbers, a universal language for learned men. I may be fluent but Asklepios is a poet. He has shown me great things that lie in plain sight, yet none of us see them.'

Always defensive when it came to numbers, Ishkun acted unimpressed. 'That must be nice for the both of you.'

'Please, don't be like that. Asklepios makes me feel like you do when you take me hunting. I cannot see the animal signs until you point them out, it makes me feel clumsy and ignorant. What is obvious to you is hidden from me so I struggle to learn and to remember. But with Asklepios what he teaches, remains. He has opened my eyes.'

'Tell me some of these simple things.'

Banipal grinned happily. 'There are numbers that cannot be divided by other numbers. For example, seven and eleven.'

'Yes,' Ishkun spoke slowly. 'So?'

'Those numbers appear to never end. Thirteen, seventeen, nineteen, twenty-three.'

Ishkun frowned, working on his fingers. 'All right.'

'And numbers go on forever. Whatever number you think of, you can always add one to it. They form an infinity.'

'I suppose so.' This was reaching a level of abstraction Ishkun found difficult. Even accepting this was true, what was the point of numbers larger than herds, or armies? There was little point in counting grains of millet or sand, you put the grains in sacks and counted the sacks instead.

'But these numbers that cannot be divided, although we cannot prove it, they could be an infinity too.'

'But they are not all the numbers there are.'

'Exactly!'

Ishkun grimaced as he tried to imagine this, then clutched his temples. 'What use is that except for making my head spin?'

'It is amazing!'

'I'm amazed you are impressed by it,' Ishkun said, though he smiled as he said it.

It was in the quiet moments like these, after a meal and listening to the two men talk, that Asklepios marvelled at his own resilience. In a handful of days he had been magically whirled first to the unimaginable future then the magnificent past. He had been robbed, nearly drowned, and become a thief himself. After taking a second look at the river he had been hauled from, he felt claiming he had nearly being eaten by crocodiles was only a slight exaggeration.

He was sure that if someone told him all this was going to happen he would have feared for his own sanity. Yet here he was, fed and clothed and in the company of strangers he believed could be his friends. All things considered, he felt fortune was still on his side.

It was strange, the thing he most regretted was losing the measuring instruments he had stolen. They had been so perfectly made, so precise. Now they were somewhere at the bottom of the river. If only he had managed to keep them. If only he had made it home… It was more than simple bad luck. Something had moved against Tim in the dream-lands, a wilful malign interference that cast Asklepios far from home for a second time. He knew one thing for certain—if he encountered that entity again he would recognise it.

The hidden blessing was that each time he travelled he learned more about his craft and its arts. He tried to explain some of this to Banipal. In the end he simply did not have the words and the conversation collapsed into shaking heads, laughter and gestures.

What he had wanted to say was this:

'I am starting to realise that much of what I did was nonsense and wasted effort. I did not know which parts of a ritual were essential and which were not. Now I see the danger, for over time rituals grow more elaborate and those complications make them prone to error. My quest is not for simplicity for its own sake, but to identify the essentials.'

One thing Asklepios was absolutely certain on was that geometry and accurate measurement were critical. The stolen instruments had clarified his thoughts, especially the half circle so neatly divided. Now, sitting here, he had another idea: why was it necessary to mark out the circle anew every time when a skilled craftsman with good tools could carve a design into wood?

Excited by the thought Asklepios interrupted Banipal's conversation with Ishkun. 'Excuse me. Excuse me kind friends.'

'Yes, Asklepios, what is it? Are you unwell?'

'No, I am very well. Please, may I ask for making something.'

Banipal listened attentively. 'What is it?'

'A bench. No, it is this,' Asklepios cursed his limited vocabulary and banged his hand on the table.

'A table?'

'Yes, a table. A fat one.'

From Ishkun and Banipal's puzzled expressions Asklepios knew he had used the wrong words. He tried again. 'Not long like this, a fat one.' Asklepios circled his finger in the air. 'Fat, big.'

'He means round,' Ishkun said. Dipping his finger in his beaker of water he drew a circle. 'Like this?'

'Yes,' Asklepios said. 'Like that.'

A Real Success

ELECTRA KEPT Tim away from Foxy and led him up a different companionway to a room with a heavy steel door.

'The ship's brig?' Tim said.

'Don't be stupid. This is an ocean vessel, all the doors are like this.'

Electra pulled opened the door and waited for Tim to go inside.

He put one foot inside the cabin. 'What's this all about, Electra? I know about the canola seed, this ship's full of it, Koponen told me. What's it got to do with Foxy and me?'

Tim met Electra's cold gaze. You're flawless, he thought. There's not a line, a mole or a wrinkle on you, every platinum-blonde eyelash is in place. It's part of why you're so intimidating.

'With you? Nothing. You were in the wrong place at the wrong time. If we'd left you behind you'd have caused problems. As for her, I can guarantee you'll never guess.'

Tim couldn't help but laugh. 'You think she's a mermaid too.'

Before he could move Electra had a grip on his wrist irresistible as a hydraulic vice. 'Don't think, Mr Wassiter, Tim, little Timmy. Do as you're told and go into the room or I'll crush your hand to a bloody pulp.'

That's the other part, Tim thought, dry-mouthed. Electra propelled him into the cabin. The heavy door swung shut with a deep, metallic boom.

Electra's voice came through the door. 'We'll come and get you later. You won't be disturbed because I've locked you in.'

As soon as she had gone Tim tried the door. Unsurprisingly it did not budge. Electra wasn't the sort of person to make simple mistakes. He sat on the narrow bed. Well done, he told himself. You've made a real success of this investigation.

As well as the bed the cabin contained a wicker chair painted eggshell blue and two corner shelves. A porthole window by the door offered a view down onto the dark docks where a sparse scatter of security lights gleamed. A steady vibration thrummed through the air, the deck canted gently and clear water appeared between the ship and the quayside. Water churned to foam at the stern, the bows swung out, the vessel was under way. Despite everything Tim felt a rising excitement, he was heading out to sea towards whatever fate had in store for him.

He checked the room again. The entire place was made of metal, the bed was steel-framed and bolted to the floor, the shelves welded to the bulkheads. There was nothing to use as a tool or weapon beyond the blanket and a wicker chair. He imagined various daring escapes: flinging a blanket over peoples' heads; stabbing them with a broken chair leg. Each plan ran up against the same obstacle. To rescue Foxy he would need to overpower the entire crew single-handed.

The lights along the coast fell far behind. Belatedly, guiltily, he remembered Persistent Smith locked in the boot of a car with an empty soft drink bottle for a toilet. With that thought came a chilling realisation: Mrs Woosencraft had been right after all, there had been four people in the Chrysler.

The Boot

EVEN THOUGH Koponen had shut him back inside the boot Smith convulsed with laughter. He had said 'Boo!' and the man with two chins had actually jumped out of his shoes. Nothing could be funnier.

He calmed down and listened to the continuing conversation outside the car. To his amazement one of the voices was Tim Wassiter's. Tim was in trouble, big trouble. These people were the RBGs, the Really Bad Guys. They kidnapped people, locked them in car boots and dressed smartly. As such, they would also have speedboats, helicopters, miniature submarines and henchmen dressed all in black and armed with sub-machine guns.

His heart beat faster as he imagined a bullet-riddled Imperial rolling down a slipway into the sea. Would that really be his own fate? This was now far more exciting than he had ever wanted an adventure to be. For a moment he wished he was back at home watching television with his parents. Smith hugged himself and hoped the voices would go away soon.

After a few minutes they did. Smith listened intently. A lone seagull cried, a ship's horn sounded far in the distance. All was quiet.

Although he had just blurted out the first thing he'd thought of when the boot was opened, Smith really did need to go to the toilet. As he lay in the dark with nothing else to think of the uncomfortable urge grew and grew. He clutched his bottle in one hand and the torch in the other and considered Koponen's suggestion. Apart from the practical difficulties of peeing into a bottle while lying locked in the boot of a car in the dark, what if the bottle filled up and he couldn't stop? And what if he got stuck? His mind recoiled from the imagery but he could feel the humiliation, the utter embarrassment of walking into a hospital with a plastic bottle sticking out of his trousers.

Mild discomfort slowly turned into actual pain. Smith rolled and shuffled then flicked the torch on. There on the inside of the boot lid was the lock and lever, down on the body was the strike-plate and catch. He had to get out and soon, or there would be some seriously Bad Peeing.

A few minutes later the boot lock clunked and the lid swung up. Smith swung his legs over the sill and hobbled urgently into a shadowed recess and guiltily relieved himself.

He'd learned something even Clive Barnett would have found more interesting than a ride in the luggage compartment of his favourite car. Getting free of the boot had been easy. The lock was designed to keep people out, not in.

He looked around the alcove. A few old overalls hung on nails, there was nothing else of interest. He peered out and saw the coast was clear. Overhead a few early stars were out, the span of the sky shading from pale blue to dusty violet-grey. An offshore breeze freshened, Smith zipped up his fleece. Apart from the fact he was by the sea at some docks he had absolutely no idea where he was.

The drive had taken a few hours, but at what speed, and which direction? There were no navy ships in sight, so it probably wasn't Portsmouth. Commercial ports were scattered all along the English south coast and this could be any of them: Dover, Southampton, even Falmouth. Smith knew the names from his train timetables, each one was an important terminus. He had never been to any of them. He had never before been out of Brighton.

He looked out across the choppy, restless harbour water, and back to the silent cranes and warehouses of the docks. The air tasted different here, the play of light, the movement of the air, all were more vivid, more filled with hidden promise than the evening skies of Brighton. It was the furthest from home he had ever been.

Wherever he was Smith knew he was not meant to be here. He should head inland, get to the town and find a police station.

A wavering light appeared at the far end of the quay. Smith stepped back into the shadows. The light resolved into two separate beams. Night watchmen on patrol.

The lights disappeared. Smith let out a sigh of relief, stepped out onto the quay only to leap back into cover as they reappeared closer.

Unbidden, the Hand reared up. 'Quick, back into the boot.'

'They'll see me.'

'Wait until they check another door.'

He could see them now, and hear their quiet conversation. As soon as they turned aside he ran to the car, clambered inside the boot and pulled down the lid. Safe, he glared at the Hand. 'What are you doing here?'

'I thought you could do with some help.'

'I told you to go away.'

The Hand, as much as a hand held into the shape of a mouth could, shrugged.

'Well, thanks, anyway,' Smith said.

'S'OK.'

They lay quietly. Two pairs of footsteps walked by.

'Um…' the Hand said.

'What?' Smith whispered.

'We should talk.'

The Lucky Ones

Much to his own surprise Tim had fallen asleep in his cabin. He jerked awake when Electra put her hand over his mouth.

That would not have been so bad if her other hand hadn't pinched his nose shut.

'You sleep like a little baby. I could have slit your throat and you'd have woken up dead.'

'You've got some great chat up lines,' Tim said. 'I expect you have to beat them back with a shitty stick.'

Electra's mouth twisted with contempt. 'I serve my master. I await him as he awaits me.'

'Isn't Koponen the lucky one.'

Electra laughed coldly.

She brought him to Koponen in a spartan dining room with a linoleum floor. Tim took in the room. In the centre a long steel-framed table covered in white tablecloths stood with places set for a meal. Koponen and Troy Jarglebaum waited at the back of the room beside an array of bottles of wine, beer, and spirits. Set in the wall behind them was a speaker grill and controls, and a dumb-waiter hatch. The sack from the car lay at their feet.

'Where is Foxy?' Tim said. 'What have you done with her?'

'Absolutely nothing, I assure you,' Koponen said smoothly. 'I have been making sure all is in order with the cargo and conferring with my captain. We're in for a bit of weather in an hour or two, low pressure in the Bay of Biscay. I hope you don't get sea sick.'

Tim bunched his fists. 'Where is she?'

Electra took a languid step forwards.

Koponen held up his hand. 'As a lady surely Ms Bolivia is allowed a little more time to prepare. Would you like a drink, Mr Wassiter?'

Tim gave a hollow laugh. 'All right, let's pretend we are being civilised. Whisky, no ice.'

'It's no pretence. You and Ms Bolivia are my guests.'

As Koponen made Tim's drink the door opened and Foxy entered accompanied by Imelda and Dolores.

'Wow, this ship is cool,' Foxy said. 'There are so many rooms and levels, it's like a building that floats.' She saw Tim. 'Hi Tim, how are you getting on with our new friends?'

'Foxy, are you all right?'

She looked at him steadily. 'Of course I am, Tim. These girls are so friendly and they've got some great clothes. Have you seen Dolores' heels?'

'I think you can see from Ms Bolivia's reaction that she's been well cared for,' Koponen said.

'Absolutely,' Foxy said. 'They're real pussycats.'

Deep under the deck the throb of the engines took on a deeper resonance. The ship gathered speed and rolled a degree to starboard.

Koponen motioned for everyone to take their places at the table. Tim sat opposite Foxy, Electra close beside him.

Koponen raised his glass. 'My plans near completion. We sail with a genetically engineered cargo towards a rendezvous with my deep-sea research vessel.' He laughed lightly, 'It's around this time an evil super-genius would explain his plans to the captive hero before consigning him to the sharks via a fiendishly intricate device—'

Troy Jarglebaum shook his leg, tugged and prodded at his groin. Koponen watched with open-mouthed bemusement.

Jarglebaum looked around a now silent room. 'Don't mind me.'

'Where was I?' Koponen sighed.

'Shark food,' Imelda said.

'Ah, yes. So, rather than that, I thought we'd have a nice meal and a friendly chat. I'm rich but I'm not evil. Tonight the fish is on our menu, not we on theirs '

Tim kept playing the game. He acknowledged Koponen's wit with a polite smile and a nod.

Koponen served more drinks, all the while keeping up a line of small-talk about tonnage, displacement and knots. Finally, he spoke into the wall-grill. 'Ten minutes, please.'

Foxy seemed at ease if a little brittle. She gave Tim a quick smile then returned her attention to Koponen.

Tim wet his lips with his own drink then put it down. After his breakfast session with Mrs Woosencraft he had lost the urge to play the hard-drinking detective. And in addition to the coercion, the pretend gun, and being locked in his cabin there was something else here, something that was not right. Koponen was used to getting what he wanted when he wanted it and no doubt was a ruthless businessman but Tim didn't feel any ill-will from him. And while Jarglebaum was rough and ready, he'd never involve himself in anything outright illegal. Jarglebaum bent the rules but he played a straight game.

There was still that vibe. Something was going down.

Foxy had said, "As far as I'm concerned they're real pussycats." She didn't like cats. More to the point she didn't trust them. Nervous fear thrilled through Tim. His instincts were right, Foxy had tried to warn him.

'Something is wrong,' Tim said.

Jarglebaum went still for a moment then vigorously scratched his ear.

'No, it isn't,' Koponen said breezily. 'I've been working towards this for years. My plans are detailed and comprehensive. You haven't heard the half of them.'

'It doesn't matter what you believe—'

Koponen wasn't in a listening mood. 'I'm not proud about the way you've been treated today. Events took on a momentum of their own. Hear what I have to say—'

'What if we don't like it?'

'Then you will have been my guests on a short voyage and will be compensated for your inconvenience.'

'We've no passports.'

'You won't need them. That, in part, is what Mr Jarglebaum is for. A man who knows the system and how to play it to best advantage. Bend but not break, isn't that how you put it?'

'Man of many talents, me,' Jarglebaum said. 'Nice to be appreciated.'

Koponen stooped and pulled a potato sized lump from the sack Jarglebaum had taken from the Imperial's boot. 'I've been carrying these around to show to the investors. White-flowered canola will earn in the long run, but I need cash now. Deep-sea mining is the plan but I'm having trouble.'

'Manganese nodules.' Tim looked down the table to Jarglebaum who winked. 'You're dredging them up from the fumaroles along the mid-Atlantic ridge.'

Foxy snapped her fingers. 'That's where I've—'

'Seen them before, Ms Bolivia?' Koponen said. 'Relatively low value on today's market, but there are other more valuable deposits. Something down there is interfering with my operations. I've lost expensive equipment.' He looked along the table to Dolores. 'I've nearly lost people too. People I greatly care about.'

'He means all of us,' Dolores said. 'He does.'

'What do you mean, interfering?' Foxy said.

'Just that. Damaging machinery, jamming electronics, frying circuitry. I sent down robotic maintenance vehicles, they never came back. I tried remote-pilot drones, they developed faults. My girls volunteered to take the submarine. They're trained marine scientists—' Koponen's voice grew tight. 'They almost died.'

'Let me clarify. I did not volunteer,' Electra said.

'I did, Markus. I'd do it again.' Dolores exclaimed.

'I won't risk it. There's some sort of field effect down there, probably geomagnetic.'

Despite the circumstances the thought of huge dredging machines labouring in the endless dark and fantastic pressure caught Tim's imagination. 'Industrial espionage?'

'My first thought. Nobody else has the technology. Not the Russians or Americans, not even the South Africans or Japanese. It's something else, something natural.'

Foxy listened intently. 'What kind of field?'

'One that left my girls weak, terribly weak. They took days to recover.' Koponen turned to Foxy. 'We've discovered one thing. The field has no effect on marine life.'

'I see where this is going,' Foxy said.

Tim looked at Koponen in disbelief. 'We're here because you think she's a mermaid too.'

Jarglebaum let out a great guffaw. 'Tim, that's dafter than a box of frogs.'

'Actually, I do,' Koponen said. 'Am I right, Ms Bolivia, or am I right?'

Foxy looked at him with dry respect. 'It was you all along. The cats, that old lady, everything.'

'Come on, she wears shoes,' Tim cried. 'On her feet. You know, those things at the end of her legs. Foxy, tell them.'

'What is it you want me to do?' Foxy said to Koponen.

Tim and Jarglebaum exchanged a look of pure bewilderment.

'Take a look. Simply that, nothing else. I'm deadly serious on this. Don't get involved, don't try and do anything. Just take a look and come back and tell me what you saw.'

Foxy leaned back in her chair. 'There is that. How do you know I will come back?'

'Because you came ashore, Ms Bolivia. You're running away from something and I don't think you want to return to the sea. Also, I shall pay you very well.'

'How much?'

Koponen named a sum large enough for anyone to start over.

'Christ on a bike,' Jarglebaum exclaimed. 'Not bad for one day's work.'

'Value for money, Ms Bolivia has unique gifts.'

'It's just about money for you, isn't it, Koponen?' Tim said bitterly.

'It's more about what you can do with it.'

'And everyone has their price.'

'You don't?'

Tim couldn't deny it. 'I did what you paid me to do.'

'Value for money.'

As they bickered Foxy contemplated Koponen's offer. Out on the ocean groups of mermen roved out of their ruined cities, tasted the water and searched for mates. Children were the future. Almost everyone had accepted the necessity. If mer society was going to survive in any form— She didn't want to think about it. Strip away civilised behaviour and what was left?

She had always felt like an outsider. Brighton had been an escape from inevitability but life on dry land had been harder than she expected. People there were so different. No merman had manipulated events with such foresight and authority as Markus Koponen, none had made her feel the way she did about Tim. What mattered was to preserve the reasons she had come ashore—to be free. To live her own life as she wanted, not according to someone else's desperate doomed rules.

And so she'd sought refuge among the people who had destroyed her own. Unknown and unregarded, the ancient mer were nothing more than a by-blow casualty of the land's exploitation of the seas.

She reached her decision. 'Afterwards, you'll leave me alone.'

'Absolutely.'

'How do I know that?'

'That's the thing.' Koponen spread his hands. 'You either trust me or you don't.'

'That's a current that flows both ways.'

'What do you suggest?'

'Pay me first.'

Koponen appeared to be enjoying himself. 'A third now, the rest when you return.'

'Half and half.'

'Agreed.' Koponen held out his hand.

'No,' Tim said. 'I don't care what you think Foxy is, you can't send her down there. Not in her condition.'

Foxy looked indignant, hurt. It wasn't the reaction he had been expecting. Across the room Dolores trilled with laughter.

Koponen regarded Tim with some sympathy. 'There are many things you don't understand.'

'Neither do you!'

Electra seized Tim's wrist without seeming to cross the space between. 'Calm down, little Tim-Tim Timmy or I'll hurt you so much.' Bone and cartilage moved inside his wrist with the unpleasant promise of imminent agony.

A dessert spoon flew down the table and walloped off Electra's forehead. Jarglebaum pointed at Electra with a steak knife. 'You let him go. Right now.'

'For God's sake, Jarglebaum!' Koponen exclaimed.

Jarglebaum didn't take his eyes off Electra. He flipped the steak knife and caught it by the tip. 'She's hurting him.'

Electra removed her hand with exaggerated care. 'A steadying hand.'

Jarglebaum snorted disbelief. 'You all right, pal?'

'I'm fine, Troy.' Tim massaged his aching wrist. 'Thank you.'

Jarglebaum gave a curt nod, flipped the knife a final time and dropped it on the table.

Koponen massaged his temples. 'I suggest we all—'

The door opened and a man in a white jacket entered to take their food orders. He took in the mood of the room. 'Mr Koponen?'

Koponen's composure cracked, he flung his glass splintering into the corner. 'Enough. I've lost my appetite.'

The waiter withdrew in the frosty silence.

'Let's go.' Electra gestured to the door.

'Foxy, I—' Tim said.

She wouldn't meet his gaze. He didn't know what to say, what to think. He'd hoped he'd at least be able to protect her even if he couldn't help her escape. Now she'd cut a deal with the man who'd tracked her down. His shoulders drooped. Electra led them out of the room.

Koponen rounded on Jarglebaum as soon as they were alone. 'It's been a demanding day but that is no excuse for such grotesque behaviour.'

'She was going to mangle his wrist. Now she's got a little bruise on her head and you don't have a lawsuit. It's a good deal. Thanks. You're welcome.'

'Act like that again and you will cease to be of any use to me. Is that clear?'

Jarglebaum took the point. 'Yes, boss. Look, I'm sorry but I had to do something. Legally you're right on the edge with all this. The wrong side of the edge.'

Koponen breathed in, then out. 'My warning still stands. For now we will put this behind us and move on.' He strode from the room and Jarglebaum was alone.

Well, that was a class-A fuckup, Jarglebaum thought despairingly. No matter what those women did Koponen just would not see them as a liability. That was what happened when you shared a mattress. He gave a snort of cynical laughter. All that bullshit about mermaids, was that the genuine angle here? What the actual fuck had he got himself involved in this time?

He poured himself another whisky and tried to guess which malt it was without looking at the label. Anything to keep his mind from worrying about whether he would still have a job at the end of the voyage.

It was just the right side of smoky, with a wonderful aroma Jarglebaum could only describe as being like old varnish and wardrobes. The superb scotch was older and therefore more expensive than any he could afford.

Even if Koponen was away with the fairies he didn't stint on the little luxuries for his staff. Jarglebaum poured another shot, determined to enjoy this one while he still could.

As Easy As…

Sunk in her wing-backed armchair in the deepening gloom Mrs Woosencraft ran the numbers through her head again and again. She'd rarely felt her age, seldom even considered the passage of years. Now she was having palpitations. Her hands were clammy, her feet cold and her heart thumped in her chest.

Sheets of paper filled with diagrams and calculations covered her ancient kitchen table, the peculiar geometries of her chosen aspect of the finite infinities of Deg Naw Wyth.

Seated at that table decades ago Ethel Godwinsson had taught an eager Dorothy Woosencraft all she was able to learn. The table had been old even then. It was Ethel's table, the place she had practised and refined her own craft, and it was steeped in her long-gone tutor's lore and magic.

Somewhere in Ethel Godwinsson's own house had been an even older table, one that had belonged to her tutor before her. It was lost now, sold off by Ethel's family. She imagined it now quietly mouldering in some potting shed or an attic playroom where young children crayoned pictures of castles, fish and faeries, spilled paint and gouged railway lines into it with biros.

According to tradition the first tables had been circular and inscribed around the edge with compass points and other geometric markers.

The kitchen table had been the only thing Ethel left Mrs Woosencraft in her will. It was the only thing she had wanted and she used it as she knew Ethel intended, as a piece of ordinary furniture. It was the right way to let the power fade, seeping down the legs into the floor, up through the chopping board or carried away by the tea tray. Out and away, back into the world.

Ethel's methods, her numbers, her steady, practical and at times crusty style still saturated the ancient pine. Mrs Woosencraft had her own table, the black oak table in the front room. It went wherever she went and it was where she explored the indivisible nineteenth way ever since that long-ago June picnic in the buttercup meadow when she and Ethel agreed the twenty-third way was beyond her.

There were still times when she liked to work at Ethel's table. Times when the subtle shove of her old-fashioned ways, the memories of abacus, slate and chalk and the cracked saucers of tally stones were a help rather than hindrance. Times like now, when she felt she needed all the support she could get.

It was not as if Mrs Woosencraft had embraced modernity. She used compass and candles, a setsquare and ruler, a row of small brass bells, a diminutive set of knife-edge scales and, almost as old as she was, her slide-rule. Heaving herself out of her chair, she went back into the kitchen for another look. Perhaps she'd missed something, perhaps she was wrong.

Heptagons overlapped circles, parallelograms butted against the sides of triangles. Lines and arcs connected this to that. One place to another. The future to the past.

Every margin brimmed with calculations. Columns and streams of them, crossed out, revised, reworked, begun again from new seed-points, new assumptions. Everything led to the same conclusion. The angles might be right but everything else looked badly wrong.

Koponen had been wrong too. Knowing she was right did nothing to help her sense of impotent frustration. Somewhere out there, wherever Tim now was, bad things were happening. For her there was nothing to do except sit and wait and see who came out of the other end.

Numbers didn't lie. They might not tell you the truth, but they never lied. They simply were what they were. She should know. They had been her way, her life, from the moment an old lady had shown a very bored young girl how they could open a path from the questions brimming inside her head to what she would eventually come to regard as the observable universe.

It was the best wet weekend she'd ever had.

Some very specific numbers had brought her through the years to today, this room, this particular variant of that constant and ever changing subjective moment called 'Now'.

Reality was a frenzy, a seethe, a simmering pot constantly rising and falling, combining and fading. Only some of it was random, the rest was probability and chance. Everything was connected, everything influenced everything else. Often it was in amounts so small they were subsumed by bigger events. Once in a while they combined to shake the earth.

One person in the right place at the right time looking through the right eyes could part the veils and see the shadows. It took enormous skill to glimpse the things that cast them.

Ethel Godwinsson had taught her how to access that layer. And how, with geometry, calculation and equation she could not only pose it questions, she could get answers too.

It was almost impossible, but only almost. The knack was to ask the exact right question. Absolutely exact. Compared to that, the rest of the nineteenth way of Deg Naw Wyth was as easy as pissing on your fingers.

'Up you come, pet,' Mrs Woosencraft lifted Morse onto her lap. 'I'll get you some supper soon, just give me a few minutes.'

He'd been all over her as soon as she had let him out of the cat box, under her feet, butting his head on her calves, winding his tail around her legs. Wherever he had been during the time he'd spent as her cat, he hadn't been getting regular meals. Out of guilt, though she knew she shouldn't, she'd let him eat all he could. Two bowls of tinned rabbit hadn't lasted long. Now he was hungry again.

All her other cats were in the room as well. They sensed something important was going on and were there to bear witness. The two Siamese sat on the curtain rail, a cluster of tortoiseshells, grey Persians and mixed tabbies colonised the settee. Others sprawled on the piano. Pedwar the Manx sat like a moth-eaten sphinx in the doorway.

All the cats in the room looked at Morse, sitting on her lap.

'All right, I'm not proud of what I did,' Mrs Woosencraft announced. 'I came here for a reason. We all did. I did what I thought was best.' Her lips tightened, deepening the creases round her mouth. 'We were down to eighteen, I had to do something, didn't I?'

And yes, she finally admitted, she had been blinded by hope, too wrapped up in what she wanted, lost in dreams of what might be. And at her age too. She should have known better.

Now there was nothing to do except sit and wait. At times like these she hated waiting. For want of something better to do, anything, she got up, went back into the kitchen, tidied her papers away and baked some scones.

Sanity

FOXY CLUTCHED Tim's hand as Electra led them along the open-sided companionway away from the ship's mess.

Below them a rolling night-dark sea ran to the horizon, above them a cloud-strewn starry sky. The ship drove steadily across the ocean through salt-tinged air.

Foxy slid her fingers along the rail. 'I like this ship, this *Sea Cucumber*. She's sailed the oceans for many years, through storms and high seas, across glassy calms, over shallows and reefs. She's seen such sights.' She squeezed Tim's hand. 'And she's always brought her crew home.'

Tim simply did not know what to make of her.

Electra descended a steep companionway to the main deck. Tim stood uneasily at the top. 'Our cabins are up here.'

'We thought you two young lovers would like to spend the night together, so we changed your room,' Electra said.

Dolores hugged herself. 'That's so sweet.'

'Does Koponen know about this?' Tim said.

'He's going to have a few surprises tonight,' Imelda hissed in his ear. Tim recoiled from the fishy reek of her breath.

'Get them down here,' Electra ordered. 'Push them or throw them, but get them down.'

'What's it going to be, guys? It's much easier to walk without broken legs.' Imelda turned to Dolores. 'Are you going to help this time, or do you just want to watch?'

'Please go down the stairs,' Dolores said to Foxy.

Foxy started down.

Tim clenched his fist impotently. Electra was below, Imelda behind, both nightmarishly strong and violent. To get away he would have to hurt one of them more than he'd ever hurt anyone before.

And then what? A mad flight around the ship in the desperate hope he'd reach Koponen before the others caught him. And how would that look? He'd be better off with Jarglebaum, at least he had some inkling of the trouble they were in.

Electra hauled open a heavy metal hatch set in the deck. 'Welcome to the bridal suite.' Metal steps led down into a dark and cavernous space.

She led them through the gloomy hold towards the bows. A single row of bare, low-wattage bulbs cast pools of dim light. One each side stacks of enormous blue plastic drums ran the length of the hold. The group stopped beside a container set on its own. A coil of marine rope lay neatly on the lid.

Electra studied the label on the drum and smiled at Dolores. 'Koponen really likes you. The old fool.'

'A fool and a loser,' Imelda agreed.

'He's been kind to me,' Dolores said.

Tim studied the label:

Kylma Kala

www.kylma-kala.com

Brassica napus (canola) var. *doloresvogler*

Re-usable container

Recyclable container (100% Cellulose)

Imelda's hand lightly circled Dolores' throat. 'You are still with us on this, aren't you, darling?'

Dolores' eyes glittered. 'We're sisters, brides, daughters, wives. I know sacrifices must be made.'

Imelda began to squeeze. 'You are completely sure?'

'Yes,' Dolores gasped.

'Prove it. Make a sacrifice.'

Dismay consumed Tim. He'd had a chance on the stairs and hesitated. Always he'd hesitated, concerned for Foxy or for some other reason. The time for killing was here. These women would not hesitate. It was always later than you think.

He took a small step back into the gloom.

Foxy shook her head a fraction and mouthed, 'No.'

Tendons stood out on Imelda's arm as she throttled Dolores.

Dolores lifted her arms above her head.

Crack.

Her little finger jutted back at an unpleasantly high angle.

Imelda released her grip on Dolores. She licked her lips. 'Do it again.'

Pale and wide-eyed, Dolores took hold of her next finger.

Snap.

This was actually insane. Tim slid another step deeper into the shadows.

Imelda studied Dolores' hand. 'Nice one. I never thought you had it in you.'

'My pleasure,' Dolores gasped. 'It really was.'

'Isn't that nice, we're all friends again,' Electra said. 'Let's move on. We have a schedule.'

Tim took a long sideways step behind a stack of drums. Out of sight of the women, he cast around for some sort of weapon, a piece of wood, a crowbar, anything to fight with.

Dolores breathed against his ear. 'I do necks too.'

He turned as fast as he could. Dolores swayed back out of reach. This would have to be fast, brutal. Tim rushed her in the narrow space. Not one punch, a dozen, a hundred. Feet stamping, kicking.

He caught her one solid blow on her cheek. She rocked back and there was just enough time for him to feel the satisfaction of the contact, register the surprise in her eyes, and feel a moment of hope. Then Dolores *flowed*, moving impossibly fast. Before he could react she took hold of his arm. In one motion she lifted, twisted, and dislocated his shoulder.

The pain was astonishing, a blinding white flare. For a moment he could neither see nor think. Then—a world of agony and worse as his shoulder bent into an unnatural shape.

'Quite a rush, isn't it?' Dolores pushed him lurching back into the light. 'Got him.'

'Little Timmy got lost in the dark.' Electra pouted. 'Did you bump into something nasty?'

Tim forced himself to stand straight, his arm frozen and useless at his side. His voice slurred with pain and shock. 'Yes, Dolores.'

'Great repartee, but don't give up the day job.' Electra gasped in mock surprise, 'No, wait, this is your day job. How's that going for you?'

Imelda held a coil of rope in her hand. 'Stand by the drum. Put your hands behind your back.'

He couldn't do it. His arm would barely move, when he tried the pain was atrocious.

Imelda hissed with irritation, grabbed his wrist, jammed her other hand under his armpit and pulled. His arm slid back into its socket with an unpleasant wet snap and more pain. Lots of pain.

Tim zoned out again, dimly aware of someone holding him upright. When he came to, he and Foxy were tied back to back at waist and ankle with their wrists behind them.

Imelda ran a second rope behind the knots at their waists, threaded it through one of the eyes on the drum and tied it off on the far side and well beyond their reach.

Hands on hips, she considered her work.

Dolores sighed as she ran a nail along Tim's jaw. 'You really are quite cute. Never mind, there are plenty more like you.'

'Goodbye forever, little Timmy. It really has been quite ordinary,' Electra said.

Tim's blood ran cold. 'What are you going to do?'

'Sink the ship, stupid.'

His head was muzzy from pain, he did his best to think. 'You work for Koponen.'

Electra's face became a blank mask of hostility. 'Not for some time. Not since that voyage he made us take down into the depths. Not since his obsessions almost got us killed. We would have died, our lovely lives smashed and ripped.' Her eyes grew wild, spittle flecked her mouth. 'Down there we met someone much stronger than Markus Koponen. Older too, wiser and stronger. He showed us things. Tuoni showed us how to remake ourselves. Tuoni told us our true names—'

'You're dry-shod yet you spoke his name,' Dolores cried.

'We're over water.' Electra flung her arms high, her body strained against the crimson silk of her dress, the tendons in her neck rigid. 'We are the sisters and she is the wife-sacrifice. Tuoni will accept our ship-gift and he will take his bride. We are his handmaidens and shall sit beside him in glory!'

Wide-eyed, Tim and Foxy shifted uncomfortably in their bonds. If there was anything worse than being tied up in the gloomy hold of a soon to be sinking ship with little hope of escape, it was being tied up in the gloomy hold of a soon to be sinking ship while listening to the ravings of a violent lunatic.

There had been times when Tim had doubted his own sanity. Confronted by Electra, all he could think of was to try and keep her talking. 'For God's sake, why are you doing this? Why does the ship have to sink?'

'You really are a little fool. Koponen wants to cool the world. We want the opposite. Tuoni was bathed by cold currents for ten thousand years. Now the water is warming and he awakes. This ship will never reach harbour. These seeds will never put down roots, their horrid white flowers will never bloom.'

'Let Foxy go. Give her a chance, give her baby a chance.'

The hold fell silent. Behind him, Tim felt Foxy stiffen.

'What baby?' Foxy said coolly.

The three women began to laugh.

Dolores held out her hand and studied her distorted fingers as if she were inspecting her nails. 'She doesn't have anything to worry about. How long do you think you can hold your breath?'

Despite having their ankles tied together, Foxy managed to kick Tim.

'I'm not pregnant.'

'Foxy, I saw—'

'I'm not. Just leave it, OK?'

Thrusting her hips, wrists twisting, Imelda danced in front of Foxy, her voice a nasty sing-song. 'When Tuoni wakes he will reach for his consort. A bride to stay by his side in his drowned kingdom. You will become Kipu-Tytto, birth mother of Tuonetar, destined to be Tuoni's daughter-wife.'

'You're all mad,' Tim croaked.

'What if we are?' Electra said. 'Soon you'll be dead.'

Imelda stopped her weird dance. 'We'll come back for you, darling. We'll find you down in the deep and the dark when the silt has settled and Wassiter's lungs are full of salt water.'

She leaned in to kiss Foxy, who twisted her face away. Imelda gripped Foxy's jaw and pressed her lips against Foxy's. She jerked back with a cry half way between laughter and pain. Foxy spat onto the deck and glared, triumphant. Imelda wiped her mouth, looked at the blood on the back of her hand, then back at Foxy. 'I'll see you later.'

'You'll drown too,' Tim said.'

Electra shook her head. 'Only if we stop moving.' She turned to Dolores. 'Sort your fingers out. It's time to say hello to the crew.'

The three women moved back the way they had come, appeared briefly under one of the overhead lights then vanished into the dark.

'They're heading for the engine room,' Tim said dully.

Foxy gave no reply.

Away towards the stern came a short, sharp crack, and a gasp, followed by a louder crack and a shrill cry.

Electra's voice echoed through the hold. 'Did that hurt? Tell me, Dolores. Tell me.'

Silence fell. Tim shifted uncomfortably, his shoulder ached abominably. 'Are you OK?'

Silence.

He tried again. 'We could try and sit down.'

'I'm fine.'

'It might be more comfortable.'

'I said I am fine.'

Tim gave a despondent sigh. His shoulder really hurt. 'I'd like to sit down.'

That close to the waterline there was less roll and pitch than on deck. The steady, rumbling throb of the marine diesels overlain by occasional creaks, distant metallic bangs and vague thuds formed a strange rhythm. Slowly the gloomy hold seemed to expand in size, reaching out in all directions to become an infinite place. Somewhere in the middle two people had been tied together, roped to a huge blue drum of seeds under a shallow pool of light.

Foxy sniffed.

Tim chewed on his lip. 'I thought you were.'

'Well, I'm not.'

'I saw your tummy and thought—'

'You thought. Well, I thought it wasn't polite to mention a lady's waistline. And while we're on the subject, where did you think I had the opportunity to get… you know… thing?'

Tim felt pretty stupid. 'I thought you had a boyfriend.'

'What? One of those fat creeps with their short little arms? I came to Brighton to get away from them.'

'It's just that you were getting bigger and—'

Foxy jerked at their bonds. 'Stop it. I'm not, all right? I'm not pregnant. It's just that time of year.'

Even though they were tied back to back, Tim could still feel her angry eyes and Foxy hear his unspoken question.

'Look, I'm gravid,' Foxy said.

'Gravid?'

'Yes.'

'What's that supposed to mean?'

'What do you mean "What's that supposed to mean?"'

'What I mean by "What's that supposed to mean" is I know what gravid means, I just wondered what you meant when you said that's what you were.'

'It means I'm, you know.' Foxy's voice dropped to a self-conscious whisper. 'Heavy with egg.'

'Um… OK.'

'But I'm not pregnant.'

'Right.'

'I just could be if I wanted.'

Tim took a breath. 'Foxy?'

'What?'

'I'm sorry.'

She went still again. Tim felt her fingertips find his and press against them. 'How's your arm?'

'It hurts.'

'I'm sorry too.'

'Foxy. All that stuff about Tuoni, they're mad aren't they?'

'I hope so.'

When it came they nearly missed it. A dull thud, a faltering in the ship's motion, a hesitation in the sound of the diesels. Then the big engines continued, their vibration a little more insistent, a little more urgent.

Slowly *Sea Cucumber* lost way. They felt it in the way the ship began to wallow. No long after they also felt a tilt in the deck, slight but growing. *Sea Cucumber* began to settle towards the stern.

'They've killed the ship,' Tim said.

'She's tough. I know her, she'll make a fight of it,' Foxy said.

Tim felt for her fingers and squeezed them. 'Don't worry, we'll be all right.'

Unseen by Tim, Foxy's eyes brimmed with tears.

Sober Up

KOPONEN BURST back into the mess. 'What the hell was that?'

'Here we go again,' Jarglebaum muttered under his breath.

'Didn't you feel it?'

'Nope.'

'Something's wrong.'

'Everything's fine.'

'I'm calling the bridge.'

'You know best.'

Koponen pressed button after button. 'It's not working. I can't get through.'

'Let me try.' Mellow from three large scotches Jarglebaum swayed over and studied the control panel. It looked simple enough, a series of domed white buttons set under a grill, each one labelled 'Bridge', 'Galley', and so on. Below the buttons was a dial labelled 'Volume', beside the dial a small electric bulb and a toggle switch labelled 'On' and 'Off'. Managing to turn his laugh into a grunting cough, Troy flicked the switch up and the bulb glowed green.

'Now try,' Jarglebaum said.

Koponen pressed the button marked 'Bridge'. 'This is Markus Koponen. Is everything all right? Over.' Koponen waited a moment. 'Come in, bridge. Respond, please. This is Koponen.' Turning to Jarglebaum he gestured helplessly. 'Nothing.'

Jarglebaum reached over and pressed the Bridge button again. He cranked the volume over to Max. 'Hello? Anyone at home? Pirates on the starboard bow. Wake up, guys.'

The speaker wasn't silent. Not quite. Over the faint electric hiss was a sound like a flag snapping in a strong breeze. Below that, faintly, a distressing low sound like wind moaning, or—

Jarglebaum's whisky-driven ebullience died in his chest. All at once he felt very, very sober. 'We need to get up there. Now.'

Then they both felt it. The ship had slowed. She was still under way but speed was falling off.

'Come on.' Jarglebaum opened the door then lurched back. 'Jesus Christ.'

The ship trailed a vast plume of roiling black smoke. Above them the bridge was furiously ablaze.

Koponen pushed past and stared up at the flames. He sagged against the bulkhead. 'Jumalauta! This can't be happening. Not to me, not now.'

The ship staggered as though something had struck it and slowed even more.

Koponen rallied himself. 'Come on. We have to help.'

'It's an inferno, we can't do anything. Where's the radio room?'

Overhead a window shattered. Jarglebaum pushed Koponen against a bulkhead and shielded their faces with his jacket.

'My girls.' Koponen stared, wild-eyed. 'Where are my girls?'

Jarglebaum shook Koponen by his collar. 'Where's the God-damned radio?'

Koponen's eyes came back into focus. 'Up a level, beyond the canteen.' He started away. 'We must save the seeds.'

Jarglebaum hauled on his arm. 'We're sticking together. That means you're coming with me.'

Bottom

SLOWLY AND by inches *Sea Cucumber*'s bows rose from the water. Down in the hold Foxy and Tim felt the deck jump beneath their feet. Their ears ached at the sudden change of pressure. Somehow they managed to stay standing.

'They're using explosives,' Tim said.

'Look at the cargo,' Foxy said.

Along with the list to stern the detonations had shifted the seed drums. One stack tipped against another, in turn pressing against a third.

Tim considered the weight of the drums and the prospect of trying to avoid them once they started rolling. 'This doesn't look good.'

'We'll be all right if the ship settles as she is.'

'I wish I could see you, Foxy.'

Their fingers pressed together again.

'Me too.'

Tim shook his head again, his ears still didn't feel right and there was something wrong with his eyes too. Down towards the stern a slow wave of blackness crept towards them across the floor. The explosion hadn't been that close, the shock wave must have affected him. He'd heard of people killed like that, with not a mark on them. He must have concussion. Inside his skull his brain was bleeding, slowly deafening him, blinding him.

The blackness moved steadily towards their feet. It carried a briny smell and Tim realised there was nothing wrong with his head. One form of fear replaced the other.

The lights went out and they both gave a wordless cry. The lights flared briefly then died. The darkness was total, the air damp cold and salty.

Tim's feet were wet.

Deep in the ship a new vibration began, a near sub-sonic rumble that steadily rose in pitch and volume to a strong, steady throb.

'Standby generators,' Foxy said. 'Emergency pumps. Someone's turned them on or they've tripped in automatically.'

Dim red lights began to glow along the sides of the hold. Five inches of icy water sloshed round their ankles.

'Koponen knew what he was doing when he refitted this old girl.' Foxy's voice filled with respect. 'You can feel her fighting back.'

'Do you think the pumps will be enough?'

'Honestly? I don't know.'

Tim thought about that for a bit. To his own surprise he felt very calm. 'If I knew was going to die on a sinking ship I'd have liked to be a bit better prepared. I'd wear a tuxedo and have a glass of brandy, maybe have a last dance while the band played on… OK, that sounds a bit unfair to the band so it had better be a jukebox. Either way I'd want to look good when the end came. Have a shave and comb my hair—'

Foxy gasped. 'Yes! Oh, Tim Wassiter, you clever, clever man.'

'I am?'

'I know how we can get out of here.'

'You do?'

'Yes. We'll only have one chance, so listen very carefully and do exactly what I say.'

Tim's mouth was dry. 'What do you want me to do?'

'See if you can touch my bum.'

A Kind of Beauty

KOPONEN WAS being violently sick, the acid stench of his vomit nauseating over the bitter reek of blood in the radio room. Jarglebaum had been a cop all his life. He'd seen things, bad things. He didn't like what he was seeing now but he could cope. Nevertheless, there was a claw of fear in his gut, gripping, twisting.

The radio was wrecked. It didn't take a detective to work out it had been wrecked by the radio operator or that he'd had an accomplice. That was because the radio had been destroyed by systematically pounding the operator's face against it.

When he was young Jarglebaum had taken firearms training with the Sussex Constabulary. For three years he'd been on call, attended armed robberies, sieges, and gang fights all without firing a single shot. Then he'd got the promotion he'd been angling for all along and never touched a gun again. There was no glamour, no cachet attached to weapons in Jarglebaum's mind. They were tools. The furthest he'd go was to admit there was a kind of beauty to their uncompromising design. Like anybody who knew guns he had an intense respect for them. Guns were good for one thing and one thing only.

How he wished he had one now.

Jarglebaum put his hand on Koponen's heaving shoulder. 'Come away, Markus. There's nothing we can do here.'

He helped Koponen down a sloping corridor. The dip to stern had increased even in the few minutes it had taken them to reach the radio room.

Sea Cucumber began to roll in the swell as she lost way. As they passed the crew's mess the door swung open. It was dark inside, the open door felt like a gaping maw.

Just through the door Jarglebaum saw a single overturned chair. He knew what he should do: he should step inside that dark and ominously silent room and take a look. He didn't want to. He could smell that sickly metallic blood-reek again. He knew what he would see.

Jarglebaum's knees were shaking, he could taste bile in his mouth. He told himself he had seen enough, that there was nothing he could do. It was more important to get Koponen safely away.

Breathe

IMELDA KNEW her knots. She had tied Tim and Foxy securely but not so tight blood could not circulate. She wanted their attention focused on each other's suffering, not their own.

Tim strained against Foxy. The ropes dug into his wrists, burning his skin as he twisted his hands struggling to touch her backside. His damaged shoulder burned with jagged inner fire.

'Wait,' Foxy gasped, 'you're not getting down far enough. We need to loosen the ropes.'

Tim leaned his weight against the rope running through the eyelets and held steady while Foxy twisted and writhed behind him. Despite being ankle deep in freezing water in the hold of a sinking ship Tim was amazed to find an erotic element to the situation.

My God, he thought. Is everything women say is wrong about men actually true?

Then Foxy slipped, her full weight went against him and the pain in his shoulder became his universe.

Foxy's voice came from a long way away. 'Tim? Tim?'

Someone was making wounded animal noises through clenched teeth. Tim realised it was him and stopped. The pain receded by moments. 'Oh Gods, that hurt.'

'I'm sorry,' Foxy gasped, breathing hard.

Somehow she had been holding him up. The water was up to their knees.

'Forget it. Let's try again.' He reached down, yelped and immediately stopped. There was no point trying if he was going to pass out. He twisted round to use his left arm. Foxy pushed up. They stretched, they arched their backs. Tim's fingertip slid past her waistband.

'There, can you feel it. My pocket.'

Tim touched the pocket's top seam. 'Got it.'

'Try and get my comb.'

'Good idea. Saw through the ropes.'

Freezing sea water surged around their thighs. Deep in the ship the pumps kept up their steady beat. Tim slid two fingers into Foxy's pocket. The seam was tight, he couldn't push down any further. He moved his fingers from side to side, his fingertips touched the comb and it slipped away from him.

'Nearly—'

Foxy strained upwards. 'This could almost be fun. In different circumstances.'

'Don't make me laugh.'

They tried again as chill salt water surged around their waists. Tim hands were submerged, getting cold, growing stiff. He growled through gritted teeth. 'Come on you bastard fat fingers.'

He touched the top of the comb again. His attention narrowed to his fingertips, the texture of the sodden fabric of Foxy's skirt, the spot on his finger where the seam rubbed his skin raw. The water softened the fabric, loosening the weave a fraction. Water that was now chest deep.

'Push up now. Hard as you can.' Tim said.

When Foxy moved he let his knees drop.

His fingers slipped into the pocket. First and second fingers brushed the comb.

'Got it,' Tim said, then lost it again. He shifted his shoulders, fought the surging fire-burn agony there, and actually had the comb pinched between his fingertips. Then he blacked out.

It was only for a fraction of a second but it was enough. The water was over his chest now, almost at is shoulders. Not long now. He knew had perhaps one more effort in him.

'Again, Tim,' Foxy said calmly.

'In a bit.'

'No, now.'

'I can't do it, Foxy. I need to let the water numb my shoulder.' He doubted it would be enough. He could barely feel his fingers as it was.

The water touched his chin. He tipped his head back and it went into his ears, the corners of his eyes. His shoulder was a cold dead lump. He blinked and gasped, sucking in lungs-full of air, hyperventilating for that long last breath.

Water brimmed around his mouth.

'Now,' Tim spluttered.

There was desperate urgency in her voice. 'Tim, I never said—'

He sank underwater and reached down as hard and as far as he could. All the sweet hells how much it hurt. Black grinding iron agony, pain that had a shape and form, a thing that had an existence of itself. He let it have the part of his body it wanted. Tendrils of pain spread out and he pushed back, pushed himself right out of his own body. For a moment he hung in the dark water and watched himself drown.

His fingers slid into Foxy's pocket. He pinched the comb between his fingers and lifted it free.

Everything was black. He tried to surface but the surface was far over his head. Dark and cold. An irresistible urge grew in his chest, soon he would have to breathe. There was not enough time to cut the ropes.

He felt Foxy's fingers against his. She tugged gently on the comb and he let go. Too late. They had tried, together. At least they had tried. Perhaps she…

Everything was black.

Behind him Foxy stroked the comb across the knots binding their wrists. At its touch every fibre unravelled.

She ducked down and freed their feet. She pulled away the rope around their waists. She put her arm around Tim and lifted him to the surface.

He choked and coughed, then took one solid glorious breath after another.

Foxy held her comb triumphantly aloft. 'My mermaid's comb. It untangles my hair when the salt and surf have been at it. These ropes were no contest.'

Rope that were now nothing but loosely spreading fibres.

All Tim could do was nod and breathe and tread water. Around them the stacks of seed drums ponderously toppled into the rising water.

Foxy took his hand. 'Come on, Ace. Let's get the hell out of here.'

Contingencies

'WHAT DOES it take to sink this damned ship?' Imelda scowled as she retracted and extended the aerial of the remote detonator in her blood-soaked hand.

Beneath her feet, the deck sloped gently down towards the stern where a towering pillar of black smoke formed a blot of solid darkness against the starry sky.

Electra leaned on the rail. 'It is sinking, you can feel it.' Like Imelda, Electra appeared to be wearing elbow-length blood-red gloves. Gloves that dripped onto the deck.

'I thought it would be more dramatic.'

'Never mind. The crew were fun.'

Dolores leaned on the rail and looked out over the rolling grey-green Atlantic. 'It's those secondary pumps.'

'Koponen's so damned thorough, so effective, so very clever with his fall-back positions and contingency plans. I worry about what he might do next,' Imelda grumbled.

'Soon you won't have to.'

'What do you mean?' Dolores came off the rail. 'We agreed we wouldn't hurt him.'

'And we won't.' Electra's mouth drew back in a cool feral smile. 'He's on board a ship sinking in the middle of the Atlantic. He'll have to take his chances like the rest of us.'

'I want him punished,' Imelda said. 'If it wasn't for him we wouldn't be here.'

Electra stretched, a lithe, liquid movement. 'I like what happened. I want to be what we shall soon become.'

'I liked being the woman I once was.'

Dolores studied her fingernails and scratched experimentally at her arm. She brushed her leg with the back of her hand and ripped her stocking open with her knuckles.

'It's happening,' she said breathlessly. 'It's already started. I laddered my own stocking. We're over water and it's happening. I'm going first.'

Imelda looked at the dark, heaving sea. 'I'm not ready. I need more time…'

'We changed once when we were growing up, now we're changing again.' Dolores rolled her shoulders. 'It itches, all down my spine.' She bent and flexed and her bolero jacket split open down the back, cut by a row of bone-white triangular ridges running down her spine.

Nervous, Electra rubbed her own arm. Moving her hand from wrist to elbow it felt as smooth as ever. In the other direction it rasped like sandpaper.

She had known this was coming, the first of Tuoni's gifts, but now it actually was happening her heart was in her throat and her mouth was too dry to swallow. People called her cold but she knew how to feel, she had emotions. She just had something they didn't, self-control.

Even before college the three of them had sought adventure, looking for lost mysteries, new discoveries and shared thrills in the wide, wild world. Now, right here, right now, was the start of something far beyond their dreams. Beyond imagination. Beyond sanity.

The entity that believed itself to be Tuoni had found them dying. In pillaging their memories it had found a semblance of identity. In saving them it remade them to share that world. Lust and terror bound them to him, a kind of madness that let them revel in what they could do, and weep at what they would become.

Imelda and Dolores' eyes were bright as the conflicting thrills of anticipation and fear surged through them. They held each other's hands tight. To make this journey alone was too awful to contemplate. Together they would survive.

Dolores laughed in alarm as her elbow split her sleeve. Imelda ran her tongue over newly-aching gums and felt a second row of teeth. She wanted to bite and chew and taste blood. She too laughed wildly though her eyes sought Electra's for comfort.

Can this really be happening? Electra thought as she felt the changes in her own body, the new flexibility of her spine, the three slits opening under each ear. Could this ever happen to a human being? Would she still be—? She cried out at the loss of what she was leaving behind. Then a colder, steadier state of mind rose up, and her fear died away.

The deck canted under their feet as *Sea Cucumber* sank lower in the water. Tuoni rose up like a new tide within them.

'Kipu-Tytto. She doesn't know how lucky she is,' Electra said.

They all knew what she meant. Birthing Tuoni's spawn was a transcendent agony they all craved.

Dolores looked down at the sea with longing. 'She's under the water already. I want to swim.'

Imelda keyed in a short sequence of numbers on the detonator and flipped open the guard on the large, red button. 'Koponen said you should always have a contingency plan. Here's mine'

She pressed the button.

It's Over

THE EXPLOSION lifted *Sea Cucumber*'s stern clear of the water. The ship smashed down, torrents of shattered seawater flew high into the air, plunged down and gushed across the deck. Up near the bows Foxy and Tim had just climbed from the hold. Knocked from their feet, the water washed them across the deck and they fetched up bruisingly hard against the base of the forward cargo crane.

High in the rear superstructure Troy Jarglebaum and Markus Koponen raced down a companionway to the main deck. Jarglebaum's feet went out from under him, his elbow slammed against an edge and he swore like the world was ending.

'Sabotage,' Koponen gasped. 'Murder and destruction.'

What else could it be? Jarglebaum hauled Koponen to his feet, wincing with the pain from his elbow. 'Keep moving, Markus.'

Koponen's hat had gone, his thinning blond hair smeared across his face by wind and sea. 'Who did this?' he shouted and clutched the air. 'Oil? Governments? Why? How? Nobody knew my plans.'

Sea Cucumber's bows slowly came up, shedding tonnes of water. With ponderous inevitability the stern sank back and she began to settle again. Clouds covered the stars, the wind was rising, a heavy swell pounded the ship's side with steady, ominous booms. Behind them rolling waves broke across the aft deck. Jarglebaum looked around with a hysterical calmness he knew was a prelude to panic.

'The hell with this,' Jarglebaum bawled. 'Where are the boats?'

Koponen clutched Jarglebaum's jacket. 'We must save the ship. The seeds, my work—'

'No way, José. You pay me to take care of you, and that's what I'm doing. We're out of here.'

'Please!'

A huge burst of freezing spray drenched them. Jarglebaum hauled Koponen round to face the stern. 'Look at her. She's sinking, it's too late.'

Koponen's shoulders sagged. 'Yes, I see.'

'Where are the damned lifeboats?'

Koponen pointed up the canting deck. 'Midships.'

As they slipped and scrambled towards the bow three figures emerged out of the dark.

'Dolores!' Koponen cried. 'Thank God, you're all safe.'

'Come with us. Now,' Jarglebaum bellowed.

Imelda blocked their way.

'Get a move on!' Head down against the wind, Jarglebaum pushed forward.

Imelda stepped aside, grabbed his arm and forced it behind his back.

'Christ, what are you doing?' Jarglebaum was on tip toe, his slabby cheeks quivered with pain.

Wind driven spume burst across the deck. Electra's platinum hair broke free of its bonds, lifted by the rising gale into a writhing, silver-white plume above her head. She pulled back her hand and gave Markus Koponen a stinging slap across his face.

Crouched behind the crane Foxy and Tim peered at the five figures through the spray drenched night.

'Can you see what they're doing?' Tim said.

'They're arguing, fighting.'

'Hardly surprising, all things considered.'

Foxy pulled Tim down. 'Keep out of sight.'

'We've got to get off the ship.'

'Don't worry, we will,' Foxy said. She narrowed her eyes. Something about the fit of the women's clothing bothered her badly.

Imelda pushed up under Jarglebaum's elbow. 'This is too easy. I could lift your arm right out of its socket.'

'Stop, I'm begging you,' Jarglebaum gasped. 'Have pity, I'm an old man.'

'You're pathetic.' Imelda shoved Jarglebaum back into Koponen and both men crashed down on the wet deck. Jarglebaum cried out as he fell and clutched his elbow when he hit the deck but his eyes were triumphant, sly.

Imelda hauled Koponen to his feet. She too slapped him hard.

Koponen's head rocked back. Blood smeared his lower lip. He looked at Imelda with incomprehension, his voice a broken whisper. 'You did this. Why?'

Somewhere deep inside Dolores felt unhappy. Koponen had been good to her; now he was going to die. She flung her arms around him and kissed his cheek. 'So long, baby. Nothing lasts forever. We had some good times but now it's over.'

'Dolores.' Koponen blinked in disbelief. 'I love you.'

'I love you too, sweetie, but there's someone else.'

Koponen's gesture took in the sinking ship wallowing in the heaving sea. 'That's what this is all about? You have a new boyfriend?'

'It's not what you think.'

'Of course not. It never is.'

Jarglebaum lurched to his feet, one arm hung by his side. 'You've done what you came for. Let us get to the boats.'

Imelda smiled a wide, wide smile. 'Sorry. This is where it ends.'

Jarglebaum hung his head, exhausted, defeated. 'I told you, Markus. I tried to warn you.'

Something had happened to Dolores' skin. Every time she moved she tore her costume. For some reason the fit was all wrong. Now she had finally accepted she had finished with Koponen she realised her relationship with her wardrobe would also have to change.

It hardly mattered. The heaving, frigid water was enticing, almost sexual. What she was wore was now little more than a collection of rags, an encumbrance. She shrugged free of her jacket, stepped out of her skirt, and kicked off her shoes to stand proudly nude except for her laddered stockings and suspender belt. Her spray-drenched skin glistened under the faltering ship's lights.

Red shoes, no knickers, Jarglebaum thought wildly. It really is true.

'My God,' Koponen gasped. 'What's happened to you?'

Dolores looked down. Although her stomach was a pleasingly flat slab of rippled muscle, the same was now also true of her chest. She considered her once magnificent bosom with a lack of concern that surprised even herself. The extra rows of teeth in her mouth and the wonderful sinuosity of her body more than compensated. The two men did look so very, very edible.

Foxy gripped Tim's arm as Dolores stood revealed. 'Shark-women! Those men are in big trouble.'

Despite the dark and the breaking waves Tim could tell there was something wrong with Dolores just from the strange litheness in the way she moved. Her chest was deep, her flanks sleek with unnaturally straight and waistless hips. She turned and under the faltering neon of the ship's lights

Tim saw a saw-tooth row of triangular fins running the length of her spine.

Foxy's voice was hoarse with shock. 'Deep Magic, twisted and gone bad. Someone— No, something has done this to them.' She looked at Tim from eyes filled with anger and fear. 'It can't be—they were supposed to have all died an age ago.'

'Who?'

'Not human, not mer. Not people.'

'Tuoni. That was the name Imelda said down in the hold.' Tim shuddered with the memory of her weird ecstatic dance and words. 'They want you to be his—'

She pressed her fingers against his lips. 'Don't say it. Please. Right now we have to help those men.'

'How? I can't fight Imelda.'

'If we don't, they are going to die.'

Tim thought fast, he needed something unexpected, from the left-field. He'd met some strange and unusual people in his time, Mrs Woosencraft, Asklepios. What would they do? It felt like it came to him out of nowhere, a gift. Asklepios. He looked up at the crane and the heavy cargo net hanging from the boom high overhead. 'Do you know how to work this thing?'

'No. Do you?'

He clutched the diamond pendant through his shirt. 'Maybe.'

Brave

DOLORES straddled the rail. 'Let's go.'

'I want to kill Jarglebaum,' Imelda said.

Electra slid free of her own costume. 'Do them both. I want to watch.'

Jarglebaum and Koponen backed away. Five meters behind the two men the deck was awash. Trapped air gouted from submerged portholes as *Sea Cucumber* lurched downwards.

Imelda kicked off her boots and paced towards Jarglebaum. Jarglebaum moved in front of Koponen and raised his fists, a brawler's pose.

Electra laughed and slowly clapped her hands. 'There's nothing wrong with your arm.'

Jarglebaum rolled his shoulders. 'Never give an old sod an even chance.'

'Now I'll break them both,' Imelda said.

Jarglebaum considered his big, meaty fists. 'I've never punched a woman before. I can tell from your dress code you aren't ladies so I'll make an exception.'

Imelda bounced on the balls of her feet. 'Are you through with the macho posturing?'

'Pretty much.' Jarglebaum grinned. 'Oh yeah, you're under arrest.'

He settled into a wide-legged static stance. Imelda danced forwards and slammed her bare foot into his groin. She yelped and hopped back clutching her toes.

'Right on schedule,' Jarglebaum laughed. 'Copper's best friend, the cricket box. Added the spikes myself.'

His uppercut to Imelda's jaw lifted her clear into the air and stretched her out on the deck. Jarglebaum swore and shook his fist. Flecks of blood glistened on his knuckles, Imelda's skin was like sandpaper. 'Christ, lady, you need to shave.'

Imelda rolled to her feet. She dug around in her mouth with her forefinger and extracted a tooth. Glaring at Jarglebaum she threw it at him. 'You want a piece of me? Have this.'

Jarglebaum snatched it out the air. The thin, triangular object didn't look much like a tooth to him. He tossed it aside. 'Hope you've got dental insurance.'

'They grow back, fucker.'

'Now I know you're not a lady.'

Imelda flexed her shoulders.

'Let's go, fat man.'

'My pleasure.'

They went at it hard. Troy came off worst.

Concealed behind the base of the forward crane, Tim pulled open the control panel cover. He looked down at a complicated bank of yellow-painted levers, toggle switches, three joysticks, a large green button, a larger red one, and an amber bulb. The light was bad and the labels on the control panel were either badly worn or missing entirely. He pushed the green button. The amber bulb glowed, flickered, glowed brighter, then died.

'Damn it.'

'Wait.' Foxy put her hands on the steel deck. 'Come on, dear *Sea Cucumber*. Remember that humans built you and put their trust in you. I know you're hurt, I know you're struggling, but there are people still on board who need your help to stay alive.'

Foxy nodded to Tim. He pressed the green button again. This time the light stayed on.

'What now?' Foxy said.

Given time he knew he could work out which control did what. Once the crane started moving it would be obvious someone was operating it, and where they were. Electra and Dolores would not sit idly by.

Down at the stern Jarglebaum and Imelda exchanged a flurry of blows that left Jarglebaum down on one knee. Behind him Koponen sloshed through ankle deep water. Imelda bounced back energetically. Obviously in pain Jarglebaum pushed himself to his feet.

There was no time. Tim knew what he had to do.

He grasped Asklepios' pendant in one hand and put his other on the crane's control panel.

'Grant me understanding,' he said.

The last diamond crumbled to black powder.

In one grand sweeping moment Tim saw the entire ship. He was the ship.

The hull was breached in three places. Down in the engine room the great marine diesels had failed, starved of fuel from ruptured lines and suffocated by sea water in the air intakes. Six emergency pumps were distributed through the ship, four still worked. Designed to operate under water, those four were at full capacity. It wasn't enough. It never could be. The last explosion had broken *Sea Cucumber*'s back and the Atlantic ocean was coming in.

So much knowing dazzled him. If *Sea Cucumber* could have sailed he could have sailed her. If she could have been saved he'd have known how. Compared to that, what he needed to know was such a small thing. His hands went confidently onto the crane's controls. He knew exactly what to do.

Jarglebaum spat blood. One of his eyes was closing up and there was a nasty bite on his shoulder. There was a worse one on his forearm and he'd sworn he'd felt teeth on bone when Imelda bit him there. He was losing blood, losing the fight, and he knew she was better than him.

Imelda moved like an eel, weaving, striking, unpredictable. Despite his wounds Jarglebaum wasn't finished yet. He kept telling himself he just needed to land one decent punch.

Electra and Dolores sat on the rail, fish-slender, brine-drenched and alien. They kicked their legs and laughed wildly as the waves broke against the foundering ship.

Koponen knew the *Sea Cucumber* was finished. On the rail a naked Dolores held out her arms and beckoned him. He was very frightened. Life had been reduced to a single unpleasant choice: how did he wish to die?

A few feet away Jarglebaum lurched and staggered. Head down, fists up, he came back to Imelda for more.

Koponen backed into deeper water. It was easy, the bows lifted higher, the slope on the deck almost encouraging. Jarglebaum went down again. Dolores and Electra applauded from the rail. Then, overhead, in the wind-racked sky, Koponen sensed unexpected movement.

Despite easily outclassing Jarglebaum Imelda was frustrated. The man simply wouldn't stay down. A canny fighter, he hung back and refused to close in the desperate hope she might make a mistake. That wasn't going to happen. Jarglebaum was old and slow but had weight and power. She had absolutely no intention of letting him use either. He'd caught her once, respect for that. It was the only chance he was going to get.

Every time she hit him he slowed. She feinted left, kicked him hard in the thigh and dodged back. Jarglebaum's riposte cut the breeze way too late.

'You can soak it up, I'll give you that,' Imelda said conversationally. He was going down soon, she could smell his sweat and fear, and over it all, his blood, a heady and appetising reek. 'How long do you think you can keep going?'

'Come here and find out,' Jarglebaum growled. Inside he knew he was beat. Probably. All he could do was hang on and stay frosty. It was never over until it was over.

Behind him Koponen stood shin deep in cold foaming water and watched the sky.

Imelda gave a savage peal of laughter. 'Stay there, old man. You're next.'

Overhead, something huge swept by.

Startled, Imelda looked up.

Jarglebaum saw his last best chance. He pulled his back fist and rushed in. 'Gotcha!'

Imelda vanished in a roar of wind.

Jarglebaum flailed wildly, desperate to connect just once before she tore him to pieces. Her counter-attack never came. He dropped into his brawler's crouch and turned a slow full circle. Imelda had vanished.

Electra and Dolores looked out to sea in utter astonishment.

A hundred feet over the far rail, fifty feet above the rolling swell, the crane's heavy cargo net reached the end of its swing. Swept from the deck Imelda hung spread-eagled for a split second then tumbled down into the heaving water.

The crane turned, the trolley raced along the jib. The net hurtled straight towards Electra and Dolores on the port rail.

Dolores yelped, rolled backwards into the sea and was gone. Electra ran for the starboard rail. The crane juddered, the net swished past with the sound of rushing wind. Electric motors raced at maximum load, cable sang on the drum, the trolley raced out along the jib. Electra dodged left, then right, and the crane kept pace. Metal banged on metal, steel cable unspooled. The full weight of the cargo net dropped onto Electra's racing form and slammed her face first onto the deck.

Battered, broken, bruised, bitten and bloody, Troy Jarglebaum was in no fit state to stand up, let alone think. He was still alive, everyone else had fucked off. That was good enough for him.

The deck lilted towards his face.

I'm falling over, I'm passing out, Jarglebaum thought serenely as the steel plating floated up. A heavy bolt was set in the decking right where he was going to land.

Oh boy, this was going to leave a mark.

Then a slighter figure was by him, staggering with Jarglebaum's weight. Troy found himself pushed back onto his feet.

'The boats,' Markus Koponen gasped. 'We have to get to the boats.'

Foxy and Tim exchanged a look of satisfaction. They had done all they could. Things had gone a lot better than either had hoped.

She laid her hands on the deck one last time. 'Thank you, dear, brave ship.'

Tim felt the vessel like an enormous living thing. Wounded beyond salvation *Sea Cucumber* was on the edge of failing but she still fought on. Foxy was right, the ship had immense spirit but now it was nearly over.

The stern half of the ship was awash, the rear superstructure still ablaze, a flaming steel island assaulted on all sides by green oceanic waves.

Air and salt spume geysered from hatches and portholes as she began her descent beneath the waves.

He saw Koponen and Jarglebaum staggering towards one of the boats and started after them. 'Come on.'

Foxy held him back. 'I won't be safe in one of those little things with shark-women in the water.'

'We can't stay here!'

The bows rose higher. Heavy chains slithered down the deck like dangerous iron snakes. A steel drum bounded past them, tumbling end over end into the waves.

Foxy's eyes were wide and clear, and steady as the moon. 'I can protect you better in the sea than any boat. The ocean is my world and they are the newcomers.'

Across the deck Koponen and Jarglebaum hauled one of the boats out onto the davits, lowering it the few remaining feet into the water. Beyond them glassy black waves heaved and tossed, a rising wind snatched spindrift from their foaming crests.

Tim hesitated. What was she asking? Ocean stretched to the horizon. 'I'm not that good a swimmer.'

'It doesn't matter. Just trust me. Hold tight and trust me.'

Still Tim hesitated.

Foxy took hold of his hands. 'You know what I am, and I know that all your life you've wanted to feel the touch of strange. Here it is. Here I am. Go to the boat or come with me. You need to choose and it has to be now.'

The two men had the boat in the water and struggled to free the ropes from the davits. There was still time to reach them.

Foxy stood at the rail, her hair a mane of pale golden fire against a storm-tinged backdrop of surging waves and dark sky. Tim had his doubts and fears but he also knew what he wanted. 'I'm with you.'

Foxy tilted her chin. 'Then kiss me. Kiss me and put your arms around my waist.'

Chastely, Tim kissed her.

Foxy grabbed his face in both hands and kissed him open-mouthed. 'My breath is your breath, your life is bonded to mine by the ancient compacts of Deep Magic. Your kiss, my breath, our touch. Put your hands around me and never, ever, let me go.'

At that exact moment *Sea Cucumber* died. It was if she had been holding on, striving beyond her own endurance until her last crew were ready to go. Now, finally, she could rest.

Down she went and Foxy and Tim went with her. Water boiled up around them. Tim took a long last breath, scared now, really scared, and really trying to believe.

'Hold on,' Foxy cried.

The vortex of the ship's descent pulled them irresistibly down, down…

Good Thinking

'I THINK we should go,' the Hand said.

Persistent Smith flicked on his torch and checked his watch. It was about an hour before dawn. 'Far too early,' he said curtly.

'All right.'

Smith felt a little sorry for being so abrupt. 'Well, we could take a look.'

He had spent much of the time in the boot of the Imperial in whispered conversations with the Hand.

'You're always popping up when I don't need you.'

'That's not fair. I've been helpful.'

Smith had to admit this was true.

'We've had fun together, adventures,' the Hand said.

Despite himself, Smith had to agree with that as well.

'Hand, when I was talking to Heidi you made me feel really embarrassed.'

'She thought I was funny.'

'I wanted to be with her on my own.'

A long silence followed during which Smith did some thinking of a type he'd done very little of before.

'Hand?'

'Yes?'

'I know you're really just me. You're not a separate thing. I made you up one day and you hung around.'

'I know. We're the same person. You needed a way to share things. You needed a friend.'

Smith thought about that for a while.

'Yes,' he said. 'You're right. Or rather, I'm right.'

'We're right?' the Hand suggested.

'No,' Smith said firmly. 'We're both me, so it's still me who's right.'

'Yes. Good Thinking,' the Hand said with approval.

Smith knew he had changed from the person who had invented the Hand. He no longer needed another voice to help him make his mind up. The realisation felt very good. In that newly empowered frame of mind, though he couldn't put a name to the concept, he knew he should be gracious.

'Hand, you are fun to have around, but you can't just keep appearing when you want to. I don't want you to go away and, seeing as you're me, I can't really do that. Just don't forget I'm the one who wears the hat in this relationship.'

Somehow the Hand contrived to look deadpan. 'You'd have to be. I don't have a head.'

Smith's laughter boomed through the car. 'Yes. I'm the one with the head, which means I get to do the thinking. Perhaps I should get a white hat like Markus Koponen. After all, we are the good guys.'

He checked his watch again. 'OK, let's get out of the car.'

Deep Magic

FOXY SWAM steadily away from the ship with powerful beats of her tail. Tim looked around filled with transcendent awe. Violet-grey sea light faded into shadowed distance. Below lay a dark void, above their heads the surface shimmered liquid silver.

Foxy really was a mermaid. He was still alive. He really was here.

The sea was filled with sound. Creaks, thuds and metallic booms came from the broken ship, elsewhere sharp clicks and trills came from unknown sources. Deep and swooping, a near subsonic oscillation vibrated through Tim's body. Knowledge came from Foxy along with her delight: whale song. She held steady in the water and they looked back.

A quarter of a mile behind them, her amber lights still glowing from portholes and masthead, *Sea Cucumber* sank stern down into the abyss. An enormous smoky plume trailed behind her from a long, ragged tear in her hull.

Not smoke, seeds, Tim thought sadly. Markus Koponen's great, brave, mad and madly expensive plan to save the world, destroyed by people he loved and trusted.

Three shapes darted around the wreck and surged into the hold: Imelda, Electra and Dolores fully transformed. They erupted back into open water, came together, circled twice, and set off in pursuit. Tim shuddered. Despite the distance, he felt their fury.

Foxy flexed her back and surged away. Tim's shoes were a dragging weight. He kicked them off and watched them jig and twirl in her wake. Away in the distance *Sea Cucumber* descended into the depths. Her last lights faded from sight and she was gone.

Now Foxy dove deeper, down into a layer of colder, denser water. They descended past a school of mackerel at rest on the thermocline, shimmering like a blanket of silver scales.

The shark-women followed, gaining fast. They burst through the shoal, scattering the fish in a whirl of panic.

Tim knew Foxy was strong but she was pulling his weight. On her own she would be able to escape.

'Don't even think about it.' Foxy's voice moved across his mind. 'If you let go you'll break my spell and drown.'

'They'll catch us.' Tim tried speaking with his mouth closed, with no idea if Foxy could even hear him, let alone understand.

Foxy swam deeper still. 'I'm going to ask for help.'

This deep the light was almost gone. Above and behind them the black silhouettes of the shark-women closed in through watery twilight. Far below Tim saw a titanic shape, shadowy and indistinct in the lower depths. Then he saw another, and another.

Tim felt the tireless energy of Foxy's body beneath him, a tirelessness he knew would not, on its own, be enough. The huge shapes loomed closer. He looked on in awe as they resolved into a pod of humpback whales. Young and old, male and female, the bulls thrumming their life-songs as they cruised the watery night.

Foxy's thoughts came again. 'I'm going to sing to them.'

Her music was so beautiful he nearly let go, transported by reefs of octaves, an archipelago of chords. The whales answered in subsonic rumbles that shivered his whole body and lifted his heart in high soaring cries. This was a language that was felt as much as heard, experienced as much as understood. Listening to it he was at once lost and found. Here was the real ocean, the source of Deep Magic and Foxy's true home.

She firmed his grip on her waist. 'The whales have agreed to help.'

Beneath them the entire pod began to circle and rise. Up above, the shark-women hesitated then swam to one side. The whales moved beneath them then ascended in a great spiral. All at once every whale exhaled and enormous billows of gigantic flat bubbles rushed upwards.

Still rising the whales herded the confused shark women towards the surface in a net of bubbles.

Foxy swam hard and stayed deep for several more minutes. At long last she slowed and began to rise towards the light.

'Where are we going?' Tim thought.

'Brighton.'

'No! Smith is locked in the Chrysler's boot!'

Foxy looked back at him with luminous green eyes. Locks of her hair slowly wreathed about her pale face. 'No need to shout. I know the way.'

The passage of time lacked conventional meaning in this eternal place. Tim slipped into a different state of mind, aware but unthinking, seeing and accepting, surrounded by wonders.

They passed among a million jellyfish, ten million. Disturbed by their wake algae shimmered with organic light as they rose with the sunrise to feed and bask. Shoals of fish cruised, and once there were real sharks, quick and grey, black-eyed and impressive. There were sounds too, the clicks, buzzes and strange whoops of sea creatures, the chush-chush of a ship's propellers. Ethereal in the far distance, whale song again.

Foxy swam steadily on.

Sunrise

Troy knew he was lying on his back but he couldn't remember where. Either the sky was moving or he was. It had to be him, shifting from side to side, rising up and down.

Salt water splashed across his face.

It all came back in a rush: The struggle to launch the boat, then, frantic and inexpert he had rowed away from *Sea Cucumber* as she slid beneath the seething waves. Then the fight against the sucking vortex of descending water while Koponen frantically baled and roared with terror.

Jarglebaum jerked upright. Tim was out there, he'd seen him across the tilted deck as he and Koponen launched the lifeboat. He worked one oar and turned the boat, an open craft about twenty feet long, and pulled back to where the ship had foundered. He rowed into a white ocean, the surface covered far and wide by sodden ruined seeds. A flotsam of splintered wood, rope, plastic bottles, empty lifebelts floated among them.

Pain tore at his shoulder, back, legs and arms from Imelda's punches kicks and bites. He refused to give up, Tim was still out there. A grey tunnel slowly closed around the edges of his vision. He drifted until his sight cleared, then rowed again, circled, drifted, rowed again. All the time looking, refusing to give up. Never would he give up.

He searched for a time he couldn't measure. It could have been minutes, it could have been years.

One of the oars was wet, it slipped from his grip. He sat looking at his hand, unable to understand why his whole arm ran red.

'Troy.' Koponen gently took the oars from him and laid them inboard.

The boat rocked and pitched, adrift on the waves.

'Tim,' Jarglebaum's voice creaked like a rusty hinge. 'Foxy.'

'They're gone, Troy. We can't help them.' Koponen looked into nowhere. 'You did your best.'

Sunrise was some time off though the sky was lightening. Waves of pain and dizziness came and Jarglebaum passed out.

'Stay still.' Koponen held something cold to his forehead. A rag pad soaked in seawater. 'You've lost a bit of blood.'

'A bit?'

Koponen smiled thinly. 'Some.'

Troy's head lay towards the stern. Koponen sat behind him with his hand on the tiller.

'I don't remember...' Troy's head swam and he slumped back with a groan. How had he even got into the boat?

Koponen put a water bottle into his hand. 'Drink this.'

Troy gulped the water down, suddenly terribly thirsty. Everything swirled, his stomach surged and he had just enough time to get his head over the side before he vomited.

Jesus, I'm a mess, Troy thought as he watched his puke swirl away into the sea. The bite on his shoulder burned like it was on fire, so did the one on his arm. Gingerly he pulled up his shirt sleeve and winced at the state of his forearm. He'd seen human bite marks and they were nasty, bestial things. This one didn't look like that. Each black and purple puncture still wept dark blood, the outline of the bite a wide triple-row of wounds.

He felt himself sliding away again and fought it. He needed a real drink. He wanted to tell himself his memories of the last hours on the ship were part hallucination, that Imelda, Electra and Dolores hadn't done the things they had done. That they hadn't changed into weird monstrous walking fish and dived into the sea. That they hadn't killed so many men.

Christ, he felt rough. He wondered if the bites were poisoned or if it was simply because Imelda had beaten him flatter than hammered shit.

Koponen lashed the tiller into position. 'There's bandages and disinfectant in the locker. Take your shirt off and I'll clean you up. These lifeboats have radio distress beacons. I've turned ours on.' He looked haunted. 'We'll be OK.'

'Sure thing. Down but not out, that's us.' Troy winced as he shrugged out of his ripped shirt. After your first cracked rib you learned to recognise the pain.

Koponen cleaned Troy's wounds. 'These are nasty but the bleeding has nearly stopped. Your arm is going to be stiff as hell but I don't—'

Something bumped against the underside of the hull. Both men froze.

The sound came again: quiet, testing.

Koponen carefully pushed himself to his feet and hefted one of the oars. He stood astride the beam of the boat, balanced, watching, waiting. Not this boat too, his whole attitude said. Not today.

Slumped against the side wall Troy looked up at the slightly built older man. Imelda ripped me apart, he thought bleakly, what chance do you have?

Not even sure he could stand, let alone wield something as heavy as an oar, Troy decided to stay where he was.

The bump came again, heavier, actually shifting the boat. A stealthy scratching, scraping sound moved towards the stern.

Troy's hands were shaking. There was a cubby hole in the prow packed with survival equipment. He rummaged through it looking for a weapon. No way was he going out without a fight.

Markus raised the oar over his head. 'Here they come.' He sounded very calm.

Metal glinted. Troy snatched it up and turned just as Markus sighed with relief and lowered the oar. 'It's just wreckage.'

Drenched in sweat, Troy looked at what he held in his fist. Koponen dropped down beside him and drew up his knees.

'This was all I could find,' Jarglebaum said.

Koponen looked at what he held and chuckled. 'A pair of tweezers.' His laughter grew and grew, then turned to racking sobs.

Troy put his good arm round Koponen's shoulders and held him close. 'It's OK, Markus. It's OK.'

Koponen fell quiet. They sat together looking across the grey, rolling sea. A thin layer of mist hung a few feet above the water. The sun rose. It was beautiful.

An Amazing Guy

CROUCHED behind the Imperial, Persistent Smith watched two anonymous silhouettes backlit by the dawn glow emerge from the water and wearily make their way up the slipway. When he recognised one of them he stepped out of cover. 'Over here, Tim. It's me, Smith.'

Tim's companion was a tall athletic woman. She looked very tired. Even so, she began combing her hair. It was the longest hair Smith had ever seen and it glowed pale gold.

Not knowing what else to say, Smith put on a fake Chicago accent. 'Who's the dame?'

Tim was in a daze. His clothes were soaked, his sopping leather jacket sagged heavily from his shoulders. Smith's words and big, eager face slowly registered. 'This is Foxy Bolivia. She saved my life.'

'Hey,' Foxy said. 'Got anything to eat?'

Smith dug around in his fleece pockets and offered a half-melted bar of chocolate and the broken remains of a few biscuits.

'Thanks.' Foxy grabbed them all. 'Starving.'

'How come your clothes are dry?' Smith said.

'BecauseImafrippinmermaidallright?' Foxy said from a mouth crammed with broken biscuits.

'Sorry. I just wondered.'

'Wellgetusedtoit.'

'Sure thing. No problemo.'

Tim stood in his socks in a puddle of sea water. He looked at Smith and tried to order his thoughts. Foxy Bolivia was a mermaid but the surprises kept coming. 'Smith, it's good to see you. How did you escape?'

Smith puffed an imaginary cigar. 'They haven't made the cage that can hold me.'

'Of course not.' Tim shivered. 'I'm freezing.'

'Wait here.' Smith darted away and returned with two pairs of overalls from the alcove he'd used as an emergency latrine.

Tim stripped off his sodden outer clothes, careful to retain the pendant. His old jacket was ruined, the leather slimy and stretched, the sleeves reaching past his fingertips. He pulled on one pair of overalls and dried his hair with the other. His skin tingled as he grew warmer. He'd spent who knew how many hours underwater and felt like he'd run a marathon. Some food would be good. Ham egg and chips. He salivated. 'Any of that chocolate left?'

'Sure.' Foxy handed him the uneaten half of the chocolate bar. She looked fine, in fact she looked great. Her skin glowed with health, her clothes were perfect, her hair shone.

Tim devoured the chocolate in two bites. 'We need to get out of here.'

Smith pointed to the Imperial. 'I found the car.'

'That was good work,' Tim said. 'Actually, it was great work.'

'I know. Let's get in.'

'No keys.'

Smith extracted the keys from the exhaust pipe with a flourish.

Tim gave him a weary grin. 'Smith, you really are an amazing guy.'

Smith looked steadily back. 'Yes, I think I probably am.'

Foxy climbed into the driver's seat. She twisted the wheel enthusiastically. 'I want to drive.'

'You can do that?' Tim wondered about the pedals.

'Humans do it all the time. How hard can it be?'

'Move over.'

Foxy slid across the front bench, Smith climbed into the rear. The engine throbbed into life. The windscreen was coated in dew.

Tim operated the wipers, held the wheel and looked through the windscreen down the long black bonnet. He'd spent a lot of time and effort looking for this car. Barefoot and wearing a shabby old boiler suit, now he was behind its wheel. The search had shown him strange and terrible things. He looked at Foxy beside him. Wonderful things too.

The metal of the accelerator pedal was cold under his foot. He pressed down and the big car surged away down the quayside. Tim swung around in a fast one-eighty and headed towards the exit.

The engine had a superb tone. Tim listened then said, 'The timing needs advancing by one half degree and the plug in cylinder three needs the gap setting.' He frowned. 'How do I know that?'

Foxy tapped his chest. 'The pendant. It wasn't just *Sea Cucumber*, it taught you the language of machines.'

It was true. The Imperial felt like a natural extension of his own body: exhaust, transmission, valves and gears.

'Look.' Foxy pointed at the Mercedes parked beside a warehouse.

The Imperial was doing fifty and still accelerating.

'Hold on.'

Tim dropped the clutch, span the wheel and hauled on the handbrake. The rear side of the heavy Imperial fishtailed hard into the Mercedes and slammed it into the side of the warehouse with a thunderous metallic bang and splintering of glass.

'Yay!' Foxy twisted in her seat. Behind them the Mercedes rocked from the impact, its windscreen was crazed, one of the tyres was flat, a hubcap spun madly across the quay. 'Tim Wassiter, you bad man!'

Tim's mouth twisted in a lopsided smile as he brought the Imperial back in line. 'Two and a half tons and not a hint of understeer.'

Smith slid around on the bench seat giggling with excitement. 'How fast can this thing go?'

'Let's find out.'

The big black car roared through the dockyard gates and tore through the empty dawn streets of Southampton. Out on the coast road they sped towards Brighton at over one hundred miles an hour, their headlights blazing to challenge the rising sun.

Perfection

The table was ready and it was perfect. Asklepios admiringly ran his hand over the smooth sanded surface. Two gold-inlaid lines divided the circular top into exactly equal quarters. He rested his cheek on the top and looked along them. Each one ran straight and true. Two finer lines subdivided each quarter into thirds, also inlaid with the precious metal.

Asklepios had been intrigued to discover the craftsmen worked in both base ten and base sixty, as did all numerate people in Babylon. He soon understood the advantages of working in a large base divisible without remainder by many numbers. Though it was difficult to learn the higher base he persisted.

Each third was further subdivided into thirty sections, each marked by a short groove on the table's circumference, with every tenth line cut twice as long.

Banipal watched Asklepios closely, happy see the pleasure in his guest's eyes.

'Your carpenters are at least the equal of the finest in Baghdad.' Asklepios' vocabulary had increased rapidly, he was grateful he could now express his thanks properly. He clasped Banipal's hands in his own. 'Thank you, my friend. This is a gift beyond kindness, beyond hospitality—' His throat grew tight, he wanted to say more but could not.

Banipal did not mind, he could see Asklepios' joy, though he was not sure the cabinetmakers would appreciate being called carpenters no matter how fine.

Once he fully understood Asklepios' request Banipal was interested in the idea for his own purposes. The cabinetmakers quickly grasped Asklepios' ideas and encouraged by Banipal's status and gold they worked fast. In fact Banipal found Abil-Ilishu, the shaven-headed and bright-eyed elderly guild leader, enthusiastic to the point of arm-waving.

'It will be magnificent! Seasoned cedar, teak and ebony, ivory—'

'Northern oak will be fine.'

Abil-Ilishu absorbed the instruction without pausing. 'Yes. Fine-grained oak, an economic choice and almost as good quality. I guarantee not one knot-hole or other flaw. I propose it is inlaid with alternating segments of ebony and ivory, the contrast will be—'

'Again, not necessary. This is a working table.'

'—beautiful.' Abil-Ilishu pouted, then burst back into life. 'A double rim around the circumference bounding the degree marks and inlaid in silver, broad and deep. The marks and radii inlaid gold, major diameters capped with rubies and minor alternating jacinth and sardonyx. I suggest chalcedony—'

The conversation wore on. After a long hour, a pause for refreshment, then further negotiations they settled on a simple medium cost design with diameters, radii and tenth-angle marks inlaid with gold. There would be no silver, rubies, sardonyx or jacinth.

'This is a prototype,' Banipal explained, feeling oddly guilty about not spending his own wealth. 'A table to your original design may well follow.'

'I understand completely.' Abil-Ilishu said, equably, his grumbling protests that a plain design was unworthy of the cabinetmaker's craft apparently forgotten.

Looking back, Banipal wondered if Abil-Ilishu had in fact got exactly what he wanted. After all, he, Banipal, had only wanted a plain wooden table.

Asklepios watched as Banipal fetched twine and began measuring the table's circumference.

May I help?' Asklepios asked.

Banipal passed Asklepios one end of the twine. 'Hold this against the table.'

Asklepios pressed down on the twine with his thumb. 'What are you trying to do?'

'The world is round. I wish to measure it.'

'What is the problem?'

'I do not yet understand how the diameter changes relative to the circumference as a circle grows.'

'It doesn't,' Asklepios said.

Banipal looked up. 'What do you mean?'

'It is the same for all circles, part of their mystery. The ratio is always twenty-five eighths.'

Banipal stared in amazement. He drew lines and circles in the air with his fingers. 'You are quite certain?'

'Completely.'

'How can you be sure?'

'It is a part of our history. Once, a group of foreign monks fled persecution because of some learned scrolls in their possession. They founded a monastery at a place called Jundi Shapur, lived peacefully and obeyed our laws. In time the emperor became ill and no cure could be found. A servant sent for one of the monks and as a result of the monk's medicines and care the emperor grew well. For a reward the monk asked only that he and his brothers be allowed to teach philosophy, medicine and astronomy from their scrolls, which were exceedingly ancient and the only copies that yet remained in the world.'

Banipal fetched parchment and drew more lines and circles. 'How can this be? How can a line grow in simple length yet the proportion of the bounding circle—?'

Asklepios spread his hands. 'I don't know, but it does.'

Banipal frowned, then laughed long and loud. 'It was me all along. My mistakes, my errors. I'm relieved, you know. I really am.'

'It happens to us all.' Asklepios remembered his own mistakes keenly.

Banipal ran his hand over the table. 'We need better instruments.'

'We do indeed.'

That evening Asklepios narrated his own adventures to Banipal and Ishkun. They listened attentively, accepting not only had he been magically transported from another land, but from another age as well.

When he had finished Ishkun sat back, his hand on his chin. 'Truly, Ea sent you here to teach Banipal. Before that could happen Marduk asked Ekad to test both of you with his river.'

Not wanting to argue religion Asklepios said nothing. Sensing his discomfort, Banipal asked him about his plans for the table. Specifically, when would he perform his magic?

Asklepios grew even more uncomfortable. 'If I could teach you ten times what I know it would not repay you for your kindness. Before I can perform a ritual I have to ask you for even more: herbs, incense, lamp oil.'

Banipal sat forwards, his eyes burned bright. 'Tell me what you need.'

Asklepios tried without success to describe the herbs and spices. Banipal clapped him on the shoulder. 'We will go to the market together. You point to the things you need and I shall buy them. That way there is no risk you will have to jump into the river again.'

Late in the night Asklepios rose and went to the table. The wick from the evening lamp guttered as the oil ran dry. Idly he traced the ritual place markings, curves and lines crossing the surface. Once again he marvelled at the accuracy of the design.

Now there could be no errors, all would be perfect.

Banipal related Asklepios' tale of the monks to Ishkun. When the story was done Ishkun wept.

'What in this tale troubles you so?' Banipal said.

'It tells me that one day Marduk and Ea will turn their backs on us. Babylon will be nothing but fallen walls under drifting sand.' Ishkun dried his eyes. 'Our achievements will be forgotten. We will be less than memories.'

'No,' Banipal whispered, half to himself. 'No.' He looked out across the glorious stepped pyramid of Etemenanki and considered the might of Babylon's armies, her foot soldiers and chariots, the strength of her double walls, the wealth of her storehouses and granaries, the grand canals and temples and tried to imagine it all gone.

It was all too easy.

The Beginning

MRS WOOSENCRAFT recognised the distinctive tone of the Imperial as the car pulled up outside. Filled with trepidation she listened to the doors open and close and the car move away. The knock on the door was no surprise. Reluctantly she prepared herself, walked down the hall and opened her front door. What would be, would be.

'I've come for Morse,' Tim said. Beside him was the young golden-haired woman called Foxy Bolivia who Mrs Woosencraft had glimpsed in the Mercedes yesterday, only yesterday.

Breathless with relief Mrs Woosencraft stepped back. 'Best come in, then.'

A dozen cats made themselves scarce.

Morse lay curled up on the tatty old sofa in the back room.

Mrs Woosencraft could hardly keep her eyes off Foxy. There was an aura of wildness about the woman. Not of aggression but of freedom. She was someone who lived and was at home in the wider world. The deeper world. The thought made Mrs Woosencraft's mouth dry with nerves.

She took in the weariness on Tim's face, the ill-fitting boiler-suit and the fact he had no shoes. Weariness, and something else.

You've come through testing times, she thought. They have opened your eyes.

'I'm glad you made it back,' she said.

Tim nodded. 'Thank you.'

'I'll put the kettle on.'

Tim sat down on the sofa, picked up Morse and scruffed the top of his head. 'Tea would be wonderful.'

Morse purred softly and pretended to go back to sleep. If cats could smile…[11]

Mrs Woosencraft was almost but not absolutely sure. Hope put a catch in her voice. One short conversation in private and… 'Would you like to give me a hand in the kitchen, love?'

'No.'

'I could use some help.'

'I'm sure you can cope.'

Mrs Woosencraft tried a different tack. 'That's Tim's cat, Morse. I've been looking after it for him.'

'I see it.'

'Not a cat person, are you?' Mrs Woosencraft said.

'What are you supposed to make of an animal that likes fish but won't get its feet wet?'

Mrs Woosencraft bit her lip. It's you, Foxy Bolivia. It really is you and you are what they say you are. Oh, my goodness gracious me.

Even with that realisation, it was cats they were talking about so she tried for the last word. 'You're not meant to try to understand them. Just accept them for what they are.'

'Some things are unacceptable.'

She means me and I deserve it, Mrs Woosencraft thought sadly. Deserve it in spades. Oh dear, oh deary me I'm in trouble now. Oh, bugger me sideways with champion leeks.

The simple of ritual of warming the pot, spooning leaves and brewing was as calming as ever. Some of Mrs Woosencraft self-confidence returned.

---

[11] *Was it affection or was it relief? No doubt a bit of both. After all, meal ticket #1 was back in town.*

This was her house, after all, she told herself. And that meant a fair bit, even in this day and age.

She carried the tray into the back room. Tim and Morse occupied the sofa. Like Electra, Foxy had chosen the armchair, the one the cats knew not to sit in.

She put the tray down, sat on the piano stool and looked Foxy up and down.

And she could not help herself, she was just too excited. Things hadn't gone as she'd hoped (there had never been a plan, just expectations). Yet now it looked as if it might work out. She rubbed her hands and beamed her best sweet little old lady smile.

'You really are her, aren't you? The one we've all been looking for. The mermaid.'

Foxy looked down her nose at the dumpy little old lady. 'And you're a witch.'

'Oh, but I knew it! This is wonderful, I'm so—'

'Sorry?' Tim said sharply.

Mrs Woosencraft dipped her head. 'Yes. You are absolutely right. Listen to me go on.' She pressed her hands together. 'Tim, I am very sorry for deceiving you I have not behaved like a friend.'

Tim looked at her steadily. So did Morse.

Sitting on the piano stool with her feet not quite touching the ground Mrs Woosencraft felt a little interrogated. She bowed her head again. 'I'm sorry for the cat-napping too.'

She turned to Foxy. 'And I'm very sorry for what you've been through, pet. Markus Koponen isn't a bad man.'

'Wasn't,' Tim corrected. 'The last time we saw him he was trying to launch a boat from a sinking ship.'

That knocked her back. She'd known bad things were coming but to have them confirmed... 'He might have made it.'

'So might Troy, but Imelda hurt him badly.' Tim sketched in the details of the fight and what had happened to Koponen's women.

'I tried to warn Markus. You were there Tim, you heard me.' Mrs Woosencraft chewed her thumbnail. 'I should have tried harder, I should have made him listen to the truth—'

There was scant sympathy in Foxy's voice. 'Yes, let's have your version of the truth.'

'Well—' Mrs Woosencraft wriggled her bottom, she scratched behind an ear. 'It's like this. You might not believe it but I was—'

'There's a lot I believe today that I didn't yesterday, so just tell us,' Tim said.

His sharp words were a verbal slap and brought her to her senses. 'I was on my uppers, stony broke and Koponen offered me money. Then I was one cat short, I'd been paid and I'd made a promise. Whatever you might think I've got my standards. I needed nineteen, you see? Nineteen cats to make it work.' Her hands dropped into her lap and she sighed. 'It all seemed so reasonable at the time. Looking back I can see how I talked myself into it. I thought it would all be all right, I'd be able to find Foxy first, we could have our little chat and you could go on your own way. All sorted out nicely. I never wanted any trouble, it's all been very upsetting.'

Tim and Foxy exchanged puzzled glances. Tim poured the tea. 'I think you'd better start at the beginning.'

The Truth

THERE SHE WAS, dressed in another variation of lace-up boots, a long skirt and scoop top in black and purple. His heart in his mouth, Persistent Smith hurried towards the Kylma Kala main entrance.

'Hello. It's me,' Smith boomed anxiously.

'So I see.'

Smith grimaced unhappily. 'Sorry I'm late.'

Heidi was incredulous. 'Late? It's not even the same day.' She headed off along the pavement. 'It's my lunch hour, I've got to do some shopping.'

Smith hurried after her. 'I could buy you lunch.'

'No, thank you.'

Nonplussed, Smith fell back. 'Help me,' he begged the Hand.

'He was kidnapped!' the Hand shouted. 'Locked in the boot of a car and driven to Southampton.'

Furious, Heidi spun on her heels. 'No you weren't. Don't you dare lie to me.'

'Yes, I was. Honestly,' Smith said.

'It's the truth, honest to God,' the Hand cried. 'Sure as the fact that I'm just a stupid hand pretending to be a person. Or am I a person pretending to be a hand? I don't know any more. You've got to help me!'

Lunchtime crowds pushed around them. 'Really kidnapped? Really?'

'Only by accident. I escaped.'

'Well, yes, I can see that.'

Smith grimaced uncomfortably. 'It wasn't that difficult.'

'You're impossible, do you know that?'

Heidi walked away. Smith bounded in front of her. 'I'm persistent.'

'Do you know how long I waited for you? I felt like a complete idiot.'

'I don't know where you can get one of those around here,' Smith said. 'I'm only part of an idiot, will that do?'

Despite herself, Heidi smiled. 'What really happened?'

'I was on an adventure.'

Heidi shook her head. 'Tell me the truth.'

'I was following someone and hid in the boot. Then they drove the car away.'

Heidi jerked her head towards the offices. 'You don't work here do you?'

'As well as being a bit of an idiot I'm a bit of a detective too.'

Heidi absorbed the information. 'Which bit?'

'The bigger one.'

They started walking.

'Then what happened?'

'They got out the car. I escaped and we drove back to Brighton.'

'We?'

'My friends. They actually really were properly kidnapped, on a ship. They escaped and swam to shore.'

It all sounded utterly implausible. On the other hand this was Derek Smith. 'So where's the car?'

'Just around the corner.'

Smith showed her.

'Oh Lord, where did you get a machine like that?'

'I just said.'

'What about the owner?'

'He drowned when the ship sank.'

'I don't know whether to believe anything you say.' Heidi ran her hand over the crumpled rear wing. 'What a shame this happened.'

'I'm going to get that mended,' Smith said.

Most of the damage was from Tim's sideswipe of the Mercedes. There were also fresh knocks and scrapes on the front bumpers. On the drive back to Brighton Smith had leaned over the front seat and studied how Tim moved his feet across the pedals and moved the gear stick. It hadn't looked difficult. When they pulled up in Tim's street he said he would take over and drive home. And they let him.

Something beeped in Heidi's handbag. 'Dammit. Look, I've got to go,' she said but didn't move away.

'OK.' Smith shuffled his feet and stared at his shoes.

The beeper sounded again, louder. 'That stuff you helped me with on the computer was really important. Thank you.'

'All part of the service, ma'am,' the Hand said.

Heidi took a step away. 'I really have to go.'

Smith took a deep breath. 'I could pick you up after work.'

The Ritual

THE WHITE-HAIRED goat gave a strangled bleat, kicked against its bonds and lay still. Assisted by Ishkun, Asklepios hung the animal by its back legs from a hook set into a roof beam. The animal struggled briefly then hung still. Asklepios placed a deep bowl under the goat, took Ishkun's proffered knife, and cut the creature's throat.

Asklepios looked at the dying animal with some regret. He knew he did not need all this paraphernalia and that simpler was better, but couldn't bring himself to give up on the ornate ritual. Not yet. For now it helped at least as much as it hindered. Experiment could come later, today was not the time for change.

While he collected the goat's blood Banipal cleared away the rushes and gouged a shallow trench all around the table in the packed earth of the floor. He cleared the debris from the trench and swept the waste outside.

'I shall send a simple message to my master,' Asklepios said. 'If he wishes to respond in person he will come. If not, his answer will reveal itself in a secondary divination.'

Banipal noted Asklepios had been careful not to mention his master's name.

Now the incense was smouldering, the lamps were lit and the correct herbs placed in the seven equidistant positions around the table. Using the table was a joy, Asklepios' insight had been vindicated and he felt his confidence grow. Already he could see how improvements could be made by adding division marks of thirds and fifths for simpler rituals, and sevenths for the more complex, like the one he attempted now.

Banipal and Ishkun stood to one side. The priest held a flask of wine, the hunter his bloody dagger.

Asklepios went outside, changed into a short-sleeved knee-length shirt of clean white linen and re-entered the room. He took up the bowl of blood and carried it slowly and carefully to Banipal, who poured in a measure of wine. The he turned to Ishkun, who stirred the mix with his knife.

He poured the mix of blood and wine into the channel, put the bowl aside, went to his allotted place, raised his hands palms upwards and began to chant.

Time passed. Banipal's feelings of awed anticipation gradually changed to the bored tension he often felt during the longer rituals in the temples at Esagila. Beside him Ishkun shifted his feet and Banipal knew his friend was itching to move.

Asklepios finished his chant and knelt on the spot he had marked on the ground, intermittently prostrating himself. As he repeated the move for the umpteenth time one of the lamps went out.

Ishkun sighed in exasperation and walked from the room.

In His Dreams

THE MORE Mrs Woosencraft explained, the more intrigued Foxy became. As her hostility faded she occasionally interjected comments of her own. She even went out to the kitchen to refill the kettle.

'Why don't you sit in your chair?' Foxy said on her return.

Gratefully Mrs Woosencraft sank into the cushions.

'Move up, Tim,' Foxy said.

Tim lifted Morse onto his lap. The cat's eyes never left Foxy and she frowned back at it.

'Never mind him,' Mrs Woosencraft said. 'He'll get used to you.'

Tim didn't find Mrs Woosencraft's explanations all that easy to follow. There were long stories and there were long stories, hers seemed to be recapitulating most of human history. He had a few questions of his own.

'You still haven't said why you really wanted to find Foxy.'

Mrs Woosencraft pursed her lips. 'Because I'm old. I'm the last keeper of Deg Naw Wyth, and only an average one at that. I've never seen Deep Magic and this felt like my last chance before I well, you know, cark it. Brown bread, pushing up the daisies.'

'Deg Naw Wyth. What does that mean?'

'It means Ten, Nine, Eight, and the name is a trick because all of those numbers can be broken. It came up from Africa centuries past and took root here. Once... Oh, that was just once and an age before my time. All that's left are a few fragments: lucky seven, everything I say three times is true.'

'Un Deg Naw,' Tim said thoughtfully. 'You named your cats after numbers?'

'Well, yes. It was tempting to be clever and call them things like Hilbert and Keith and Heegner, but to be honest it made them easier to remember.'

'It's not very affectionate.'

Mrs Woosencraft shook her head. 'They don't mind, and they've got their own names. Secret ones like 'Scrwch' or 'Yrowl' they don't want us to know about. We were all in this together. They wanted to see a mermaid. Don't ask me why, cats just like looking at them. Me? All I wanted was to meet someone who knew one of the old ways.'

Foxy took over. 'Our magics don't overlap, we'd lost contact. My mother warned me about cats but she didn't know why, it was just something we knew. We had forgotten they could be a sign, a request for a meeting.'

'Such a shame.' Mrs Woosencraft shook her head sadly. 'Poor little scrap.'

'What happened to her?' Tim said.

'I did,' Foxy said regretfully. 'I'd only just come ashore and straightaway she was there, following me. I decided better safe than sorry.'

Tim could believe it. He remembered her reaction to finding Morse in her flat and shifted uncomfortably. It was a difficult thing to discover the woman you— He had to know. 'Did you—?'

Foxy shook her head emphatically. 'I scared her off. A lot.'

Mrs Woosencraft squeezed Foxy's hand. 'We've both made mistakes. I want you to call me Dot. All my friends do.'

'All right.'

Despite their reconciliation Mrs Woosencraft was exceedingly glum.

'The skill is gone. Nobody is interested in the old ways. I don't have a student, not even a chubby little goth girl in black lace, with purple hair and a nose ring. Soles on their boots like breeze blocks, some of them. Nineteen isn't very far to go at all. Ethel managed twenty-three and a bit of twenty nine. Her tutor mastered thirty-one. These days hardly anyone even knows their thirteen times table.'

'There isn't enough room in our minds for everything,' Foxy said. 'New things push aside the old. Then the new becomes old and the very old ways return in a new form.'

'I think she's right,' Tim said. 'Foxy and I managed a divination with maps. And I—' He became self-conscious under Mrs Woosencraft's suddenly penetrating gaze. 'I can make things happen in my dreams.'

Mrs Woosencraft cocked her head. 'Tell me more.'

Tim narrated his experiences with Asklepios.

'That's right,' Foxy said.

'You knew all this too?' Mrs Woosencraft exclaimed.

'I was going to get around to it.'

Mrs Woosencraft flapped her hands with excitement. 'Show me his pendant.'

Tim pulled it out from his shirt. Mrs Woosencraft cupped her hands around it without touching.

'Hmm,' she said. 'Whatever was there, it's gone.'

'You don't believe me,' Tim said.

'I do, but I'd like to see you do it.'

'It's not that easy,' Tim said. 'I have to be asleep.'

Mrs Woosencraft settled back into her chair. 'Well, I think it's just about time for my nap.'

All She Needed

His parents' front garden was exactly as Smith remembered. Shoulder high dahlias flanked the path; blue pansies, pink daisies and orange marigolds still clashed in the flower bed.

Why shouldn't it be the same? He had only been away a few days.

It felt like forever.

The garden gate clicked shut behind him. 'My, what a lot of flowers,' Heidi said. 'They're so, um, colourful.'

Smith pressed the doorbell. Soft chimes rang in the hall. I'm not nervous, he told himself as he reached for Heidi's hand. I'm excited.

A slightly stooped female figure swam into view through the hammered glass of the front door. She stood still for a moment, fumbled the catch and flung the door wide. Violet Smith looked joyfully up at her son.

'Hello, Mummy,' Smith said.

'Who is it?' Albert Smith called from upstairs.

'Derek,' Violet said quietly. She called out louder: 'Albert, it's Derek. He's come home.'

Furniture bumped upstairs, a door slammed. Unbuttoned cardigan flapping, bifocals swinging from the cord round his neck, Albert Smith erupted onto the landing and thundered down the stairs. 'By God, my lad, where have you been? Your mother's been worried sick.'

'Albert,' Violet cautioned.

'Whatever you've been up to, my lad, it was not Good Thinking.'

Violet's voice carried an edge. 'Albert. Derek has a friend with him.'

'Actually, it was very Good Thinking indeed,' Derek said. 'Hello, Daddy, this is Heidi.'

Albert Smith lurched to a halt, reassessed the situation and stuck out his hand. 'Hello, my dear. Won't you come in?'

It didn't take long. Violet knew she could be good at this sort of thing if only she had the chance. She'd waited such a long time.

'So tell me, where did you meet Derek?' Violet said.

'In the office where I work. Del helped me out with some calculations.'

She calls him Del, Violet thought happily. 'He's always been good with numbers. Lists and timetables, things like that.'

'Did you come over on the bus?' Albert said.

'No, in Del's new car.'

Albert looked through the lace curtains, gaped and turned back. He managed a rather high-pitched, 'Derek, where did you get that car?'

'It's not mine, I borrowed it.'

'When did you learn to drive?'

'It wasn't that difficult.'

That wasn't the answer Albert had been looking for. He opened his mouth, lifted a finger.

'I like your front garden,' Heidi said a little loudly.

It was all Violet needed.

'Come out back and see what I've done. Derek, go and show your father the car.'

She's nice, Violet thought to herself as the two women toured the garden. Her top is cut a bit low, but I expect that's just me being old fashioned. It's not every girl who'd pretend to be interested in flowers to please her boyfriend's mum.

Later in the front room the two women looked out the window at the men. Albert knelt beside the wing of the Imperial making circular motions with his palm over the dented bodywork. Derek helped him up and they stood back, arms folded, heads nodding slowly.

Violet took a deep breath. 'You and Derek get on well.'

Heidi smiled to herself. 'We've really only just met.'

'I know, dear. I can't help it, I'm his mother.'

Out by the car Derek said something. Hands stuffed in his pockets, Albert roared with laughter. Watching them, Violet felt her feet were about to leave the ground. She blinked hard, it had been a long while since she had last felt this happy.

Albert and Derek came inside. Violet put her arm round her husband's waist and gave him a hug. 'I'd like to go to the garden centre. Heidi suggested I put a purple clematis over the trellis,' Violet said.

'Derek and I need to go to the car shop.'

'Why don't we go together,' Heidi said.

'I've decided to become an accountant,' Derek said.

To Sleep…

IT WASN'T EASY to fall asleep when people expected you to. Although Tim was very tired and comfortably settled onto Mrs Woosencraft's settee he just couldn't do it.

Once Mrs Woosencraft drew the curtains she dropped off with no trouble. Now she lay in her chair with her hands folded over her tummy and her feet on a low footstool. Despite being asleep there was an air of expectation about her.

Tim's mind was still full of the past day's astonishing events: the sinking ship, the great swim, Jarglebaum and Koponen's unknown fate, the shark women's transformation and wild revelations.

A shadow passed over Tim's face. Foxy kissed his forehead. 'I'm going into the kitchen,' she whispered. 'Go to sleep.'

Tim found himself thinking about the flies under the lampshade in his room. During their swim to shore he had seen small shoals of fish circling under floating mats of weed, discarded fishing nets, waterlogged pallets and other debris. Foxy had said such places were refuges, the fish were hiding.

What were the flies hiding from, he wondered? They were safe, he didn't mind them being there. They should land and have a rest. Maybe it was safer for them to keep on the move. He zoomed in closer and flew with the flies. His office expanded to became a titanic space filled with vast objects like the valleys of Colorado.

I think I'm asleep now, he thought.

And he was.

Tim opened his eyes into a room bled dry of colour. Mrs Woosencraft looked up at him from her sleeping body. He reached down and drew her out. She took one look at her own form, and nodded. In the kitchen Foxy sat colourless and still, both she and the room looked like they were drawn on pieces of paper in astonishing detail. Tim led Mrs Woosencraft into the garden.

Gale-winds blew out to sea, the monochrome sky streaked with tattered clouds streaming like wind-torn banners. Mrs Woosencraft jumped up onto his back, lighter than a feather. Tim thought a single word: Asklepios. For a moment he struggled against Mrs Woosencraft's inertia then surged up into the sky. The ground fell away below their feet. The wind whirled them in four directions, then one.

Moving On

ELSEWHERE in Brighton an overweight middle-aged man became aware of someone sitting beside his hospital bed. It was a young woman, one who now wore her hair in a black rooster-cut with a red fringe.

'Hey,' Gabby said.

'Jeez,' Troy struggled to sit up and not to let the pain show as the stitches pulled. 'I didn't expect to see you here.'

'You visited me.'

Jarglebaum winced, gave up and lay back. 'I was interviewing you.'

'Seven billion people in the world and I had one visitor. I don't care about the reason.'

Troy looked at her narrow face with its too wide mouth and too long nose, her pipe-cleaner arms and her really quite lovely brown eyes and wondered why someone like her would go out of the way to visit a copper old enough to be her father.

'Pass me some of that water, love. These hospitals are too damned hot.'

She carefully poured water from the jug and handed it to him with her left hand. She saw him watching. She held her head up and looked right back.

'How are you doing?' Jarglebaum said as gently as he had ever said anything.

'I'm meant to say that.'

'So tell me.'

Gabby looked down. 'OK, I guess.'

'The shop going all right?'

'I've hired a manager. I went back for a bit but every time the door opened—'

That was all it took. Troy was back on the *Sea Cucumber*. It was dark, the ship was sinking and Imelda was kicking nine different types of hell out of him.

Gabby touched his arm. 'Troy? Are you all right?'

'Yeah, sure.' Troy breathed hard, sweat prickled across his back. 'It comes and goes. How's the hand?'

Gabby tried to make a fist with her right hand but it wouldn't close. 'I can't hold a mug, I can't write. I don't think it will ever be the same.'

'I'm proud of my scars, you should be too.'

'At least I can tell when it's going to rain.'

'That's my girl.'

Gabby tried a smile. 'All I ever wanted to do was run a pet shop and sell fluffy little animals and goldfish to nice people.'

'Yeah, well, you shouldn't let God hear your plans. I always fancied a bar on a beach somewhere hot. Babes in bikinis queuing for pina-coladas. That's why I ended up in the public sector with three-quarters of fuck all for a pension.'

'I think I'm going to sell up.'

Troy thought things through. 'Look, Gabby, I know who hurt you and I reckon you're safe. I know their names and I know what happened to them. I honestly don't think they'll be bothering you again.'

Gabby's eyes widened. 'That sounds heavy.'

'It is, but not how you think.'

'A long story?'

'Yeah, one for another day.'

Gabby sat on the end of the bed. 'What are you going to do?'

'Take a break. I'm out of the service and there's a rich guy who owes me a favour. Apart from that I don't want to risk screwing it up by talking too much.'

Gabby looked out the window. 'I'd like to hear that story when you're ready.'

Look at her, Troy told himself. You're such an idiot. She's been through tough times and she's all alone. You're just some kind of father figure.

He tried to keep his voice light, conversational. 'It's a deal.' He held up his arm with the saline drip attached. 'I'm out of here tomorrow, looking forward to a better drink than this.'

Gabby jumped to her feet. 'I could get you something from the hospital café. How about a strawberry and banana smoothie?'

The thought of all those vitamins made Troy's stomach recoil. 'I was thinking of something stronger.'

'Gooseberry and rhubarb?'

Oh Christ, this is never going to work, Troy thought, but he was laughing so much it hurt.

A Ghost

BANIPAL STRETCHED out the ache in his back. After Asklepios' failure he had returned to his own studies and spent longer than he intended bent over his bench inscribing clay tablets.

He rested his head in his hands and closed his eyes. He was avoiding the obvious question: was Asklepios a fake? Was the man he had pulled from the river, the man now sleeping beside the expensive round table in the other room, making a fool of him?

If so then he was being tricked by a well-educated man. Banipal had already incorporated some of Asklepios' number secrets into his own work and solved problems he had previously struggled with. No, to doubt Asklepios was to doubt the Gods. Ishkun was right, this was a test of tests. If the Gods so chose they would reveal their purpose when it suited them.

The last time he hunted with Ishkun the lion had taken their final quarry. It was a clear message from Ninurta, Lord of the Hunt, that they had hunted enough. So far there had been no such sign from wise Marduk.

The strangest feeling came over him. Unbidden, he found himself looking towards the door of the room where Asklepios slept.

The feeling grew and grew. He felt oddly separated from the room in which he sat. Somehow he had become distanced from it, yet remained within.

The door drew his eye powerfully. Still seated, Banipal simultaneously felt himself rise up and move forwards. He passed through the door without opening it. Three ghosts stood there.

Charcoal grey and semi-opaque, the apparitions stood braced against a wind Banipal could not feel. For a moment he was frightened, certain they were three of Anu's terrible demons. Then he saw one was Asklepios. And here was another wonder for Asklepios' body lay sleeping on the mat. The second ghost was a tall, dark-haired young man. The third had the form of an old woman.

The ghost of Asklepios turned to Banipal and solemnly raised his hand. Without quite knowing why, Banipal did the same, and realised Asklepios was filled with a great joy. He wanted to speak but before he could Asklepios faced the tall ghost and they both vanished.

The ghost of the old woman turned her cold grey gaze on Banipal. Their eyes met and—

Banipal lay at his scribing bench, his face pressed on the desk. One of the fired clay blocks pressed uncomfortably into his cheek.

He stood, filled with a transcendent sense of connection to his vision. This had been no simple dream. As he opened the door into the other room he was certain what he would find. He was right, Asklepios was gone.

Origin

BLOWN LIKE thistledown by the dream-winds Tim sensed Asklepios' location in the blustering blue-grey clouds as nothing more than a sense of rightness in one direction more than any other. He swept closer, Mrs Woosencraft a growing weight on his back. When they had set out she had been no burden beyond a slight inertia, the further they travelled the greater her weight had grown.

Asklepios resolved into the same pinpoint of blue-white light Tim had seen on the beach during his first dream-flight. His light rose to meet them, hung steady then plummeted like a falling stone. Tim dropped down after it and broke free of the mists. Above him stars glittered in a moonless sky, far below a double-walled city stood beside a broad river on a winding plain, the very place he had brought Asklepios. Free of the mists that had plagued him on his first journey Tim saw the city was on a grand scale with wide, brick-paved avenues, two and three story buildings, and towering stepped temples. Temples were everywhere.

Asklepios' soul light glowed inside a room at the base of one of several buildings around a plaza. To the west a bridge with a dozen arches spanned a wide energetic river. Immediately to the north an enormous stepped pyramid thrust into the sky.

With no sense of transition they were inside the room beside Asklepios' sleeping form. Mrs Woosencraft dropped from Tim's back though her weight, the effort of carrying her, did not. She looked around in wonder, especially at the table.

Tim reached for Asklepios' hand and drew him out.

Asklepios and Mrs Woosencraft's spirits recognised each other immediately.

Asklepios thrust out his splayed hand. 'Servant of Bez! Begone from this dream. I cast thee out!'

'You can talk, interfering meddler. I'm glad to finally clap my eyes on you.'

'You know each other?' Tim was dismayed at their mutual hostility.

'She is the root of all my troubles,' Asklepios said.

'He broke my teapot.'

Tim clutched his head. 'What?'

'Remember the bee and the glue? That was this idiot,' Mrs Woosencraft said.

'I was helping Tim,' Asklepios said with affronted dignity.

Mrs Woosencraft looked at the two men in sheer amazement. 'You two were working together?'

Asklepios bowed serenely. 'Indeed we were.'

'Foxy was plagued by cats,' Tim said. 'I didn't know it was you.'

'Oh—!' Mrs Woosencraft clenched her fists, opened her mouth and struggled to find the right words. 'Just forget it. Water under the bridge.'

'A gracious offer I gladly accept.' Asklepios turned eagerly to Tim. 'Have you come to take me home?'

'This isn't it?'

'Sadly, no.'

Mrs Woosencraft cleared her throat. 'I can only apologise.'

'All right, we've been working at cross-purposes, but I can put things right,' Tim said. 'Asklepios, I can take you home but I'm not strong enough to carry you both.'

'Leave me here,' Mrs Woosencraft said without hesitation. 'It's the simplest way.'

'I've only done this once before. It's not easy—'

'Nothing worth doing ever is.'

'If something wakes me up—'

Mrs Woosencraft folded her arms. 'I'll take my chances. You and Foxy, you've made it all worthwhile, see? I want to look around. Especially at that table.'

Reluctantly Tim agreed. If he did wake then she could end up marooned here like Asklepios. 'I'll be as quick as I can.'

'I'll be fine, *bachgen.*'

'The people here have been kind to me I would like to say goodbye,' Asklepios said.

Tim opened the door and saw a shaven-headed man with a long, plaited beard dozing at a table. He was neither fully asleep nor awake. Tim tried to draw him out and to his surprise the man's spirit emerged and stood in front of them.

'This is Banipal, the man who saved me.' Asklepios raised his hand and Banipal returned the gesture.

'Goodbye, my friend. May your gods bless you,' Asklepios said but Banipal gave no sign he understood.

'He's in his own dream, he cannot hear you,' Tim said.

Asklepios accepted the fact calmly. 'I shall miss him.'

'Are you ready?'

'To go home?' Asklepios beamed with pleasure. 'Always.'

He was not as heavy as Mrs Woosencraft but heavy enough. In a trice they were high above the city, then higher still. Asklepios cried out and clung on. Mist enfolded them and he relaxed.

'I see you wear my pendant.'

'I had to use the last charge.'

Asklepios' disappointment was palpable.

'It helped save people's lives.'

'Then I am glad.' Asklepios became thoughtful. 'Now it is uncharged please be careful when you remove it.'

'What will happen?'

'I have no idea.'

Tim smiled to himself. 'I'm going to miss you, Asklepios.'

'And I, you. In the past few days I have lived an entire lifetime of enlightenment and adventure. Now I am ready to go home.'

'Then show me where.'

Asklepios fell silent. Far across time, distance, and possibility, a dim red light shone. 'There.'

Travelling the mists was not getting easier. Tim struggled against a rising wind, a growing pull to wakefulness. Unbidden thoughts of Mrs Woosencraft's back room intruded. He saw himself asleep there clearly, it would be such an easy thing to open his eyes. He pushed onwards, determined not to let Asklepios down a second time.

The winds grew contrary, gusting hard in one direction then the other. 'Think of home, Asklepios. Remember the street, your rooms, your family, every little detail.'

'My doorstep has a chip where my son dropped the bucket.'

'Yes.'

'My children, my dearest wife—' Asklepios' voice dropped a tone. 'I shall bathe more.'

It worked. A steady breeze built behind them first countering then cancelling the push against Tim. For Asklepios there was a rightness to this direction of travel. He was going home.

At long last the dream-mists parted. The two men stood in a monochrome alleyway of tapered arches in mud-plaster walls. Nearby stood a particular doorway familiar to Asklepios.

'I am home.' Asklepios dropped to the ground, knelt, and kissed the packed earth.

Exhausted, Tim leaned on the wall, the urge to wake almost overwhelming. To wake and sleep again—

Asklepios gestured apologetically and backed away. 'Master, my children, I am anxious—' Colour bloomed around

Asklepios as he stepped into the waking world, red-mud plaster on the walls, a patch of blue sky, a waft of orange blossom.

'Farewell.'

Colours faded and with them Asklepios and the alley. Tim was alone in the mists.

Wind slammed against him. Asklepios had brought him close to the waking world. Tim pushed increasingly vivid memories of his own home from his mind and began the wind-torn journey back to Mrs Woosencraft, each moment an act of sheer will.

She shone far brighter than Asklepios and for this Tim was grateful. It was so very far…

Brighton. The shingle beach front, happily screaming children, music on the pier, the sunshine on his face. Morse asleep on his bed.

Thunderheads of black and grey cloud piled in front of him, the winds against his chest like a forbidding hand. In the far distance a scatter of bright motes blew: dreamers like himself. Most went with the winds but one drove headlong into the dream-winds towards some far destination on a dream-quest like himself.

That brief moment of kinship gave him strength. He drove on through air so dense it felt solid. Grab and pull, grab and pull. Mrs Woosencraft was still far away. A trembling fear built in him, the growing certainty it had been a big mistake to leave her. Dark clouds circled all around, the wind a soundless hurricane. Weary beyond measure Tim veered and swooped towards her beacon light.

When he finally breached the mists she was terrified.

All that remained of the city was Asklepios' room. Outside there were no buildings, no city, just a windswept charcoal-black tornado through which pinpoint lights tore round and around.

The corners of the room sloughed into smoke. Mrs Woosencraft clung to the table, the last item of furniture in the room.

Then the walls of the room were gone, rubbed away into nothingness. They stood on a corroding circle of floor within black storm-winds spattered with bright motes.

The look she gave him was half gratitude, half incomprehension. 'Leave me. Wake up, be safe.'

All around was a maelstrom of dark dreams, nightmares and terror.

'Out there—its madness.'

He was right and she knew it. If he left her, even if she woke. Her face set hard, she tried to push him away. 'Save yourself.'

He did not need saving, this was still his dream and he would always be safe from his own nightmares. But they would tear her apart.

The power of the dream-storm was daunting. They climbed onto the round table and clung to each other. If they were going to go it had to be right now. Tim lifted Mrs Woosencraft onto his back. His knees buckled, her weight was astonishing. The idea of going into those winds with her on his back an impossibility.

He couldn't do it.

Mrs Woosencraft climbed down. 'It's all right, Tim.'

'I'm sorry.' What else could he say?

She squared her shoulders and looked down at her feet. 'I never thought I'd go out like this. Look after the cats, won't you?'

'I'm here to the end, Mrs Woosencraft—'

She took his hand. 'Dorothy.'

'I won't leave you. Dorothy.'

The dark winds touched the table and it resisted. It resisted and even here, even now, Mrs Woosencraft gave a great laugh. 'I knew it! That Asklepios, he's the bloody one.'

They stood inside a dream-tornado of black wind spattered with whirling motes of light, other dreamers blown by the dream-winds wherever they took them. The thought shook Tim like a thunderclap. He had brought Mrs Woosencraft with him, her spirit was connected to his dream. Therefore— Those lights were dreamers, if he could attach himself to one of their dreams—

The mad black winds were close enough to touch. Tim clutched Mrs Woosencraft's hands and flung himself towards the nearest light.

Inanna

Asklepios was gone. Unbidden, a tear welled in Banipal's eye. He laughed at his own self-pity.

Praise the Gods for the gifts they give, he chided himself. Don't weep because you wanted more.

He would go to the temples and seek understanding. Ishkun's philosophy came back to him: head, hand and spirit, all must be provided for. Of late Banipal's days had consisted of little else but his work, the hand of Marduk showed strongly in the pattern of his life. He had not kept his promise to Ishkun and had neglected his physical aspect. It was obvious which deity he should petition for help.

The courtyard below his workrooms opened onto an open plaza. On the far side, flanked by double rows of squat oval pillars, the high bronze-banded cedar doors to Inanna's temple stood ever open. There the priestesses offered their own bodies to honour the goddess. For a lesser donation they would bathe, oil and massage the supplicant's body. For less still they would dance. For nothing at all they did as they pleased.

At the doors Banipal removed his sandals, washed his feet in the ceaseless stream that flowed from the twin cisterns and went inside.

The interior of Inanna's temple was cool, pooled with light and shadow from small oil lamps burning here and there. Banipal made his way through the silence to the purifying rooms. There he gave over his offering, a nugget of natural gold, and was admitted.

Alone in the peace of a cool-water pool he stripped, bathed, then floated for a while in the dim silence. He rose from the water, dried himself and walked naked into the next room, where a muscular male priest oiled and scraped his skin with a strigil carved from the shin bone of a lioness.

The priest departed. Banipal lay face down on a low wooden couch padded with cushions. The chill of the pool and the rough tingle of the strigil faded to a pleasant glow. He tried to clear his mind and seek Inanna's peace. It wasn't easy, his thoughts kept returning to the ghosts, Asklepios, the geometries on the table.

Warm hands pressed on his shoulders. Unheard and unannounced one of the celebrant priestesses had entered the room. She began to massage his back.

She was strong and skilful, kneading and pushing the muscles and tendons under his skin. Banipal groaned as she found a knot of tension above his shoulder blade and was rewarded by a satisfied, feminine laugh, relaxed and easy. Shoulders, spine, hips, thighs and calves all yielded to her skill. She pressed her palms onto his kidneys, her hands burned like hot bronze and sent warmth deep into his entrails.

She touched his shoulder. Banipal turned onto his back.

The priestess was a woman neither young nor old, still in her prime. The grey veil of the celebrant covered her face. Her oiled skin gleamed copper red in the lamp light.

Her hips were wide, her breasts full and heavy. She had given birth at least once, her belly marked by a spreading fan of pale stretch-marks.

Banipal admired all the aspects of her beauty, each one emphasised by the shadows pooling in the hollows and curves of her body: her female form; her mother-marks; that carrying and giving birth had altered her body. He felt a pang of envy, her whole body was Inanna's gift in ways he would never know.

This he knew he must accept. Her gifts also brought great risks. Men too had their gifts, their lives held different dangers.

'This evening I am weary,' he informed her politely.

The priestess understood. She laid her hands on his brow, his heart, his stomach. 'I am a vessel of Inanna's peace.'

'I am in need of that peace' Banipal said.

'What is your offering?'

'I am my own offering.'

'For now?'

'Now, and always. My whole self.' Banipal said, completing the simple ritual.

He closed his eyes. A gentle breeze moved across his stomach and thighs but he felt no arousal. The priestess pressed her palm onto his brow again and he exhaled. As he did he felt his entire body loosen, limbs sinking, spine settling, all sinking towards the supporting wood beneath him. Peace filled him—Inanna's first and last gift. He felt her presence beside him, within him. The warmth of her body, the soft pressure of her stomach against his scalp.

So Banipal slept, and dreamed the strangest dream of a city without streets, of buildings without doors or windows. Mud brick dwellings stood crammed together like eggs in a nest, each with a single entrance in the common roof, both door and smoke hole. The whole city was built upon the ruins of an earlier age. Beneath that lay older ruins, and older still. Over the centuries a great *tel* of rubble had risen above the surrounding grasslands with the current city on top.

He stood above the entrance to what he knew to be his own home. Storm-light flickered ominously. Every other inhabitant was safe in their homes, safe from the storm and the creatures that made it. He was the last, and alone.

Banipal climbed down a wooden ladder with a centre-rail into the darkness of his single room home. Lightning flashed and a few heartbeats later thunder rolled across the plain. He blew the embers of the fire into life and added a little kindling.

As he built the fire two people dropped into the room, a lean young man and an old woman. Strangers seeking refuge, they knelt with palms upraised until Banipal touched their shoulders and accepted them as his guests.

Both were weary and far from home, exhausted by a long and arduous journey. The fire caught and in the growing light Banipal saw the tattoos on their bodies, patterns of the clustered dots and lines, circles, arrows and angles. Numbers, he realised with a start, they had numbers even in these ancient times. They understood the abstract and measured things beyond the seasons.

The storm circled the city. All three curled beside the fire and slept. Dreamers within a dream inside a dream.

Down to a time before legends—

Where tall ships lay at berth in a grand harbour beneath a city of pillared domes and bright spires. A city unwalled, where a roofless temple of marble steps and gilded columns stood in the green foothills of a towering, cloud-bannered mountain. A city that glowed with light at night, where machines had minds, and winged platforms slid across the sky. The kingdom, the city, of many names: Thule, Ys, Atlantis…

The three of them stood on the sweeping quay under the shadows of marble gods and saw the city was past its glory days. The harbour breakwater was a tumbledown ruin, one city quarter was abandoned, another had been smashed to rubble by something enormous that had rampaged through it.

Beyond the harbour a titanic segmented creature was being towed out to sea by a flotilla of three-masted ships. The creature was alive and strove mightily against the massive chains that bound it tight. The flotilla headed towards the cold heart of the ocean. There, the beast would sink. There, like all the others of its kind, it would die.

Only one living thing could be so gigantic.

Tuoni

The word beat inside Banipal's mind as if spoken by another voice.

The name broke his dream. Startled, he hovered in the formless darkness of his own mind. Who is there? Who spoke?

A crone voice came: 'Wake up, *bachgen*. I see the way home.'

Instantly Banipal was wide awake on the couch. Above him the veiled celebrant pressed down on his breastbone with the heel of her hand. Between his legs his manhood was achingly erect. He could only have slept for moments.

The priestess sensed his confusion. 'What is it?'

'A vision.'

In one graceful movement she swung her leg across his hips and mounted him. 'Tell me,' she said.

The sensation of her engulfing him was incredible.

Tim's eyes jolted open at exactly the moment Mrs Woosencraft's leg jerked and sent her stool flying across the room.

She returned Tim's wide-eyed gaze with aplomb. 'Well, that takes me back. Not the kind of ride I imagined. Very impressive.'

Foxy and Tim spent the rest of the day with Mrs Woosencraft. First Foxy insisted on hearing about their dream journey while it lay vivid in Tim's mind. He told her of Asklepios and the nightmare winds, the tattooed men and women from the honeycomb city of manmade caves, and the bright city and the beast on the ocean.

They discussed what it all meant. Mrs Woosencraft summarised: 'Warm waters have woken something from the first great days of mankind. Something that was supposed to die. The ancients created it, then they tried to destroy it.'

'That creature controls minds and changes bodies,' Foxy said. 'Deep magic cannot do that, nor can your numbers. It knows things we don't.'

'*Sea Cucumber* is lost, the crop destroyed. Koponen didn't know what was going on,' Tim said. 'He was trying to save the world, now he might not be alive. I feel sorry for him.'

'Part of the world doesn't want to be saved,' Mrs Woosencraft said gloomily.

Tim shared her mood. 'So much has happened so fast. I really feel out of my depth.'

Foxy burst out laughing. 'That's such a funny thing to say.'

It relieved the tension in the room. Things might not look good but Foxy and Mrs Woosencraft were becoming friends. The old witch gave Tim her best advice:

'You've started to find a way through the veils we wrap around ourselves. I do it one way, Foxy uses another, now you've found a third. I'm sure there's a part of us that doesn't want to see things as they actually are, it prefers to make up its own rules and pretend they are true. It's strong but when it's confronted by things that it can't explain some people break free and cast about for new ways, new answers. The veils grow thin, an open mind glimpses the unseen path.'

'You think that's what happened to me.'

'Stress is kind of a crash course to open your inner wossname.'

'It's hard to realise I actually went to those places,' Tim said.

'You did, and in a way you didn't,' Mrs Woosencraft said. 'Like all magic there are limits you shouldn't push past, dangerous ones. You took chances and I let you. Worse, I encouraged you. I should have known better.'

'We found out a lot. Where do you think we were?'

'More a case of when,' Mrs Woosencraft said. 'That first was Babylon, the second somewhere very old, but the third, that golden ruin on the island was older still.'

'Foxy, that's where you're from, isn't it?' Tim said.

Mrs Woosencraft settled herself down in her chair. 'It's where we all came from.'

Old Tuoni

THAT EVENING as Tim walked home his head still spun from what he had done and everything he had learned. Even the street had looked different. The next day it was the same. The pavement, sky, trees and houses all had a new clarity as if they had acquired extra dimensions of colour and shape.

It was Tim who had changed. He saw with different eyes and had learned to take far less for granted.

Morse had changed too, only slowly returning to the cat he used to be. Tim had carried him home but next morning the cat was waiting by the door to go back to Mrs Woosencraft at number 23.

Overnight someone had dumped a battered cream-coloured Mercedes convertible across the road. One of the hubcaps was gone, the side window a taped-up sheet of plastic.

Tim stopped dead in his tracks. With its broken headlights, crushed wheel-arches and cracked windscreen the car had known better days. Days when three women who liked to wear red drove it.

Uneven footsteps hurried behind him. 'Hang on old buddy, I don't go that fast.' It was Troy Jarglebaum.

Tim turned, delighted. 'Troy. You made it.'

Jarglebaum was still big in the belly but his face was gaunt, he looked older and moved less easily.

'Most of me, I guess.'

The two men looked at each other. They'd had their differences but after what they'd been through on the *Sea Cucumber* they were small things.

'Troy. On the ship. I saw you fight.'

Jarglebaum's eyes briefly lost focus as he relived those last dreadful minutes fighting Imelda on the sinking ship. He shuddered, then flashed those tombstone teeth of his. 'That was you with the cargo net.'

'Yes. Me and Foxy.'

'You saved my life.' Troy stuck out his hand. 'Thanks, Ace. Nice one.'

Tim didn't know what to say. The main reason was the way Jarglebaum had said 'Ace'. He accepted Jarglebaum's hand. It seemed natural to follow through with an embrace.

'Not so tight,' Troy wheezed.

Tim stepped back. 'How did you get here?'

'A short-wave radio in the lifeboat and GPS on Markus's mobile. We called the *Iron Herring*, they picked us up and the supply chopper flew us ashore. A couple of pints of blood and some bed rest and here I am, right as rain.'

'Koponen's alive?'

'Last time I looked.' Jarglebaum raised his voice. 'You're still with us, aren't you, Markus?'

The passenger door of the Mercedes creaked open and Markus Koponen emerged, dapper as ever. He settled a new white Stetson on his head and crossed the road.

'Thanks to you two.'

'I'm glad you made it,' Tim said.

Koponen bowed stiffly. 'Though perhaps not so glad to actually see me. I can hardly blame you. How is Ms Bolivia?'

Out of the corner of his eye Tim noticed Jarglebaum grow attentive. Careful not to look towards Mrs Woosencraft's house Tim said, 'She's well, and quite safe.'

'I am pleased to hear it. You're a resourceful man, Mr Wassiter. I underestimated you.'

'I have my methods,' Tim said knowingly.

Jarglebaum chuckled. 'You got lucky.'

'That,' said Tim, '*is* one of my methods.'

'And I don't dismiss it lightly.' Koponen drew himself up. 'I won't be stopped, Mr Wassiter. I can't be. Too much is at stake. More now than ever, now we know there are people… Things…' Koponen took a deep breath. 'Well, now I know where so much of Kylma Kala's profits went. I was blind and foolish, so very foolish.'

'She's not completely human any more,' Tim said. 'I really don't think you'll see her again.'

Koponen's eyes glistened. 'There's still part of me—'

Jarglebaum put his hand on Koponen's shoulder. 'Markus, this is getting you nowhere. They ripped you off big-time, sank your ship and tried to kill you. Whatever they are, they aren't your girlfriends.'

'I know it, Troy,' Koponen sighed wearily. 'And you were right, I didn't listen. Ah, well. Mr Wassiter, I hope you still believe I'm one of the good guys.'

'I'll accept you're not one of the bad ones.'

'That will have to do. I'm not going to give up. If I have to start again, I will. Sisu. We Finns never give up.'

'I believe you,' Tim said.

'I'd like you to come and work for me. You and Ms Bolivia.'

'I can't imagine she'd be interested.'

'Even after what she saw aboard *Sea Cucumber*? Don't you want to find out more about what happened to those women? And that thing, whatever it is, is still down there, still damaging my operations.'

'They called it Tuoni.'

Koponen went very still. 'By the old Gods, did they? What else did you discover?'

'They wanted to marry Foxy to him, for her to give birth to his daughter, a second bride.'

'Tuonetar, the daughter-wife,' Koponen half-whispered. 'This is… crazy.'

'Yes. How do you know?'

'The Kalevala, Mr Wassiter. The more you research legend and myth, the more truth you find. These stories form part of my country's gestalt, they are part of what I am.'

'Legends are in the past.'

Koponen gave a thin smile. 'Isn't your King Arthur the once and future king?'

'Guys,' Jarglebaum broke in. 'You have totally and completely fucking lost me.'

'It appears something dangerous and ancient is trying to return,' Koponen explained.

Jarglebaum's instinctive guffaw died in his throat. 'OK, I can go along with that.'

'Whatever it is, it is very powerful and believes it is Lord of the Underworld. This new Tuoni is not something we can ignore any more than we can global warming,' Koponen said. 'Mr Wassiter, please talk to Ms Bolivia, then call me. You know where I am.'

Tim couldn't help but be amused by Koponen's persistence. 'I'll mention it.'

'I ask for no more. Whatever she decides I would very much like to hear about your trip back to shore.' Koponen prepared to cross the road. 'Troy?'

Jarglebaum shook Tim's hand again. 'See you around, Ace. Look after yourself.'

'You too.' Tim walked him to the battered Mercedes. 'A pint in the Bat and Ball?'

'Only if I'm buying.'

Koponen doffed his hat before climbing into the car. 'You can keep the Imperial. It's time I had something less ostentatious, less traceable. Something with a white roof.'

Tim walked away then looked back at the Mercedes. Under his shirt the pendant pulsed. 'Your Merc is fine apart from the bodywork. Change the water pump at the next service.'

'How's the Imperial?'

'I don't have it,' Tim called back. 'I don't even know where it is.'

Koponen found that highly amusing. 'What goes around, Mr Wassiter.'

'I prefer the 55 Belvedere.'

'Work for me and I'll buy you one.'

Twenty-Three

MRS WOOSENCRAFT'S door was off the latch. Some things never change and that was no bad thing. The world was a now a very different place. Or rather, it was always as it had been except some of what had been hidden was now revealed. That reality was very different to the one Tim had hoped it might be and feared it actually was.

He noticed the smell first: oceanic, tidal, a blend of ozone, seaweed and shellfish. Beneath it all lay a familiar and unwelcome stink of cold, sweet decay.

Cats streamed down the stairs and into the back of the house, the sound of their paws a rolling patter like muted thunder. At the foot of the stairs the Manx, Pedwar, glanced at Tim then hurried on.

From the back room came the spine-tingling sound of fifteen cats hissing.

Tim ran after Pedwar. Foxy was right there, wide-eyed, her shoulders against the wall. She gave him a look of worried gratitude. 'They're here.'

Old Mrs Woosencraft blocked the kitchen door. At her feet an arc of cats spat and hissed with arched spines and bottle-brush tails.

Electra Vaughan put one bare webbed-toed foot on the kitchen step. Her mouth was bloody, the limp corpse of a silver tabby hung in her hand.

The left side of Electra's face still held her cold beauty. The other was a ruin ridged with livid half-healed scar tissue, her right eye a blind pearl-white orb.

Dolores and Imelda were in the kitchen. There was a frightening similarity to them now, something terrible about their hairless heads and atrophied ears. Things had been added and taken away from their bodies and their minds. They were shark-women on dry land and no longer human. Each held the limp corpse of a dead cat like an offering.

Mrs Woosencraft's mouth hardened, her eyes grew cold as flint. 'You horrid, horrible creatures.'

Electra let a sad little body drop to the floor. 'No more tricks from you, old lady. We've broken your magic.' She turned to Foxy. 'You hurt me a lot and HE still wants his bride. You made us come back so now you will suffer.'

Tim wanted to do—something. What could he do? He'd seen what Imelda had done to Troy. All three of them were here and he was not Troy. He subsided against the back wall, watching, thinking, waiting.

'Get out of my way, grandma.' Talking was difficult for Electra. She breathed hard, a dribble of clear liquid oozed from the three slits each side of her neck.

'How about I kick your arse so hard you taste brown-eye calamari?'

Back in the kitchen Imelda's smile stretched to her ears exposing a triple row of triangular teeth. 'I knew you'd be like this.'

Mrs Woosencraft clapped her hands. 'Out now. Scat! All of you. My house, my rules. Foxy, Tim, you too.'

The surviving cats didn't hesitate. All except for Morse. Mrs Woosencraft lowered her arm and Morse sprang onto her hand and up to her shoulder. She looked back at Tim. I need this one, that look said. Trust me.

Tim found that he did.

Together the cat and little old lady faced the shark-women.

Tim pulled Foxy down the hall and out into the street.

'Bye, Tim. Tim, Timmy,' Imelda called after them. 'We'll see you very soon.'

'I haven't thanked you properly for my eye,' Electra said. 'I see such wonderful things with it now.'

Mrs Woosencraft looked down at her slippered feet and checked her position on the carpet against the battered piano, her scruffy chair, the cat-scratched curtains. It wasn't as if she'd deliberately brought any of this about but she was at least partly responsible. She'd made mistakes, stupid selfish mistakes. For a while she'd become old and foolish, she'd lost her vision. She'd hurt her friends and done strange things to cats. Now she was prepared to do what needed to be done to make amends.

Her position was good, centred in the triple axis of the window latch, doorknob, and the foot pedals on the piano. Under her feet, the carpet. It had such an interesting pattern. Nobody ever noticed.

In the end this was what life came down to, moments like these. If she could not give the youngsters a chance she knew she was not worth a cat's fart in a hurricane.

Muscles rippled across Imelda's shoulders. 'Ready or not, here we come.'

A worried frown appeared on Mrs Woosencraft's face. She yanked the waistband of her skirt round, settling her knickers.

Electra tipped back her head and laughed. 'Ten Nine Eight, isn't that what you call it? Deg Naw Wyth. Your old dead magic.'

Not dead, not yet. Mrs Woosencraft didn't move a muscle.

'How does that go?' Dolores stepped into the room. 'Ten.'

'Nine.' Imelda's mocking smile was cold as ice and very, very toothy.

Electra looked through her bad eye. 'Eight.'

Dorothy Woosencraft was old, her life had been rich, her last wish had been fulfilled. These three didn't understand.

All their numbers could be broken but she had a number, the first, the indivisible. She touched Morse on her shoulder. She felt strong, so very strong.

'One.'

Tim and Foxy made it to the street. They held hands and looked at the open front door. Tim knew they had to go back inside. 'Foxy—'

For one timeless moment blood ceased to flow in their veins. Cars paused on their journeys, bees hung in the air. The wind ceased to blow. The very sun hung motionless in the sky.

Then, like all things, this too passed.

He could not remember running down the street but there they were, outside another house. Things like that happened in emergencies, your body took over and did things without thinking because thinking took too long.

Foxy pulled on his hand. 'Come on.'

They went back but went too far. Outside number 21 they turned. Straight away they were at number 25. They looked back and forth between the houses. It didn't make sense but there it was.

Somebody needed to state the obvious.

Tim trembled down to his boots, his voice a hoarse whisper. 'It's gone. Her house isn't there.'

There was no gap in the terrace, there was simply no longer any room in the street for Mrs Wocsencraft's number 23. It took a while to sink in.

Tim frowned and rubbed his face. He looked back at the place the house wasn't. 'Poor old Morse. I loved that cat.'

Foxy's arms went around him. 'Cats have nine lives, remember.'

'Seven,' Tim said miserably. 'Mrs Woosencraft said it was seven. Seven can't be broken.'

The sun shone, a bus went past the end of the street. Life went on. However she had done it, Mrs Woosencraft had kept them safe.

A feeling approaching pride tugged the corners of Tim's mouth. 'I didn't know she could do that.'

'It's a good one.'

'She was all right wasn't she, Foxy? In the end.'

'I think she probably was all along.'

'Where do you think they've gone?'

Foxy slowly shook her head. 'Somewhere. Somewhen.'

Tim struggled with the differences between memory and reality. He'd been there, inside a house that wasn't there. He'd drunk cups of tea and eaten flapjacks, had arguments and revelations. Bumblebees and glue. It had been the home of a nice little old lady whose company Tim had enjoyed, and who was more, so very much more than just that.[12]

Foxy hugged him. 'Are you OK?'

He hugged her back. 'Yes. How about you?'

'I was frightened, I'm not now.'

Tim remembered Dolores Vogler perched coquettishly on the edge of his desk, one leg swinging.

'What shall we do now?'

'Let's go down to the sea and watch the waves.'

---

[12] *Most of them are. Try talking to them, and the old men too. You might be surprised.*

The Girl from a Thousand Fathoms

THE NEXT MORNING Tim woke early, padded down the hall to the bathroom and showered. With a towel wrapped around his waist and about to return to his room, he couldn't resist the urge to look in on Foxy.

There she was, curled up on the settee fast asleep. Golden hair pillowed around her face, the blankets tucked under her chin. Was she beautiful? Yes, but far more importantly, she was who she was.

Pedwar perched on the top of the filing cabinet next to the settee. The other survivors of Mrs Woosencraft's cat pack had disappeared, only Pedwar seemed to want to be adopted. Tim more than didn't mind, he needed a cat and he and Pedwar got along.

Pedwar meant 'four', a nice sounding name.

Now Pedwar gazed down at Foxy in utter fascination. He tentatively extended one forepaw into the air and shuffled his bottom in readiness to jump.

'Pedwar, no,' Tim hissed.

Foxy stirred. Pedwar flumped down on arm of the settee, then the floor.

Foxy stirred sleepily. 'What's going on?'

'I thought Pedwar was going to jump on you.'

Foxy sat up under the blankets and fixed the Manx with a cool stare. 'You and I are going to get along.'

Pedwar looked away first. He sniffed the carpet then nonchalantly walked behind Tim.

Tim remembered he was only wearing a towel. 'Good morning. Did you sleep well?'

'Very well, thank you.'

Pedwar sharpened his claws on the threadbare carpet.

Tim winced at the ripping noises behind him. 'He likes you. Really.'

'We'll see. What's for breakfast?'

Pedwar looking thoughtfully up at Tim's towel. He snagged it with his claws and tugged it free. Too late Tim snatched at the tumbling material.

Way too late.

'Woah! What's that!' Foxy pointed between Tim's legs.

Tim snatched up the towel. 'It's— Well, it's my thing. You know.'

'No I do not know. What's it for?'

'What do you mean? Don't your men—?'

'I'm a mermaid. Mermen don't look like that. It's called streamlining.'

Sartorial indisposition notwithstanding, Tim was intrigued. 'So how do you—you know?'

'What?'

'Get it on?'

Foxy shuddered. Mer society had collapsed. Memories of pursuit through the water… 'We, ah, swim alongside each other and waft.'

A kind of frottage without the clothes. 'So how does a mermaid actually—?' Tim gestured with his hands. Foxy stared, fascinated. Tim realised what he was doing and whipped the towel back into place.

Foxy looked up at the ceiling then around the room, anywhere but at Tim. She could have been looking for inspiration or the nearest exit. 'We have these muscles.'

'Oh?' He'd never seen Foxy blush before. It made her look even more lovely. It sent his thoughts in a certain direction and as a result his body began what it believed were appropriate reactions to those thoughts. He held the towel a bit further away.

They fell silent. Tim, naked except for the towel he held in front of him, Foxy on the sofa. Despite her having slept in her clothes they looked perfect with not a rumple or crease in sight.

'How about you?' Foxy said.

'You mean how do we—?'

'Yes.'

So Tim told her.

Foxy's eyes grew wider and wider. 'That is so very kinky!'

'Not as such…'

'Tim.' She slipped out from under the covers and kissed him.

'Foxy, you're a mermaid.'

'You're my true detective, Sherlock.' Foxy kissed him again. 'A girl can't help how she's put together, can she?'

'Very true.' Tim kissed her back. 'Foxy, you and I, we might not be physically— Also, I mean, well, I'm a man.'

'I noticed.'

They kissed again, properly. When they came up for air Foxy said, 'I've wanted to do that again ever since the time poor *Sea Cucumber* sank.'

So had Tim. They tried it again.

'Kissing really is very, very sexy,' Foxy declared.

In no way could Tim disagree.

Foxy stepped back and looked down.

Tim followed her gaze. The buttons on her blouse seemed to fall open all on their own. Underneath there was nothing but mermaid. Tim was mesmerised by her uptilted, green-nippled breasts.

Both pairs.

That day it had rained and Foxy had run. Now he understood.

Foxy raised her arms over her head. 'What's the matter, Ace? Cat got your tongue?'

'You're beautiful, Foxy.'

'So are you, Tim. Let's get rid of that towel.'

An eavesdropper at the door would have heard material being cast aside with some enthusiasm. Immediately afterwards came Foxy's gasp. Then she said:

'Can I—?'

'Yes. Ah—'

A long languorous silence followed. Low laughter, soft groans, the softest sound of skin moving against skin.

'I don't think that's—'

'Try—'

'Oh.'

'Yes.'

'Oh.'

'Ooh.'

Some time later Foxy cried out: 'I love how everything's on the outside. Ace Timewaster, you are one hot mammal.'

The End

Beginnings

THAT WAS HOW Tim and Foxy finally got it together. If this was a fairy tale all that would need to be said is that they lived happily ever after. In the real world endings are never the end, they're just another name for the start of something else.

Over the next few days there were several other endings, including the one about the overweight middle-aged reactionary cop and the teetotal vegan libertine. He's wearing a brand-new Hawaiian shirt, cut-offs, Jesus-boots and white socks and he's waiting in the departure lounge at Gatwick airport. His entire future hangs on the promise of a young woman with crazy hair, a fondness for small animals, and a hand that can no longer make a fist.

One dewy morning Foxy led Tim up to the roof and opened the door to the chicken coop. Shoulder to shoulder the three birds emerged. They peered this way and that, tipped their heads and scratched and pecked at the gravel, moss, and ants on the flat roof.

The cool damp air was invigorating, a day for new things, a day to begin again. The sun rose higher, copper-red light pushed across the walls. Away to the south gulls cried and circled above the eastern pier. Hearing them the chickens lifted their heads and beat their wings.

Dusty hopped up onto the low balustrade edging the roof. A sense of imminence grew in Tim's stomach. He took hold of Foxy's hand.

A flock of pigeons skimmed overhead, flight feathers whistling. Squawking with excitement Dusty took off after them on clapping wings, shedding white down. For a full thirty seconds she battered her way through the morning sky then crash-landed on a chimney stack three houses along the terrace.

A few feathers drifted on the air.

'Chickens don't fly very well,' Tim said.

'So I see.'

At their feet Patch and Shy clucked anxiously, button-eyes glittering. Teetering on the edge of the distant chimney pot, Dusty slipped, scrabbled for balance and regained her poise. Head tilted to one side, she worked her way around the pot and back again as if she were looking for something. Then she reached down and pecked at a lump of mud with five feathers stuck in it until she worked it free.

With the mud and feathers in her beak Dusty faced the offshore breeze and leapt into the sky.

'Look at her go!' Foxy clasped her hands with delight. 'Fly, little bird. Fly, feathery sky fish.'

Higher and higher Dusty rose. Higher than the pigeons, higher than the gulls until she was a distant speck in the far blue sky.

The lump of mud dropped from her beak. Wheeling and diving, one of the gulls caught it, shrieked, and spat it into the sea.

Dusty tumbled out of the sky like she had forgotten how to fly. Fifty feet above the rooftops she pulled out of her dive and barrelled between aerials, chimney pots and washing lines. Wings fanned wide, she thumped into Tim's chest. It looked like she was hugging him. Very few people, Tim included, have ever been hugged by a chicken.

Tim carefully put Dusty down. She walked in circles, scratched behind her ear then trotted into the coop. Patch and Shy looked up at the sky, down at their claws, and hurried after her.

'I think they like it here,' Tim said.

'Now it's their choice.' Foxy said. She took Tim's hand. 'It's my choice too.'

Epilogue

In another time and place Asklepios established his reputation as philosopher and magician with a series of essays entitled Conversations with Infinity. Having squandered the resultant wealth on a folly of white marble with elaborate onion domes he departed on an expedition accompanied by his family and a round and intricately carved table.

A note nailed to the door of his home proclaimed they headed north, to the lands of the long evenings, to seek a race who will build a city by the sea. Most probably he is never heard from again.

And where are Mrs Woosencraft and Morse, and Dolores Vogler, Imelda Marchpane and Electra Vaughan? All five are born survivors, though not all have the same number of lives.

Where in fact is the house with its two rather special old tables?

Electra has discovered she can see much better with her blind eye than the sighted one. She comes to think of her good eye as an inconvenience. In lonely moments she thinks how easy it would be to dig into the socket with her fingers—

Dolores looks at her and remembers the forty-fifth rune of the Kalevala: Blind daughter of Tuoni, Old and wicked witch, Lowyatar.

And she wonders where exactly does reality end and myth begin?

About the Author

David Gullen was born in Africa and baptised by King Neptune. He has lived in England most of his life and has been telling stories for as long as he can remember. He currently lives in South London behind several tree ferns with the fantasy writer Gaie Sebold and the nicest cat you ever did see.

www.davidgullen.com